Ember's Center
Book #1
The O-Line Series

Jillian Jacobs

To: Claudia

Find your Center!

Jillian Jacobs

Cover art: Shelby Bertsch www.shelbybertsch.com

DEDICATION

To: J.W.

ACKNOWLEDGMENTS

During the initial writing process of this book, I sent out a pivotal scene to a group of critique partners. What I received in return created the intensity needed to make this book what it is today. So, thanks to that group of gals who played the "let's fix Jillian's scene" game. Critique partners rule!

I would also like to express my gratitude to editor, Linda Carroll-Bradd. www.lustreediting.com. Any errors are my own and not due to her fantastic skills. She made this story richer, and put all the commas in the right place.

CHAPTER 1

As he waited in line at the coffee shop, Xander Kane flipped through missed messages on his phone. Good. Ember had called and texted. Twice.

The poor dear really needed him right now, but he'd let her wait until after his two o'clock class. His plans for their future were ready to move forward, yet they required a touch of finesse.

He offered a tight smile to the girl behind the coffee-shop counter. "I'll have a vanilla non-fat latte with only two squirts of syrup. Last time, you gave me four when I specifically asked for two."

The girl, Macy, according to her nametag, just nodded and rattled off his total.

Imbecile.

Xander glanced at the pastries behind the glass and considered how far he and Ember had come. Before his influence, he knew she'd have seen no problem with inhaling two or three of the sugar-filled concoctions, but under his tutelage, she'd gained control over her less-than-healthy eating habits. Now *he* filled the empty space, sating her hunger with friendship and understanding. He'd spent considerable time directing her along the correct mental and physical path. Though her life continued to have major setbacks, she was becoming a new woman—his perfect woman.

His drink appeared on the counter, and he took a sip before leaving. *Much better.*

The coffee shop was in a bookstore beneath Visions Clinic where he was completing his final year of psychology clinicals. As he walked down the bookstore's center aisle, he ran a hand over the glossy book covers. Soon, his name would appear at the top of best-seller lists, to be followed, of course, with guest spots on top talk shows. Leading psychologists would seek *him* for answers.

Ember was his golden ticket.

Xander held open the bookstore door for a woman with a cumbersome stroller occupied by a crying baby. A towheaded toddler whined and tugged its mother's sleeve.

Come on, lady.

She smiled. "I'm sorry. Thanks for holding the door."

He nodded. *Whatever.*

He shifted his satchel strap on his shoulder and walked around the side of the building, grateful this was his last year lugging the heavy burden of books and notebooks. He threw his satchel in his Volvo's backseat, and then headed out of the parking lot toward campus.

Xander stretched his neck from side to side, limbering up for the hour-long class that would teach him nothing new. Real-life dramas were the true classrooms. From the first, Ember's story drew him. Psychology textbooks scripted her life on every page. Her chapters lay titled in bold black font: abusive mother, negligent father, unhealthy lifestyle, teenage trauma, and sibling suicide.

He'd met Ember during her sophomore year of college, when she'd worked behind a fast-food counter. Teased and taunted by drunken customers about her weight...and yet, she never batted an eye. Right then, he knew she was the one.

After a few more nights of observation, he introduced himself and worked past her initial misgivings. Delving into her life story and helping her overcome her issues ranked him smarter and wiser than his peers. Ember was the perfect test subject. He watched other students waste time on recreational pursuits, but he allotted time with Ember, honing his knowledge, digging deeper into her psyche.

And now, the time spent grooming her had come to fruition. His patience and guidance would lead to their mutually beneficial future together. Carefully planned construction was necessary in

the next phase of Ember's development—love.
He alone held the hammer.

CHAPTER 2

"Get your ham hocks off the table." Owen Killion shook his head while glaring at his teammate's flagrant sprawl. "I'd rather not be on the receiving end of coach's lecture on how your size thirteens broke this advertising agencies high-dollar table."

Ignoring his request, Jason lounged on the steel-gray couch, and left his feet propped on the glass-deco coffee table covered with marketing magazines "So, where are we eating after this?"

"Are you serious? We ate two hours ago." Owen sighed over his fellow player's uncouth behavior. His Marauders teammates thought of only three things in varying order: football, food, and females.

Bronco, his left guard, frowned over the top of his hardback book.

Owen shifted in the metal chair digging rivets into the sides of his thighs. "What are you reading anyway? Is that the same book you were reading last week?"

"No, different book, same author. Now, shut up. It's not my fault you didn't bring anything to pass the time."

Owen kicked Bronco's leg in response.

Bronco ignored him and kept his nose buried in some sci-fi mystery by R.W. Hardcastle.

As the center for Ohio's Manchester Marauders offensive line, Owen didn't have time for leisure reading. Most days were spent combing through playbooks and keeping an eye on the cast of heathens making up his team.

Thumbing through his tablet, he brought up the TV commercial script and read over his changes. "Did you see this script?" Ad-copy writers penned lines for football players with the assumption they hadn't passed the second grade.

After heaving a sigh, Bronco shoved his gum-wrapper bookmark into his book and snapped the tome closed. "Yeah, I read it. Why? Did you change something?"

Owen handed over his tablet.

"Let me see." Jason swiped the device out of Bronco's hand.

They had arrived early for their Breast Cancer Awareness commercial shoot. In the football world, showing up on time meant you were late. On the first day of college ball, Owen had arrived at the practice field on time. Or so he'd thought. Coach ordered him to lie on his side, roll all the way down the field, and then roll all the way back. After which, Coach told him to stand and run. Running after rolling made his head spin, his legs wobble, and his stomach churn. Lesson learned.

Millicent Brown, their commercial director, emerged from behind glass doors and greeted them. An assistant stepped out from behind her.

Owen rose when the ladies entered. He zeroed his gaze on the vision before him. Ms. Assistant was tall and brown-eyed with dark auburn hair clipped up like a rooster tail at the back of her head. Her gray suit hung on her body, and she clutched a laptop under her arm.

Although he wasn't hungry before, now Owen reconsidered—a handful of Ms. Assistant would certainly satisfy. Her eyes were puffy and red, as if she'd been crying. His protective instincts kicked in gear. A distraught woman reminded him of all the times he'd wiped his sister's tears.

The director left after speaking to them like pre-school dropouts, but the assistant stayed behind.

"Is there anything I can get for you, gentlemen?" Her husky voice stirred his body even more.

"Gentlemen? I don't see any gentlemen around here." Jason waved his hand around the lobby. "You must have us confused with—"

"Jason," Owen snapped. "The *lady* asked you a question."

After years of playing football together, Jason merely raised a brow at his imperious tone. Glancing at the assistant, he gave her a quick once-over before returning his gaze to Owen, and then he turned and studied the woman once more, as if solving an intricate puzzle. Meeting his gaze again, Jason flashed a wide-grin.

More like brothers than friends, Owen assumed the mischievous sparkle in Jason's eye meant he recognized his interest in the woman. Owen glared in warning.

Jason smacked him on the shoulder. "Well, I'll admit I am a little hungry, but I think Owen here is near starved. What is it you're hungry for, Big O?" His cocky grin made clear he didn't mean food.

Bronco bashed Jason on the head with his hardbound book. "Excuse these poor examples of the male race, Miss...sorry, I didn't catch your name."

The lady in question shuffled her laptop from one arm to the other. Owen stepped back. Perhaps they were intimidating her since all three were well over six foot, with their weight tipping over and around the three hundred mark. At six-four and two ninety-eight, he came in as the shortest and smallest of the trio. He waved at the sorry excuse for a chair. "Would you like to sit?"

Ms. Assistant took a deep breath, and then offered a bland smile. "Thank you, no. I would be happy to see to your refreshments before we start, though."

"You could start by telling us your name." Owen popped a piece of gum into his mouth.

She stepped around the coffee table and offered her hand. "I'm sorry. Ember Brooks."

"Nice to meet you, Ember. I'm Owen Killion." He shook her hand and kept her fingers clasped in his, blocking the others from the pleasure of her cool touch. "This is Warren "Bronco" Murray and Jason Stafford. We make up part of the offensive line for the Manchester Marauders."

"I'm familiar with your names because my brother Elliot is a huge fan. He will be so excited I'm...um...that I..." Her expression blanked.

"What is it? Ms. Brooks?" Owen rubbed her overly-chilled hand, offering his warmth.

Her bottom lip quivered.

Ah, hell. He led her to the couch and sat with her hand

clasped in his. He waited a moment before asking, "Is it your brother?"

Ember sniffled and stuck her index finger in the corner of her eye.

Why women thought putting their fingers in their eyes would stop tears from falling was beyond him. Owen squeezed her hand. "Tell me what's wrong."

"I'm sorry. This is very unprofessional." Edging off the seat, she landed with a plop when she met his grip's resistance. "Really, please." She patted his hand, which was still locked around hers. "I need to get back to Mrs. Brown. She's expecting my assistance in setting up your commercial."

Owen kept her at his side. "You mentioned your brother is a big fan, right? If having us meet him would erase your tears, we could do that. Hell, send him over right now."

"I can't," she answered with a small voice. "He died last week."

"What?" He tipped her chin in his direction, needing clarification for this travesty. "Why the hell are you working?"

"Owen," Bronco chastised.

He grumbled, but placed an arm around her shoulder. "I'm very sorry about your brother."

"What happened?" Jason stood before them with both arms crossed over this chest.

Bronco shoved him, "What kind of question is that? Can't you see she's upset?"

Ember cast Owen a sideways glance. Tears pooled in her eyes, and then spilled over. "I'm not sure, but I'm going to find out. I went to the police department today... but...he didn't kill himself." She shook her head. "He didn't."

"No, of course not." Owen squeezed her shoulder.

A silky russet tendril brushed against his hand. Her scent reminded him of those flowery bath soaps his younger sister had lined along the shower's ledge when they were kids. He ran his hand up and down her arm. Her floral scent wafted through the air and clung to his skin. Unbelievable. This woman had him thinking about flowers and showers. Which had him skipping to showers and sex—with her.

What? Stop! She's mourning...morning showers and sex. Move away, now, you inappropriate ass.

Ember stood and tugged down the sleeves of her ill-fitting jacket. "Please forgive me. His death just hits me at times. The loss is all so new, and I...I shouldn't be discussing this." She cleared her throat and shuffled her laptop in her arms. "What would really help is if you would let me get you something."

He could practically see her mind repeating a saying that had been pounded into his brain over and over again—*Keep your head in the game.* Professional and strong-willed. Back to work after suffering the loss of her brother. Her display of resiliency added to her appeal.

At sixteen, Owen had taken care of his family after his father died of cancer. Twelve years later, his mom and sister Maude still lived with him. He knew only too well the emotional devastation of losing someone you loved.

"Ms. Brooks. I think we could use some refreshments. What do you have?"

She offered her first true smile.

The warm glow almost knocked him off the couch.

Obviously grateful to be back on a comfortable field, she rattled off a list of what was available. One thing he didn't know was whether or not *she* was available, but he'd find out. Later.

CHAPTER 3

After a long day of shooting commercials with the Marauders, Ember sat at her desk, writing ad copy for a new sports drink. Ironic, since she'd never played a sport in her life.

Well, school sport anyway.

"Ember."

A husky baritone called for her attention. "One sec." She raised her arm and lifted an index finger, finishing the perfect tag line before she forgot. After correcting the script, she clicked 'save,' swiveled in her chair, and then shot straight to her feet. "I'm so sorry. Had I known it was you, I wouldn't have kept you waiting." Her boss would use her face as a dartboard for making him wait.

Owen Killion leaned with one solid arm spread along the top of her flimsy gray cubicle wall.

"I'm sorry," she repeated, then stepped around her chair, almost tripping on the wheel. Her tiny cubicle shrank now that his brawny frame occupied the space. His team's mascot suited him perfectly—Marauder. A vision flashed of Owen single-handedly rowing a Viking vessel across stormy seas to plunder riches from a village. A towering force, he embodied everything she found attractive in a man.

Huge feet in brown boots led to sturdy legs covered in dark-washed denim. His muscular arms bulged under the short sleeves of his hunter green jersey. Shoulders so broad she doubted she could fully wrap her arms around them. His thick brown hair lay neatly trimmed, and his brown eyes were heavy-lidded, yet welcoming, like a sad hound dog. And what was it about certain men's noses that, when combined with the rest of their features, resulted in masculine perfection? The only thing missing was sexy stubble.

He smiled when she finally met his melted-chocolate eyes.

Seemingly aware she'd given him a once-over—a very blatant once-over. *Awkward.* She clasped together her trembling hands. "Was there something you needed?"

"Yes, actually."

His voice matched his body: deep and heavy, and she bit back a sigh.

"I have a small problem you might help me with."

"Absolutely. What is it?" She folded both arms across her chest. *Where are my shoes? Can he see the tea stain on my shirt?*

"I'm glad you agree. You see, I hate when women cry."

What? That was quite the non-sequitur. Laugh lines appeared beside his eyes. Unsure what her answer should be, she replied, "I hate when women cry, too."

Not comfortable around men, especially huge, handsome ones with square jaws sharp enough to cut ice, Ember calmed her breathing and tried stilling her pounding heart. The Marauders' center stood in her cube entry.

Her entry. *Oh no! Where has my mind strayed?*

Did he live up to the rumors? The "O" in Offensive-line raised many a woman's curiosity across social and traditional media platforms since all the players were extraordinarily gorgeous. Not hard to imagine Owen's reputation for bedroom proclivity was very accurate since his shoes were so big, which meant he was big everywhere. *Ridiculous.* She would not stare *there.*

Maintain eye contact. Keep it!

Since she stood at five-eight, she was used to most men being of similar height or a few inches taller—not so with Owen Killion. Her chin actually lifted in order to meet his gaze. Then there was his mouth, which was speaking—

"Ember?"

"I'm sorry. What were you saying?"

"Sometimes talking to a stranger helps. Let's grab a bite to eat." He lifted her jacket off the back of her chair. "We'll go somewhere close by, since we're already downtown."

"What are you talking about?" He wasn't asking her out. Men didn't ask her out. She didn't date, especially not unbelievably gorgeous professional football players. Jocks didn't date chubby wallflowers. Wait, she wasn't that girl anymore. Was she?

"Dinner. I'm talking about dinner." He chuckled and shook his head, evidently amused by her confusion. "We'll walk across the street to that steak place."

"I really, I don't—" She glanced around, unsure how to continue or to determine what alternate universe she had entered.

"Really don't what? You eat. I eat. It's time to check out for the day. Come on." He held open her jacket. "I'd like to hear more about your brother."

The gesture was just like the leading man in a movie. But she didn't eat dinner, at least, not a large dinner. Her health plan entailed tapering off for the evening meal, and she didn't stray from her meal plan—ever. "I usually eat soup for dinner."

"I think I can handle that." He glanced down at the jacket he still held in mid-air.

"Did something happen during the commercial shoot?" Some other explanation existed for why he was here. Why he was helping her slip on each jacket sleeve and taking her arm.

"Let's go." He nudged her lower back.

Shivers shot to her toes. Toes currently shoeless. "Sorry, I need to grab my purse and shoes." After hearing his deep sigh, she glanced back and caught him jiggling his keys. "Owen, you play center, right?" As she slipped on her shoes, she turned and faced him.

"Yeah." He raised a brow. "Why?"

With an index finger, she poked his hard chest. "You're bossy."

"You have no idea." He smiled and took her hand, leading her out of the building.

This surreal moment topped her life's unbelievable encounters list. Talking to Owen about her brother would provide another perspective. And that was all this gesture was about—her brother. Elliot hadn't missed a single Marauders game. So, she would have a cup of soup in tribute to his football fandom. Staring down from a heavenly cloud, her brother was no doubt blown away a member of his favorite team was in her presence. The vision made her smile, her first heartfelt smile since he died.

And then a familiar ringtone pealed from her phone, and her smile disappeared.

# # #

Owen polished off a porterhouse, baked potato, and some sort of salad with pears. As Ember continued sharing her brother, Elliot's, enthusiasm for the Marauders, she fiddled with the spoon in her empty soup bowl. Not once had she mentioned his death, but instead spoke of his excitement over her ad agency's plans to work with so many players today. Her brow creased when she discussed her visit to the police station. Frequent heavy sighs and slouched shoulders painted a picture of a discontented female as she railed against the detective's refusal to conduct further investigation.

While Owen sympathized with her concerns over her brother's case, he wanted to learn more about her as a person. What did she do on Saturday nights? Why did she eat only soup for dinner? What would that mass of red hair look like spread across his king-size pillows?

"So, what about you, Ember?" He shifted forward in his seat and fiddled with the candle on the table. "Doesn't seem like you're much of a football fan. What occupies your spare time?"

Her phone rang again—fifth time. She fussed with her hair and re-clipped the loose curls in that crazed tail, ignoring the call. Since nothing irritated him more than talking to someone while they flipped through their phone, he appreciated her unwillingness to answer. Yet, with each ring she seemed to pale, and her words came across more brittle and edgy. Her hand shook as she lifted her water glass.

"Is there some emergency you need to handle?"

"No, why?"

"You must be a popular girl, then." On edge, he tapped his butter knife against the table. Was a boyfriend on the other end of those calls?

"What? Popular? Not at all." Her glass, in hand, stalled midway to the table, and she frowned over the rim. "I should probably go. Thanks for the soup." Dishes clinked together when she brought down the glass.

"Whoa. Hang on a sec, what just happened?" Owen did a mental backtrack of their conversation. "What did I say?"

"Listen, I appreciate the dinner and enjoyed talking about my brother, but I need to go." She stood and struggled to remove her purse strap from the side of the chair. Giving up, she threw her hands in the air and sighed heavily.

He held back a chuckle. "All right, Ember, we'll go, but after you tell me what's going on in that red head." He sat back in his chair and folded both hands across his stomach. "What's with all the phone calls? Is someone bothering you?"

She laughed. "I think I've divulged enough family secrets tonight."

Her laugh seemed tinged with something, as if on the edge of hysteria. He rested his elbows on the table and leaned forward. "Oh, but I love family drama. I live with my mom and sister. Plus, considering all the "girls" I work with, everyday is a fucking soap opera." He winced. "Excuse my language. I'm used to being around men all day. I apologize."

"No, it's understandable." She made a show of looking around for the exits, and then turned back, brows raised.

He remained seated and used his butter knife and spoon to tap a tune on his scrap-filled plate. The ting morphed into a raging drum solo, causing curious and perturbed stares from other diners. As hoped, he was gratified when she laughed at his antics. "Sit back down, Ember. Please."

She sighed and crumpled into her seat. "The phone calls...it's my mother. She's...um...she's a bit...I'm sorry. I can't really explain. I'm unsure about a lot of things right now, and I refuse to speak with her. She's always been very—"

There went that index finger poking into the corner of her eye again. "Very what?" Owen shifted forward in his seat and dismissed his need to clasp her hand, to make her stay.

"I'm sorry. I can't do this right now. Thank you, though. You've been very kind." She bit her bottom lip and avoided his gaze. "Good luck with your football stuff. And well, just...so yeah, thanks." She fussed with the tablecloth, brushing at invisible crumbs.

Odd girl, she seemed so unsure of her place. *Very endearing.* No one would ever accuse him of not knowing the exact play to make and the exact time to make it. He was a lot smarter than people gave him credit for, a stigma that came from being a football player.

He pushed back from the table and offered his hand. "I'll walk you to your car."

"Thank you." She flashed a small smile.

Though willing to leave her deeper story for another day, he'd delve again soon. Once outside, he waited for the walking signal to light on the post across the street and glanced at that thick mass of red hair. She appeared unaware of his interest in her as a woman. This girl was one he'd take home to Mom. Most women he dated came across more interested in who he represented on the field. With Ember, he believed her concerns would center on who he was in life.

Placing a hand at the small of her back to direct her across the street, he felt her flinch. *Skittish thing.*

Both were quiet as they made their way through the dimly lit parking garage. Pigeons cooed and fluttered along the concrete ledge. Mid-August in the upper mid-west still offered some muggy nights. Perhaps it would rain later. With his first pre-season game coming up, Owen hoped this warm weather was long gone by then.

Ember stopped by an old white Buick and thanked him again.

Sorrys and thank yous came readily to this woman. A habit she'd have to break. Owen twirled a red-brown strand around his finger. "Ember, what an appropriate name for a girl with hair the color of fire." He leaned down and placed a soft kiss upon her lips.

Her body remained statue-stiff, except for her hands, which rose against his chest.

Honey, I've spent my life holding back defensive lines, you don't stand a chance.

"Ember Brooks, I'll see you soon." He nudged her chin to close her slack mouth. While keeping his finger in place, he made sure to catch her gaze before slightly tilting his head and kissing her again. A short, quick caress to clarify he meant to kiss her again and often. A smile he couldn't contain not only crossed his face, but also spread across his heart. Getting to know this woman would take time, but in

15

the end, and with that curvy body, damn, she'd be worth every tick of the clock. Whistling a happy tune, he turned on his heel with the smoothness of a running back spinning away from a tackler, and headed toward his truck.

CHAPTER 4

Owen's cheery whistle echoed through the empty garage. All while Ember remained rooted in place, gaping at his retreating back. He'd kissed her. Twice. A honk from outside the parking garage startled her from her frozen state, and she brushed two fingers across her lips. Sweet kisses, like he'd give his sister. *Right?* Right. He'd only felt sorry for her—end of story. And yet, her lips were the only warm part of her body. Affection from a man was outside her comfort zone. After growing up with an absentee father and spending her teen and early college years extremely overweight, she remained unfamiliar with any sort of male intimacy. Even Xander, her best friend, had never touched her intimately and, while disappointing at first, she now held a more clinical view of their relationship. In the beginning, Xander made clear his intention to guide her through the morass of her past. Together, they'd succeeded.

As she started her car, she glimpsed a lighted icon on her dash. Tire pressure. Great, changing a tire in a skirt—*What fun.* Not that she knew how to change a tire.

After resting her head on the steering wheel and counting to ten, she unbuckled and stepped out of the car. Sure enough, the front passenger tire was deflated, and the round silver circle thing touched the ground.

As she clicked open the trunk, she noted her back tire was flat, as well. Hmmm? Her heartbeat kicked up. Had someone purposely slashed her tires so they could attack? She glanced around the garage then hustled to the driver's seat and grabbed her phone.

"Ember?"

At the sound of Owen's voice, she jumped and banged the back of her head against the doorframe. *Ouch!* Rubbing one hand across her chest to fend off her heart's impending explosion, and with the other hand checking her head, she turned and saw him leaning out his truck window. "You scared the daylights out of me."

He parked, and then came around the back of his truck to join her. "What's wrong?"

"Flat tire." Dang, her head really hurt. She removed the clip that had smashed into her head when she'd struck the door.

"Are you all right?" He removed her hand and took over with a soothing massage. "What happened?"

"I banged my head when you scared me." He smelled amazing this close, like leather and citrus mixed together with gooey caramel.

What would he do if I leaned in and took a bite?

"We'll get you some Ibuprofen." His other hand brushed her hair away from her face. "Which tire?"

"Uh, two." She mumbled, half-asleep from his ministrations and dreams of floating in caramel seas.

"Two flat tires?" Owen walked around the car and bent to inspect the sunken rubber. A frown marred his handsome face. "Not flat, slashed. Piss someone off?"

"I have no idea."

"Got a spare?" He raised her popped trunk lid.

"Pretty sure. Yes." She leaned against her car and peered inside the trunk.

He lifted away the fabric lining and huffed out a curse. "Do you know how to change a tire?"

"Sorry, no, but I can look up a video on my phone."

"You sure as hell can't change a tire if you don't have a spare *or* a jack." He gestured to the empty hole in her trunk. "What if I hadn't come along? Woman…" Jaw clenched, he stepped back and slammed shut the lid.

Woman? She'd been independent for years, and true, she'd never changed a tire, but there was a first time for everything. "I don't know where the tire and jack went. They were both there when I bought the car. At least, I checked for that." She hadn't asked him to stop and play the hero. And she wasn't about to tell him her assumption her own father was behind the stolen items.

"I'll have you out to my garage sometime to teach you the essentials." He grumbled about females and tires as he made his way back to his truck. While standing by his truck's passenger door, he placed a call on his cell.

Hearing only his side, Ember stifled laughter over his high-handed manner. He certainly had no trouble throwing around his authority. "Don't give a shit…Who pays your check?…Tell her you're saving a damsel in distress… Who? Why should that matter?…Get your ass here." He hung up, and then inspected her passenger side tires again. "My mechanic, Jake, should arrive shortly. Now…" he crouched by her tire and pulled on a rubber flap. "Two slashed tires is no accident. Tell me what's going on."

"Nothing. I don't understand, perhaps this was kids playing a mean trick." She sank beside him. "I'm sorry. Please, don't feel you have to stay. I can wait by myself."

"Enough with the 'I'm sorrys' and 'thank yous'." He stood and offered his hand.

While she appreciated him helping with this tire situation, she didn't appreciate the officious attitude. "Common courtesy," she mumbled.

"What?" He barked through gritted teeth. "I don't need courtesy. And I don't expect your constant thanks for helping."

Her worry over replacing two tires, along with the stresses of a long workday, made accepting his brashness that much harder, not to mention all the other worries swarming through her mind like a hive of bees ready to strike. Was this man the same person who kissed her so sweetly less than fifteen minutes ago? "You're being kind of growly."

"Well, two slashed tires fires up my inner mechanic. People do this shi—stuff and don't realize the expense of replacements." Hands jammed on his hips, Owen paced in the empty parking spot beside her car, continuing the verbal rampage. "On top of that, you don't have a spare or a jack. You would have been stranded here, facing who knows what? Then you feel the need to thank me when I don't abandon you in an empty, dark garage."

"I'm very sor—" She slapped a hand over her mouth.

He glared.

She became very interested in a pavement crack. Xander had chastised her many times about taking so much blame on herself. Yet, here she was, thinking Owen's anger was directed toward her and not the circumstances.

"Let's get you home." He clutched her arm and tugged her toward the passenger side of his truck.

"Wait." She dug in her heels by her driver's side door. "We can't just leave my car here. I need my stuff." She grabbed her purse and phone out of her car's front seat. "And another thing, I'm not some player on your team you can just boss all over. Plus, how will I get to work tomorrow?"

"I'll take care of your transportation. Don't worry." Flashing a cheeky wink, he grasped her shoulders and kissed her nose. "Get in the truck. Please."

There he went kissing her again. She settled into the passenger seat, more confused than ever. He shouldered into the driver's seat and placed a call, all the while unaware he'd just kissed a girl who'd never technically been kissed before today.

After barking out more orders at some unfortunate on the receiving end, Owen hung up and slid a glance her way. "Sorry about that. Where do you live?"

Oh no. He probably lived on some lakeside mongo-mansion, while her duplex was a total dump. But the hovel was her home, so she zipped off the address.

He plugged his phone into the USB port and shouted orders for his playlist. "I'll meet Jake at my shop, and we'll fix your car."

"Well, I'm not supposed to say thank you, so I won't." She clutched her purse in her lap and stared out the side window. "Why aren't we leaving? I thought you were in a hurry?" She thrummed her fingers against her leather purse.

"Why would you think that?" He chuckled and nudged her chin. "Seriously, you need to consider who might want to cause you harm. Could be kids, but two tires seems excessive."

Ember decided his growling was due to his alpha-dog nature so she'd forgive him—this time. "I need to go to work tomorrow. How will I get my car?"

"Don't worry. I'll have your car back by then."

How he planned to fix her car in the middle of the night was beyond her, but he seemed confident in his abilities. Only, he shouldn't work for free. "I'll pay you back."

"Do I need to remind you of our previous conversation?" He reached over and squeezed her knee.

Her mind boggled at how, within seconds, he could go from domineering to affectionate. After arriving at her duplex, she remained unsure of the next step.

Will I see him again? How is he going to get tires this late?

Owen turned off his engine. "So, this is your place?"

"Yeah, not much, but this is what I can afford."

"Wait here." He jumped out of the truck, jogged around to her side, and helped her down. He clasped her hand and walked her to the door. "Hand me your house key." After unlocking the door, he grasped both her shoulders with his hands.

Strong, capable hands, finely sprinkled with dark hair. How would those coarse fingers feel traveling over her body? Not that she'd ever know; the ride in the golden chariot was over, reality would return in a blink.

"Now, don't worry, I'll return your car in the morning."

Since she wasn't allowed to express her gratitude, she was at a loss on how to respond. Since "Don't leave" was what she wanted to say, she handed over her car keys before she blurted that embarrassingly needy statement. "Good luck with your season." *Oh, that's brilliant.*

"I'll see you soon, Ember Brooks." He slid her a sideways grin and marched that sturdy body down the sidewalk to his truck, at ease with the world. A seemingly unencumbered strength she coveted. What was it like in Owen Killion's world? She barely knew him, yet as she watched him leave, she wished just once for a happily ever after.

"Bye," she whispered. And with the vision of him inked across her heart, she opened her apartment door. Why did she feel an urge to cry, like she'd lost a chance at something special? Would a normal girl have known what to do in that situation? Was inviting him in for after-dinner drinks standard procedure? Would tea count as an after-dinner drink?

These male-female relationship games remained a mystery. As she stepped into her apartment, she was surrounded by silence. She already missed the deep timbre of Owen's voice.

She sighed and headed to the kitchen to end the evening with the only reliable man in her life—Earl Grey.

CHAPTER 5

Ember rose early to carefully dress and primp, adding three layers of mascara instead of the usual one. When her cell rang, she jerked, which caused a lovely black smear under her eye.

"Good morning, Xander." As she checked her cabinet for eye-makeup remover, she switched her phone to speaker mode.

"Sorry I missed you yesterday. I tried to reach you after my class."

"I was in the middle of a commercial shoot. My boss was on red alert, so I couldn't return your call." She fingered through her tote until she found the purple bottle.

"How was your visit to the police station? Was the detective able to help with Elliot's case?"

"I'm running behind this morning. Can we talk about what happened during our Thursday session?"

"How about we try something different? Let's meet for lunch today."

Ember held back a sigh. Usually they met for a counseling session on Thursday nights. They'd never had lunch before. He must believe she needed extra time due to Elliot's death.

"I'm not sure I can do that, Xander. I'm having car trouble, and I may have to visit the garage at lunch to settle the bill." She dipped a Q-tip into the eye-makeup remover and carefully removed the black smudge. Her hope that Owen would ask her out made her hesitant to plan anything with Xander.

"Car trouble?"

"Two flat tires."

"Two? Why didn't you call?"

Now that was another odd statement, since she couldn't envision fastidious Xander changing her tire, let alone knowing how.

"One of the Marauders' players from the commercial shoot was in the garage, and he helped me." She stepped into her bedroom and slipped on her black heels. "I'm actually expecting my car this morning, so I need to finish getting ready. Can we do lunch another time?"

"You do seem distracted, dear. We missed last week due to your brother's funeral, so we'll need to make up that time Thursday night. Why don't you stay an extra hour?"

"Perfect. Sorry about lunch." And there she went apologizing again. *Owen wouldn't be pleased*. She stifled a chuckle.

"Don't let these minor inconveniences sidetrack you. How are you faring?"

While she loved Xander, she didn't have time for a long chat this morning. "I'm not sure Elliot's death has become real yet. I just put on mascara, so I don't want to discuss my feelings right now. Would you mind waiting until Thursday?"

"Certainly, we'll discuss your denial stage then."

Denial—never a truer word was spoken. Xander always pierced straight to the heart of her emotional state. Maybe she should be grateful for the distraction of flat tires and handsome football players. Denials, distractions—anything to keep from dwelling on the fact her brother was no longer a phone call away.

As she peered through her front window blinds, she dug her front teeth into her bottom lip, making a groove. *Don't cry*. She clenched her jaw, breathed deep through her nose, and slowly exhaled. Just get through the next minute, the next hour, and the day will pass.

The day will pass.

#

From her window perch, Ember watched her car arrive with a brown-haired man sitting behind the wheel. Her heart fluttered with excitement. He'd come. She grabbed her purse and rushed out the front door. As she drew near, she realized the driver wasn't Owen.

She halted at the end of the sidewalk and tamped down her disappointment.

A husky kid, likely in his early twenties, hopped out of the driver's seat and approached. "Ember? Ember Brooks?"

"Yes." She glanced down the street. Perhaps Owen was arriving separately.

"I'm to deliver these keys and this note." The guy handed over her keys and a folded piece of notebook paper.

"Thank you." She smiled and nodded.

"You're all set."

Not really. All set would entail a handsome football player handing over her keys. She sighed, all that extra primping for nothing.

Ember noted the embroidered name on the kid's smudged shirt—Jake. Was he the unlucky recipient of last night's distress call? "Busy night for you?"

"Yeah, but no problem." He shrugged. "See ya." He passed her, heading down the sidewalk that was still damp from an overnight storm, and hopped into the passenger side of a tow truck with a Killion's Service logo on the side panel.

With jittery hands, she carefully unfolded the note.

When is the last time you had this car serviced?

The stark accusation was scrawled in bold black ink along with a checklist of all the services performed on her car. Unbelievable. Owen must have worked through the night. Why would he go to the trouble? Grease, or some sort of black grime, had left fingerprints and smears on the paper.

Ember never learned about proper car care, because her father was more likely to steal her vehicle than offer service advice. She tucked the stained note in her purse as a memento of a time when a handsome stranger made her dream of happier things—if only for a little while.

CHAPTER 6

Days after her brush with football fandom, Ember slouched in the padded leather booth, entranced by the action on the big screen TVs lining the sports bar's walls. Both teams faced off on the field at the twenty-yard line. Since they'd stolen the ball, Owen's team now had a long way to go.

Not stolen, recovered the fumble.

His strong leg muscles were nicely defined in hunter green pants. She'd giggled when his severely perturbed face appeared on screen during the initial announcement of the offensive linemen's college and team position. She hadn't realized he was the one who threw the ball back to the quarterback.

Snapped the ball. Geesh, all this football lingo is frying my brain.

Owen seemed quite limber. She should call and tell him he was doing great. Looking great. Where was her phone? Did she have his number?

"What are they doing now?" Ember chewed on a maraschino cherry stem. "How many times can they throw the ball again?"

Kelly, her co-worker and friend, grabbed her shoulders and jostled her back and forth. "Ember, you're driving me crazy." She held her at arm's length. "How can you not know one single thing about football?"

"I just don't." Gesturing wildly, she knocked over the salt shaker. "Oops." She blinked and then carefully righted the container, scooping the loose particles into her hand at the edge of the table.

Kelly's shaking had stirred her alcohol-laced stomach contents, creating a moment of queasiness. Ember brushed at the stuff on her hands. Why was there salt all over her palms?

After Pilates class yesterday, her friends had talked her into meeting at a sports bar to catch the Marauders first pre-season game. The plethora of big screen TVs offered a full shot of Owen Killion charging forward, clashing against his opponents over and over again.

Ember texted Xander. *@ Bandits stop by.*

Then, she thumbed through her contacts to see if Owen Killion's name would magically appear.

Icy rum drinks were barely coating the surface of strain caused by her mother's continuous passive-aggressive phone messages. The calls added a frequent reminder that she still hadn't dealt with her brother's death, or the alleged cause. With each cocktail, reality fogged and painted over the pain and uncertainty of her life. She hadn't told anyone about Owen Killion's pity date on Monday. She'd locked away the moment in a deep spectrum of her mind and refused to dwell on the soft cushion of his lips. She burst out laughing. Ah, soft cushy lips, that was funny when he was so hard. Oh geez, she really needed to have sex. Maybe some random bar dude would do. She laughed again. *Gross.*

Kelly shot her a look that suggested she'd lost her mind. Perhaps she had. If she drank another rainbow-colored slushie, would the alcoholic haze lead to a pot of gold? A treasure she could exchange for a normal family and her brother's return.

Oh Lord, I am full of lucky charms.

Time for another drink.

As she waited at the bar, she felt someone tap her shoulder. "Ember? Ember Brooks? Oh my God, is it really you?" Chelsea Day, lead "sitter", looked her over with a wide-eyed stare and gaping mouth. Ember had dubbed Chelsea and her friends "sitters" back in high school, because she'd been the stumpy, shy girl ridiculed by all the pretty girls sitting huddled together, whispering and teasing.

"Hello, Chelsea." *Now go away, Chelsea.* Maybe if she drank one more drink, she'd be brave enough to actually tell her to bugger off. She glanced at the screen and saw the solid wall that was Owen Killion jarred against two players from the other team.

27

Is it hot in here?

"Jessica," Chelsea yelled at "sitter" number two.

Of course, they were still friends.

"Jess, look at Ember. Can you believe this?"

"Ember Brooks? Wow. You've lost like, a ton of weight." Jessica offered a fake smile and continued scrolling through her phone.

Obviously, there were more interesting people to speak to. *Or fat girls to taunt or salads to puke up. Stop it!* Time to act like a grown-up. "Jessica, nice to see you again."

"I just love that dress. Where'd you get it?" Chelsea asked. Not surprising, her priorities hadn't changed in the seven years since high school.

The bartender appeared and saved Ember from answering she'd bought the dress at Goodwill. She didn't owe Chelsea a breakdown of her shopping habits.

"What can I get you, Red?" the bartender asked with a wink.

They'd been flirting all night—or she had, anyway. Since she'd always been a good tipper, she considered, perhaps, he was only expressing gratitude.

"I'll have another rainbow slushie."

He nodded and walked off.

Leaving her with her personified nightmares from age fourteen to seventeen. Would the scruffy, hot bartender let her hide behind the bar? This high school reunion would not end well.

"So, Ember, who are you here with?" Chelsea asked. "I heard about your brother. Elliot, right? That is so horrible. Remember Candice Ferguson? They found her body in the shower."

"I need to get back to my table. Excuse me." Ember's stomach churned from memories of these caustic girls. Plus, how dare Chelsea speak about suicide that way? Not that Chelsea, "lead-sitter," ever considered how her words affected others.

With the overabundance of liquor after eating only a tiny bowl of soup, Ember's stomach broke into opposing factions—carrots and peas on one side and rum drops on the other. *Should have added crackers.* Alcohol's foot soldiers would surely win the war. Maybe one more slushie wasn't such a good idea.

"You look much better, *Stember*." Jessica laughed.

Chelsea hid her smile behind her glass and elbowed Jessica's side.

Fun times.

# # #

After heavily slashing through the X in his signature, Xander passed the check to the hovering waiter.

On the table, his phone lit up with a text from Ember. Why was she at a bar on a weeknight? When they'd met earlier, they hadn't discussed their plans for the evening. Although, she had seemed a bit preoccupied.

He'd scold her for this behavior. Her friends were a corruptive influence, not pure, like his fiery rose. Nor was she defiled, like the woman seated across from him, drinking an expensive glass of red wine. She'd pay for ordering that glass. A woman of refinement would know the proper way to order wine in a restaurant. What kind of person ordered a single glass from a bottle lying around the bar for who knew how long? Positively dreadful swill. He rolled his eyes at her ignorance. So, he'd been forced to purchase the entire bottle. Plus, the fool had ordered red instead of white, which would have complimented her fish.

He planned a special reimbursement for her wasteful spending. If the way she'd pawed him all night was any indication, she was eager to please. As secretary for the Dean of Psychology, she'd cheated on her husband with college students many times over, but had finally been caught. She admitted her divorce only disturbed her because her single status took away from the excitement of adultery.

Faking an interest, he nodded at her dissertation of her daughter's gymnastics class. Good thing he'd ended his meal with coffee or he'd be nodding off. "Shall we go?" He came around the table and pulled out her chair.

They retrieved their jackets from the coatroom and headed for the parking lot.

As he opened the passenger door, he stated, "Once we get to my apartment, you'll come inside."

"Yes." She grasped his shoulder and attempted to kiss him.

Suppressing a shudder, he pressed two fingers against her lips. "Anticipation." He would not kiss her foul mouth, especially with that hideous pink lipstick. No stain from this woman would remain on his skin after he finished using her for his purposes.

After fastening his seat belt, he turned on the radio to discourage conversation, but she blathered on anyway.

"I'd always hoped you'd notice me, but you seemed so remote. I've had fantasies about your body." She ran a hand up his thigh. "I'm glad you called."

"No touching." He removed her wandering hand, setting it back on her lap. Irritated that arousal had followed her touch. "Eagerness is unbecoming, dear."

"Is it? Well then, I suppose I'll have to be disciplined."

Really? Were all woman now masochists? The more she talked, the more she ruined the mood. Perhaps he should dump her at her car; but no, he needed physical release. This unquenchable hunger came upon him at times. While he understood sexual repression was unhealthy, he hated sullying himself with creatures like this woman. Unable to have the woman he really desired, he settled for substitutes. These stand-ins didn't require more than one night, and they were willing to accommodate his special requests without question or shame.

Upon arriving at his apartment, he tossed his keys on the side table and shrugged off his suit coat. "Leave your things on the kitchen table."

Anger stirred that his physical response was not under his control. He tried tamping down his excitement. Clearly, he'd waited too long between interludes. Exchanging bodily fluids with this tainted woman would be foul and dirty. Only with Ember would the act be pure.

As she draped her jacket and purse over a chair, the woman glanced around his kitchen. "May I have a drink?"

"No. Come." Refusing to taint his bed sheets, he stepped down the hall to his office. "Are you fond of games?" He waved her through, and then locked the door.

"Always." Licking her lips, she draped her arms around his neck. "I'm up for anything. Are you?" She ran a hand over the bulge in his pants.

"You agree to role-play then?" He untangled from her grasp.

"Sure."

He led the woman to his psychologists' couch. Ember's

sweet floral scent still lingered from her perch on the seat earlier this evening. He breathed in the purity, focusing on his fantasy of her still in the room. "Kneel on the couch, facing away. Do not speak unless given permission. Your name is Flame." Digging into a side cabinet, he pulled out his props. "Put on this wig."

She turned to take the wig.

He slapped the side of her thigh with a wooden ruler. "Did I ask you to turn around? Face away." He placed the red wig on her head. She was tall like Ember, but her skin wasn't as fair. Still, the decoy worked until he could have the real thing beneath him.

Unzipping her skirt, he tugged until the fabric bunched at her knees. He ran a hand up and down her back, and then around to pinch her peaked nipples. With his other hand, he fisted his cock.

Pink blotches rose across her skin. He fingered her wet folds and entered her with a finger. The flame-red hair shimmered in the desk lamp's light. "Oh, my Flame, do you like that?"

"Yes."

Closing his eyes, he envisioned Ember's red lips and the tight shirt she'd worn over her full chest. He would make this good. Satisfaction would come from his hand, his body. He worked his fingers with studied motions until she arched and came. Heat from his steamy rose spilled over his fingers.

"Xander. I want—"

Opening his eyes, he slapped the side of her hip with his hand. "Don't speak." *Damn it!* The woman was ruining the fantasy. After slipping on a condom, he slammed inside her wet core.

"Yes, just like that."

"Don't make me gag you." He spanked her again, and then increased the depth and pace of his penetration. Deeper and harder. Close to release, he opened his eyes and watched the red head bobbing under each heavy plunge. His flame was beneath him now. He had to make her feel everything, to know only he could bring about her satisfaction.

Her breathing increased and whimpered moans poured from her throat. She shook and her fists clenched on the couch before she panted out her release.

He fisted her hair in his hands, squeezing and kneading the silky red mass until he shuddered and finished, nudging deep with his final thrust.

Withdrawing from the woman's body, he shook the vision of Ember from his mind. How revolting to associate her with this woman. His skin felt clammy under his shirt. "Please dress. I'll meet you in the front room." He refastened his pants and left the room.

This perverse act was just practice. Just practice. When he was alone, he'd remove all traces from his body. He heard the toilet flush in the hall bathroom. Good, she'd leave soon.

She entered the living room, studying him as she ran both hands down the sides of her skirt. "You're odd."

"And you're a whore who bent over for a twenty dollar bottle of wine."

In a fine fury, she yanked her jacket off the chair and stormed toward the door.

"Come now, darling. We're still playing, aren't we?" He followed her into the entry. "The words are part of the game. No need for offense"

"Calling me a whore is not part of a game." She jabbed a finger against his chest. "What is wrong with you?"

"If I had called you my sweet whore while you were writhing beneath me, would my use of the label be acceptable then?" He leaned in and lightly kissed her lips. "Don't pick and choose when to play, lady."

She flicked a glance from beneath lowered lids, stalling before opening the door.

"That was...pleasant." He brushed a hand through her hair. "We'll have to meet again sometime."

As she met his gaze, she furrowed her brow. "Seriously?"

"Come now. I thought you were adventurous."

"I'm not sure."

"We both found pleasure, didn't we? I doubt you'd want anyone to know how easily I bent you over that couch?" He ran a hand along the side of her neck into her hair and gripped it, snapping back her head as he kissed her neck.

She wrapped her arms around him. "I could stay."

"No. You'll wait for the next round." He licked her neck, and then bit her ear. "I'll see you Monday." He had to make sure she didn't reveal his secret proclivities. His personal life was separate from his professional persona. This was why he chose women who were well-used. People were less likely to believe their tales.

After he delivered the woman to her vehicle, he returned home, stripped, and washed her from his skin. He remembered the red hair grasped between his fingers. Soon, he'd have the real thing, silky and fine, flowing over his hands and his body. He'd be Ember's first. His breath caught, as he thought of her writhing body, hot from his touch. He'd teach her how to please him. Until that time, he'd suppress his urges. No more false puppets.

He poured a quarter-size dollop of body wash onto his hand and circled the soap over his belly, then moved lower.

Only with Ember could he extinguish this lusty blaze; in the meantime, he'd make do.

But soon.

So very soon.

CHAPTER 7

Walking across the player's parking lot toward his truck, Owen shoved Jason's shoulder. "Slow as molasses."

Grinning, Jason shoved back. "You're pissed because I recovered the fumble."

"The hell I am. That play won us the game. You're just lucky you didn't drop the ball. Coach would've had you doing up-downs 'til you puked."

"Thirty yards. You see me truck that guy." Jason bumped him, trying to relive the play. But, unlike the players on the field, Owen didn't fall against Jason's assault.

"All right, you saved us, now shut up." The sound of his sister's ringtone echoed across the empty lot. Owen sighed before answering. "Hey."

"Hey, yourself. Good game tonight." Maude's voice was barely audible with the loud background sounds on her end of the line.

"Thanks." He shifted his duffel bag on his shoulder and swatted at a buzzing mosquito. A warm late-summer breeze ruffled through his damp hair. He couldn't wait to go home and ice his knees.

"So, what are you doing?" Maude's overly jolly tone alerted something was up. Fake conversation was not his sister's forte.

He pinched the bridge of his nose. "Maude, why are you calling?" Why was she beating around bush? He wasn't in the mood for any more games tonight.

"Maude's calling?" Jason tapped his shoulder. "She okay?"

Owen put his finger over the phone and shoved Jason. "Back up, Mole-ass-ass."

"What?" Maude said in his ear.

"What's going on?" Jason grabbed for the phone. "Why's she calling so late?"

Owen glared at Jason and mouthed a very foul set of words.

Jason retaliated by punching his stomach.

Maude asked, "Who's with you?"

"Jason, if you want me to find out what's going on, then quit dickin' around."

"Owen?"

"What?" Owen didn't know which annoyed him more—the stupid mosquito, his sister, or Jason.

"My date's weirdly obsessed with Chewy. And I might have had a tad too much to drink." She was silent for a moment before muttering, "and Carrie left."

Chewy was their tall, blond quarterback. Everyone loved Charles Hendricks. Owen snapped him the ball each game, which meant Chewy's fingers had a very familiar relationship with his undercarriage. The man practically gave him a testicular exam during each game. Their relationship went deeper than most on the team, because trusting someone around the family jewels didn't come easy.

"Is Carrie coming back?" Owen had a sudden premonition he wouldn't be heading home.

"Owen, could you just come get me please?"

"You can't be serious." Heaving a sigh, he opened the truck's back door, threw in his bag, and elbowed Jason away from his side. "Where are you?"

"Bandits."

"Bandits. Chewy's sports bar?" Leaning his forehead against the cool metal side panel of his truck, he heaved a heavy sigh. "Do you realize what that place will be like? Especially since we won."

Silence reigned for a moment on the other end of the line. "Fine. I'll call someone else."

Ah, there went that petulant little sister tone. He even envisioned her pout. He whipped open the truck door and gritted out, "I'm coming." He disconnected and tossed his phone in the cup holder.

"What's going on?" Jason shook his shoulder.

"Get in the truck. We've got to pick up Maude at Chewy's bar." He settled in the driver's seat before slamming shut the door.

"Hell, no." Jason hopped into the passenger seat and yanked the seat belt across his lap. "Are you joking? What happened? Was she on a date? Did the guy do something?"

"What are you doing? Writing a report?" Owen shot him a sideways glare. Jason always seemed overprotective of Maude.

Jason shook his head. "You've lost your mind, walking into that place."

"I'm aware." As Owen drove out of the lot, he waved at the guys in the security booth.

"Why the hell does she go out with these losers anyway?"

"She's just trying to figure things out like the rest of us."

Jason remained silent for the rest of the short trek from the stadium to the bar.

Upon arriving, Owen spotted no parking spots along the front of the building. He swore and ran through a yellow light on his way to the parking lot. He had planned to go home, relax, and call Ember. Now he was stuck circling a bar parking lot. A bar he had no desire to enter.

"Why are you wasting time? Just valet park." Jason waved a hand toward the young guys in green suits.

Just to be an ass, Owen circled the parking lot once more. "I'm not paying twenty dollars to valet park for five minutes, because then you have to tip a hundred bucks or you end up in the papers looking like a cheap ass."

"You are an ass. Your sister needs you inside. Valet park before I kick your ass myself."

"Valet parking is for pussies."

"You know, this is why you don't get any, because you're not a gentleman."

"Oh, I'm sorry. Are we on a date? If so, you can blow me."

Owen swung the truck alongside the valet stand, handed over his keys, and tipped the kid sixty bucks.

The kid, who looked like he couldn't weigh more than a buck twenty, shook his hand. "Good game. Is Chewy coming?"

Owen sighed. That's all anyone cared about, fucking Chewy. "I don't know, kid. Maybe." He caught up with Jason outside the bar's entrance. "You do the schmoozing."

"Why me?" Jason threw up his hands, highlighting his fitted black suit and green silk tie.

"Because, you look like a schmooz in that suit." Owen laughed and opened the door.

Once they stepped inside, they were instantly recognized. Murmurs began and people hollered out, "Hey, O-line." A crowd formed around them. Everyone got caught up in the excitement of the Marauders' win. Cocky, tough guys slapped him and Jason on the back. A couple of girls asked to take pictures, which brought more people. More than a few girls lowered the necklines of their tops and offered fleshy signature pads. While these girls were pretty, none appealed like his redhead. These fan-photo moments were for players like Jason and Chewy, who absorbed attention like a sponge. This O-line moniker the press had given them caused nothing but trouble and unrealistic expectations.

"Where's Maude?"

Jason had stayed by his side which was unusual since plenty of "goal-diggers" were making the fact known they were available. "I'll text her." Owen pulled out his phone. "My thumbs are too big for this shit."

Whre ar u?

Bench outside bathroom.

Owen skirted around the bar patrons toward the restrooms in the back corner. They found Maude sitting alone on a padded bench. Her head rested against the wall. A half-empty glass tipped in her hand.

"Where's your date?" Jason demanded, arms braced across his chest. "What did he do?"

Maude blinked open her eyes. "Owen, why is Jason in my face?"

Jason shook his index finger. "Because, you date these guys Carrie sets you up with, then the night ends with her off banging some guy, and you stuck alone."

"Watch it, Jason." Maude glared. "Carrie is my friend. Besides, you have no room to talk. I heard all the ladies screaming—'O-line, Oooo, it's the O-line. Are the rumors true?

Oh, Jason, show me, baby.' If I wasn't nauseous before, hearing that bit of ridiculousness will send me to the porcelain goddess, pronto."

"Let's get you home." Owen interjected as he assessed the quickest route to the exit.

"I'm sorry to call." Maude took his hand and stood. "I know bars aren't your scene, especially after a game."

Jason scoffed. "This shouldn't be your scene, either. You're half-drunk. Dumped by some asshole outside of a bathroom. What's the matter with you?"

"What's the matter with *me*?" With both hands, Maude pushed Jason. Hard.

He bumped into a tall redhead and knocked her down.

"Oh, my God," Maude cried. "Are you all right?" She bent to check on the woman.

Owen could only stare. On the floor was *his* redhead, wearing high-heeled black leather boots with a red sweater dress that accentuated every curve—*every well-rounded, sweet Jesus curve*. He took her arm, helped her to her feet, and patted her butt. An automatic reaction on the playing field, but the pat made her gasp and swat at his hand.

"Owen, what are you doing?" Maude slapped his shoulder. "She's not one of your teammates. I'm so sorry for my brother's manners."

"Ish fine," Ember slurred.

Well, well, his woman was drunk off her ass.

"Owen, nice to schee you." She patted, and then ran her hands over his chest, as if checking he was real. Her hand lingered for a moment over his heart and a secretive smile crooked her lips.

He swore she whispered something about "lucky charms" before she bobbed her head and wobbled away. "Whoa." He blocked her by bracing his hands on her waist. "This is fortuitous. I planned on calling tonight."

"For-tu-it-tous," She tapped two fingers against his lips with each syllable. "Nish mouth." Her grin went goofy. "Nice man."

He chuckled, and then he slipped an arm around her. She still smelled like flowers. This unplanned stop to his evening was working out mighty fine. Her dress was damp at her hip where she'd landed on the floor. "Jason, I think we've found a couple of very toasty ladies tonight. Good thing our taxi services are available." He couldn't hold back a grin.

A lanky guy in a Chewy jersey rounded the corner and stopped in front of his sister. "Maude, there you are. You left and never came back."

"This your date?" Jason jerked his thumb in the guy's direction.

"Who's this guy?" "Jersey" boy raised a brow.

Jason towered over him, glaring down. "Who am I?"

"Enough," Owen reprimanded without much heat. "Coach will bench you for fighting again."

"So he gets to disrespect your sister?" Jason jabbed a finger against Jersey's chest.

"What? I didn't—" Jersey glanced back and forth between Maude and Jason, hands raised at his sides.

Maude grabbed Jason's arm and tugged him toward the exit.

With an arm around Ember's waist, Owen steered her in the same direction. "How much did you have to drink anyway?"

"Oh, they have zees yummy rainbow slushies." Her head lolled back, and she shot him a sloppy grin. "I need my stuff."

"Always holding things up." He smiled into her dazed eyes. "Where's your table?" His spiffed redhead still seemed unclear as to where she was headed. Good thing he knew how to steer. He craved a taste of those red-stained lips. Images of her in nothing but burnished lips and those black leather boots would haunt him until the vision became reality.

Ember headed for her table, but she stopped when two blondes blocked her path. Owen heard one pipe out, "Hey, Stember. Aren't you going to introduce us to your friend?"

Ember shouldered past them.

The girls approached and smiled in unison.

"Stember? Why are you calling her that?" The woman's tone spelled trouble, and he locked gazes with the lead blonde.

"She's a bit of a stump. Well, she used to be anyway. Stumpy Ember—Stember." Both girls laughed, causing their drinks to spill over the glass rims.

Light bulbs switched on in Owen's mind, illuminating another level of Ember Brooks. She had some "stems" all right. And right now those stems were in full view as she bent at the waist, revealing a finely shaped ass draped in red. One hand leveraged on the table as she dug into the booth for her purse. When she turned and saw him with the "mean" girls, she frowned, and then started muttering to herself.

What is she doing?

He jerked his head and waved her over. A buzzy chatter continued from one of the blondes, but he tuned out her words.

Ember completely ignored the girls and took his hand, leading him out the door. "Those girls…" Once outside, her whole body shivered. "They called me St—"

With a quick kiss, he silenced her.

Her warm breath puffed against his lips.

Damn if she wasn't half-gone with drink and he still wanted to bury his tongue so deep down her throat that all she'd care about was taking her next breath. Girl bullies would be the last things on her mind. And she'd understand he was the last person to care about nicknames. She'd obviously never been in a locker room full of rowdy football players.

"Let's go home, Stems."

"Don't call me that." She shoved against his chest and stalked off.

Stretching, he grabbed her arm and led her in the opposite direction. He had a feeling this wasn't the last time he'd point her north when she tried to go south.

CHAPTER 8

A loud moan vibrated through her pounding head. Ember tried wetting her mouth, but an overnight invasion by a vacuum cleaner had sucked her dry and emptied a vat of dust bunnies. The furry beasts had reproduced and now ran rampant, creating fuzz on both sides of her cheeks and her tongue.

She refused to open her eyes, knowing any light would cause all the bunny ears to blow out the top of her head.

How did I get home last night?

"Ember."

At the deep rumble, she sprung her eyes open. Her already unsteady stomach flipped the soured alcohol like gooey green pancakes in her stomach. *Oh no, Where am I?*

Owen Killion lay on his side, his arm bent at the elbow. An open palm propped against his head. Owen. Killion. Bed. Shirtless. Was this a post-alcohol delusion?

She refused to look anywhere but his face, well, maybe her gaze flashed to his chest for a second. Even that tiny motion had those bunnies hopping up and down with their huge bunny feet.

She closed her eyes. Perhaps if she opened them again, she'd wake up in her own bed.

"I brought you a Gatorade. The color's red, like you." There went that low rumble again, accompanied by a tug on her hair.

Her eyes opened—overly curious little buggers. A nicely matted chest was blocked by a bottle of red liquid. She croaked out, "What time is it?"

41

"Eleven."

"Tartar Sauce!" She shot upward, and pain lanced across her temples. "I am so late. My boss will have a major breakdown." She massaged each temple with two fingers and swallowed, holding back the impending reversal of each rainbow-colored drink. No gold waited at the end of this rainbow, only head pain and perhaps a visit to the toilet rim. No way was she getting sick in front of *him*.

"Ember, lie down. I've already spoken to your boss." Owen dangled her phone between them.

She flicked him a sideways glance from her perch on the pillows. "What did you say to Millicent? Oh my gosh, you didn't tell her I'm hungover, did you?"

He smiled and shook his head.

Which made her stomach do this weird little flip, only this one wasn't green, but rosy and pink. How could anyone be so gorgeous? Seriously. There should be laws.

"I have four Advil. They should help with your headache."

"Do I have to move to take them?" She covered her mouth with her hand, sure her breath emanated a foul, skunky stench that would melt his stubble-covered face.

She heard rustling against the comforter, and then felt fingers against her temples. He gently kneaded away her pain. Owen Killion, pro-football player, was touching her. Rainbow hangover world was a heavenly place.

"Whose bed am I in?"

"Mine."

That word, coming from that deep voice, had her mind screaming one thing and her lower anatomy screaming another.

What is the football word for escape? Return? Retreat? Reverse?

"I need to use the bathroom." As she spoke, she placed her hand over her mouth to deter any wafting of her horrid breath.

A corner of his lips curved. He'd probably seen every emotion a girl could have. He probably had a new girl each week—each day. *Retreat,* that was the word. Who cared if the term was accurate?

Owen brushed her hair behind her ear. "I'll get you a towel, Stems. You'll feel better after a shower." He nudged her hip and got out of bed wearing nothing but faded workout shorts with a

Jolly Roger imprint on the back. "I've grabbed some of Maude's clothes. Get up. Drink this with your Advil." He handed her the pills and waited while she swallowed them before leading her to the bathroom.

At the bathroom door, she blinked hard, a vivid understanding forming in her mind. This man was rich with a capital R and maybe even capital I-C-H.

Owen grabbed a remote off the counter, hit a button, and a TV appeared inside the mirror, which, of course, broadcasted ESPN. A fireplace embedded in a wall flickered to life with warm, soothing flames. Beautiful wood cabinets were topped with copper bowl sinks. Faucets sprouted from the mirror over their rims. The rustic cream-colored tile felt warm under her feet. And a wooden bench sat in the center of the room.

How much money did a professional football player make anyway? His bathroom was bigger than her entire apartment. If the bathroom was this amazing, she'd be even more out of place in the rest of the house. She had grown up in a stink hole trailer. Her apartment was a slightly bigger stink hole where she lived by herself. She was buried in student loans. Her car barely ran. While, he probably had a four-car garage filled with four cars that cost more money than she would ever make in this lifetime. Talk about being in over your head. This was the second time Owen had rescued her from tumbling into an emotional abyss. Expecting him to catch her before she fell was a dangerous game. What would happen if she opened her heart and he punted her out of the end-zone?

#

As Xander sat before the Dean of Psychology, he flicked a stray piece of lint from his pants. This past week he'd allowed his Dean, Dr. Drew Jordan, to review the first three chapters of his book. This glimpse into his book was more of a courtesy than any need for a critique.

"Very well done, Xander." He adjusted his oversized glasses, and then handed over a stack of papers. "I added some comments and suggestions. You've always been such an excellent student with a ready grasp of the human mind." He ran his fingers through his short, silver-streaked hair.

Xander shifted forward in his seat, ready to leave this droll man's presence.

"How are things outside of campus life?" Dean Jordan leaned back in his chair and studied him. "I worry you focus too much on your academic pursuits. This writing step is worth pursuing. However, you'll need to refine a few points. I'll offer as much guidance as I can."

"Thanks." *As if I need pointers from you.* "I take ample time to indulge in social engagements." Why had the dean taken such a patronizing tone? Had the secretary mentioned their date?

"How are your parents?" Dr. Jordan stirred in his leather chair.

This familial lie Xander had perpetuated served him well. No one had ever discovered the truth. "They are well. I don't see them much."

The truth was his aunt had obtained guardianship after his parents' death in a car accident. He'd been six when they died. His aunt's household staff and a continual round of tutors trained him to obey like a stray dog. Quite ironic that the puppy he'd given his aunt for Christmas got tangled around her feet at the top of the stairs, causing the domineering bitch to fall to her death. What a sight—her crumpled body splayed across the floor, the dog yipping at her feet, and the startled screams of the housekeeper. Half his dear aunt's considerate estate had gone to an arts endowment, and the rest to him. He'd been twenty at her death, and used the funds to reinvent himself and his past.

"I need to head over to the clinic." Xander stood and shook Dean Jordan's hand. "Thanks for looking over my work." He took the red-lined papers from the desk. Once he got home, he would shred them.

As he walked out, he winked at the receptionist.

She smiled in return and mouthed, *"Call me."*

Dean Jordan's fatherly attitude rankled. He didn't need this man offering advice on how he conducted his life. This ridiculously wasteful meeting only added to his agitation at being unable to reach Ember. He hopped in his car and headed to the clinic, eager to meet with his clients. *They* needed him. They appreciated his interpretation of their troubles.

This morning, he tried calling Ember before she went to

work. No answer. Called her work desk. No answer. Texted. No reply.

Very odd.

Where is she?

Those girls she worked with were a bad influence. She should rely on him. Need only him. Spending time with other people and having her decisions based on others' guidance was unacceptable.

Arriving at his assigned parking spot, he considered how their negative effect would stain her perfection. He understood Ember never had a chance at normal social interactions in college. This rebellious stage was common for children of abusive parents. Still, he would not tolerate any defiant behavior or breaches in his plan. Shaking off these unwelcome thoughts, he loosened his grip on the steering wheel, took a deep breath, and headed for his office.

Earl Grey would soothe his overtaxed mind. A habit he and Ember shared. He dropped the tea pod into his office coffee maker. Then, after checking his phone and seeing no response, he dialed Ember's number.

Once more, he left a message. "Xander again. Where are you, dear? I'm starting to worry. Call soon." Using endearments in their conversations advanced his subtle courting. After being friends for so long, they should ease into these changes.

Uneasy, due to his errant charge, he tapped his letter opener against his notebook. Five minutes remained before his next client. He logged onto Ember's Facebook page. No new posts. She rarely engaged in social media. Although, he noted, she'd recently liked the Manchester Marauders page. This made sense, since her company had just shot commercials with the players.

After logging out, he thumbed through the dean's edits on his chapter about Ember's relationship with her father. He rolled his eyes at the suggestion his opinions of "parent hunger" weren't aligned with past studies. Xander had theorized friendships and support from others could ultimately overshadow or overcome any deep-seated need or "hunger" for a mother or father figure. Replacements could be found through others. The dean disagreed.

Jaw clenched, Xander fisted the letter opener in his hand and ground through the paper over the dean's words. He threw the shredded mess in his backpack for disposal later.

A tap sounded on his door. "Mr. Kane?"

"Good morning, Alice." He came around his desk and led his first appointment to her seat.

"This box was outside your door."

"Wonderful, come on in and sit down. Did you get your things moved in?"

"Yes, I can't thank you enough…"

Xander tuned her out and grabbed his Leatherman's tool from his desk drawer and carefully opened the box. Inside were the books he'd purchased for Ember. They shared a fascination with American history and the real truth behind the building of this nation, so he'd ordered a couple books on the Reconstruction era after the Civil War.

If only he knew the truth of where she was. The idea of her constructing her own life was out of the question. He hadn't spent time creating her to his specifications for nothing. These gifts, chosen just for her, added to his courting. Together, they'd write their own history, and together, they'd rise to fame and fortune. All his plans for their future would come to fruition.

"…so again, thanks for letting me stay at your place for a while."

"What's that?" He'd forgotten the girl's presence in the room. "Oh, right, no problem, Alice. I'm sure we'll be able to work out some kind of rent structure." As he sank into the leather chair behind his desk, he smiled and showed her one of his new books. "Do you read much American history? "

"Some during high school, but not so much anymore."

"Well, feel free to read from the books at my apartment. Let's go ahead and start your session."

CHAPTER 9

"Owen!"

Ember visibly jumped when a muffled female shout sounded from the other side of the bathroom door.

Owen heaved a heavy sigh. "Give me a minute to get rid of her."

Ember's eyes went wide, and she held her towel against her chest. "Who?"

"My sister. She lives with me."

"Oh, that's right." Ember nodded, then winced and rubbed her forehead. "I sort-of remember now."

"You should, since the two of you spent the whole ride home singing AC/DC's "Big Balls" at the top of your lungs."

Her cheeks reddened, almost matching the flame in her hair.

"I'll see what the little pest wants." He smiled before shutting the door. The awed look on Ember's face when she'd glanced around his bathroom had amused him. Her color was a little green, so perhaps leaving her for a few minutes was best anyway.

Still, he glared at Maude and crossed both arms over his chest. "Why are you in my room?" His knees were killing him. He needed ten minutes in an ice bath. He'd already missed the team's traditional after-win breakfast of omelets and pancakes. Typically, he lost between five and seven pounds during each game, and by skipping that breakfast, he'd lost his chance to inhale carbs. So, this unwelcome sibling visit wasn't adding cheery vibes to his mood.

"What are *you* doing?" She rocked up on her toes with her hands in her pockets.

"I'm not having this conversation now."

"Going to help with her shower, are ya?"

He scoffed and shook his head. "Again, I ask, why are you here?" Heading to his dresser, he opened a drawer, and picked out a T-shirt.

"Mom wants to know if you're eating before going to the training center."

"She doesn't need to fix me anything." He shrugged on his shirt.

"Seriously?" Maude cocked an eyebrow. "She knows you have a girl up here. She's probably icing a wedding cake as we speak."

He grabbed his sister in a headlock and ruffled her hair.

"Hey. Stop it, jackass."

"Stop going out with asses, and I will."

"Do not say another word." She drilled a hole in his chest with her finger. "Jason lectured me enough last night. By the way, great game." She always knew how to change the subject.

"Thanks. Now, out."

A light tap sounded on his door, and then his mother stepped in the room. "Owen, can I make you something before you go?"

His rock, his home, his mom stood there in her jeans and an orange shirt with bright flowers along one sleeve. A shirt likely purchased on sale at Cracker Barrel. Her curly red-brown hair was nicely styled. She'd like his Ember. Both were very resilient women. However, his mother wasn't really here to ascertain his meal options. "Ma." He shoved his hands in his gym-short pockets.

She sniffed and brought her hands together at her waist. Waiting for what, he couldn't guess. An apology? A full meal request? A promise to marry the woman in the bathroom? Who knew?

"I'll take something before I head to class, Mom." Maude wrapped their mother in a big hug. "I appreciate you. See, Owen, this is why I'm the favorite." Out of her mom's sight, she stuck out her tongue.

"I'll let you be the favorite if you both leave."

His mother raised a single brow.

He winced. "Sorry, Mom."

She just smiled and shook her head. "Let's leave him to romance the girl on his own." Nancy Killion, mother-extraordinaire, hooked her arm in Maude's and led his nosy sister out the door. He really needed a lock.

With a bolt.

And chain.

# # #

Ember sat on the bathroom floor, leaning against the tub. The edge felt wonderfully cool against her clammy neck. After hearing the door creak open, she lifted one lid. "Owen, I don't need a shower. I can just go." She picked at a loose string on her towel. "I'm sorry for all the trouble."

"No more 'I'm sorrys.' You'll feel better after a shower." He opened a cabinet and rooted around inside.

His clanking around made more noise than a hundred howling monkeys. "I'm not undressing with you in here."

"No?"

"No."

"Well, now I'm sorry." He smiled and winked before leaning against the sink with a toothbrush multi-pack in his hand.

"Ah, don't make me laugh. Every movement is excruciating." The effort required to move facial muscles threatened to renew her temple pain. Life's light moments were rare. The bunnies had retreated to build acid mines in her stomach, and her brain was throbbing under her skull, but she was happy—with him. Although, while he visited with his sister, he had donned a shirt, quite unfortunate, as she'd enjoyed viewing the hard planes and valleys of his chest.

Oh, to go exploring across that terrain.

At floor level, she had a nice view of his legs. Solid, defined muscle led to big feet. What would he do if she leaned over, grabbed a calf, and held on for dear life?

"What was all that about?" He knelt beside her while pulling a pink-handled toothbrush from the multipack.

"What?" Which *that* did he mean? She took the toothbrush

49

and slowly crept to the sink, away from his largesse and the odd feelings of attraction she would decipher at another time.

"The drink-a-thon." He supplied a neatly rolled toothpaste tube.

The answer to his question was too involved a conversation to delve into with a slushie-fueled hangover. So, she stalled their heart-to-heart by spending a long time removing the remnants of her night's drinking from her mouth. "I might've gotten a little carried away."

"Why?"

Why? Her world was full of whys. She refilled her Dixie cup twice.

Owen leaned a hip against the sink and took the cup before she could refill it once more.

She sighed and rubbed sleep from her eyes. "I don't...my brother...those slushies had a higher alcohol content than I realized." Explaining her insane and chaotic life to a man who had marble countertops seemed a rather cracked idea. She sat on the tub edge and twisted her fingers together. "Why does it matter to you anyway? I mean...that came out rude. I guess I don't understand why you're being so nice." She peered from beneath lowered lids.

As he crouched by her side, he furrowed his brow. "Why would I be mean?"

"I'm just saying...each time you're nice, I'm surprised. And I'm glad you're not mean."

"A few Vegas Vagrants players may differ on that point after last night's game." He brushed her hair behind her ear, and then stood. "Take a shower, Stems. I'll bring you some breakfast."

"But—"

Owen pressed a finger against her lips then left.

Always walking away before she was done discussing matters. High-handed man. After locking the bathroom door, she rubbed her aching temples.

What am I doing here? And why is the TV still on?

This whole encounter was extremely humiliating. Wait, had he called her Stems? *Lovely.* Why be worried about what he thought anyway? As a super-mega rich football player, he wouldn't be interested in "Stember" Brooks from the trailer park.

She sighed and snatched the rectangular remote off the sink. Where was the power button for the TV? After thumbing through the options, she pressed mute. Ah, blessed silence.

Hanging her towel on a hook outside the shower, she quickly undressed. Sweater dresses and hangovers did not mix. Might as well enjoy this luxurious shower while she could. She studied the shower's electronic panel, most likely created in an alien futuristic space-lab. Buttons, levers, and a lighted number pad. Rich people really overcomplicated the simplest things.

Where is the hot water button? And is there a brain massager programmed in there somewhere?

CHAPTER 10

Owen settled in the truck beside her. "Once I'm done watching film and working on the playbook, I'll stop back by so we can pick up your car."

With her eyes closed, Ember slumped against the headrest. "I forgot about my car." She shielded her eyes with her hand to block the sunlight burning holes through her retinas and into the core of her still-thrumming hangover. At home, she'd down more aspirin and lie quietly in the darkest corner of her apartment.

"I'll pick you up around six. We'll grab something to eat while we're out."

Ember considered his statement for a moment then blurted, "Why?"

"Why? Because I'll be hungry. I have to re-hydrate and eat loads of carbs the day after a game." Owen flipped on his turn signal and shifted into the left lane. "Jason brings in this orange juice and wheat grass mixture. We guzzle down that concoction, too. Keeps our immune systems going. He's into that organic health shi—stuff."

"No, I meant, why are you doing all this?" She waved her hand back and forth between them. "Helping me? I'm just some girl you met at a commercial shoot. Don't you have a model to date?"

"Not my style." He winked. "Drink your water."

Bossy, and yet, so handsome. Why she found that combination so attractive, she'd delve into her psyche later to figure out. Having a man around was comforting. Before now, she'd never relied on members of the male species, except for her brother, and her brother had let her down, hadn't he? He'd ended his life, taking part of her heart with him to his cold grave. And then there was Xander, but Xander was…indefinable.

Stray thoughts of her brother were not helping her condition. "So, you've never dated a model?"

Owen grinned. "How's that red head doing?"

If he avoided answering questions, so would she. "Your mom was really nice." She didn't want to talk about the discomfort in her head or stomach. "I like Maude, too. You're lucky to have such a nice family."

"Sorry they fussed." Owen took the exit ramp leading to her duplex.

"I didn't mind. Sort of nice, actually." Lord knew, her own mother was never overly-concerned about her welfare, unless it directly affected her own well-being. She'd never made tea and toast or patted her hand. The motherly warmth exuding from Owen's mom, Nancy, made her wonder: what would hugging a mother who actually loved you feel like?

"You probably don't want the radio on, do you?"

"No, sorry. This whole situation is not flattering, at all. I mean…in general."

And speaking about unflattering, a familiar minivan was parked in front of her duplex—her mother's van.

Ember gasped and glanced at Owen. She should always expect the unexpected. Always assume a golden moment in her life would tarnish. She took short, quick breaths to fight back the rising panic rumbling through her mind and crashing into her stomach.

How can I avoid this encounter?

Owen meeting her mother was not on her to-do list. Ever.

Anytime her mother was involved, the experience ended in disaster. She clenched her fingers around the truck's door handle and closed her eyes. So exhausted—so tired of confrontations, tired of happiness slipping through her fingers time and time again.

Ember glanced at Owen's handsome profile. In her heart, an ache erupted and screamed that she would remain alone and lost in misery forever. Facing her mother was inevitable, but she hoped to dismiss Owen before things hit the south side of Diana Brooks town.

She'd successfully avoided her mother since her brother, Elliot's, funeral. But since fate liked playing havoc with her life, of course, her mother would choose today to darken her door. Why should her luck continue along any differently than the past twenty-five years?

Owen pulled in front of her mother's van.

Ember spared a quick glance in the rear-view mirror. Her pounding heart blocked out all sound. *Is the Tell-Tale Heart beating in my chest?*

"Is it all right if I park here?"

Her mother stepped out of the van.

"Ember?" Owen squeezed her hand.

Her cane struck the pavement as she wobbled toward the truck.

"What's wrong?"

Dizziness overwhelmed her vision, and Owen's voice buzzed in her head. A sweaty sheen dampened her face and body. She unlatched the seat belt, opened the door, and crumpled to the ground. Landing on her hands and knees, she retched into the narrow grass strip alongside the road.

Seconds later, Owen lifted her hair away from her face and brushed a hand along her back. "Let's get you inside."

Her mother shrieked out something imperceptible, and the horror of this moment went from slightly embarrassing to mortifying.

Still shaky, Ember attempted to stand.

Owen supported her by wrapping an arm around her body.

"What have you done?" Her mother shoved Owen's shoulder.

The force bumped him into her. Ember fell onto the grass, dirtying Maude's borrowed clothes. A harsh tug on her hair wrenched her to her feet. She gritted her teeth against the all to familiar pain.

"Where have you been?" Her mother's grip practically pulled a hair chunk from the roots. "Out all night. Not coming home until the next day. Have you no shame?"

Ember remained frozen as if in a Technicolor nightmare as her mother drew back her hand and swung.

No.

Not in front of him.

The slap stung upon connecting with her cheek, but the pain was nothing compared to the humiliation of Owen witnessing the abuse. Strong arms gripped her, and suddenly, she faced Owen's broad back. Everything in her wished to wrap her arms around his burly body, but she knew better than to reach for things she couldn't have.

"What the hell, lady?"

Diana lifted her stumpy arm and swung with her cane.

"Mom!" Ember tried to block Owen from the blow. "Don't."

He grabbed the cane mid-arc and yanked the weapon from her mother's hand. "I wouldn't."

Ember took a deep breath and attempted to diffuse the situation. "Owen—please, I can explain."

"Who is this person?" Glancing over his shoulder, Owen jerked a finger in her mother's direction. "What the hell is she doing here?"

"I'm her mother, you shit." Fury lit her mother's face.

"Mom, that's enough." Ember steadied herself with one hand against Owen's truck. Shivers racked her body. "Owen, please just go. I'll handle this."

"She slapped you." He turned and gently touched her opposite cheek. With his thumb under her chin, he tilted her head and studied her face.

Thank God, he couldn't see the internal cost. Her stinging cheek could never match the red shame burning inside her body. Perhaps that was why God had gifted her with red hair, so all the fury would have an outlet.

"Get away from my daughter." Her mother poked a pudgy finger against Owen's arm.

"You." Scowling, Owen pointed at her mother. "Quiet."

"As if you have any right to—"

"Lady, I'd stop right now." Owen glowered, standing at his full height.

Ember grasped his hand, wishing she could hold on to his

strength, but knowing she had to let go—and that hurt so much more. "Owen, please. She won't stop. It's best if you just go."

"So she can slap you again? I don't think so."

"Please, leave." Knowing she had no choice, she pressed against his chest. "I don't want you here anymore." She swallowed and tasted her humiliation. Her cheek was on fire, matching the flare of longing in her heart. But no, a relationship with Owen was inconceivable.

"I'm not comfortable leaving you here." He maintained his stance between her and her mother.

Her mother nudged her cane out of his hand. "Haven't you done enough? Bringing her home sick, full of drugs, alcohol and who knows what else? What kind of man are you?"

"What kind of man am I?" He turned with both fists locked against his hips. "I'm the kind of man who doesn't like watching mothers slap their daughters. I'm the kind of man who—"

"Owen, stop please." Trying to reason with her mother would get him nowhere. Nothing penetrated her clockwork-orange mind. She should know. She'd been trying for years. "Just go."

He scraped a hand across his face and allowed silence to fester before throwing both hands in the air. "Fine, you want me gone. I'm gone." He pounded his fist against the truck hood before vaulting into the driver's seat, slamming his door, and driving away.

Ember took a single step toward the road.

Don't leave me. I can't do this anymore.

Her face stung, a foul taste lingered in her mouth, and she still had to deal with her mother. Heartbreak would come later. Her needs always came last, why should today be any different?

"Who was that?" Her mother grabbed her arm.

Ember glared at the offending hand before yanking free.

"Are you over that silly fantasy you dreamt up about your brother's death yet? You can't truly go without seeing your own mother."

"I refuse to discuss Elliot with you, and believe me, I've done fine without you." Ember dug through her purse for her house key.

"I can see that, coming home at all hours, sick from your

night out. You're doing *just* fine." Her mother's pudgy hand waved toward the road. "Who was that man? He seems familiar."

"I owe you no explanations." Heat from the mid-morning sun added to the sick sweat covering her body. Cobwebs shimmered, and a lone spider greeted her from the post on the porch outside her apartment door. Normal, everyday things. Focus on those. The burning bush along her front windows blazed with bright fall-red. She unlocked the door, anxious for silence. Ready for this nightmare to end. But would it ever?

"He's more than a friend if he's dropping you off in the morning," her mother wheezed out, persisting in her trek along the sidewalk, and then stopping before the small cement porch. "Awfully nice truck. He got money? If you want to keep a man like that around, you'd better not get fat again."

Ember refused to respond. The blatant truth was quite clear. She wouldn't be keeping 'a man like that around.' Not after today. What would have happened between them, anyway? What did Owen want from her? She'd never know, and all because of this woman beside her. Dear old ma always found a way to suspend happiness, like a wheel that never had any spokes, because each time one was built, Diana Brooks would shatter the fine wood in her meaty hand.

"*'Don't get fat again, because he's got money,'* words of wisdom from Diana Brooks." Ember glanced over her shoulder at the constant encumbrance in her life. "Congratulations, you've won this bout." She jabbed a pink-chipped nail against her mother's chest. "But let me tell you this, if I find out you had anything to do with Elliot's death, I will be the one who wins. Stay away from me, because all I have for you is disdain."

"You think you're something now because of your college education. Well, who paid for that? How would your brother feel about you abandoning me? After all I did for the two of you, raising you both by myself..."

The throb in her cheek matched the throb in her head, in her heart. Same voice, same words drilled through her mind every time. Me, me, me and the blame—the never-ending blame. Diana Brooks could only function in this world by assigning others with her faults.

Ember stepped into her apartment, and then slammed the

door in her mother's ranting face. Since her brother's funeral, she stopped catering to the selfish, heartless woman whose needs could never be satisfied. Throwing her purse on a chair, she hobbled into the bathroom. As she stared into the mirror, she saw a redhead with blood-shot, puffy eyes—a pale girl with a pink handprint of defeat on her cheek.

Tear after tear escaped and trickled down her face, leaving an itchy trail. Her knuckles went white as they clenched the sink's edge. "Why? Why do you do this to me?" Her hands fisted in her hair as she cried out the accusation. "Why can't I have just one thing?" With a moan torn from deep in her heart, her soul, she let the heartbreak of losing her brother, her mother, and a new friend coalesce, and she collapsed onto the bathroom floor.

An unceasing knock against her front door grated against her last nerve. Ember kicked closed the bathroom door and shut out the world. Huddled on the floor, she let the sadness of her life escape her emotional stronghold.

The one person who truly understood her was dead. And while true, she had Xander, he couldn't possibly understand the unending emotional drain of living in that house—of the continual trench she trudged across each time she dealt with her mother or father. Only Elliot had understood, but he left her behind.

Owen brightened her dark world with a ray of hope. Hope for a strong shoulder. Hope for a steadfast friend. Hope for love.

Hope now gone.

She knew better.

CHAPTER 11

At the training center, Owen tore into his assigned spot, slammed the truck in park, and tugged his bag out of the back seat. The strap got tangled around his headrest. "Son of a mother fu..." An inventive mix of colorful language poured from his tongue as he wrenched the fabric free.

Once inside, he dug through the ice-filled trough set up on a table in the lobby for a Sportade. Red was the only available flavor. *Unbelievable. Un-fucking-believable.* Rage over the morning's inconceivable events finally broke through, and he grabbed the trough on both sides and shook the stupid metal piece of shit. Pissed at his limited options. And that thought pissed him off even more, because limited options were how he lived, how he puzzled his way through his life and his job. What were his options now? Was he out of his element with this girl? Following an unknown play was a foreign concept, and he didn't do indecision.

Under his breath, he cursed another blue streak while heading for the ice bath, downing his sports drink to the last drop. He'd never felt this strongly about someone he'd basically just met. This overwhelming state of emotional attachment pissed him off all over again. Why couldn't he detach his mind?

He needed to cool off. Get his mind right. And yet, he could still picture the horrified look on Ember's face, her red-rimmed eyes and the ruddy blotch on her cheek. Why had he left? His main job was protection, and he'd failed.

He punched open the steel double door.

"How long in the ice bath today, Big-O?" Doug, the head personal trainer, glanced over from where he was draining a defensive lineman's fingernail.

Something he should probably do to his own thumb since the appendage had been smashed between a couple of Vagrants' helmets yesterday. "Well, my knees need five to seven, but I could use a little longer for my head."

Doug nodded to the lineman. "Stick your thumb in here for a bit before we wrap. Come back by before you leave today, and we'll dip in the solution again. Owen, come on back."

"How are things with Steven?" Owen stripped down next to the ice-filled tub.

"Going well." Doug's smile went coy. "Thanks for asking."

"As long as you don't go into any details, man. We're good."

"You're such a Neanderthal." Doug threw a towel at his head.

"Probably." Owen settled into the ice-bath, and several of his body parts scrunched in search of warmth. While some people had doubts about the efficacy of an ice bath, others believed once a person left the ice bath, blood pumped back into tissues, which stimulated oxygen and nutrient supplies to areas needing repair. All Owen knew was his knees always felt better afterwards. Perhaps he'd trained his body and mind to believe ice baths worked, perhaps not.

"Sounds like you do need a soak. Woman trouble?" Doug swished a hand through the water.

"Ain't it always?"

"Not for me."

Owen smiled and threw an ice chunk at good ole Dougy. That was all the fun he could muster today.

After drying off and dressing, he met with the offensive lineman in the film room. Throughout the replay of yesterday's game, he pointed out every fault and misstep. Chewy and Jason sat in the back—quiet for once. Smart. After a particularly bad block, he shot out of his chair, knocking it over, and jabbed his metal pointer against the screen. "The pass protection was horrible, and you weren't picking up the blitz."

"Owen." Bronco spoke his name evenly.

"I can't watch any more of this piss-poor play." Owen kicked his chair against the wall and thundered for the door.

Bronco blocked the exit with an arm.

"Move." Ice laced Owen's tone as he glared.

"No."

"Move." Owen growled out between his teeth. The more he thought about leaving Ember behind the more livid he became. She'd taken the hit. He'd considered himself tough, grinding in the dirt each week, but Ember had lived her life in the muck. How many hits had she taken? How was she still standing?

His job required balance in body and mind. Every day he led with power at the point of attack, but today he'd gone stiff. Hadn't stopped the violence from erupting or seen the hit coming.

Bronco moved aside. "What's up your ass today?" He walked alongside, bumping against his shoulder as they moved down the hallway. "I realize we always need to improve, but we played pretty tight last night. Your attitude doesn't do much for morale. Leave your personal shit outside the door." Bronco halted him with a hand on his shoulder. "How many times do you tell us that? Yet, you come storming in, trailing along a whole stinking pile of something."

"You *are* weak on your traps." Eager for a confrontation, Owen poked Bronco's chest. "How about we work through that pile of stinking sh—"

Bronco shoved his shoulder, knocking him against a recycle bin sitting in the hallway. "Enough, I'm not running through plays with you in this mood."

"I'll go." Jason piped up from behind them.

Chewy was beside him, leaning an arm against Jason's shoulder.

A cocky smile lit Jason's pretty-boy face. He stepped forward and smirked. "What's the matter? Find out she wasn't a natural red head?"

"Outside." Fists clenched, Owen stalked toward the field. If Jason wanted natural, then Owen would go full-scale ancient warrior king.

Once on the field, Jason charged.

Jason's weak tap against his jaw brought some release for the excess adrenaline surging through his body. He couldn't take out his anger on an older woman with a bad dye job, but he could take out this frustration on his guard. He landed a blow and heard the satisfying "Ooof" from Jason.

Together, they hit the ground.

Bronco, along with the offensive line coach and Chewy, pulled them up and dragged the pair apart.

Chewy tugged Jason toward the locker rooms, but Jason continued his instigations. "And you bitch about *our* weak blocks after bringing that love tap. Come on, Big-O, I thought you wanted to play?" Taunting, he spread both arms before him and flicked his fingers into his palms.

Chewy said something inaudible.

Jason laughed and elbowed him. "You coming, Bronco? Or you gonna kiss it and make it better?"

Bronco laughed and cupped his balls. "I've got something you can kiss."

Coach pressed against Owen's chest and cuffed him on the head. "Get your head straight. I don't need you on the disabled list."

Owen sank onto the turf and rested his elbows on his bent knees. He took a deep, calming breath, ran both hands over his stubbled face, and through his hair. Coach was right.

What am I doing?

A sentiment echoed by Bronco. "What are you doing?" He placed a hand on his shoulder.

Owen shrugged him off.

Bronco planted his feet in front of him and folded both arms across his chest.

Fucker would wait forever, too. Owen huffed out a few choice curses under his breath. "The redhead. She's different." He shook his head and glanced at Bronco. "And this morning... I don't even know how to explain what happened." He scratched his chin. Damn, should have shaved.

"Different? That's the first sign of trouble. Different gets you thinking."

"I'm thinking she's more than I can handle." He pounded a fist against the ground. Could he walk away? For real?

"More than you can handle," Bronco scoffed. "Am I hearing this right? From the man who never backs down? The man who fights his way to the second level during every game." Bronco nudged his leg. "What happened?"

"I dropped Ember off this morning, and her Mom's waiting outside her place." He scrubbed a hand over his face as he considered the best way to explain what had happened. "She comes over screaming and waving around a cane before slapping Ember across the face. Slapped her. Right in front of me."

"That ain't right."

"I don't know how to handle that kind of situation."

"Violent behavior?" With a shove from his size sixteen, Bronco knocked him over. "I'd say you got a good bead on that."

Bronco was right. Wasn't preparing for violence his whole life? On a daily basis, he prepped his body and mind for the pounding coming the next time he stepped up to the line. Why should his tactics be any different with this girl? He wanted to pursue her. And shouldn't the drive to have her be even stronger now?

Owen extended a hand, tired of sitting when he should be moving forward. "Help me up."

Bronco grabbed his hand, yanked him off the ground, and out of his sorry mental state.

Ember had grown up with that cane-wielding psycho as her mother. She needed a strong man in her life. Her brother was gone, so what kind of support system did she have left? He'd always had his mother and sister. True, he'd lost his father, but he still had a rational, loving family, but not Ember. Not this girl now stuck under his skin.

He needed a playbook for this relationship. A strategic map, and in the end, he would win. Never had he backed down from an adversary. And when that opponent was a beautiful redhead with mile-long legs, deep brown eyes, and a body that fired his fantasies, she was worth the extra prep.

Back in the locker room, he grabbed his keys. "Hey, Bronc, thanks, man."

Bronco nodded. He sat on the wooden bench beside him, chewing on a protein bar.

"I'm not walking. I'll get an angle on this girl."

"She did have some nice angles." Bronco just laughed at his glare. "Careful, Big-O, figuring out a woman always leads to trouble. Their mysteries are better left to philosophers and poets."

"I can handle her. I'm heading out." He punched Bronco's shoulder. "I'm done with this pansy-ass heart-to-heart."

"I sure hope so." After a quick fist bump, Bronco closed his locker and followed him out.

Out in the parking lot, they caught Jason leaning against Chewy's truck.

Jason blew him a kiss.

Owen responded with a middle finger salute before hauling himself into his own truck and heading out of the lot.

Should he take this big of a step? Did he want a relationship? Granted, starting something at the beginning of the season was not an ideal time. Although starting slow with this woman might be his best option, since he was already in deeper than was wise. How long had Ember's mother been abusing her? Now, her brother's suicide made a little more sense. Where was her father?

With Ember, he could release his softer side. He wouldn't allow her to push him away again. Thrown by the strange encounter, he'd gone off-center today, but he'd adjusted to the play, always would. Mind made up, he wouldn't back down. Plus, he had to concede she was hungover, which made her disoriented and cranky. Not only that, she was probably embarrassed she'd tossed her cookies in front of him. He zipped onto the interstate, meshing with traffic as he headed for Ember's side of town.

She was different. Fragile, lonely, and a tad insecure, but there was more beneath the surface. He would add fuel to the dormant flame—a match to light her inner fire.

They'd burn together—a slow, rising heat. He shifted in his seat, his body already prepared to meet hers on that elemental level.

He turned up the radio, singing along with the hard rock song, at ease with the world and his game plan.

CHAPTER 12

The digital clock on his truck's dash read four sixteen instead of six. Owen glanced at Ember's duplex. Was she inside? Probably should have called first. The mature trees planted street-side had turned from green to gold. As he walked up the sidewalk, he noted the grass needed mowing. A couple red and yellow fall-type flowers sat in pots on her front porch. A jagged half-piece of plastic lingered as her doorbell cover. A muffled buzz sounded when he pressed the remaining half.

Out of the corner of his eye, he caught movement by the window. A moment passed before Ember opened the door. Her bright pink cheek matched her red-rimmed eyes and the rosy tip of her nose.

"Hi," she croaked out, and then cleared her throat. "Hello, Owen." She hesitated before stepping aside. "Why did you come back?"

He liked that she was unwilling to hold back her thoughts. The earth-tone color blend in her apartment was warm and inviting. A small dining table sat off to his left, and on the right, her living room was set up with an L-shaped couch and a wide green recliner.

"You like that word. Why. Kind of goes along with your usual sorry and thank you." Smiling, he chucked her chin.

Ember shrugged and fiddled with her fingers.

He sighed. "I came back because I said I would. We made plans."

"Why?"

"Are you serious?"

"Sorry." She winced. "Look, I don't think you should come around anymore." After grabbing a tissue from a box on her table, she sank onto the arm of her recliner. "There's a lot you don't know about me."

Now that is an understatement. "I get that. I saw that. So tell me." He sat in the recliner and pulled her into his arms.

For a few heartbeats, she remained stiff, drew a shaky breath, and then she relaxed and snuggled against his shoulder.

As he rocked them in the chair, silence reigned. Had she fallen asleep? He ran his fingers rhythmically along her arm and almost drifted off, too.

She shifted and drew a circle on his chest with her finger. "Owen?"

"Yeah."

"I'm sorry about this morning."

Her finger kept up that small circle and the caress spun to life other portions of his anatomy. He kissed the side of her head. The fragrant, flowery scent offered a soothing balm to his senses. "I came back because I understood there was a lot more going on in that moment. I'm sorry I left."

"I didn't want you to leave. Not really." She ran a hand over his chest, sliding down to his bicep where she squeezed. "You're so strong. I try to be solid like you." She tilted her head on his shoulder so she could meet his gaze. "As a kid, the environment you grow up in is your normal. You have no understanding about your world being different, but the older you get, the more you see, the more you come to understand, the life you're living is wrong. But what can you do?" She shook her head and fiddled with his shirt collar. "I have an abusive mother. My father only comes around for money, or to steal stuff."

"I'm sorry." Unsure whether he was apologizing for her messed-up life or his straying carnal thoughts. Fuck, this was erotic. Her on his lap, her voice a husky whisper in his ear, her light touch, and that glorious scent all created an inappropriately timed response in his lower body.

"You're not supposed to say that." She poked a finger against his chest.

He chuckled and kissed her nose. "Sweet little thing." Damn, this woman was something else. The decision to come back was the right one. Offering her comfort was the least he could do, for now. He understood she didn't want anything else. Ember would never expect more, because after a lifetime of disappointment, why would she? He brushed her hair behind her ear and dropped a quick peck on her cheek.

She fiddled with her fingers again, so he grasped her hand in his.

"I live an emotionally damaged life, Owen." She wiped her nose with the tissue. "I was overweight. Depressed. Angry. I went to college and did everything I could to change my path. Luckily, I got a great job, made some friends, but my family always finds a way to drag me back." She twisted the fingers on his hand now, pressing on the tips of each nail. "Owen?"

"Yeah."

"I've never dated."

Hold up. This new information would alter his playbook. "Never dated?"

"What happened to your finger?"

"Smashed it. So, you don't date?"

"Yeah, kind of goes back to the whole overweight, insecure, mental-parents thing."

"All right." He wouldn't let her sincere disclosure slip into self-doubt. Explaining her past couldn't have been easy. He would have no difficulty leading her off the path of sexual inexperience. "We'll build this slow." He wrapped his arms around her and nuzzled the top of her head.

"Build what slow? Why are you here?" She straightened and peered into his eyes. "I gave up hope for this. Whatever this...I don't..." Her shoulders slumped, and she drew in a shaky breath. "I don't know how to do whatever you think we'll do. I've had enough games played during my life, so if you're looking for something quick and easy, I'll warn you now, that isn't me."

"You have no idea how welcome your honesty is." She was so beautiful in this moment. So real that his heart faltered and knelt at her feet.

"I'm weird," she whispered, as she ripped her ragged tissue into shreds.

"No, listen." To meet her gaze, he lifted her chin. "I could give you a lot of come-on lines. Believe me, I've heard some good ones, even used a few myself, but not now. Not with you. I will work to be nothing but honest with you. I will not let you down."

She glanced away.

"Ember, look at me. I understand, for you, what I said are just words. You need actions. Proof." He tweaked her nose with his finger. "So let's go."

"Where are we going?" Her brow furrowed as she rose from her slouch on his lap and brushed off her tissue pieces.

Bracing her head between his hands, he kissed her lips. "Well, you're not ready for quick and easy, so let's grab a bite to eat and get your car from the bar parking lot." He brushed her lips again with his, savoring her honest innocence. "For now."

#

He'd come back.

Her heart fluttered one way and her mind fluttered another.

"You want a bite before I dig in?" Owen offered her his sandwich. Sitting beside her in his truck, he crumpled up a sandwich wrapper covered in Italian dressing.

Since she hadn't eaten since toast this morning, she took a big bite. The mix of meat, cheese, and seasonings exploded in her mouth. Although, she wasn't sure her stomach was quite ready for something so spicy. She'd already finished a small cup of soup with loads of crackers. Soup was so boring, like her. She should live a little, maybe add some tortilla straws, or eat a cookie.

She sneaked a glance at Owen. He was so sure of himself. Probably didn't worry about calories, cookies, or psycho parents. To possess one tenth of his strength would be a real life-changer.

What was life like for a professional football player? Were their nights full of parties, and women in hot tubs? What was real? Where had he gone after he left today? He'd said something about watching film. What film? Did he have a publicist? She knew the team had one, because her agency had worked with the gal to set up the breast cancer commercial. "Owen, you said you were going to watch film. Why? What were you watching?"

"We watched film from yesterday's game. Analyzed where we need improvement, then we prep for the next game. If someone has an injury or soreness, we'll deal with that today, as well." He took a deep draw from his soda.

She'd never seen anyone eat so much. He'd devoured two twelve-inch sandwiches. They were loaded with veggies, though. Owen had run through a drive-thru on their way to retrieve her car, after claiming starvation. Ember doubted that, but was fine with letting him pick where they ate.

"Not much of a football follower, eh?" He crunched on his final chip before wadding up the bag and adding it to the trash pile on the floor.

"Some, but no, not really. I'm trying to learn more though." Oh no, he'd think she was a stalker. "Well I mean, because...I...my friends, they're into the Marauders, so I thought I might as well join in. Then you came to do the commercial shoot so...with the whole O-line thing... and anyway."

Idiot with a capital I, Ember.

He met her gaze and smiled—a knowing smile. Obviously, her stuttering explanation made more than obvious her new-found interest in football was due to him. Which was true, and so what if it was? He should be glad to have another follower.

"Since you are interested in 'the whole O-line thing'"—He threw up air quotes, but stopped when she smacked his arm. "Sorry. Sorry. You were just so cute going into that whole explanation."

"Oh yeah, cute." She tried to pinch him, but he grabbed her wrist. He really was quick. Warmth from his grip trickled into all her hollow places.

He wrapped her hand in his. "Listen, we've just started the season. The position I play requires extra time. I work with coach on playbooks. And in-season, I spend a lot of time mentally and physically on the field. You're a distraction. A welcome one, but nonetheless, please don't be disturbed if I don't call you all the time, or if I don't stop by much. Each week, I get one day off." He squeezed her fingers. "Do you understand?"

"It's fine, Owen. You don't owe me anything."

"See, Stems, that's where you're wrong. This isn't a brush-off. I don't explain myself or my personal plans to anyone." He leaned back against the truck door, placed his arm along the back of the seat, and ran his fingers through her hair. "I know you need a slow build, so that's how this relationship will develop. We don't have much choice in the matter, anyway."

She pinched off a corner of Owen's chocolate chip cookie. Savored the melting chocolate in her mouth. Something that tasted so good, and yet was so bad for her. Was that true of this man beside her? Could she take the chance at hope again, only to collapse in pain and dashed dreams? She wanted to believe, but in her world, optimism didn't come easy.

"Owen, no matter what happens, please know I appreciate your kindness. I don't have a lot of experience with reliable men in my life, so you can understand if I have trouble believing any of this is real. I know it's cliché, but this doubt is all on me, not you. I have a lot of insecurities." She broke off another piece of the cookie and popped it into her mouth. "I'll sort through my issues, though. I have no idea what to expect from a relationship, so your belief I have expectations is incorrect. I'll be surprised and pleased if you come by or call. Truly."

"We'll get there." He pulled the other two cookies from the bag. "You want another cookie? I'm surprised you can survive eating only that flavored water."

Crap, she'd eaten the whole cookie. *Stress eating. Never a good sign.* "No, sorry. I shouldn't have eaten that cookie as it is. I don't burn calories like you do." She handed him her empty bowl, then took a sip of her lemonade.

"Lots of ways I could help you burn calories, Stems." Owen dropped her bowl into the fast food bag then pulled her across the seat. His fingers continued to comb through her hair, tucking loose strands behind her ear. He locked his hand against the nape of her neck. "How was the cookie?"

Her mouth was so close to his, she felt every word brush her lips. "What? Good, it was good." She shivered and ran her tongue over her dry lips.

"Let's see."

With steady reserve and care, his warm lips pressed a delicate kiss to hers. A wet glide swept across the seam of her lips.

On a gasp, she parted her lips and she allowed the rough slide, the thorough invasion of his tongue. An ache built at her core and her body went sleepy-relaxed. She imagined melting into a puddle of root beer-flavored Owen. Only this root beer got you drunk on the flavor, made you crave the taste time and again. A needy purr, a sigh of surrender, escaped from deep in her throat. Fear kept her from returning his silky caress.

She pulled away and watched as he licked his lips. She wanted to lick them, taste the dampness left from their kiss. "I...can I..." What was she asking? She'd never been kissed before and now that she had, how could she ask for more without seeming needy?

"I what?" Owen teased. He brushed his thumb over her lips before he briefly kissed her once more. "You're so shy." The tip of her nose received a quick peck. "We'll work on turning up the heat, Ms. Ember."

"That's clever. How are you planning on doing that?" Her voice was husky and her gaze remained on his lips. She'd meant her words as a joke, or had she? She wasn't sure. By the heated look in his eyes, she understood saying something like that could be viewed as a challenge. Or that she was being flirtatious. Maybe she was. "I didn't mean, I only meant..."

"I know what you meant, and believe me, I'd have no trouble showing you. I think a flame is building already. Too bad I can't check and see just how hot." He squeezed her upper thigh then winked. "Come on, let's get you to your car, before I lose all good sense."

Good gosh, what was she doing? He'd probably been with hundreds of women, and here she was Miss Virgin USA, who didn't even know how to kiss properly. She didn't have a chance in hell.

Her door opened, which brought about the realization she'd been staring off into space.

Reality check, Brooks.

"Right, let me find my keys." She hopped down from the truck and just eyed him standing so close. Suddenly, a strange emotion overran her mind—need, happiness, excitement, and lust. Something had her wrapping Owen in a tight hug and holding on for a timeless moment. Oh, he smelled good. She breathed deep, savoring his heady male essence until the next time she could be in his arms.

"We fit together pretty good, don't we?" He swatted her butt.

She squeaked out a "Sure" between her gasp and laugh at his antics.

He took her keys and unlocked her door. "Be careful driving home, Stems. I'll call soon. All right?"

Ember nodded and slipped into her car, conceding a much happier end to the day. She checked her face in the mirror, glad this time her pink cheeks were from her blush.

But as always, her happiness was short lived. When she turned the key, she heard her car crank over but it didn't fire. After trying again, the engine still whirled and wheezed, but wouldn't start.

Owen knocked on her window. "Pop the hood."

How awkward was this, since they'd already said goodbye. She pulled the hood knob, then got out and stood beside him as he dug into her engine. Perhaps she was still dazed from his kiss, but she had no idea what she was looking at.

"The trouble is with your coil wire." He scratched his chin as he leaned a hip against the car's front-end. "Ember, is someone angry with you?"

"Probably."

"I'm serious." He shook her arm. "First, your tires get slashed, and now someone's removed your coil wire. That's too much of a coincidence. Not only that how did they get under your hood?"

"Huh? I don't know anything about cars." She fiddled with the cap on some container, trying to remember her checkbook balance. "How much will the wire cost to replace?"

"Coil wires are an easy fix. Lock the doors. I'll call Jake."

"You can't keep fixing my car." She stepped back as she watched him drop the hood. The loud thump along with concern over these continual car troubles had her rubbing her temples, staving off a return headache. "I can pay for the service."

Owen shook his head. "Do me a favor, and let my guys work on your car."

He seemed so sincere in his worry. "Owen, this makes me uncomfortable. I'm not used to people doing something for nothing."

"My father was a mechanic."

"Um…that's nice."

"We spent a lot of time at his garage. I ended up following a different career path, but I still love working on cars." He shoved his hands in his pockets and rocked back on his heels. "I kept his business going. He was always fair, every time. Lots of people don't understand how cars work, but he did, and so do I."

"You kept your dad's business going?"

"Yeah." He shrugged.

As if keeping the legacy alive were no big thing. But it was. "So, you won't rip me off then?"

"Nope." He shook his head and flashed a crooked grin.

"Fine. Please fix my car, Mr. Mechanic."

"Back in the truck with you, then." He shuffled her over to the passenger side of his truck. "We'll wait at my place for Jake to bring by your car."

She hopped back up into her seat in the truck. Her seat. *Yeah, right.* "Thanks, Owen." How sweet of him to share that part of his past. The emotional roller coaster she'd been riding today just kept taking all kinds of dips and curves. Xander would need to schedule her for two hours next Thursday. Maybe he could squeeze her in on Monday, too. She had a lot to discuss. But then again, perhaps she would keep these moments with Owen all to herself.

"Want to listen to some music? A little AC/DC, maybe?"

"Very funny." She rolled her eyes. "No, I don't want to listen to any "balls" songs. I have to be drunk to appreciate that fully."

"Just flip through the songs on my phone until you find something, then."

She scrolled through the songs on his phone. Found his rock playlist and plugged in the USB port. A text came through from Jason titled Red Bush. "Jason just sent you a text, I think."

"What's it say?"

"Red Bush."

As Owen wrenched his phone from her hand, he swerved a little into the other lane. "Fuck...I mean, sorry...let me see." At a stoplight, he read the text then slid his phone in the front pocket of his workout pants.

"Jason seems to be a good friend."

Owen huffed out a laugh as he shook his head. "He seems to be something, all right." Bumping along a gravel driveway alongside Owen's three-car garage, they ended at a pole barn that sat back and off to the side surrounded by trees. Car parts, a couple rusty heaps, and a cool-looking old truck sat in the grass.

"Since we'll be working on your car tomorrow, you can drive one of mine. I want to make sure whoever removed the coil wire didn't damage something else."

"I'm not sure about driving one of your cars." Ember followed him to the barn's side door.

Stepping across the threshold, she halted, momentarily surprised by the modern conveniences found inside. She brushed past Owen and shook her head at the sight. A kitchenette with all the necessary amenities was to the right of the door. On the counter, an open loaf of bread rested beside a random car part and a pile of well-used tools. A metal sink was topped with a huge orange bottle of soap. The steel fridge was covered with notes and Marauders paraphernalia. "So, this is your side business?"

Owen threw his keys on the counter, then took her hand and led her over to a black car. "Working on cars is like painting a blank canvas. When you're done, only certain people can see the actual artistry." He drew her deeper into the garage and flicked on a flood of overhead lights. "Look at that Thunderbolt. You wouldn't know by looking, but she has a high-rise 427 with six hundred plus ponies. Then my '69 Boss 429, she's like me, not overly nimble, but we've both got earth-twisting torque."

So here it was—his passion. His voice seemed almost reverent as she heard him continue.

"That '72 Ranchero, she's ugly, but she can do sixty miles per hour in less than six seconds."

"Did you work on these cars yourself?" Ember ran her hand over the hood of the one he'd said was like him—The Boss. Aptly named.

"Yeah, the 429 I did with my dad." He shrugged. "Rebuilding cars actually relaxes me. I come out here, turn on some music, and fiddle around. I've got the money, and this is really my only hobby." From behind, he wrapped his arms around her and rested his chin against her head. "The house is more for Maude and Mom. I could live out here and be good."

"I don't know." She glanced back and smiled. "That shower of yours is pretty fancy."

"I still can't figure out that thing."

She laughed. Bent over at the belly laughed. The fact he couldn't figure out that ridiculous shower panel struck her as hilarious. Maybe they weren't so different after all. Here she stood in her raggedy old sweats and a faded purple sweatshirt, being held by Owen Killion. Could this get any more surreal?

He chuckled and turned her in his arms. "Why is that so funny?"

"I don't know." She wiped the tears from under her eyes. "I think I'm still hungover. I'm being silly." His wide smile lit the room and shined a tiny ray of light on the dark recesses of her wounded heart.

He rocked her back and forth in his arms before kissing her smack on the mouth. "Silly girls get to drive Audis. A safe car. I'll let you drive her until we get your car straightened out, plus an unknown vehicle might confuse whoever is bothering you."

"I don't know." Ember fingered the outline of the pirate flag on his T-shirt. "What if I wreck it, or get pulled over?"

"Yo, Owen!"

Sweet mother! She jumped about a mile out of her running shoes.

"Hey, Jake." Owen grasped her fingers and headed toward the kitchen area.

When she'd first entered, she hadn't noticed the recliners and big screen TV in the opposite corner. There was some kind of gaming system placed on top of what looked like a flipped-over truck bed.

"Hi Ember." Jake ambled into the garage, still wearing the same type of shirt as before, only this time paired with faded, hole-filled jeans.

"Jake, right? Sorry my car is causing trouble again." He shrugged a shoulder in a move similar to one she'd just witnessed by Owen.

"Doesn't sound like the trouble is from your car, but from someone messin' around."

"Give us a minute, Jake." Owen led her to the back of the garage, next to a silver Audi.

This car she recognized and knew was super expensive, but super beautiful.

"Jake and I will inspect your car." He tilted her chin with his thumb. "I trust you. I'll give you a call later on this week to see how you're doing." He opened the car door and pushed a button on the dash, which opened a garage door behind her. "I've got game prep all weekend, but when I come up for air, I'll call. I'd like to see you eat more than soup." He flicked her nose, and then dangled the keys before her eyes.

He didn't need to hypnotize her, she was already under his spell. Rising on her toes, she kissed him. There was a first time for everything, and she wanted every first time to be with him. But, because she knew Jake was watching, her kiss was one of gratitude and hope for more. This press and slant was the best she could do with her current skill set. When she felt the wet glide of his tongue, she pulled back. She met his gaze and felt the rise of nervous laughter.

He quirked a brow and tilted his head.

An expression indicative of solving an intricate problem.

No. No! Don't figure out I'm an inexperienced freak.

She should change the subject.

What subject?

Food. Go for food. She sputtered the first thing that came to mind, "I can cook. I'll make you something."

"Is that so? Well, well, I'm learning something new all the time about Miss Ember Brooks." He lowered his head as if to kiss her again.

"Then you could write a novel." She backed up, pressing against the driver's door. "As a matter of fact, there's a bio being written right now. Lots of words, and I don't even know what else. Probably no one will read it, but...I mean...who cares about my messed-up life, right?" Another one of those bone-melting crooked smiles appeared.

"I see." He studied her a moment before taking her hand and placing the keys in her palm. "Be careful driving home, Stems."

"I will. Thanks again." She smiled and got in the car, grateful for the reprieve.

He knocked on the glass and gestured for her to roll down her window. "Stems, understand this, next time you won't get off so easy."

She froze in the act of fastening her seat belt. "Um...okay."

After catching his pirate's smile, she tossed the key fob in the cup holder and prayed she'd back out of the garage without crashing into something. "Uh…got it…great…thanks again, bye."

With *her* ignition already lit by the heat of his words, she pushed the start button on the Audi's dash. The engine roared to life. As she drove off, she shot Owen a quick wave through the window.

On the way home, she may have pushed a little too hard on the gas a couple times, but this car was meant to move.

You didn't have to be a car-girl to figure that out.

CHAPTER 13

At the end of a horrendous Monday, Ember logged into her bank account. Since missing Friday due to over-imbibing, she'd had Millipede as a burr on her butt all day.

"Great." She sighed as she read her checking account's balance. Too much money spent at Bandit's Thursday night. ATM machines in bars were an evil bank conspiracy.

Kelly stopped by her cube. "Hey, what are you still doing here?"

Ember bumped her forehead against her desk's edge. "Despairing." She studied a scuffmark on her shoe.

"Over what?"

"Lack of funds." She logged out of the bank page, and then swiveled in her chair to face Kelly. "Lack of life."

"Oooh, this is deep. Do tell?" Kelly dropped her bag on the floor and leaned a hip against her desk.

"Remember when those football players came to shoot commercials last week? Well, Owen Killion stopped by afterward and took me to dinner."

"He what!?" Squealing, Kelly grasped her shoulders. "Why am I just hearing about this now? Are you serious?"

"I went to dinner with him Friday night, too."

"You're dating Owen Killion?" Kelly wrapped her in a lung-busting embrace before pulling back, her wide eyes enhanced by a huge grin. "O-line Owen Killion? I'm shocked. Shocked. How did this happen? And set me up with his friends. Now, please. Kelly needs her a football flavored, sugar-daddy."

Ember shook her head at Kelly's crazy-talk. "I'm driving his Audi."

"Shut your mouth." Kelly shoved her shoulder.

Ember snickered. "I know, right? I said, what if I get pulled over? No one will ever believe I didn't steal his car. But my car is all messed up, and since he fixes cars as a hobby, he's working on it. And I don't have a credit card, so I can't get a rental. My mom showed up after I spent the night at his house and she freaked out, so I honestly don't know what I'm doing." She threw both hands in the air. "Cause he's so... and I'm so... and it's so insane. I don't even know why I'm talking about this."

"Hold up." Kelly lifted a hand, palm up, right in her face. "Back up a sec. Spent-the-night-at-his-house?" She spaced each word separately, as if foreigners were using her tongue. "Let us go back to that statement and extrapolate, expand, and extol. Feel free to give as many details as necessary. Go on." She rolled her hand in an encouraging wave. "I'm listening. Enraptured, even."

"Did we spend a little time in the E-section of the dictionary today?"

They both burst into giggles, like grade school girls discussing their first crush.

"I am grateful Owen is letting me use his vehicle. My mother racked up a ton of debt on my credit card, and since I just paid everything off, I'd rather not incur the expense of a rental car."

"Irrelevant. Back to Owen and naked night spending." Kelly poked her with her key.

"No nakedness. I was buzzed Thursday night, and he took me to his place. You were off talking to that art student." She shrugged. "We didn't do anything."

"Bow-chica-bow-wow." Kelly gyrated into porno dance moves. "Ember's getting her some O-line loving." She batted her eyelashes and stuck two fingers by her lips, like a silly Betty Boop. "Oh, Owen, it's soo big."

Ember rolled her eyes. "Why do I talk to you?"

"Apparently, you don't."

Ouch. "I'm sorry. I've never dated a guy before. I have no idea what to do." She fiddled with her purse strap, unable to meet Kelly's gaze. "He's too good for me."

Kelly jabbed her shoulder with a single finger. "That's your mother talking."

"You're right." She rubbed the spot Kelly had stabbed. *Double ouch.* She must have power fingers. Ember heaved a sigh. "So…Owen met her."

"How?" Kelly gasped. "When?"

Ember explained how her mother had been waiting when she arrived home with Owen. "I was this close to slapping her when she raised her cane at Owen." She wasn't fool enough to forget the anger and destruction Diana Brooks could cause. Her budding relationship with Owen had survived the initial storm, but who knew what lightning and rolling thunder Momma and Daddy Brooks had in store.

"I'm so sorry, Ember." Kelly patted her hand. "But hey, Owen stuck around afterwards. That's a good thing, right?"

Ember nodded. Trust Kelly to find the rainbow in the storm clouds. There'd been plenty of past fights. Her high school years were full of family altercations and visits to the police station. But she'd left that girl behind, refusing to follow the same abusive path as her mother.

Emitting a familiar trill, her phone lit up on her desk. "It's Xander. I should probably answer. We'll talk later."

"All right, but don't hold out on me anymore. Details, Ember. Details." Kelly forked two fingers, pointed them at her own eyes, and then pantomimed back and forth between hers and Embers. "I'm watching you."

"Would you go before you accidentally poke out an eye." She smiled as she waved Kelly away. "Xander, sorry, I was talking to Kelly."

"Ember, dear. Can you meet for dinner?"

"You have no idea how much I'd love to do just that."

"I'll come by your place and pick you up. I've made reservations for seven o'clock at Shipman's Cove."

"Wow, fancy." Her vacant checkbook flashed through her mind. "I'm not overflowing with funds right now."

"Let this be my treat."

What would she do without Xander? "All right, I'll see you then."

Time and time again, she'd bared her soul to him, but she'd

never joined him for a fancy dinner. Tallying the number of therapy hours she'd spent in his dorm room and now his apartment was near impossible. His life was so different from hers. He'd grown up with loving parents, and yet, he helped her analyze her every word and feeling. She loved him as deeply as possible. He was her rock in the tumultuous sea of her life. Working through the pain of losing her brother was only tolerable with his guidance. Which reminded her, she should give Bethany a call. How was her brother's girlfriend faring? She'd been wrapped in her own budding romance and had neglected her friend.

Ember scrolled through her contacts and pushed Bethany's number.

The phone rang four times. She almost gave up until Bethany answered.

"Oh, Ember." The words came across choked and muffled.

The sounds evoked the picture of a sobbing, tormented girl. A vision she recognized, since losing her brother. "Bethany? What's wrong?"

"H-h-how c-c-could he?" Her staccato voice hiccupped out words between sobs.

"How could he what?"

The only response was sniffles and rushed breathing.

"Bethany? What's wrong?" Only more muffled cries. "I'm on my way."

As Ember walked to her car, she remembered her dinner plans with Xander. "Shoot." She whipped out her phone and thumbed a quick text.

Bethany upset. Dinner tomorrow? My treat? Sorry.

Luckily, she was still using Owen's Audi, which helped her whip around corners and perhaps, go a little faster than was legal, but the handling and speed was a thrill. She arrived at Bethany's apartment in record time.

Bethany answered the door with one arm folded around her body. A tissue wad filled her free hand, and her eyes were a puffy red. She retreated to the living room and slumped onto the couch. Used tissues and old take-out boxes lined the coffee table along with a mound of opened mail. Bethany huddled into a ball and covered herself with a pink camouflage blanket.

"Why are you so upset? What happened?" Ember sat beside

her and patted her knee. Was her brother's death finally becoming real?

Ember refused to acknowledge the vice tightening her chest, faltering her breathing. She kept her gaze on Bethany so she wouldn't see her brother's belongings throughout the place and lose her tenuous emotional hold. In her hurry to arrive, she hadn't taken into account her feelings when sitting in this apartment again. This retreat her brother had created with Bethany, where he had found happiness, acceptance, and love. So then, why? Why? Would she ever know?

Bethany blew her nose with the crumpled tissue in her hand then handed over an open envelope.

A bill.

Addressed to her brother.

From a jewelry store.

Ember unfolded the paper, her heart pounding fast and hard. That tortured organ very aware of the coming disaster, even before she recognized the danger. The room became a vacuum, and all she could see were the tiny black figures at the bottom of the paper.

First payment $127.25. Due September 5th.

$3,657.77 total for a ring.

An engagement ring.

She shot off the couch, bumping her knee against the coffee table.

Red haze filmed her vision. A muffled knock sounded on another apartment door. Bethany sniffled. Water dripped from the kitchen faucet. Stench from the take-out cloyed in her nostrils. Goosebumps formed on her skin. Every sense merged into one overwhelming moment of clarity.

Engagement ring.

$127.25 due on September 5th.

But this meant… this meant…

Struggling to escape this madness, she glanced at the floor and drew in a steady flow of air. In and out. In and out. On her way to the bathroom, she stumbled and fell to the floor. Crawling to the toilet, she pulled up on the rim, stared into the pool of water, and heaved her lunch. Crumpled and confused, she balled up on the floor, for hours, minutes, days.

Who bought an engagement ring then went home and pulled a trigger? No one. Not her brother. No. Wrong. Wrong. Wrong. She'd finally slipped past that edge. Wrong. Wrong. She yanked a towel off the rack, wiped her mouth, and then held the cloth against her mouth, stifling her building scream.

Nothing added up. Why?

$127.25. Payment due.

He'd bought a ring. He'd had hope. He'd had love.

And *she'd* taken everything.

She'd done this. The fault had to lie with her. She'd been there. She'd killed him. Ember bit the towel. Hard. Had he told her about the ring? Was that why?

Where was the ring?

And where was the gun now? How would *she* like the loaded barrel pointed at her crazy head?

Intent solidified, Ember straightened, splashed water on her overheated face, washed her hands, and left the bathroom.

"Ember, where are you going?" Bethany asked from her perch on the couch. Tiny and small, her voice was incapable of penetrating Ember's supreme focus.

Ember grabbed her purse off the coffee table. "Elliot didn't kill himself. That duplicitous bitch is going to pay."

"Wait, Ember." Bethany shot off the couch and clutched her arm. "Don't."

Ember just glanced at her grip and raised a brow.

Bethany released her arm. "Elliot wouldn't want you to do anything rash."

"Well, he's not here to stop me, is he? And all because...all because..." Closing her eyes for a moment, she drew a deep breath. "No. I can't."

No time for conversations that offered no answers or release from acidic anger eroding her very sanity. She had to leave.

She needed to see her mother about a bullet.

# # #

Xander sat outside Ember's duplex, thumb raised over the delete button. He regulated his breathing, calming the storm before his anger rose out of proportion to the situation.

Ember breaking plans was extremely irresponsible and

discourteous. They had made an agreement, therefore, she should stick to her end of the bargain. Hadn't he always stuck to his?

After guiding her, day after day as they delved through her past, he deserved better treatment. His knuckles went white as his hand tightened on the steering wheel.

"You're lucky, Ms. Brooks, that I don't have my ruler." He'd derive great pleasure in pinking her bottom and tugging relentlessly on those red locks. He released a shaky breath. Perhaps, he should call the secretary again and relieve some of this pent-up aggression.

Apparently, her brother's death wasn't enough to keep her home at night. Instead, she gallivanted through the streets, not turning to the one person who could direct her through her despair. Who was Bethany in comparison to him? Nothing, and yet, she'd rated higher. This would never do.

Ember's adoration had always been evident, but he'd never acted on her wishes. Now, he'd have to make his intentions clear. Speak plainly of his plans for their future.

Giving her homework after their sessions would occupy her time and mind. He fiddled with the Leatherman tool on his key ring—a Christmas gift from Ember. She'd held his hand and said, "I hope this tool serves for you as you've served for me." Lies. All lies. He pounded his palm against the steering wheel.

They would work on her priorities. He intended to keep her as his own, since he'd groomed her for his pleasure.

He flicked open the tool and ran the knife-edge along his empty water bottle. *No. Don't do this. Don't. Calm down. Calm.* He used his breathing exercises. Nothing to worry about, she was just helping a friend. That made her special, proved she cared. Proved once she gave her heart, nothing stopped her from those she loved. In the very near future, her heart would be content serving only him. He'd make sure of it.

He threw the shredded bottle onto the passenger side floorboard and started his engine. He deleted Ember's text and thumbed through his contacts until he found the secretary.

"Hello, pet." He rubbed his damp palm along the front of his Dockers. "Do you have plans this evening?"

CHAPTER 14

Ember yanked open the trailer door, slamming the trashed screen against the outside wall. She stormed into the double-wide and, after her vision adjusted to the dark, she saw her mother slouched in her recliner.

Grabbing her mother by her pajama top, she lifted her so they were nose to nose. An abundance of adrenaline made her capable of lifting her obese mother from her overburdened seat.

"What are you doing here?" Blinking herself awake, her mother dug her press-on nails into Ember's forearm. "Let go of me."

Ember tightened her grip on her mother's shirt and shook her. "Why? Why did you kill him?"

"Who do you think you are, storming in here? You said you don't need me or want me in your life. So, why are you barging into this house?"

"Shut. Up." Ember pinched her forefinger and thumb together and shoved them right before her mother's eyes. "I am this close to slapping your face. Elliot bought Bethany a ring. A ring," she roared, lost in fury. "So, you know what that means? He didn't kill himself. Now, let's get to the truth." Once again, she yanked hard against her mother's shirt, ripping the collar from the stained top. "What did you do? What happened that night?"

"Engagement ring." Her mother smirked. "Is that what that little witch told you? She probably bought the ring and now wants you to pay. Did you see it? If so, that's *our* ring. You need to get it back."

Ember's world went from red to ultraviolet. "Get it back?" she jarred out the words between clenched teeth. "I'm here to talk about Elliot, and all you care about is the ring?" Ember bit down hard on her back teeth, refusing to cry. She would not let the rage and desperation turn to passive tears. Would not weaken in front of this monster. "I want the truth."

"He's dead. You can't change what he's done."

"What *he's* done?" Ember shook her head in disbelief, looking away from the woman in disgust. Something caught her eye. Something different. "Is that a new TV?"

Her mother's shoulders sank, and she fell silent, refusing to meet her gaze or answer her question.

"How can you afford a new TV?" Where had she gotten the money for such an expense? Her disability checks wouldn't cover a nice flat screen like this one. So where…

Holy smokes—life insurance. Why hadn't she looked into that before? "Did Elliot have a life insurance policy?"

"How do you think I paid for the funeral?" Her mother took a big swig from her yellow diet soda. "I'll get the ring from Bethany. Now I'm watching my shows." She waved Ember out of the way. "I'm not going through the whole mess about your brother again. Get out."

"What happened that night? What did you say?" Ember remained infuriated that her mother sat in her faded brown recliner passing judgment on the world, taking advantage of anything and all. Never offering any answers, any succor. Diana Brooks never had and never would. Why should she expect any different?

"I'll call the police, if you don't leave in the next minute. Wouldn't that look good for your fancy uptown job?"

"Go ahead. Then I can inform the police you killed my brother to get his life insurance money." She thumbed through a sheaf of food-stained papers on her mother's side table. Proof of something had to be somewhere.

"You can't handle the fact he left you." Her mother rocked back and forth in her chair. "You made your father leave, and now your brother. Can't keep a man around, can you?"

"What?" Ember crumbled the papers in her hand.

"You think that fancy football player's going to stick. That's right, I figured out his name. He's interested in one thing from trailer trash like you, and you've already given that up. Your only hope is getting pregnant, since that's the only way you'll profit."

Ember would not let her mother's vitriol sideline her purpose. "We are talking about Elliot. What happened? He was your son. Don't you care? Don't you want to know why?"

"I know why." As she sat up in her chair, her mother hurled the remote across the room. "He was a loser like his father. If you were still living here, he wouldn't have killed himself. But you left him behind and went to college. Made him wish for greater things. Got his hopes up. We both know he was never meant to succeed. He was stupid in school."

Ember huffed in disgust then tossed the wadded papers onto the floor. "If that helps you sleep at night. Pretty bad, you didn't know your own son. Too busy beating us down to see we were fine together. We didn't need you. You're the one who can't keep anyone around." Ember shoved a finger in her mother's face. Close, so close to losing control.

"I sleep fine at night because you were to blame. Where were *you* that night? Certainly not here, supporting him. Feeding him. Maybe you're just jealous because his last moments were with me. Always thought you two had a weird relationship. A little too close, if you ask—"

Ember slapped her mother's disgusting mouth.

Her mother sat stunned a moment before rising from her chair with a wild scream.

Ember slapped her again.

Lost in violence.

Lost in hate.

Her mother swayed, and then crashed into the side table, falling with a loud thunk against the trailer floor. Her soda bottle tipped over and fizzled onto the carpet next to her face.

Shaking with rage—with horror—Ember had tears streaming down her cheeks. She'd finally done the one thing she swore she'd never do. She'd become her mother, brutal and violent.

Blood trickled from the gash on her mother's forehead.

She'd killed her.

How do you check a person's pulse? Is she dead? Is that even a bad thing?

How could she even think that?

Shame engulfed her. Diana Brooks had turned her children into killers. Violence was never the answer, and yet, all the therapy she'd done with Xander evaporated when dealing with this woman. She'd let her mother's words seep beneath her thick skin. The insinuation she and Elliot had...no...too disturbing to consider. And how dare her mother speak such a thing? But why was she even surprised at the twisted words spewing from her mother's mouth?

Why couldn't she view her mother like a stranger? Detach completely. Why was Diana Brooks who she was? How had she become this grasping, evil person?

And why am I following the same path?

Only one choice before her now—she had to face the consequences. When would the violence of her life stop? How would she find peace? She ran a hand under her sloppy, wet nose. *Where are the tissues?* She should invest in a life-long supply.

After taking a deep breath, she dialed 9-1-1. "My mother needs an ambulance."

"Extent of her injuries?"

"She has a gash on her head. I've either knocked her out, or she's dead."

CHAPTER 15

Ember studied the violent hand resting on the pay phone's handle.

"Ember, you need to make your call." Her neighbor and city cop, Clayton, patted her shoulder. "Do you have someone who can pick you up and post your bail?"

Lucky for her, he'd been at the station when she was brought in earlier. When she'd first moved into her apartment, her libido had stood up and said, *Hello*, the first time she saw Clayton. Tall, with dark hair and blue eyes, but those eyes carried a sadness, or a warning that he wouldn't let you close. He'd always been kind, but never anything more. After living beside her for two years, he was aware of her rotten family history. Had even broken up a fight between her brother and father a few months ago.

Do I have someone to call?

Why was Owen's number at the forefront of her mind? A number she'd memorized from her cell contacts.

The arresting officer was surprisingly kind after her mother regained consciousness and released a verbal tirade that would make a pirate proud. Though, Ember knew she also had Clayton to thank for her treatment. Not that she deserved his support, after her appalling behavior.

"Let's go, Rocky. I haven't got all night." Clayton smirked as he stood beside her, flinging his handcuffs around his index finger.

Why did girl fights entertain men so much?

With bail set at a grand due to her mother filing a battery charge, Ember now faced the potential of one year in jail or a five thousand dollar fine. Bonding out would cost ten percent, which was a hundred bucks. *Owen has the money.* Great, now she really did sound like her mother. Again, his number ran through her mind. Did she want him to see her this way? Broken and defeated by her unconscionable behavior?

She could call Xander, but then she'd have to endure a lecture. Not really what she needed to hear right now.

So what other choice did she have, really? Owen had been so kind and understanding. Gently teasing her. Taking care of her during her troubles. She shouldn't rely on him to save her every time. Don't get in too deep. But why not, her heart couldn't possibly break any more, could it? And so what if it did? She'd welcome any future pain if right now she could feel his solid arms wrapped around her, offering comfort and warmth. Would he help her once more?

She lifted the germ-ridden receiver.

The robotic collect call voice asked her questions.

Then Owen accepted the call. A trickle of relief coursed through her from just hearing his voice. "Owen."

"Ember? What's wrong?"

"I'm at Manchester Central police station. Do you have a hundred dollars I could borrow?"

"Police station?"

"Yeah." She scratched the hair at her temple. Were lice jumping from the receiver to her head? Why was she so itchy? "I sort-of got into a fight with my mother."

Clayton bumped her arm and scoffed, "Sort-of."

Everyone probably thought her an evil abuser. They didn't understand the pent-up restraint she'd let off the leash tonight. Still, her actions were shameful. She wouldn't blame others for their less-than-sympathetic thoughts. This wasn't her first time at Manchester station. Many childhood nights were spent here after her parents' sparring matches. Lovely memories.

"I'll be right down." Owen mumbled something to someone in the background then said, "Will you shut up?"

"What?"

"No, not you, Stems. I'll be there as soon as I can. Don't

worry. All right?"

She bit down hard on her trembling lower lip before answering. "Yes. Thanks, Owen." Tears leaked down her cheeks. Amazing she had anything left to cry out.

He was coming.

She needed to mentally prepare for his questions. His rebuke. She waited in the cell until Clayton appeared again and led her to the lobby.

There he stood by the exit, papers in hand. He met her gaze and flashed a tight-lipped grin. So handsome in a trendy pair of jeans and a long-sleeved, hunter green Henley. He looked like a Marauder—resolute and inexorable. Was he angry? Had he been in the middle of something? A date?

"Ember."

Owen's deep voice shattered through her thoughts, and the reverberations echoed through her chest.

"Let's go." He tilted his head toward the door.

She stepped toward the exit then stopped, afraid to leave. A sturdy arm appeared in front of her and pushed open the door. She felt Owen's steady presence at her back and wanted nothing more than to fall, to escape into his arms.

He latched onto her elbow and led her to his truck. Not speaking.

The early days of fall had finally settled in, and a light drizzle cooled her overheated skin. Darkness came sooner in the evenings now. A few light posts illuminated the parking lot. Moths buzzed around the lights, seeking warmth. She knew exactly how they felt. There was always a barrier to that heat. She could never seem to break through to the light. Halting at the back of the truck, she squeezed his hand.

He met her gaze with a raised brow, and then blinked against the raindrops landing on his face.

"I'll pay you back."

The questioning brow lowered into a glare. "Get in."

With a trembling hand, she opened the passenger door, climbed up, and sat very still in her seat.

"You want to pay me back?" Owen snapped the seat belt over his shoulder. "Then tell me what's going on."

She sighed and sneaked a quick glance at his resolute face.

"I'd really rather not."

"I'd really rather you did."

She scratched her head. Had she left the police station with more attached to her person than she'd come in with? What time was it anyway? "Why are you all dressed up?"

"Ember. Answer the question." He squeezed her knee.

"I think I got lice."

Owen drew in a deep breath and released it slowly before speaking. "We are not leaving this parking lot until you explain."

"I'm sorry."

"Ember!"

She jumped. *Geesh.* Someone was touchy this evening. "Fine. My mother is an evil, selfish monster. Verbally and physically abusive, as you've witnessed." She picked at a hangnail on her thumb.

"Go on." He unlatched her seat belt and pulled her across the seat. "What happened tonight?"

"My brother met Bethany about a year ago. They moved in together. I thought he was happy with her." She rested her forehead on Owen's shoulder and released a couple shuddering breaths. Too late to stop the story now. If Owen wanted to know the truth, and he did deserve to know, he would get the whole story. "Elliot apparently bought Bethany an engagement ring. She received the bill today."

She focused on Owen's scent, so clean. Calming. She wouldn't think about those numbers. Wouldn't go back to her moment of insanity. "I can't prove my mother killed Elliot. The police have ruled his death a suicide. I refuse to believe he would do that to me. To Bethany. To himself." She squeezed his upper arm with both hands, holding back the building fury. "There's so much more, and my mother won't tell me what happened that night. The not knowing is tearing me up inside." Rubbing a hand across her breastbone helped ease some of the ache. "People don't go around buying engagement rings and then shooting themselves. They don't. He didn't."

"All right, baby. Calm down." Owen took over massaging her chest, then worked his way up to the side of her neck. "We'll work through this."

"I can't calm down when my brother's been murdered by my

psychotic mother. I have to figure out what happened. But she won't tell me, and then she said…she accused me of…the thought is so foul, so I slapped her. I thought for a moment I might have killed her." Ember straightened from her slouch against his shoulder and met his gaze. "That's the kind of girl you have in your truck right now. A girl who doesn't care if she committed matricide."

"I know what kind of girl you are." He cradled her head between his hands.

She clutched his bicep and held tight. Just held tight. Warmth shot from her hand all the way to her toes.

"What can I do?"

"I don't know," she whispered. Pulling away, she offered a weak smile and returned to her seat. "Do you think we could go now?"

"Sure, Stems."

The cab remained quiet as they pulled out of the station and maneuvered through downtown. A previous thought occurred. "You smell fantastic. Did you just shower? I'm sorry, I only meant…did you have a date or something? I didn't mean to interfere with your plans."

"Ember, stop. I was headed out to dinner with Bronco and Chewy. No big thing."

"I'm crazy, you know. Go back home. Meet your friends." She pointed out the window. "You can drop me off on that corner. Please, salvage your evening."

"Too late for that now." He chucked her chin with his knuckle and flashed a grin that crinkled the corners of his eyes. "I'm sorry about your brother."

How did he always know the perfect thing to say? Lord, he was a fine specimen. She'd love to conduct extensive research all up and down that fine body. There he sat, looking like the millionaire he so obviously was, and she was still in her work clothes, covered in jail germs. Welcome to Fantasy Island. Wasn't that some funky TV show like a zillion years ago?

He took the exit leading to her duplex.

The rain stopped, and the windshield wipers screeched out a tune before he shut them off. Lights from local businesses blurred as they drove by. Cars with people in their own worlds, with their own problems, sped alongside the truck. Masses of wet leaves filled the crevices along the sides of the streets. The seasons continued, the world continued—with or without her. But with her, tonight, who had she become? Did she have no control over her emotions? Why was her life always in such chaos?

Owen pulled alongside the curb, shifted into Park, and stepped out of the truck.

What was he thinking? Was he really willing to take her on? She wanted to invite him inside—her life, her heart, her body. Just put out everything for him to take as he wished. Just once explore the nature of a relationship with a man. But deep-seated fears kept her from saying the words, because how would this end? What was the point?

In silence, they walked up the sidewalk. Owen shook her keys out of a yellow manila envelope and unlocked the door. "Have you had dinner?"

"No." However, the payphone cooties running rampant over her body were, no doubt, experiencing a moment of fine dining. "I'd really like to shower, so…"

"Go ahead. I'll dig around the kitchen."

"You don't have to stay. I believe I've tapped out on favors."

"Damn it, Ember. Don't do that." Heaving a heavy sigh, he tossed his keys on her table. "Don't act like I'm just some guy who does you favors. The implication is insulting."

And there went her stomach, falling to her knees. "I apologize, but in truth, I don't know you. Not really. I'll admit you've been reliable, and for that I'm grateful, but I can't expect anyone to save me. I have to survive on my own." She placed a fist against her pounding heart. "Based on everything I've told you, you should see that. I can't fall at your knees, because I'll never get back up when you leave."

He scrubbed a hand over his face. "Lady, you're complicated." Facing her with both hands on his hips, he shook his head. "We're playing this out. You *will* know me. And as you see, I'm not leaving." Stepping close, he gathered her in his arms. "We're in this together. I expect you to ask for help. Don't hesitate."

She nodded against his chest. Her happy dance would wait until she was alone in the shower. "I haven't been to the grocery store in a while."

"Go take your shower. I'll figure something out."

She nodded, but kept a tight grip around his waist. He smelled amazing. A citrusy, gooey caramel smell that had her wishing she was made of nougat so they could meld together forever in an airtight wrapper. "Thank you."

Realizing she was pawing his body, she retreated to wash the evenings mental and physical stains from her body.

# # #

Damn, if that woman wasn't playing with fire. She had him lit from one end of the wick to the other. Talk about tumultuous relationships. The level of heat coming from his body right now could burn down the walls of this apartment—half from lust, the other half from anger over her situation.

Owen rummaged through her kitchen cabinets, not surprised at finding only soup and a couple boxes of oatmeal. When he'd received her call, he'd been on his way to dinner. A collect call meant the situation was not good. When he'd heard Ember's shaky voice, his protective instincts kicked in high gear. What had she suffered during her life? Had her mother really killed her brother? Was she involved in some kind of therapy to deal with all this?

He fully comprehended how she ended up at the station, especially after meeting her mother. After posting her bail, he'd heard the story from a cop named Clayton. Apparently, he was her neighbor and had witnessed Ember's colorful family many times before.

The strength of Owen's feelings toward her should have surprised him, but they didn't. He'd known upon first seeing her, she was different. She had the potential to mean something more. *The one.* Fine by him. A strong woman who wouldn't back down or agree with everything he said was exactly what he needed in a partner. Now that he'd found her, he'd convince her of the legitimacy of his intentions.

Dressed in sweats and a T-shirt, Ember slid into the kitchen, ruffling her red-gold locks with a big green towel.

He glanced down and caught a glimpse of toenails painted siren red. He pulled the towel from her hands and took over drying her hair, edging her backward against the counter with his hips.

"You're supposed to squeeze my hair dry, not fluff it up." She poked his chest, grabbed her towel, and then combed her fingers through her hair.

Aligning his fingers with hers, he helped her work through her wet strands, tilting her head in perfect alignment with his.

Her gaze dropped to his lips.

That was all the invitation he needed. He kissed her with a light, seeking kiss, attempting to soothe her worries.

Ember remained stock still, not returning his pressure.

While he understood she had limited experience with men, he assumed involvement in at least a few intimate encounters. But based on this lack of response, he reconsidered.

She braced her hand against his chest. "Why are you still here? I expected you to run for the hills." Frowning, she fiddled with the button on his shirt. "I'm the crazy red-headed girl. You deserve someone normal."

"Ember, there is no normal." He lifted her chin with his thumb. "We all live along the edge. One person's normal may be completely insane to someone else." In an effort to soothe, he brushed a hand up and down her arm. "But then you make a connection with a person, someone you want in your inner circle. Someone whose normal you want to know." Slowly, he stroked his fingers through her damp hair. Wet silk, releasing a heady floral scent that fed his already raging need. He adjusted his stance, holding back all thoughts of throwing her on the kitchen table and devouring every portion of her body.

Focus, man. She's not ready.

"My life revolves around my job. I eat, sleep, train, and work with the same guys every day. I need more. You think you're different, but in truth, you're so much more. So strong. A survivor. You've built a beautiful character to go along with your absolutely beautiful body."

"You have a way with words, Mr. Killion. Must come from all those locker room pep talks." She ducked her chin and whispered, "But I'm not beautiful."

"I disagree." He trailed a finger along her cheek, tipped her chin, and kissed her.

She drew away.

"Where you headed, Stems?" With a gentle nudge at the small of her back, he pulled her lower body closer. "I understand, you know."

Her busy little fingers were buttoning and unbuttoning his shirt. "Ember. Look at me."

She heaved a heavy sigh. "No."

He chuckled and squeezed her waist. "I know you're inexperienced with men."

"More like having no experience," she mumbled. "I don't know how to do this." She shoved away and paced off into the living room, arms flailing wildly as she explained, "I wasn't interested. And they weren't interested. So I don't know what I'm supposed to do. And here you are, all super-hot in your nice clothes and caramel brown eyes. And I want so much, but I don't know how to take...I want...will you...maybe you should come back in a couple of years, and I'll try to garner some experience between now and then."

"Hell no." He tugged on her wrist and brought her to a halt before him. "I'll teach you. I'll garner the shit out of you." He kissed his way down the side of her neck.

With a shuddering breath, she admitted, "Do you know how embarrassing this evening has been? My life is one disaster after another. And now, I have to explain to Mr. Hot Sex in Boots, that I don't know how to kiss him."

"Stop. Your lack of experience is nothing to be ashamed of." Owen walked her backward until her knees hit the couch. He sank down and pulled her onto his lap. "I'm here. I want you. I don't give a fuck about anything else." He lightly brushed her lips with his. "Trust me." Damn, this was dangerous ground with her all soft and vulnerable. And him thinking he could be some kind of sex professor. *As if.*

With one hand supporting her back and the other locked around her jaw, he held her still as he tilted his head and bent closer, softly pressing his lips to hers. Adjusting the angle, he toyed with her mouth until her lips softened and shaped to his.

Her warm, minty breath fanned against his lips as she released eager little whimpers and shifted closer.

These feather-light kisses were driving him mad. She wasn't

the only one shaking and breathless with need. Fortunately, Ember had no idea how far gone he was. He wanted nothing more than to pillage, to claim, but this mild exploration served for now.

She clutched his shirt, gripping the fabric tightly in a fist. Her breathing became erratic, and she panted against his lips.

"Shhh, all right. Just breathe."

"I'm sorry."

"No, don't apologize. Just relax." He held her face between his hands, stroking her cheeks with his thumbs. "This time, part your lips."

Her eyes were wide open as she nodded and maintained her claw-like grip on his shirt.

Lowering his head, he settled his mouth firmly on hers. Then with a silken glide, he broke past her parted barrier. The hot tangle of his tongue against hers shot raging heat through his body. A deep groan escaped his lips as he slanted his mouth over hers, driving her to follow his frenzied pace.

Sexy cries escaped from her throat, vibrating down his spine, firing across his over-kindled erection.

"That's right, baby, purr for me." Fuck, this was hot. He ran his thumb along her damp bottom lip. "It's your mouth, your lips are such a deep red. So soft."

She shifted on his lap and ran a hand along his cheek.

"Close your eyes, Stems." He wrapped her hair in a fist and held the mass aside as he feasted on the fragrant field of her neck.

She gasped and clasped the back of his head, drawing him close.

Working his way along her jaw line, he returned to her plump lower lip and nipped with his teeth. Frantic need replaced all caution. He seized her mouth and plunged rhythmically, using all she had learned and pushing her to accept more. At her eager response, Owen charged to the next level, moving his hand under her shirt, across her warm, soft skin, he brushed a thumb over her peaked nipple.

She jerked and pulled back. "So, um…okay, I'm—"

With a smooth caress, he rolled the tight bud between his fingers. "Stop thinking."

Her lids went heavy and she hauled him closer, kissing him

hard.

With a degree of wildness he'd never encountered, he felt her work her hands through his hair and then over his shoulders. His overeager little steam engine was obviously a quick study. He let her play and learn, certainly willing to be her test subject.

Finding pleasure in her exploration and her eager pants, he let go of all conscious thought and allowed himself only to feel. When had he ever been this hot? This strained? His cock was on the edge of eruption like some adolescent first-timer.

A cool tingle from her light touch brushed across his stomach. Then her journey became more intent as she traveled south.

Damn, she was brave. He took over the kiss. Teasing her mouth until he heard her moan for more.

She rose above him, wrapping his head in her hands as she straddled him. Her body rocked against his jutting erection, until she unbuttoned his jeans and relieved the pressure.

The tip of his cock peeked out from the top of his briefs. He gripped her hips and matched the thrusts of his tongue to the thrust of his hips against her core. A yearning ache built inside, a need only she could assuage. How many more steps could he take? Could he hold back his warrior nature and not plunder the bounty before him? And what a bounty she was. Full breasts, red lips, trim waist that fit perfectly between his hands. She fit, everything about her. There was more he could do for her, to her.

He straightened from his slouch and quickly twisted so she was beneath him on the couch. He rose above her, and his heart almost stopped at the sight. Red strands framed her face. Her chest heaved and her lips were ruddy-red from his bruising kisses. The needy look in her deep brown eyes said more—give me more.

"Owen?" Ember trailed a finger along his jaw. "Is this...am I doing all right?"

He answered her with a hard, quick kiss. "You are the sweetest fucking thing. I've got the taste of you burned on my tongue now, baby."

Her knees spread wider, and she arched her hips against him. "You kiss like you play football. I feel like you're tackling me, driving me to fall. But I want... I want to go down." She peered upward from beneath lowered lids. "And I want you to tumble with me."

"Believe me, Stems, I've fallen." He kissed her, once more overcome by the intensity of his feelings. Never before had his heart been so aligned with his body, leading the path to completion together. The intensity of sheer lust for this woman would sustain him for a lifetime and beyond. His hands shook as he brushed her hair away from her face. Her fearless drive into this physical field defeated him. Everything he thought he knew about sex became new with her. Only her.

Through meshed lips and exploring hands, heat burned between them again. Their bodies flexed in time with their grinding kisses.

A sound broke through his flaming lust. A triple beat, beat, beat mirrored his pounding heart and the blood pumping to his cock. Thump, thump, thump.

Someone was knocking on her door.

He groaned against her mouth.

She pulled at his neck, drawing him back.

Probably for the best, someone had sounded a two-minute warning. Had those few minutes gone by, he'd have thrown her over his shoulder, marched into her bedroom, and broke through every sexual boundary she'd ever raised. Twice.

He sat up and adjusted his aching erection. He'd rather face a herd of defensive lineman than deal with the discomfort of neon blue-balls.

"Owen?"

Ember's husky whisper fired another round of heat through his body.

"Do you want to go to my room?"

Hell, yes, he wanted to go to her room. What time was it anyway? Why was some asshole knocking on her door in the middle of the night? Better not be that cop, or they'd have words. Not a fair statement, but considering the ache in his unrelieved body, anyone interfering deserved a punt into next week. "There's someone at your door."

"There's someone at my door." She blindly repeated his words, still lost in the moment.

"Yeah, Stems." He chuckled at her confusion then massaged the crease in her brow. "You want me to answer?" He brushed at her wild hair, patting the fluffed strands against her head.

"Not really."

He grunted at her honesty, since he felt the same way. "Listen." He gripped her chin. "You get an A plus for that first lesson. However, we'll have to retest to be sure."

She rolled her eyes and slapped his arm. "Go answer the door."

At his raised brow, she added a please.

Adjustments made and clothes realigned, Owen opened the door, and then studied the well-dressed fellow across the threshold.

"Excuse me, is Ember here?"

The guy, a slim-but-fit blond with glasses, stepped inside, brushing shoulders with Owen as he passed.

Owen shut the door, mumbling, "Sure, come on in." He spun on his heel and saw Ember standing by the couch, shrugging on a sweater.

The guy wrapped her in a hug then held her at arms' length. "I was worried about you, dear. You didn't call, so I contacted Bethany. She told me how agitated you were when you left. Are you all right?"

Who the hell is this guy?

Ember glanced over and met his gaze. Her top teeth were practically chewing a hole in her bottom lip. "Owen, this is my friend, Xander Kane. Xander, this is Owen Killion. He's one of the Marauders' players I met the other day."

"Her friend" was boldly running his hand up and down her arm.

Too late, buddy. She's taken.

The guy was not her type—too fastidious and patronizing. A trait made obvious by the fake smile currently lining his face. Owen stepped back into the living room.

Xander nodded then turned away. "Ember, I'm sorry I was unavailable. I was in the middle of a session. What can I do? Should we sit? We've talked about this. You can't revert."

"But, Xander, I have proof now."

Xander shot him an uneasy glance accompanied by oh, yeah, there it was, the supercilious smile.

"Owen, is it? I've got this now. We appreciate your

assistance."

We? He was still hot as hell, still throbbed with lust from every pore, and this stick waltzed in and thought to take over his woman? Why wasn't she kicking Xander's ass out?

His marks stained her skin. Her lips were bright red, and pink blotches appeared on her neck from *his* whisker burn. And yet, some pompous ass breezed in and brushed him off.

"Owen, I'm sorry. I should discuss things with Xander."

Ember remained next to Xander like she hadn't been arching under his body moments before. She looked at this guy like a lost puppy who'd found her leash. Owen pinched the bridge of his nose and huffed out a laugh. "Any time." After grabbing his keys off the kitchen table, he headed for the door.

What was he doing? He didn't back down.

Halting, he turned and stomped across the room, pulled Ember into his arms, and waited until she peered at his mouth before kissing her. This hard mark ran along the same lines as pissing to mark his territory, but he was a pirate at heart. And they plundered. They claimed. Best that she and this Xander stick understood that now.

He pulled back—point made.

Wide-eyed, Ember blew out a breath and pressed her fingers to her lips.

He was halfway to the door before she spoke. He glanced over his shoulder.

"Owen. I'll wait...I'll be here, I mean...for...ah...you know...whenever." Her arms flailed all over the place again.

"I'll see you soon, Stems."

Xander followed him to the door. "I'll see you out." He walked alongside and, upon arriving at the end of the sidewalk, finally deigned to speak. "I'm afraid Ember hasn't mentioned you."

"No?" So, they were going to do this now. *Good.*

"No. Her brother just died, so she's emotionally vulnerable. As her psychological adviser, I'll direct her away from situations that can exacerbate her issues." Xander locked his hands behind his back and rocked back on his heels. "I appreciate any assistance you offered her this evening. However, future endeavors won't be necessary. I've had Ember in hand since college. Our relationship is expanding, so you'll kindly step aside. You do not possess the qualities necessary to engage in a relationship with Ember." He raised a blond brow. "Am I making myself clear?"

Owen looked Xander over. Football was really a mental chess game. So, he knew how to play against a worthy opponent. "You know, there's something about Ember I still haven't quite figured out." This pretentious prick was under the impression he had Ember controlled and contained. Even more of a mistake, he thought he had Owen pegged.

"Oh, what is that?" A polite smile flashed, and he waved his fingers between them. "Perhaps I could help."

"It's a conundrum."

"I know her very well." Xander folded his hands together at his waist.

"I gathered that." Owen winked. "So tell me, is it roses or carnations?"

"What?"

"Her. You get close enough and her scent overwhelms you. She's a heady mix. I'll solve the puzzle soon though, son. Don't worry." Owen clasped Xander's shoulder. "I'll break her down piece by piece then put her back together again."

Xander shrugged Owen's hand off his shoulder. When he met Owen's gaze, he exuded an icy emptiness from his narrowed eyes before he spoke with cutting precision. "One word from me and she'll never speak to you again."

Owen popped a piece of gum in his mouth, allowing the mint to fill his senses before replying, "I'm really leaning more toward the roses." He shifted toward his truck, took a couple steps then turned to deliver the final blow. "And speaking of words, she hasn't mentioned you, either."

CHAPTER 16

Holy chocolate cupcakes. What was she doing? Why was she letting Owen leave? Perhaps she'd been stunned stupid. Or was her main reason fear? Alarm bells tolling at the intensity of physical desire overwhelming her body made her hide behind Xander's timely arrival.

With every rasp of Owen's tongue, she'd been ready to devour him, to let him breach every boarded wall in her body and mind. Her body still called for an ending she knew would only be obtained with him.

So why had she latched onto Xander like he was the only life vest floating in an endless sea? How could she dismiss Owen after he'd been so kind and patient? Rudely, she'd basically said, "Thanks, and see ya." *Brilliant, Ember.* Relationships were obviously not her forte.

And why was Xander coming by so late? She needed a huge glass of water. No, make that ice water. Her body was still on high heat from Owen's magic hands, magic mouth, magic bulge in his jeans.

How would she explain this to Xander? And what was taking him so long? She sank into her recliner and rocked back and forth, then shot up. Lunch, she'd prepare her lunch for tomorrow. Right now, occupying her mind and stepping away from the couch where she'd almost forfeited her virginity was a necessary move.

She heard the front door open, but kept busy organizing her lunch contents, although she'd pulled out the ketchup instead of the mustard.

"Ember?"

"In the kitchen." She didn't want to discuss Owen with Xander right now. Not until she had time to process these foreign emotions on her own.

Xander stood in the kitchen doorway with his hands stuffed in his front pockets. "I find I'm quite curious." An inquiring brow rose. "In all our recent discussions, you've failed to mention this man."

Oh no. He was angry. She'd never heard him use such clipped tones.

"Let's adjourn to the living room, to discuss this void in our dialogue."

Ember sealed the package on her lunchmeat, opened the fridge, and let the cool air soothe her overheated skin before following Xander to the living room.

He patted the couch.

Like a recalcitrant child, she sank onto the seat beside him.

Xander cleared his throat. "I cannot fully diagnose and counsel you if you do not provide all the necessary information. Do you understand how difficult my job becomes when I'm not given all the facts?"

She nodded. Yet compliance while sitting on this couch with a different man had her more confused than ever.

"And do you understand how beginning a new friendship would be relevant to our discussions?" He reached over and held her hand. "I've always been your friend. Your one true confidant. Why should there be secrets between us now? Is this man asking you to hide your relationship?"

"No." Owen hadn't asked her to hide their relationship, but he hadn't asked her to talk about it either. So, what did that mean? Did he want them to remain secret?

"This man, why was he here?"

"I'm sorry I hadn't mentioned him. I...there wasn't... I didn't feel there was anything to say." She flicked her free hand in the air. "I met him a week or so ago. He's been helping me with my car. He's a mechanic, of sorts. We met at the office. He's a player for the Marauders." Her explanation spilled out, not making any sense at all.

Xander straightened and ran his hand along his knee. "Ahhh, now I see. You've associated him with a white knight. A hero complex. Is this the case?" He shook his head and patted her hand. "Ember dear, haven't you suffered enough? This dark cloud you're under will only grow if you pursue this man with unrealistic expectations. He's not your type. Unintelligent. Unavailable. Men like him enjoy the hunt. They seek out weak prey and once obtained, they devour and gnaw through the bones. I'm sure interest from such a man does much for your self-esteem. But, dear, beware the fairy tale. He's not your hero."

He held her chin in his hand and met her gaze. "He does not hold your ruby red slipper. I do. We've belonged together from the beginning. We've grown our friendship until we were prepared to move forward." He tucked a strand of hair behind her ear. "We will begin that path now. I've known for some time that you were attracted to me, but felt pursuing that course unwise."

"Xander, I'm very confused." She sank back on the couch, pulling her hand free from his hold. "You've never indicated those sorts of feelings. I did fancy myself in love with you at one time, but I gave up." She had loved him, did love him, but she had always wondered how much was gratitude and convenience versus a heart-pounding true love. Even now she felt a pull toward him, a thread of love, but the feeling wasn't the same as what she'd just experienced with Owen. No ache formed in her chest, no muggy heat formed under her skin at his touch. So what did that mean? Could she change? Find those feelings for Xander once again? Did she want to?

"I know this may come as a happy surprise, Ember, but I've always meant for us to come together." He traced a single finger down her jawline. "Always meant to remain by your side. I'm sorry I haven't made that more clear. I plan to remedy that now."

Conflicting emotions roiled through her mind. This was Xander. In truth, she'd denied an attraction to him for many years. He was her security blanket, her calm in every storm. He'd always been so professional, never allowing any other relationship but patient and doctor to develop. So she'd buried those long-ago feelings. How could she dig them up again, when they were covered by a huge heap of Owen Killion?

And yet, Xander had never led her astray. He'd always shown

her the true path. So, then, what was she doing? Was he right about Owen? She had no experience with such matters. "Xander, I'm not sure you're right about Owen." She gathered a throw pillow and held it against her chest. "He's been very kind. I don't believe he's some sort of villain intent on wrecking my heart. I agree I may view him as a hero, but can't I just escape into that for a while? Can't I try something new?"

"I won't let you ruin our progress by pursuing a man who seems exciting, who is the epitome of the bad-boy, because this only leads to emotional collapse. This thrill ride isn't worth the devastation when you go off-track." He threw her pillow onto the floor and gently nudged her head against his shoulder. "Men like that brute don't have intentions for the long term. In his career, too many temptations are present, dear. Don't believe you'll be the one to control him. That myth never becomes reality."

Never becomes reality.

Her body was on sexual overload, and now her brain hit a red light.

Two men—one night. But no clear path or direction.

Everything Xander said made absolute sense. She was safer and could develop so much more with him. They'd already laid all the groundwork. He knew everything about her. There would be no surprises. So, why not? Why not try?

Once again, she was pulled against a strong male body, and once again warm lips pressed upon hers. This kiss was strong and did everything to convince. Skilled and seductive, but her heart didn't beat, her body didn't melt. No thoughts of pursuing more, of touching his body, occurred. She met his kiss, able to match him with her recent tutoring, but this kiss felt wrong. Forced and awkward. Why did Xander have to choose tonight to propose this change in their relationship? Would she hurt him with a solid rejection? Should she reject him? She was flying down a track without a safety belt and her mind, her heart, screamed stop.

She drew away. "Xander, please. I've been through the emotional wringer tonight. First, the engagement ring shocker, next I ended up in jail, then Owen, and now you. I can't process anything right now."

"I'm sorry." Xander clasped her chin and met her gaze. "Did you say jail?"

Oh boy, why had she let that slip? "I was only...you see...Bethany showed me...Elliot bought this ring...and Mom..." Ember shook her head, unable to continue.

"Start at the beginning, dear." Xander brushed her hair behind her ear. He held her hand as she explained her fury, which led to her altercation with her mother. As she expected, she found him disappointed she'd resorted to violent behavior.

"Ember, this is why you should only rely on established relationships. You're still in turmoil over your brother's death, and are unable to control your emotions. Normal people do not react in such a violent manner. I believe this man is provoking additional strain and causing you to act out in other areas."

"Perhaps, you're right." She rose from the couch. "I'm tired, and I have to work tomorrow." She hated feeling like an errant child. One who didn't know her own mind or heart. "I think not analyzing everything in my head would be nice."

"Let me worry about what's going on in your head." He rose from the couch and kissed her softly before wrapping her in a quick hug. "We'll talk again soon. I'll give you some time to process our new direction."

What direction?

Nothing made sense. Maybe he was right. Delving into a new relationship without knowing how, without a guide, might not be the smartest move right now. But sometimes, she felt like Xander held her back, kept her from exploring new areas by keeping her mired in the past.

Which man was right? With Owen, sparks flew, but was he just a flash in the pan? And so what if he was? She deserved one walk on the wild side. Just once, taking an escape into madness with a pirate—to sail across those stormy seas to find treasure and bliss. What was wrong with having such an adventure?

At the door, Xander kissed her cheek. "You have no idea how happy claiming you as mine makes me. I'll check in tomorrow. I know I've given you a lot to digest."

From longstanding habit, she simply nodded. What else was there to say? She'd spent the first half of her life digesting things until she'd become poisoned, both mentally and physically. How much more could one girl swallow in this lifetime?

Which would she choose—Xander, a steady staple, or Owen,

a foreign delicacy? She already knew which flavor remained on her tongue. So, how did she tell her best friend she couldn't choose him? How could she explain her feelings to a man who had held her deepest secrets in his hands for so many years? And what if Xander was right about Owen? Was she just some bounty for a playboy Marauder? Did she have enough strength to release her heart and find out?

Maybe she should stop whining about her own life and think about poor Bethany. Maybe she could investigate this new information. Maybe she should focus on finding answers about that night.

Maybe she should snuggle under her bed sheets, read a steamy romance about pirates, and fall into an endless slumber until her true white knight came along.

And just maybe I've lost my mind.

Ember grabbed her towel off the kitchen floor, tossed it onto her overflowing clothes basket, and then stumbled to her bedroom. Surely, all the maybes could wait until tomorrow.

CHAPTER 17

Ember stabbed a fork into her salad, trying to pierce the last tiny tomato square. "Do you think restaurants have some sort of special tool that dices tomatoes so small?" She'd forgone her packed lunch, as she was in desperate need for some blunt advice from the one person she knew would tell her straight.

"Ember, you're stalling." Kelly swirled her tea with her straw.

"When I wanted Xander to like me, he didn't. And now, I don't know if I ever really liked him, or if the feelings were based in gratitude. Now that I've learned he's interested, I feel obligated in a way, but that's unfair, because I don't feel any sexual attraction toward him. But with Owen, I feel…I guess the best way to describe the feeling is lightened. Free. And really, just happy."

"Xander is a nice-looking guy, but Owen is on a whole other level." Kelly took a bite from her fish taco.

Ember sighed, wishing she'd ordered the same, instead of boring salad.

Why am I never happy with what I have?

"Xander isn't my type. Not for a relationship. I don't understand why, of all people, he doesn't see we are not meant to be a couple. Changing our labels will just make everything awkward." Ember picked through her salad, searching for one more tomato square. "Anyway, I'm baffled by his sudden interest."

"Well, you are hot. If I was a guy, I'd do you." Kelly blew an air-kiss across the table.

"What?"

"Guys look at you all the time, but you put off this don't-approach-me-vibe, so they don't."

"Owen approached."

"He's a smart cookie. Don't let all that crap Xander was trying to feed you about Owen sway your opinion." Kelly wiped at the salsa dribbling down her chin. "Ah, messy." She tossed her napkin aside. "Listen, Xander is just trying to get in your pants."

"I'm still like, why me? Owen is gorgeous, and he has an amazing body."

"Really, and what parts are amazing?" Kelly held her taco mid-air, and then set the crumbling mess back on her plate. "List them in slow detail, please, or fast, whichever."

Smiling, Ember shook her fork at Kelly. "I don't know *all* the details."

"Not yet," Kelly quipped.

"I have like zero sexual experience, you know that. I've never done anything with a guy. He's got to think I'm weird."

"He's letting you drive his Audi, Ember. He's seriously interested." Kelly took the last crouton off Ember's bread plate. "If I could learn how to kiss from anyone, I'd choose Mr. Fine-from-the-O-line."

"Hey." Waving her knife in the air, Ember sent her friend a mock-glare.

"Calm down, Miss Real Football Wives of Manchester." Kelly laid her hand upon her chest and swooned in the booth. "Teach me, Owen. I'm all yours."

Ember choked on her iced tea, laughing so hard. "I'd love to be all his, believe me."

"High–five on that one."

They slapped palms.

"I say, hit the end zone with that O-liner." Kelly rocked in her chair as she sang, "Like a Virgin". Loudly.

And why not, the song was appropriate. Trust Kelly to take her lemon-lined life and make lemonade. "Don't quit your day job." Actually, Ember would admit having the interest of two dynamic men was exciting—until someone got hurt, anyway.

At a diagonal table, a couple of guys observed Kelly's garish display.

Ember rolled her eyes and shook her head.

Both guys laughed.

Huh? Am I flirting?

She glanced at Kelly, who now smiled at the men, as well. *Good lord.* "Kelly, if you're done with your 80's flashback, can we return to the prior subject? What about Xander?"

"Explain you want to keep the patient-doctor relationship, and you're not comfortable with anything else. Including playing doctor." She snickered, covering her mouth with her napkin.

"You're the one who needs a doctor. But what you said makes sense." So why then did Ember think explaining her decision to Xander wouldn't be so easy? He was very goal-oriented and driven. She'd been the object under his magnifying glass for so long, she felt perhaps he was the one confusing emotions. Plus, if they began something more personal wouldn't that interfere with their professional association? Weren't there codes against patient relationships? Not only that, they'd never really delved into his personal life. She knew he dated, but wasn't sure if any were long-term relationships.

With that in mind, she decided she wasn't being a very good friend. She should question Kelly about her personal life. That's what friends were supposed to do. She shouldn't hog all the social time with her mad world. "So, what happened with the Roth project? Did you work things out with Paul?"

As Ember listened to Kelly, she realized how grateful she was to have the woman as a friend. And while she did owe a large part of her ability to maintain healthy relationships to Xander's therapy, she had also worked hard on improving herself. He was the torch, but she'd kept the flame alive. What more could she give him? She couldn't lie to herself, or him, and feel something she didn't and most likely never would.

Her salad churned in her stomach. She hoped her decision didn't rip apart their relationship. She'd grab a hot tea on her way back to the office. Earl Grey never asked anything of her. He was there for her, all the time. Warm and smooth—like Owen Killion.

She wasn't sure about what was happening with Owen, but she knew what happened to her libido when he was around. Why not explore that attraction? Take good moments when they came.

And if a bad moment happened in her relationship with Owen, she'd remember the good. She was strong, and could survive anything life threw her way.

Except maybe jail time. But she'd see what she could work out with Clayton on that later. Her mother had left a lovely message this morning about filing battery charges. Maybe Ember wouldn't have to worry about picking between two men, because she'd be in jail worrying about two women—with shanks. *Great.*

# # #

After a seemingly never-ending Wednesday full of team meetings, weight training, and studying the new playbook, Owen checked his phone on his way to the parking lot. He'd driven the '69 Boss 429 today. Matched his mood—fierce.

He flicked open a text from Ember. Her standard 'thank you' was capped off with a yellow smiley face. Good, she'd received his roses. He hadn't mentally delved into the Xander factor since leaving her Monday night. Though Owen was not quite sure what position Mr. Patronizing played in Ember's life, he'd not allow jealousy to interfere with his feelings or plans.

He thumbed a quick text: *So you liked the roses?*

Seeing Ember tonight wasn't an option since he'd scheduled a crack-of-dawn interview at a local radio station, plus his evening was booked with two other meetings.

As he started the engine, he barely heard his phone's ping. The engine's chest-rumbling purr was a symphony to his soul. "Sorry, baby," he patted the dash. "Someday soon, we'll grab that redhead and let those horses run."

He read Ember's text. *Yes, thank you. They are beautiful*

Owen turned off the engine, settling in for a little text talk with his woman. *What are you doing?*

Heading home after a workout.

Get all sweaty?

Maybe

I'd like to see. Owen shifted in his seat and opened the car door in order to let in a cool fall breeze.

I'm here.

I have two appmt tonight.

Ok

You ok?

I talked to Clayton about engagement ring bill. Know a good lawyer?

Why?

Nothing

Why?

Mom's pressing charges. Think you could slip me some cigarettes

I'll see what I can do

K

He sighed. His first meeting tonight would hopefully clear up some of her family issues. Since he couldn't explain by text his intentions and didn't want to cause her any alarm, he simply responded: *I'm meeting with my agent. I'll call when I get back in town Sun. We'll find something besides soup, k?*

Yes good lick Owen

What? Good lick? He chuckled at Ember's obvious thumb-slip.

Luck. Good Luck.

Where's your head woman?

Where's yours?

Damn. How could she make him hot with just text messages? Cheeky little witch.

What exactly are you asking, Ms. Brooks?

Simple curiosity.

I am more than happy to satisfy any questions you have. Right now gotta scoot.

Sorry ok bye

He pulled out of the parking lot and headed downtown. Pushed the car a bit, because after his little flirtation, he was not only sporting a raging erection, but he was running late. Releasing his frustrations by pressing on the gas pedal would pose no problem for this engine. His phone pinged again, and when he stopped at a red light, he read another text from Ember.

Have a good game. Hope you win.

Sweet thing, yet she occasionally added a little spice in the mix. Some prim-and-proper miss would never do, he wanted his fiery Ember. He punched up the volume on the radio, and used 2-60 air conditioning—two windows down and cruising at 60 mph. Fall in the upper northeast corner of Ohio saw temperature changes from fifty degrees one day to eighty degrees the next.

Tonight, a warm front had moved in, but luckily over the weekend, the temps would turn mild again. His baby didn't have air conditioning, and on a hot late-August night like this, he reconsidered his decision.

He wasn't, however, reconsidering his appointment with private detective Rachel Harris. His first meeting of the night was scheduled to discuss Ember's situation.

The detective's office was in a high-rise building nestled between the five or six main buildings downtown. He hated leaving his baby in a parking garage, so he traveled to the very top row and parked in a lone spot, then made his way across the lightly lit lot and headed for the stairwell. After entering the appropriate building, he stopped at the security guard's desk. Unfortunately, the guard recognized him and decided to go into a dissertation about how the team could improve.

Owen thanked the guy for his support, slapping him on the back. "I hear you, brother. I've got to head up. Have a nice night."

"Will do, sir." The guard shuffled back to his desk after giving a salute.

The detective's instructions led him to the third floor where he swung a left, then stood stymied when he arrived at the offices of Harris and Blackstreet Law. Pulling open the door, he was met by a smiling receptionist. He asked the whereabouts of Rachel Harris, and the secretary smiled and led him through the maze of executive offices to a small office in the back.

At his knock on her open door, he held back his shock over her appearance. She shut a folder full of photos, then stood and greeted him. Ms. Harris was a pretty, petite thing—with long brunette hair, a pert nose, strong chin, and an athletic body. Not his type, but attractive nonetheless.

As she came around her desk, she held out her hand.

"Didn't realize you were a lawyer." He shook her hand then took a seat.

"That's my uncle. He set me up here, thinking if I'm around enough, I'll switch. Sorry my desk is such a mess."

A couple of R.W. Hardcastle books were haphazardly stacked on the corner of her desk.

"My buddy, Bronco, reads those books." He ran his finger along their spines. "Has his nose buried in one all the time."

"Does he?" A single, sculpted brow rose. "So, what can I help you with, Mr. Killion?"

He glanced around the room, not sure what he'd expected from a detective's office. Having an office based in a lawyer's den made sense, he supposed. And her desk was far from a mess. As a matter of fact, he felt sure if she ever saw his desk, she'd reconsider her definition. Books on a broad range of subjects lined a wide set of shelves behind her, from gun safety and serial killers to organic chemistry and gardening. Bronco would feel like a kid in a candy store in this room.

"Mr. Killion?"

"Sorry." He shifted forward in his seat, bracing his hands on his knees. "Now that I'm here, I'm not quite sure where to start."

"You mentioned a friend and her brother."

"Right. A friend of mine, Ember Brooks, believes her mother killed her brother. The police have ruled the death a suicide, but she disagrees. I'd like you to investigate the case."

"No problem." She folded her hands on the desktop. "I hate to say this, because you are obviously a well-paying client, but the outcome will most likely remain suicide."

He'd considered that outcome, but paying for another pair of eyes on the matter was worth the risk. Perhaps the results would give Ember some closure. "Ember's pretty adamant. I'm not so sure either, after hearing her story." He shrugged. "Plus, I trust her instincts."

"All right." Rachel nodded and gathered a pen and notepad. "Tell me what you know."

After he gave her what little he did know, he listened to her explain the route she would take to investigate Elliot's death. They agreed on a fee, and then talked football for a few minutes.

"Thanks for your time, Ms. Harris." He stood, reached across the desk, and shook her hand. "You've got my cell. Call with any questions."

"Will do, Big-O."

On his way out, he felt a slight niggle between his shoulder blades and turned back. "One more thing. Ember has this friend, Xander Kane. I'd like you to run a check on his background, whereabouts, the usual investigation."

"Xander Kane." Harris penned his name in her notes.

"Why?"

"Instincts."

"Why do I get the feeling that's not all?"

"Apparently, you have good instincts, too." He winked then mimed firing a pistol with his index finger and thumb.

"Hey, Killion," Rachel called, leaning against her office door. "I'm figuring you're a leftie, since you always snap a bit to the right."

Owen snorted out a laugh and rubbed the back of his neck. "Uh...maybe."

"And tell Bronco to get out of the blocks quicker when he's pulling."

Owen cringed. "Now that advice may be a little hard to deliver."

On his way down the corridor, he checked the time on his phone. He thumbed a quick text to his agent, saying he was running a few minutes late.

He hated being late, but would sacrifice a little time to help Ember. He sprinted down the stairs, rather than waiting for the elevator, glad he'd chosen Rachel Harris. Any woman who understood football was a treasure indeed.

CHAPTER 18

After over-analyzing her text exchange with Owen, Ember sipped her smoothie with a ridiculous grin on her face. The sandwich shop patrons probably thought her headed for the loony bin when she'd repeatedly laughed out loud earlier. Not many people came in for ham and turkey on bread for dinner. Just one couple remained, snuggling in a front booth.

Xander breezed through the door, confident and handsome. His personal trainer kept his body highly toned. Unfortunately, she didn't want to get personal with that body. A huskier, hardier body was more to her taste. She smiled as Xander slid next to her in the booth.

"Which smoothie did you get?" He pointed to her half-empty drink.

"Pineapple-coconut with a protein blast."

"Not willing to try a new flavor?"

Did that question mean something more? Why was he sitting so close? This was already awkward, especially when she meant to reject his relationship offer.

"I see you're still following your diet plan." He nodded toward her drink. "Very good, Ember. Big protein breakfast, medium lunch, tiny dinner. A healthy lifestyle is all about calories, dear."

"I know." She refrained from rolling her eyes. They'd gone over her nutrition plan ad nauseam until she could repeat a calorie's definition verbatim. *A calorie is the energy it takes to raise the temperature of 1 gram of water 1 degree Celsius. In dieters' terms, a unit equivalent to the large calorie expressing heat-producing or energy-producing value in food when oxidized in the body.* Not that the definition made any sense.

Basically, she only took in what she could burn off, and if she wasn't burning calories, then she ate less. Simple enough concept, yet, one she had struggled with for years. She liked living a healthier lifestyle, even if she sometimes craved a gooey grilled cheese or huge stack of syrup-covered pancakes.

"I'm glad that in your grief over your brother's death, you didn't revert to bad habits as a form of comfort."

"No." Any man should know by now that discussing a woman's weight was a danger zone lined with many, many land mines. She didn't know why he continually brought up her weight. A few months ago, she'd worn a sweatshirt and jeans to his office and had received a half-hour lecture on her sloppy presentation. "Were you going to eat?"

"I'll grab something in a moment." He clasped and squeezed her hand. "I'm so glad you called. I feel dates like this are a great start."

"Xander, I'm sorry." She pulled away her hand. The coconut and pineapple from her smoothie started dancing the cha-cha in her stomach. "This isn't about starting anything. I'm glad you mentioned that, though, because I'd like to talk about what you suggested the other night."

She folded her straw wrapper into a tiny square, hesitant to begin. "I was very surprised. You're right. At first, I did like you, ah…as a girl…you know…likes a guy. You are handsome and dependable." She flashed a close-lipped grin. "I finally had someone who cared, but then I realized our relationship was only clinical, so I let those feelings go. Perhaps, we've just been together so long you're comfortable with me and are therefore mixing emotions."

"No, that isn't the case at all, dear. It's you. You are finally ready for the relationship I want." Xander brushed a strand of loose hair behind her ear. "Your true personality is finally shining through, finally ready for an intimate relationship. With time and dedication, we'll establish a level of desire between us."

"I'm not sure." Ember sank back against the booth, putting

space between them. "I've come too far from that girl who idolized you. You know everything about me, and the more I consider this relationship idea, the more I realize I don't know much about you."

"Times like this are perfect opportunities to ask questions." He cupped her cheek in his hand. "Realign your thinking. As before, I'll guide you. You'll see."

"But, I…what about the patient-doctor—"

He placed a finger against her lips. "No, give this time. We're already in a very intimate relationship. We'll slowly add the physical component."

This conversation had strayed far from her planned course. She was actually a bit confused now and didn't even know why. "I'm seeing someone else." She hadn't wanted to play that card, fearing the words would upset him, but he'd given her no choice.

"I assume you're referring to your visitor the other night?" He raised a single blond brow and shook his head. "As I said before, I believe you've developed a type of white-knight infatuation with the man. Crushes fade, dear. What we have is everlasting. Built on a foundation of years together. Continue your fixation with this man, if you must. I'd rather you removed him from your system. And when he breaks your heart, I'll be here, and we can discuss your feelings. Just promise me one thing." He gripped both her shoulders and peered into her eyes. "Don't give him your innocence. Save that for a worthy man."

Fantastic. He really did know too much about her love life.

"Do you understand?"

Huffing out a laugh, she nodded. Although, this whole conversation had taken a complete nosedive that just continued its spiral downward, because he drew her close and kissed her. Stunned, confused, and frozen in place, she had no idea which direction to turn.

Xander pulled back and met her gaze, then gently kissed her once more. "We will continue with our Thursday night sessions, but will also see each other socially. I'll allow you more time to consider." He tweaked her nose with his index finger. "Good night, Ember."

She nodded, then watched him leave.

What was she going to do? He hadn't listened. She hadn't

made him listen. Where was this sudden interest coming from? All their Thursday night sessions had seemed so cold and clinical. Never had softer emotions come into play. At times, she actually felt like a lab mouse. And now, she was a mouse who'd crashed face-first into a maze and couldn't find her way out. The idea of a physical relationship with Xander was too much to comprehend.

She needed to shift her primary focus. Bethany needed her. She'd called earlier asking Ember to come by the apartment. Good plan. She would take another look through her brother's things and find out if Bethany had any details on his life insurance policy. This exercise would keep her mind from over-analyzing Xander's comments—and kisses.

And yet, one remark had burrowed deep. His classification of Owen as her white knight didn't resonate. For so many years, that had been Xander's role. He had saved her. Arrived with his psych books in tow and carried her away to a new world—a better place. A fact for which she would remain eternally grateful. However, she no longer craved the white knight.

She wanted a pirate.

A plundering, dirty Marauder.

CHAPTER 19

Shivering against an autumn morning breeze, Ember clicked down the sidewalk in her new black heels to Owen's car. Today was chillier than she'd thought. Tonight she would see Owen again, and these killer heels were purchased with him in mind. Killer being the operative word since they were literally killing her feet, but her new mantra was feeling positive about her future, no matter the consequences. Why not start with shoes that made her look sexy? Or at least feel sexy. He'd called after his win Saturday night, and they'd conversed until the early hours of the morning. Tonight was his only day off before he began serious prep for the next game.

How much longer would he have her car? Not that she minded driving his Audi, but using the vehicle on a daily basis seemed an imposition.

Oh, holy fish paste! What the hell?

The Audi's entire driver's side was dented and streaked with what appeared to be black paint. Someone had sideswiped Owen's car.

Oh, sweet mother have mercy.

He was going to kill her. Would her insurance cover this?

She glanced down the street for a long-gone perpetrator, then hobbled through the grass strip to check the passenger side. Her heels speared the grass, and she grasped the car's hood for balance.

Why am I checking this side?

No one could get to the passenger side unless the car hopped the curb and drove down the sidewalk.

Should she call Owen? She had to, didn't she?

She walked around the front. The driver's side door was a dented mess. After a few tugs on the handle, she shrugged off her jacket and wiped her brow. No go. *Great.*

Placing her purse on the hood, she dug through it for her phone, found the stupid thing in a side pocket, and then dialed Owen.

His sleepy voice answered.

"Owen, I've got something really awful to tell you."

"Mmmm..."

"Are you awake?"

"I'm getting there."

"Well, I wouldn't have called so early, but well, um, your car's been sort of," she paused for a moment, then forced the word from her lips. "Dented."

"Don't worry about a dent, Stems. Why don't you come by before work?"

"What? I can't do that. Besides, dent is actually an inaccurate depiction. This dent sort of affects the whole driver's side and has left a variety of black streaks. I'll call my insurance company and see if they'll cover the damages."

"Wait, what? Are you all right? Did you get hurt?"

The worry evident in his voice, touched her heart. "No, no. I just came out this morning, and your car was damaged. I'm so sorry, Owen."

"Hold on. I'm not quite awake yet." She heard rustling on the other end of the line. Rustling in sheets—warm sheets. What did he wear to bed? *Seriously?* Why did her mind always stray to sex when he was involved?

"Do you need a ride to work?"

Work, right. Millicent would be furious if she was late. Her boss would just titter out, *"Well, you should have a back-up car for occasions like these."*

"I'll call and tell them I'll be late. Not a conversation I'm looking forward to."

"Tell that boss of yours to kiss your ass. Someone sideswiping your car isn't your fault." She heard a dresser drawer or some such thing slam shut before Owen barked, "I'm on my way."

Perhaps he was her white knight after all, but he'd more likely arrive on a huge black charger wielding a broadsword as if it weighed no more than a twig. She hated being the damsel in distress. Leaning against the trunk, she texted Millicent in order to avoid an early morning verbal confrontation.

Shortly after, Owen arrived, riding shotgun in a black tow truck.

Jake hopped down from the driver's seat and headed over to inspect the damage. "Dang." He blew out a long whistle. "You weren't in the car, were you?"

"No."

"Good thing."

She nodded, worried about Owen's response. Standing beside him, she chewed on her thumbnail and tried to think of ways to fix what just might be unfixable.

Owen ran his hand along the side of the car. After shaking his head, he said, "Cars don't seem to agree with you, Ms. Brooks." He rose from his crouch by the car, positioning his large frame inches from her own, and then ruffled her hair.

She pressed a hand against his chest and met his gaze. "Are you mad?"

In response, he wrenched her close and kissed her.

Perhaps he hadn't had breakfast yet, because he devoured her like a man starved.

While maintaining his grip on her hips, he pulled back and smiled. "Good morning, Ember."

His hooded eyes cast a sleepy look, which had her thinking of warm sheets again. She fiddled with the strings on his work out pants, "I'm not so sure it's a good morning. Owen, I—"

He kissed her again, longer, deeper. Then, after finishing a bone-melting series of light, teasing kisses against her mouth and neck, he asked, "Good morning yet?"

"Yes," she answered, breathless from his kisses.

"Come on. Let's get you to work."

The only work she wanted to do required two tools—a soft bed and a naked Owen.

"Got her hooked up, Owen." Jake hollered from beside the tow-truck.

"We'll run Ember by her office on our way to the garage."

With her head turned down and away, Ember glanced at Jake and held back a smile. His presence had been overshadowed by a big bowl of cheery-O. Plus, what would her neighbors think of her out on the street, kissing a man like some kind of girl for hire? Speaking of that, what grand acrobatic maneuver could she perform to enter the truck in her short skirt and high heels? She started with one foot on the running board.

Owen grabbed her hips, and then reached around her body to brush fast food wrappers, gum packs, and papers onto the floorboard.

The position set her bottom squarely between his thighs. He was certainly having a very perky morning. What possible excuse could she use to get him into her apartment? Now. Her brain frantically searched for any possible reason, then sparked and short-wired when he gave her bottom a long fondle before nudging her into the seat. If she was going to burn, then so was he. She wiggled against his very impressive erection before sliding onto the seat.

His sharp intake of breath preceded his husky groan against her ear. "Put a girl in heels, and she becomes a siren." Owen rested his arm against the seat back and brushed his fingers through the hair at the back of her neck.

Heat shot through her body. She considered grabbing the steering wheel and begging Jake to turn back. Boldly, she placed a hand upon Owen's knee and squeezed.

Two could play at this game.

In retaliation, he massaged the back of her neck.

Her gaze met his, and then flicked to his lips. She leaned closer, forgetting where she was, only what she wanted. When she felt the truck bump into a pothole, she jostled against his side and braced her hand against his chest.

Owen flashed a wicked grin and gently squeezed the back of her neck. "I'll pick you up after work. Call when you're ready."

She nodded, still hypnotized by those strong lips and how they made her feel. Would she get any work done today? "Are we still on for dinner?"

"Let's just say I'm having a hard enough time letting you leave this truck. So yeah, we're on for dinner." Curbside in front of her building, Owen helped her down. "Don't fret that redhead about my car, either." He ruffled her hair. "That's why I pay guys like Jake. Your car's ready anyway."

"Oh, good." She had a hard time concentrating on car talk, when her focus was on the way his gray T-shirt fit his upper body. All those bulging muscles. Sometimes she forgot the massiveness of his presence. His strong, steady build, honed by years of athleticism, was certainly on display today.

"Come on." He tugged her along toward her office. "I'll walk you inside."

"Oh...um...all right." She double-stepped to catch up. A tad happy, no, gloriously happy, she'd had a reason to see him this morning, even though a beautiful car paid the price. Maybe she should get a tank. Then she wouldn't have these car problems. She could run over anyone who got in her way. And she and Owen could hide away inside.

How much room is inside those things anyway?

As Ember stepped into the office, she noticed Millicent in her cubicle, rifling through the papers on her desk. Perhaps a rocket launcher would be a good investment, as well.

Ember picked up the pace, curious as to the purpose of Millicent's search.

Millicent hadn't detected their approach and continued to shuffle through her papers.

"Good morning, Ms. Brown." Owen's deep timber resonated across Millicent's frantic search.

Her boss stiffened, patted her hair, and then turned with a bright, white-toothed smile. "Mr. Killion, what a pleasure to see you again." She offered her hand. "Ember, good to see you in one piece."

"It is, isn't it?" Owen wrapped an arm around Ember's shoulder and smiled like the big bad wolf before he blew your house down.

An awkward silence pounded through Ember's ears as she studied Millicent and could practically see her evil mind churning, deciding which move to make in front of a past client.

Millicent cleared her throat. "Well, Ember, I was looking for the Green Moose Beer file. When you find the information among this pile of—"

Owen jangled his keys and shifted forward.

"Just find the file and come to my office." Millicent nodded to Owen. "Mr. Killion."

Ember dropped her bag on the floor. *Odd.* Her bright green GMB file was right on top and she picked it up. She tapped the folder against Owen's chest. "Thanks for...well...just everything this morning." She sighed and forced steamy thoughts to the back of her mind, since Maleficent Millicent was agenda number one this morning. "I should probably see what Millicent wanted with this file."

"Yeah, I'll let you get to it." He tilted her chin with his index finger. "Do me a favor. Stay away from moving objects."

"Very funny." She whacked his arm with the folder. "Get out of here. I've got work to do."

As she watched him lumber down the hall, she contemplated a thought that had been churning in her mind for a long time now—

"Owen?"

"Yeah?" He turned, but his gaze was on his phone, thumbs busy on his screen.

She wanted to ask if he thought perhaps all these car incidents were related. For some reason, someone certainly didn't like the idea of her having transportation. Who? And to what end? Did she really need to burden Owen with what could quite possibly be just an overactive imagination?

"Um, I just wondered...do you think...should I bring anything tonight? For dinner, I mean." Not what she wanted to say, and perhaps she should have spilled her concerns, but he might think she was a paranoid loon.

"No, it's all good, Stems." He winked, waved, and headed back down the hall. She was still staring at his very fine form when he turned back and said, "You could bring those heels."

And wasn't that just something? Even when worrying about how her life could possibly be filled with some psycho stalker who had a fetish against her vehicles, every word that came out of her Marauder's mouth made her feel like her world was one happy bubble.

Made her believe that together they'd sail life's stormy seas, if only he understood how much she needed to just let life flow.

How much she wanted to be swept away by raging water until free-falling over a rushing waterfall, arms spread, enjoying the plunge, finally jumping off the ledge she'd been frightened of her whole life, but this time, she had every hope a very fine pirate would break her fall.

CHAPTER 20

Ember sliced her chicken breast into bite-sized pieces and topped each with an even dollop of bruschetta. Apparently, Owen had started dinner prep around three. He'd made the tomato, cheese, onion, and basil mixture himself. Adding in the cooking factor pushed his hotness rating to an undiscovered level.

As they ate, they discussed Saturday night's game. His insider info was filled with fascinating football facts she tried storing in her brain for use when watching his next battle on the field. Sitting across from such a dynamic man, she could hardly believe her luck. His mom had stopped by earlier, but left after peeking at the chicken and taste-testing the salad.

Ember built on her morning revelation throughout her hectic day, eager to begin this new let-it-flow direction. This journey would not dwell on her past or focus on any future heartbreak. Her forecast showed only sunny skies for each day in this normal boy-girl relationship. She wanted to feel the bright rays of love and the balmy breeze of passion. No more hiding under the thundercloud of Stember Brooks.

Her hormones screamed for action. Such perverted little suckers, screaming all kinds of lurid thoughts from her special place clear up to her brain. They were certainly on high alert tonight, ready and eager to respond to any touch Owen deigned to give.

Her phone rang again, which pulled her from thoughts of Owen as a caramel-topped dessert.

She glanced at the screen—Xander. He'd called twice this evening. She'd been avoiding his calls since their Thursday night session where he'd not only become touchy-feely on the psychologist couch, but he'd also asked inappropriate personal questions about Owen. Feeling hedged in, she'd faked a headache and left. Not again, though. With this new plan in mind, she'd make clear her stance. Owen was the man she wanted. No question.

"Is everything all right?"

She hesitated before answering. "Xander keeps calling."

"I see. Do you need to give him a call?"

"I've never really explained my relationship with Xander, have I?" With the tip of her knife, she swirled a tiny tomato around on her plate.

Owen tapped his half-empty beer bottle against the tabletop. "Hold on. I may need another beer for this."

Ember shook her head, "Owen, it's not like that."

"Gimme a minute." He tipped the bottle and finished his beer before grabbing another from the fridge. "You want one?"

"No." She took a deep breath and began. "You're aware of my childhood. Pleasant though walking down that road may be, let's move on to my college years."

Owen leaned against the counter, beer bottle in hand. "Sure, let's."

After taking a long drink from her water, Ember continued, hoping she'd find the right words to appease Owen. "Xander was a true gift. Finding someone willing to help me, to listen to my problems, and not use every word I said against me was initially hard to comprehend. He turned my life around. I am a healthy person in body and mind because of his guidance."

"He shouldn't be crossing the line with a patient. Using what he knows about your past to manipulate you into a relationship, isn't fair." Owen ran his thumb along the side of his bottle. "I think you had a lot to do with your changes as well, Stems. You're a very strong woman."

"Maybe, but Xander was the catalyst. I grew up believing I was nothing, hidden, ashamed, afraid of everyone and everything. He opened the cage I'd lived in my whole life. And I need you to know I care very deeply for him. He is a very large figure in my life. He understands me in a way no one else ever can, because of his psychology studies, of course, but also because during our time together, I've shared everything."

"Everything." Owen nodded, finished his beer, then turned to the fridge and grabbed another.

"Everything in my mind." Ember stood, took the bottle from his hand, and after a long drink, she met his gaze. "At one time, yes, I would have shared my heart with Xander, but not again. Not now." Reaching around his still form, she placed the bottle on the counter, and then braced her hand along the edge. Not sure of Owen's reaction, she decided to be proactive and kissed his chin before moving to his lips.

Receiving a less-than-enthusiastic response, she rose on her tiptoes and locked a hand around the back of his neck. "Kiss me back. I'm yours now, Owen. Only yours."

Apparently still digesting her words, he responded with two quick pecks before holding her at arm's length. "I know you have to work tomorrow. Let's play a couple rounds of pool before you go."

"Owen, please don't do this." She brushed a hand down his arm, following a vein trail along the inside of his bicep.

"Come on, we'll go downstairs." He grabbed another beer before following her to his fully stocked man-cave. All the required items filled the room: big screen TV, gaming system, huge couch, bar with a not so mini-fridge, and a case full of trophies. But the best thing about this atmosphere was the fact it was a cave. She could hide away down here and explore her primal side. Her reveal about Xander had affected Owen and put a damper on their pleasant evening. So, she would do what she could to realign the mood.

Deep breath in and exhale.

Now Mr. Sulky, prepare for your seduction.

Leaning her hip against the table, she set the pool stick between her legs then flashed what she hoped was a sultry smile. "Is your stick bigger than mine?" Ember reached for the chalk, got hung up by the stick, and stumbled in her heels.

Owen huffed out a laugh. "What was that?"

"Nothing, I suck at this," she mumbled as she pitched a striped ball down the table.

"What'd you say? You suck at what?"

"I'm sorry if I upset you by talking about Xander, but I don't want to dwell on that tonight, because I'm tired of waiting. Tired of talking about my stupid life." Ember dropped the solid yellow number one ball in place at the top of the triangle. "I want to move forward." She placed the eight ball in the center. Now she needed one solid and one stripe for the bottom corners. "Where are all the stupid stripes?"

"Hey, what's going on?" Owen wrapped his arms around her from behind.

Good, now she wouldn't have to face him while she revealed what she wanted. "I don't like you stalling because I'm a shy, inexperienced girl. I want to try things."

"Is that so?" He brushed the hair from the side of her neck and kissed his way to her shoulder.

"Quit teasing." She pressed her hips back against him and thrust his arms from her waist. "Let's just play."

"You want to play?" He turned her to face him and spread his arms. "Well, I'm right here."

"I'm well aware of where you are." She threw a chalk square at his chest.

He chuckled and shuffled her closer. "If you don't want me thinking you're shy, then change my mind."

"Is that one of your side-line taunts?" She raised her arms to his chest and brushed the blue chalk mark off his shirt. "Aren't you clever?"

He nudged her chin. "I can be very, very clever." Between each word, he kissed her.

Tonight was her night. Her declaration of independence from a war she'd been fighting her whole life. She rose on her toes and kissed him back. No more shy shrinking violet, but a bright burning rose.

Placing her hands on his shoulders, she boosted onto the pool table's edge, and pulled him between her thighs, while sliding her arm down his sides and gripping his hips. "Listen to me, please. Don't hold back. I want this."

His warm breath fanned across her lips before he settled his mouth on hers.

Desperate for more, she wrapped her legs around his waist

and arched against him. Mindless fever broke through any lingering restraint. Her hands explored the solid strength of corded muscles under his shirt. Hot skin singed her fingers and sent heated signals to her aching core.

With trembling body and eager pants, she fervently returned each searing kiss. Beyond her control, she curled her restless hand along the large ridge in his jeans.

A raw sound rumbled deep in Owen's throat, and he broke their rhythmic kiss.

"Sorry." Her hand shook as she caressed his face.

He kissed her palm, and then unzipped his jeans. "Touch me." He placed her hand upon the tip of his engorged shaft peeking out from under his briefs. "I need your hands on me."

With a single finger, she circled the slick tip, catching a wet bead of his desire.

He hissed out a breath.

This was what she wanted—primal, heated sex. She tightened her fingers around the bulk of his swollen head, stroked his steel ridge in her hands, and used his heat to fuel her own. "Can we go to your room?" Maintaining her caress along his rigid flesh, she rested her forehead against his heaving chest.

He stilled her hand. "You're not ready for that."

"Yeah, I am." She met his gaze. "Beyond ready, actually."

"We're taking this one step at a time." He lightened his refusal with a kiss.

"How about we take big steps?" When she resumed her teasing play, she felt his erection twitch in her hand. "I want big steps."

"Little."

"This feels pretty big to me."

He chuckled. "Whatever the lady wants."

As she resumed her touch, she fantasized about all that solid flesh breaking past every barrier in her body. She glanced up and caught him watching each stroke.

His hooded eyes caught her gaze.

Her breath hitched as the atmosphere stilled and heated. "Take off your shirt." She watched him lift away the barrier to his skin, and then she eased his pants further down his hips. A mat of soft brown hair trailed down to his erection, now resting against his stomach. Unable to keep still, she placed both hands on his chest and ran her fingers down the silky trail.

"Do you have any idea how close I am to taking you right here on this table?"

His deep, husky voice hypnotized with each rumbled word.

"Keep up the teasing, Stems. But remember, my playbook is vast and varied." He wrapped her hair in his fist, tugged back on her neck, then possessed her mouth—plundering deep.

Each thrust of his tongue, revealed his skill. With unsteady breaths, she basked in each deep caress. His hands stole under her shirt and skimmed the undersides of her breasts before he circled each peak.

Momentarily breaking their connection, he removed her shirt, and tugged the bra straps from her shoulders. He coaxed her sensitive tips from beneath their cotton covering, and then bent his head and grazed each tip with a coarse brush of his tongue.

As urgent longing rose to a boiling point at her center, she cried out. A hot shiver shot through her body and, holding his head in place, she raked her nails through his soft brown strands.

Owen gently eased her against the green felt, working her skirt up her thighs. He stood between her legs. "You okay?"

In answer, she spread her legs wider and scooted her lower body closer to the edge. "Show me, Owen. I want to know."

"Curious little thing, aren't you? You want to know what I know." He ran both hands along her calves then over her knees to the tops of her thighs. "I know I've never seen anything more beautiful than all that red hair against the green felt. I know I've never felt such craving for a woman." He brushed a finger against her soft mound. "And I know I'll find satisfaction between the thighs of a shy, inexperienced woman."

With the first slip of his finger over her wet cleft, she practically bounced off the table. His teasing fingers continued to play then, when she arched against his hand, he relented and broke past the barrier. Skating back and forth through her silky heat, he drove her beyond any sensation she'd ever known.

"I'd love to slide right here."

"Yes, please," she panted as she gasped for breath. "Slide."

"No, that isn't how we'll play this game." He lifted her against his chest and slanted his lips fiercely over hers. The brush of his chest against hers and his touch within her hot core created a combustible combination.

Each breath marched in time with her pounding heart. All straining toward a swirling edge she couldn't wait to dive off. "Owen…please…I want…right there…"

In answer to her desperate plea, he brushed his thumb against her swollen clit, and he drew her nipple deep against the roof of his mouth.

She stilled, holding her breath, relishing that absolute pinnacle of pleasure before the fall. Time stopped, her body froze at the precipice, rigid and tight. Then Owen pushed her over the edge with a hot sweep of his tongue over her lips as he pinched her swollen nipple between his fingers.

Free falling as she'd wished, breaking through pleasure's surface as wave after wave crashed against her body. She fought to breathe, to hold back the raspy pants and moans escaping her throat. Using his shoulder as her bit, she dug her teeth against his skin as she fought to control each spasm breaking across her body. Resurfacing, she buried her face in the curve of his neck.

With a grip on the back of her neck, he drew her from her burrow and studied her face.

Happiness spread to every corner of her body, and she smiled.

Owen mirrored the image, hummed out a laugh, and then kissed her. Light, calming kisses that didn't ask for more, just reassured and made her feel cherished.

His erection remained rigid between them. Though sleepy, she wanted to give him the pleasure he'd given her. Wanted to watch his face as he found release at her touch. She trailed her fingers down his chest, but was stopped by his grip on her wrist.

"No," he whispered against her lips. "I am teetering too close to my pirate side. Don't, please."

Scoring the nails of her free hand down his chest, she said. "But I like your pirate side."

Owen shook his head and released a pained laugh. "We'll get there, just not tonight." He pulled on his jeans, but didn't zip or button them. Then he caught her gaze and smiled. "I like that I'm the only man for you."

"Good, because I've made the decision that I don't care…I

mean, not that I don't care that I'm with you, just that I'm not going to worry so much. I want to appreciate my time with you, and not worry about every unforeseeable outcome." She took his hand in hers, lifted his palm, and traced the etched lines. "I may get hurt, but at least I played, right?"

Owen wrapped her in a stifling embrace. After rocking her back and forth, he released her then chucked her chin. "I'd pick you for my team anytime." He dropped a quick kiss on her nose and gripped her chin between his forefinger and thumb. "But the thing is, babe, when you play, sometimes you get hurt. I know that and so do you, but we'll work through those tumbles, all right? I'm not afraid to step up to the line. To meet you there, eye-to-eye. You with me on this?"

She wiped at the tears trickling down her cheeks. "You make me smile at odd times of the day. You've rescued me when I had no one else. But, most importantly, you make a pretty mean bruschetta." She laughed and pulled him close for a kiss. "So yeah, I'm with you."

CHAPTER 21

Relaxing after their Sunday night win, Owen grabbed a handful of pretzels and contemplated the cards in his hand. After weighing his odds, he swirled and swallowed the final dregs of his beer. Last one, since he had to drive home. A slight buzz eased his aching body after their win tonight, although, he could use some caffeine. Quite comfy and feeling a bit lazy, maybe he would propose a side bet and the loser would have to grab a soda from Chewy's fridge. With his killer hand, he didn't want to move until he finished collecting his winnings from his adversaries across the table.

Football players approached poker like they did everything else—winner take all. The Madden 25 X-box tournament taking place in the living room occasionally halted their game when a physical altercation broke out between players.

Too bad, his good luck charm wasn't in attendance. Somehow, after their lunch date on Friday, he and Ember had ended up in her car's back seat. He shifted in his chair as he thought about how eager she'd been under his hands. Incomprehensible that he'd walked away from that encounter. His little redhead burned for progress on the physical front, as did he. However, due to repeated disappointments by the past men in her life, he felt an obligation to first build a solid foundation of trust.

The salt from the pretzel burned against his tongue, and he focused on that sensation, instead of the discomfort of his semi-erection. He refused to recall each well-developed curve of her body—how each dip and mound fit perfectly in his hand. No, instead he should consider these continued odd incidents with her vehicles.

Ember's repeated harassments troubled him, so he'd called Detective Harris and brought her up to speed. Harris indicated she had some initial case data and would like to meet. Since she'd been unwilling to discuss her findings on the phone, she'd scheduled their appointment for the beginning of the week.

"Owen, where you at? You in or what?" Bronco flicked ash from his Cuban cigar into an empty red Solo cup.

Sitting across the table from Bronco posed a unique challenge, because he didn't have a tell. "What's the ante?"

"Pay attention." Bronco threw a handful of pretzels at his head. "Quit dreaming about that pretty redhead."

The ribbing continued around the table until a commotion erupted outside the French doors. Jason plastered his face against the small square window and licked the glass, imitating some sort of fucked-up cunnilingus.

Owen chuckled at his antics. The freak probably did practice moves on various household items.

Jason opened the doors, trailed by no less than four women. Not only a pretty-boy, he exuded layer upon layer of charm, which got him laid on a regular basis.

No wonder, he always had a cocky grin on his face.

"Sweetheart, if you're still looking for him, here he is." Jason pointed a finger in his direction.

"Jason, if you aren't playing, get out," Bronco grumbled around the hefty cigar stationed between his lips.

"Here who is?" Though annoyed at Jason's interruption, Owen figured this was his best bet of getting that soda. "Go get me a Coke, would ya?"

Ignoring his request, Jason ushered two girls around the table. "You've got a couple fans here. Ladies, meet the Big-O."

"We're in the middle of a game." Tired and on the edge of irritated, Owen rubbed his eyes and yawned. "I've got fifteen hundred riding on this hand."

"The lady just wants a picture, O. Come on." Jason shoved his shoulder and laughed. "Show this pretty thing some appreciation."

"Hurry the fuck up," Bronco grunted and stubbed out his cigar. "We aren't in the middle of some pansy-ass photo shoot."

"Are you Owen Killion?" A petite blonde, wearing skinny jeans and a Marauders shirt that looked like a baby jersey, leaned against his chair.

"Yes, he's Owen Killion." Bronco fingered a poker chip and glowered at the girl. "Why would you ask who he is if you're a big fan?"

"I'm...I'm just nervous is all. You're Bronco Murray, right?" She winked. "I've wanted to meet you for a long time, too."

"That so?" Bronco raised a brow.

"Owen, could I take your picture?" She squeezed between him and the table. Sinking onto his lap, she lifted the phone and snapped a picture.

He disengaged her hand from the back of his neck. "All right, photo-op is over."

"I'm Izzy." During her introduction, she ran her nose along the side of his neck. "I'm told a center is good with his hands. That true?" She nibbled his earlobe.

"My hands are occupied with another lady." He gently separated her wandering lips from his neck. "Sorry, Izzy."

"Is she here?" Seemingly unwilling to give up, she ran a hand over his chest.

"Yes, she is." Not physically, but in his heart Ember had set up shop, and he'd be damned if he let this girl compromise him in some way.

She smiled and placed a kiss on his lips.

He flinched, and then wiped the back of his hand over his mouth. "Thanks for following the team." He stood, which disengaged her from his lap. "Have a nice night."

Ms. Izzy left the room with another girl, whispering and giggling.

After watching them leave, he glared at Jason and returned to his seat. In an effort to remove any leftover neon pink lipstick, he scrubbed both hands over his face and neck. "Jason, do me a favor. Keep the girls to yourself. I'm fine with who I've got."

"She said she was your number one fan." Jason ruffled his hair. "Probably your only fan. I figured we should get a photo to mark that occasion."

"How about I mark the occasion with my boot up your ass? Get out of here so we can finish our game."

Jason tisk-tisked as he leaned against the wall behind Bronco. "Owen, I feel we should discuss this fascination you have with other men's asses."

Refraining from laughing, Owen lobbed his empty bottle across the room, aiming for Jason's head. The glass bounced off his shoulder and landed on the table, scattering chips.

"Come on!" Bronco erupted. "Get out, Disruptor." Apparently done with Jason's presence, he shoved out of his chair and tackled Jason to the floor.

After an entertaining scuffle, they both stood and continued their bout with the expected verbal taunts.

Jason combed his fingers through his tousled hair. "We going to eat later?"

"I could use some pancakes." Owen nodded. "Give us an hour. And bring me a Coke. Least you can do for disrupting our game."

"Anything else, Mighty-O?"

"Nope, that should do it."

"Before I go, I honestly feel I should say one thing." Jason shuffled his foot against the carpet. "In all seriousness, guys." He came over and clapped him on the shoulder. "Owen, my center, my friend…there is a secret I've been meaning to share for many years now." He heaved out a long sigh. "*I'm* your number one fan. Can I take your picture?" That said, he bent and kissed Owen straight on the mouth while snapping the shot with his phone.

Jason managed a couple clicks before Owen shot out of his chair and knocked him to the ground.

Bronco poured an entire bowl of popcorn on his head.

Jason sputtered, "Oh dear, does that mean I won't be seeing your pig skin tonight?"

CHAPTER 22

After her lunch hour, Ember shoved her keys in her purse and hustled back to her desk, anxious to finalize the script for the sports bra line she'd been working on so she wouldn't be late for her evening with Owen.

Practically skipping down the aisle to her cubicle, she felt something niggling along the base of her spine. Something strange. Was she imagining things, or had everything and everyone suddenly gone quiet? She glanced around the office and noted several people bundled together, eyeing her oddly before looking away and whispering. Had she done something wrong?

Was Millicent on a rampage?

She sank into her chair, took out a compact mirror, and checked her face for signs of strange bumps or second heads. Nope. Same freckled mug as always.

"Hey, Ember." Kelly's reflection appeared in the mirror. "Are you all right?"

"Maybe." She waved Kelly closer and whispered, "What's going on?"

"Um…you haven't heard the news?" Kelly chewed on her thumbnail and sank against her desk.

"Oh, no. Am I getting fired?"

"You really didn't see the news?"

The salad she'd just eaten churned in her stomach. "What news? Tell me."

Kelly leaned over and shook her mouse, waking her

computer. After a few clicks, she brought up the ESPN home page.

A square box appeared behind the anchorman with a photo of Owen and a headline that read: "Killion Goes Off Center."

Ember adjusted her laptop's volume. "*Allegations have surfaced from a woman attending quarterback Charles Hendricks' celebratory party Sunday. The girl claims she halted Marauders' center, Owen Killion's, advances. Allegedly disappointed by her refusal, Killion struck her. The Marauders' camp has indicated they will respond to these accusations with a press conference at 6pm.*"

"There's no way. I don't believe it." Ember sank back in her chair and wrapped her shaking fingers together.

"Ember—"

"No." She pounded a fist against her desk, and pens rattled in their mug. "Owen wouldn't do this. He's not violent."

Kelly cleared her throat and patted Ember's shoulder. "Uh,…well, violence is what he does for a living."

"No. No. She's lying." Ember's throat went dry, so she pulled her water bottle from her purse.

"I hope you're right."

Was she? Men in her life had no problem raising their hand to women, but Owen was different. He *was* different. But then, how had the girl come by her injuries? Owen had told her about playing poker and going for pancakes after Sunday's game. Had he pursued another woman? Did he understand she believed they were exclusive?

"Have you heard from him?"

"Yeah, he texted me this morning. We're having dinner."

"He'll probably cancel. They'll have him in isolation."

Twisting the water bottle on her desk, she nodded and clicked the news off her screen.

"I'm so sorry, Ember." Kelly embraced her in a one-armed hug. "Let me know if you need anything."

Great. Seemed Kelly believed Owen was guilty, which sort of made sense. Athletes were frequently plastered across the news for roughing up women or cheating on their wives. Even if they hadn't committed the offense, the tarnish remained against their character.

Unnerved when her phone rang, she jostled the water bottle

in her hand and glanced at the screen.

Killion, Nancy

Ember took a deep breath and answered while wiping up the water drops with a tissue from the box on her desk.

"Ember, dear, I'm sure you've seen the news by now. Owen asked that I call to make sure you're all right. He'd like you to come by tonight. He'll be late, of course. They had an emergency public relations meeting and a conference with the coaches. The team takes these accusations very seriously."

"I imagine." Ember grabbed her purse in search of an antacid to soothe her rioting stomach.

"He didn't hurt that poor girl."

"Oh no, of course not."

"I understand if you have doubts. I know you're just getting to know him. But my son would never hurt a woman. Never. Based on your upbringing, you might find this hard to believe, but not all men strike out. And certainly not my son."

Wouldn't having a Mom who believed in you no matter what, be wonderful? Ember sighed. "Is he all right?"

"To put it lightly, he's a tad angry. Luckily, Jason being Jason, he took a bunch of photos of their night together. It's a long story, but just know those photos clear my son. That unfortunate girl doesn't realize the impossibility of being in two places at once."

Two places at once. Impossible. And yet, why did it feel as if her heart had left her body and was gasping for blood at her feet?

"Ember?"

"Yes. I'll be there after work."

"You're a dear. Maude and I will keep you company until Owen returns."

Mothers had such unyielding faith in their children—at least, normal mothers. Her mother would've come out on the side of the accuser, then wrote a book about her ordeal, and starred in the movie.

Speaking of starring roles, which would Owen play in this drama? The vile pillager, or the vindicated buccaneer?

# # #

143

Although a large meal wasn't appetizing on a sour stomach, nor was such a large piece of chocolate cake, Ember hadn't refused, since cooking seemed to occupy Nancy's mind. Pilates in the morning would burn the extra calories.

Owen's mother and sister regaled her with tales of Owen all through dinner. Both so very warm and inviting, which was a complete reversal from her own family dynamics. She'd offered to help with the dishes, but was scooted off to the basement. Though she refused to watch any news, Owen's story still replayed in her thoughts. Question after question tumbled through her mind, leaving a trail of doubt bolstered by years of insecurity. Head aching, she closed her eyes.

"Hey, Stems. Wake up."

If she pretended to sleep would he just lie beside her? The denial option seemed much better than hearing he had a different perspective on their relationship.

"Ember." The couch dipped at her side.

She stretched her arms above her head and blinked open her eyes.

"Look at you. All ruffled and warm." He bent and kissed her like a man starving or searching for something—forgiveness, understanding, or maybe control.

Since she was barely awake, she let him have his way, following him in the kiss. Until she remembered the pictures, and the woman sitting on his lap with her face buried against his neck. "Wait." She eased away.

With a tilt of his head, Owen met her gaze, his arms braced on each side of her body. "Ember, baby." A muscle ticked in his jaw. "Please say you don't believe the lies."

"I don't believe...you hit her." She fiddled with the button on his shirt, avoiding eye contact.

He tipped her chin, forcing her to meet his gaze once more. "A very select statement. What do you believe?"

"She was sitting on your lap. Kissing you."

"Jason brought her into the room to take a picture." Owen stood and paced beside the coffee table. "She said she was a fan, and then yeah, she got a bit handsy. I explained I wasn't interested, and shoved her off."

Ember straightened on the couch. "The pictures

looked...intimate." She bit her lip to hold back tears. She would wait to hear his truth before letting the dam break.

"This whole thing seems like a set-up." Owen dropped into a side chair. He ran both hands over his bristled face, rubbed his temples, then clasped a magazine in his hand. He tapped the rolled newsprint against his palm for a moment before he continued. "There are women who try to extract money from players all the time. Jason has time-stamped photos from the entire night. Would you like to see them?"

His appeal seemed in earnest. A twinge of guilt surfaced for doubting him, but her stomach still churned with worry he'd find her replacement at one of these parties. "I'm not sure the photos are the real issue."

Owen sighed and tossed the magazine back on the table. "Jason was taking my picture as a way to give me a hard time after the girl came in. Good thing he's such an ass, because those photos clear me from being anywhere near her later."

Ember believed him, but long-held fears still rattled through her mind. What about other nights? Other parties? Her mother's voice slithered through her thoughts and struck with venomous words. *You were never good enough for him. He has tons of women on the side. You're stumpy and stupid.*

"I imagine there are always grasping girls at those parties." She tapped her fingers along the couch's arm.

"Yeah." He shrugged. "Some girls use those opportunities to score with players. Sometimes their strategy works, sometimes it doesn't. I know not all women are 'goal-diggers.' I just happened to run into one who had a game plan before she even entered the building." He sat forward in his chair and rubbed his chin. "But, why choose me?"

"Didn't look like you were overly distressed when she was nuzzling your neck." Ember chewed on her fingernail, avoiding Owen's gaze.

"Don't."

"I'm tired, Owen." Tired was a cop-out, because fear was ruling her heart. Fear of where this conversation would lead, but she'd been afraid of life for too long. She needed the truth. Heading to the kitchenette, she grabbed a water bottle from the fridge. "I believe you," she said as she settled on a stool. "But I have been green with jealousy all day. I'm angry with you, angry with myself, angry at the news, angry at the girl..." Since her voice shook a little on that last one, she stalled by taking a long drink. She twisted the cap on and off. "I'm angry, because I'll never belong in a world with football players and parties. Who do I think I am? I need stability and calm."

"Calm?" He shot out of his chair and grasped her shoulders. "You're not calm. You have a fire burning inside." He held her chin between his forefinger and thumb. "You have every right to your anger. Every emotion you felt today was normal, except one. You do belong. Everything I did today was for you. I didn't want any of this nonsense hurting you, or disturbing what we're building together." He shook his head. "Talk about angry, I was more pissed about how this affected you than anything else." He wrapped her tight in his arms, holding her for a quiet moment before he whispered, "Don't doubt me."

Don't soften. Don't. Oh man, he smelled good and his arms enveloped her entire body, making a comforting cocoon. But could she really find solace here? "I don't know if I'm equipped for this. You're so big. Larger than life." She drew a ragged breath. "I feel overshadowed sometimes. I'm not starring on some reality show with a bunch of football wives. That's not me."

"That lifestyle isn't me, either. I'm just Owen and you're just Ember, and what's between us doesn't need to be analyzed or viewed by anyone else. The way we feel, the path we're taking, is exclusive. I won't let you go." He pulled back and met her gaze. "You just got spooked."

Peering into his pleading brown eyes and hearing his sincere tone, she melted a little. He *had* sent her a picture of him and Bronco at the pancake house, pouring syrup into each other's mouths. They were crazy. She was crazy. "I did get spooked."

He kissed her softly, and then delved for more. A primal and needy sound rumbled from deep in his throat.

As she was drawn tighter against his body, she felt the solid ridge of his erection press against her core, but she wasn't feeling the emotional connection. Lust, sure, but too many conflicting thoughts were crisscrossing circuits in her brain.

"What's wrong?" His husky murmur blew across her dampened lips.

Retreating, she sat back, resting both elbows on the counter. "Owen, will our relationship always be like this? Spread all over the news for everyone to analyze?"

"Absolutely not."

"Did you turn on the news today?" She fisted her hand in his shirt, remembering her concern over his constancy.

"The story got picked up because we were at Chewy's." He pulled away. "Anytime newscasters can spin a negative story around a star quarterback, regardless if he's involved, they'll run the story so far past the end-zone, they wind up in some alternate reality." Heading for the bar, he wrenched open the fridge and grabbed a beer. "Ninety percent of the time, we're the irrelevant other guys. No one cares about our personal lives. We only get noticed if we do something wrong."

"You have a nickname in the press. The O-line, heavy emphasis on the "O" for your supposed abilities in the bedroom."

"Stems, there's no supposed about it." He winked and tipped his bottle in her direction.

She rolled her eyes. No doubt, he was excellent in the bedroom. Well, wasn't that just good news for her then.

He stood between her legs and ran his hands up and down her arms. "We'll work on my 'supposed' abilities together until we get every move just right."

Heat rushed through her body as he kissed the side of her neck. *Could the human body liquefy?*

"In the meantime, I won't let the outside world hurt you."

"It hurt me today," she whispered.

"I'm sorry, baby. But I never meant to hurt you, nor did I hurt that woman."

She squirmed under his continued assault on her neck, her ear, and finally her lips. While pressing a hand against his chest, she turned away. "I should... I would like to go home."

Frowning, he studied her for a moment. "Don't let this come between us. The girl is a liar."

"I know. I just need some space. You're so huge." She ran both hands across his broad shoulders. "I feel like I lose myself in you. In the past, I let people overshadow me. I'd like us to be equals. Standing together. I thought I had confidence, but in this sphere, I still need work." Why was there always some roadblock in her path? Couldn't she just have one relationship without the emotional struggle? She picked at the chipping polish on her thumbnail. "Give me time. I'm sorry. I know I'm a lot to take on."

"Look at me, Ember, please."

She straightened her shoulders and met his gaze.

"Eye to eye, that's what we'll be." He pressed a finger between her brows. "I will meet you right here every time. I believe you are strong enough to hold your own when we face each other across the line. I know you've been pummeled by life." His tone turned soothing, intimate. "But understand this, you can always make me listen. Make me stop and take notice."

"That's the problem, Owen. I'm not so sure there are things about me I want you to notice. Like I don't...don't..."

"Don't what?"

Spit it out, expel it, or she knew the worry would eat her alive. "I don't want you with other women." There. Take that, Killion.

A smile lifted one corner of his lips.

Irritation had her reaching for a bottle of whiskey to pummel him. "I'm glad you find being faith—"

With a commanding press of his lips, he silenced her.

Showing without words, demanding without pity, her complete belief in his intentions. Taking every breath from her body and every beat of her heart, until she had to break free or die, but oh, what a death. The kiss continued on and on. Lazily he took her on a slow journey, seemingly unwilling to cease.

The fervor slowed, but picked up once more before, with a teasing series of touch and retreat, he eased away. "I'll take you home, but don't think for one second I'm letting you go. I'm doing as you wish. Granting you the space you need. Just remember, there are two players in this game."

While she appreciated his team spirit, she knew the scoreboard of her life had yet to post any victories. And yet, still lost in the play of his heated kisses, she decided losing to him might very well count as a win.

CHAPTER 23

Xander wrapped Ember in a tight embrace the minute she walked in the door Thursday night. The poor girl was obviously distraught, and no wonder, when her knight had taken such a public fall from his horse. "How are you faring?" He breathed in the warm, sensual fragrance of her hair.

She met his gaze with a small furrow between her brows. "I'm great. I've figured out some things. Made some decisions."

Well, this promised to be interesting. Perhaps, she was ready to discuss their relationship now that her 'supposed' boyfriend was out gallivanting and abusing other women. He suppressed his grin. Wouldn't want to appear insensitive during her troubled time. "Ember, honey, let's sit in the living room today." He reveled in the feel of the smooth skin on her upper arm as he led her to the couch. "Can I get you some tea?"

"No, I won't be here the whole hour." She remained standing, with her hands buried in the front pockets of her dress pants.

"Not staying?" Her condition must be worse than he thought. "Ember, I've seen the news. I can only imagine the devastation you must feel. I'm so sorry that man created such a scandal. He was always unworthy. Don't take the blame. Brutes like him are not accustomed to treasuring a true lady such as yourself."

"True lady," she scoffed and rocked back on her heels. "I don't know what that means. I wasn't raised proper. And I do think Owen is worthy. Whether or not I'm the right fit for him is the question."

This was ridiculous. The man had thrown glitter in her eyes. He cleared his throat and sank onto the couch. "But surely after those news reports, you understand his life is filled with cruelty and promiscuity. His competitive nature allows no room for deviation or denial. We haven't built you up only to have that man tear you down." She'd come from nothing, and now she coveted this man and all his worldly possessions. Was she such a materialistic bitch? "Why should you allow such a man to sully you? Does his money hold sway? If so, I find that quite appalling. I believed you better than that."

"Xander, please." She ran a hand through her hair. "Money isn't a consideration. Could we just…there is something I came here to say. Will you listen, please?"

Perhaps he'd read the signals wrong. Was she nervous about asking his forgiveness? Would those full red lips plead for understanding? For comfort found only through him, now that she'd been betrayed by another? Of course, he'd let her momentary indiscretion slide, but he'd make her sweat for a moment first. "I'll always listen. Please sit, Ember. You seem quite troubled."

After settling on the sofa beside him, she popped up again and paced in front of his couch. "I was thinking…that I…that I should only come for therapy once a month now. We've been meeting every week for almost six years. I feel sometimes our sessions are actually more of a detriment to my progress. When I'm here, I'm reminded of where I came from and every horrific moment of my childhood." She stopped before him and pinched the bridge of her nose. "I'm tired of rehashing my past. So very tired."

Her voice became muffled as all the air left the room.

Not come back.

Once a month.

Unacceptable.

He'd found her as a jagged, gray rock and polished her into a rare stone. This conversation was ludicrous. She'd never survive without his counsel. He tuned back in as she continued her ridiculous proposition.

"When I discuss my past, I actually get more depressed. I will always be grateful for your guidance." She knelt before him and took his hand. "I hope we can become true friends instead of this current clinical relationship."

"Ember, please think this through. To make an abrupt stop in your counseling would be absurd." He took her hand while considering his next words carefully. Her infatuation would not interfere with his plans, nor would this idea she no longer needed therapy. "I hate to discuss such a horrid subject, but consider, please, your brother failed to communicate, which ended in his death. I realize you're thrilled over this new man in your life, but don't abandon our relationship."

Breathing steadily to maintain control, he tightened his grip on her hand and drew her closer. "Is this man asking more of you? Is he trying to control you? Is he so petty and insecure he won't allow your involvement with another man?" Aware his clipped tone verged on rage, he took another moment to breathe deeply. He wanted nothing more than to take her to his room, tie her down, and thrash her for this obscene disloyalty. "This man has already deceived you once. He enjoys a fast-paced lifestyle. Sports figures are never held accountable for their actions and constantly manipulate what others see while the truth remains hidden."

"He didn't do anything wrong." Ember sighed, and then sat next to him on the couch.

"Honestly, Ember." He shook his head. "The fact he attended such an affair in the first place was a betrayal. He may not have strayed this time, but what about the next? Your interest in an intimate relationship is gratifying after all our hard work. However, you risk much by choosing this man as a trial run."

"You have a lot of preconceived notions." Removing her hand from his grip, she leaned against the side of the couch.

"Notions proven correct by this latest debacle."

"No." She sniffed. "That isn't what happened. The girl set him up."

Why would she believe such a story? He'd been her adviser for many years, yet she denied his counsel on this subject. This would never do. He clenched his hand against the couch cushion, staving back the fury at her witless refusal to see the facts right before her eyes. "You say you wish us to be friends, yet you force me to take the role of adviser due to your blindness concerning this man. I've defined all your relationships over the years, so I'll entertain this notion for a brief moment. Define who this man is to you." His tone had become quite abrupt. But, let her see behind his confidant's mask. He would make clear his disgust that she'd fallen at this man's feet. Let her recognize her foolish pursuit of an unworthy man when a greater choice sat before her.

"Xander, please don't be angry. I know you thought our relationship might take another direction, and I'm sorry, but I don't believe that is the best course. Not when I feel so much for Owen." Her gaze focused on the tips of her shoes, and as she spoke her next words, her voice softened. "I think I could love him. Not that I truly understand love, but the way I feel when I'm with him is everything. I don't know how else to describe my feelings."

Loved him. Blood roared, like a crashing, white avalanche in his ears. He studied her pale cheeks, counted the twenty-six freckles on her nose. He knew every curve and flicker from this girl. He'd underestimated his opponent, thought the game an easy win, but no matter, he'd begin a full court press. Switch up the plan. "All right, dear, but please be cautious. Your emotional state is fragile. Just a few weeks ago, you were in the police station after striking your mother. What will you do when Owen hurts you? When he rejects you, or leaves you for another? Only through our meetings are you able to maintain a hold on your inner turmoil and quite unsteady rage."

She released a heavy sigh, and then spoke just above a whisper. "Why can't you be happy for me?" Sad brown eyes appeared as she flicked a quick glance his way. "I worry your reaction is due to my interest in Owen, instead of you."

This was no rejection, only a slight speed bump. "Absolutely not." He let a tinge of affront brisk his tone. "I am capable of separating my emotions. I am your doctor. I have studied cases like yours for years. My reaction is due to knowing you better than you know yourself. I worry that if you suffer an emotional hardship, I'll have to medicate you again." He took a deep breath, kissed her hand, and met her gaze. "Or I'm afraid...terrified, actually...that you'll leave me as your brother left you."

"How can you say that?" Ember shot off the couch, her gaze shooting daggers. "That isn't a fair statement."

"Not fair, but realistic." Soon, she would see the truth. Her only path forward was by his side. No other man would remove her from his grasp.

"No, not realistic. Should Owen choose to leave then, I'll do what women throughout all time have done. I'll grab a box of tissues and a gallon of chocolate ice cream, and then listen to sappy love songs on my phone while crying in my room for weeks. But, then I'll move on, because that's what I do. That's what you taught me to do. To move on."

"Ember—" He rose to take her in his arms.

"I'm sorry, but I *am* moving on." She waved him back. "I feel we need some time apart, so I won't be coming on Thursdays for a while. I'm sticking with Owen. I'm sorry." She stepped toward the door then turned back. "Maybe after a few weeks, we can meet again as friends. Start anew." She stepped forward then, with tears falling down her cheeks, and hugged him tight. "I'm so sorry, Xander. If I've ever loved any man, it's you. But I need to discover if I can love another in a different way." She rose up on her tiptoes and kissed his cheek.

A chaste kiss, as if pacifying a loyal dog. He fisted his hands at his sides, knowing if he moved, he'd lock her down—allow no escape.

This time, she'd slipped through his fingers. But what did predators do when their prey escaped? They waited, hunkered down, and prepared for the next attack. Then when the time came, they pounced. She wanted to run like a scared rabbit, well, he'd oblige and play the seeking wolf. Once he held her in his strong jaw, his teeth sunk deep, he'd make sure she'd never again break free.

CHAPTER 24

Before his Friday night date with Ember, Owen thumbed through the folder containing the initial report from Detective Harris.

"I spoke to Ember's brother's girlfriend and his co-workers. Everyone was shocked by his suicide. His best friend was pretty emotional." Rachel sat back in her chair. "I reviewed the police reports. I'm investigating the gun's source now."

"Sounds like you've got a good start." He'd tucked her notes in the folder, unsure why this information necessitated a face-to-face meeting.

"Now for the hard part." She tossed a yellow folder across the desk.

"What's this?"

She huffed out a breath and flicked a finger toward the file. "Open it."

Doing as directed, Owen flipped open the file and found an 8x10 of Xander Kane with his lips plastered against Ember's. He shot up, knocking over his chair. "What the fuck is this?" His blood pressure spiked to a dangerous level. "How the hell could she do this?" He scanned through the rest of the photos, acid anger rising with each glimpse of the truth. Each betrayal. Crumpling the last shot in his hand, he headed for the door, and then faltered when something hit him hard between his shoulder blades. The object spun at his feet. A football. He turned to give Ms. Detective a piece of his mind. "What in the hell do—"

"Sit. Down. I'm not having you leave my office in a rage."

She raised a brow and waited. "Weren't *you* in a photo scandal only days ago?"

He glared and remained standing. While true he had suffered through a photo "situation," he hadn't caused the events to unfold. Based on this photo, he had every right to his fury.

She rose and stabbed a finger at the toppled chair. "Pick up that chair and sit your ass down."

Who the hell is she talking too? "Lady, you got a lot of nerve."

"Thank you." She flashed a tight-lipped smile. "Now shut up and listen."

He righted the chair but didn't sit.

"Ember meets with Xander every Thursday night."

"I'm aware of that. He's her counselor. At least, that's what she said," he scoffed. He knew Xander was interested in Ember, but he hadn't thought the interest was reciprocated—until now anyway. Damn, his chest hurt.

"May I finish?"

He leashed his tongue and his wayward thoughts for the moment. But only because he hoped she could explain, could erase some of this foreign pain rushing through his body. Was Ember with Xander even now? And why? Just why?

"As I was saying, they meet on Thursday nights, always for an hour, maybe fifteen to thirty minutes more. However, last night she only stayed for approximately twenty minutes. On the occasion marked by the photos..." she waved her hand at the nightmare on her desk. "They met for dinner on a Wednesday night. I situated myself in a booth beside them. Based on what I heard, she tried to break things off. However, this Xander guy is good. A master manipulator. But, she did not, I repeat, did not welcome his advances. After he left, she seemed a bit dazed, and she was sniffling into a tissue. You were right about him, some things aren't adding up, but right now, I'm awaiting feedback."

"May I speak?" This time, Queen Harris deigned to wave a hand in his direction. "If everything seemed so innocent, why show me the photos?"

"Full disclosure." She tapped a finger against a photo. "Maybe I read the situation wrong. Unlikely, but still...I think you should speak to Ember yourself. Figure out your own relationship shi—situation." Clearing her throat, she walked around her desk and leaned against the front edge. "I don't usually make assumptions on a single nights study, but this girl, I don't know, she seemed decent."

"Fine, yeah, decent. Can I take these folders?"

"All yours, Big-O."

"If Kane is a 'master manipulator,' then keep digging. He's crossing way to many lines—professional and personal." He jerked open her office door and stomped down the hall. Rude, but he didn't care.

That sly dog had touched his woman. Why hadn't Ember said anything? What was she hiding? He'd give her a chance to explain, since she'd offered him the same courtesy just a few nights ago. Hell, who was he kidding? He'd forgive her, and then make sure she understood he didn't share.

Not one inch.

# # #

Owen slammed his truck into Park, yanked the folders off the passenger seat, and hopped onto the curb. He ignored the cool autumn breeze. Nothing could break past the barrier of his red-hot fury. Resisting the urge to knock down her door, he rang the doorbell. Lucky for her, she was quick to respond.

She moved aside as he blasted past and dropped the folders on the coffee table.

He studied her for a moment. She was still in her work clothes. Her eyes were wide and her head tilted a bit as she studied him.

Is that innocence an act? "I believe I mentioned I hired a private investigator."

"Yes."

Her smile seemed a little forced as she nodded. "You realize then that she's investigating."

"Why? What did she say? Something about Elliot?" Her words rushed out, and then she visibly swallowed before sinking onto the arm of her recliner.

Damn it! He refused to feel any sympathy and contained his wish to offer her comfort. She had some explaining to do. "I thought we were exclusive."

"Oh, I wasn't sure. I'd hoped, and based on the other night, I assumed, but I am glad you feel the same." She brushed at a string on her pants as her cheeks turned a beguiling shade of pink.

He wouldn't be deterred by her enticements. "When people are exclusive, they don't kiss other people."

"Of course not…I would never…wait… you just came from the investigator so did she say something?"

"She didn't have to say anything. The pictures pretty much speak for themselves." He dropped an offending photo on her lap. "She took this picture a few days ago. Is that why you needed distance and space? Stringing two guys along does take time, I imagine."

Her eyes widened as she studied the photo. "I can explain." With an unsteady hand, she placed the photo back on the table, and wrapped an arm around her waist. "That night after you picked me up at the police station, Xander revealed he had feelings for me." Her voice wobbled, and a few tears trickled down her cheeks.

Undeterred by her tears, he strove for the truth. "That photo isn't from the night I bailed you out."

"No, that's when I met him for dinner."

A feral growl rumbled from deep in his throat. Could he really listen to this?

"I met Xander to explain I didn't want our relationship to change. He is a dear friend, and he's counseled me for years. During that meeting, I tried to explain my reservations, but he twisted my words."

"Looks more like he was twisting your lips."

"Owen, please, my relationship with Xander is hard to explain. I didn't kiss him back." Her hands twisted together in her lap. "I told him I'm done with our Thursday night sessions. I can't keep rehashing my past." She met his gaze. "I need to live in the now. I said if he wants to be friends outside of the clinical environment, I would like that, but nothing more."

"Why did you keep this from me?" He combed his fingers through his hair.

"I thought I'd made my refusal clear that first night, but he persisted." Ember sighed. "He holds this high ideal of who I am, but I'm not that woman."

"So, he's clear now? Because if I see him again, I'll make

clear how things stand between us, and I don't think he'll enjoy my methods."

"That isn't necessary. Don't you dare bully him." Ember rose and stood before him—nose-to-nose and eye-to-eye.

Damn, if her tough side didn't turn him on. "He needs to get his head straight, and so do you."

"So do I?" She poked a finger against his chest. "So do I? Perhaps you've forgotten the other night when some girl was cramming her tongue inside your ear. And that was some girl you didn't even know, so don't throw my friendship with Xander in my face." She grabbed his shoulders and held him at arm's length. "We're on an equal line now, remember? Or didn't you mean what you said?"

"I'm here, aren't I? Standing toe-to-toe." He jabbed her chest right back. "I don't care if this is high-handed. Xander may know you, may have helped get you where you are today, and for that I'll remain grateful, but don't think, for one second, you owe him more."

Her gaze faltered. "I am working on my conflicting feelings, because I—"

"How about I help you along?" He hauled her into his arms and kissed her, making clear his unwavering resolve. Untamed and unfettered, he claimed with each stroke and thrust of his tongue.

"You still conflicted, baby?" As he teased his lips across her neck, he reveled in her tight grip in his hair, her sure hand trailing over his body.

"No," she purred. "How do you like *my* high-handedness?" She stroked a palm along his erection then stepped back, wiggling out of her jeans and kicking them aside.

There were no words.

He lifted his shirt over his head, and then walked her backwards to the couch.

They tumbled with lips locked in a flagrant kiss that stoked every nerve-ending in his body.

Like a fuse on dynamite, their explosion was imminent, but that didn't mean the blissful trail would be short. He released her lips and eased back to study her face. Her lips were deep red, her hair fanned around her face, and her restless hands continued their frantic study of his body.

"Owen." She traced a finger over his damp lower lip. Her voice was low and husky. "Please, believe in me."

Did he believe her? Such open innocence stared back from her eyes' deep chocolate pools. Treachery didn't exist in this girl, even though she'd been bottle-fed that existence. "I believe in what we have together. Any mixed feelings you have about anyone else are done."

In answer, she sat upright, removed her shirt, and switched their positions. "Take off your pants." From her mounted position, she unbuttoned his jeans and slowly tugged down the zipper.

He stayed her hand. "You're not ready."

"You said steps, right? Well, this time, I'm not climbing the peak alone." She scooted off the couch and grabbed a fleece blanket off the recliner. After fixing the blanket on the floor, she flicked a finger in his direction. "Get naked."

Though his mind said no, his body said yes. He toed off his shoes and dropped his jeans to the floor. "Ember, are you—"

"No. You want to know how I feel? I'll show you. Lie down."

After raising a brow, he received a "please" in response.

Whatever happened to Ms. I'm sorry and thank you? Not that he minded, especially when she braced her well-curved body above him, and buried his face in the fall of her hair as she kissed him. She'd come so far, so fast. Heart focused on her, lips moving in perfect rhythm, he let go his earlier angst and believed her words. With each brush of her lips, he fell deeper and deeper, knowing he'd never surface, but satisfied in the drowning. Her greedy mouth worked down his neck to his chest, then across his stomach.

When his full erection was deep in her mouth, he shuddered and released a few choice curses. Sweet, blissful torture continued as her untutored mouth enthusiastically learned everything in a matter of minutes. Aching, heart pounding, breath panting, he eased himself out of her mouth before he found satisfaction. He would find release, but they would share the pleasure.

"Stems, I want to try something." He grabbed her by the waist and rotated her body so her sweet center lined up with his mouth. Up on his elbows, he licked her wet sheath.

Her entire body shook.

He felt her throaty moan against his cock.

With determination, she worked his thick erection in and out of her mouth.

Not to be outdone, he slid two fingers in time with his tongue, stroking, roughing her pink bud with each brush.

She gasped, and the hot breath stroked over his over-stimulated head. After catching her breath, she continued her tight suction, then glided.

Closer now, she squirmed against him, but he would show her no quarter. He glanced down and saw his cock buried deep in her mouth.

He shuddered and moaned, then concentrated on intensifying her pleasure—rasping, driving, and seeking her full surrender. Lost in her body, in his will to drive her past bliss, he teased with his tongue until he felt her spasm, draw taut, and then break.

She cried out and bit down hard on his thick cock.

"Fighting mean, Stems?" Delivering payback, he stroked with his tongue and fingers until her body stopped shuddering.

Her hard bite on his tip, and her moans vibrating along his cock shot racking pleasure down his spine. He caught the vision once more of that mass of red hair spilling over his thighs. Her body still shook with release as she ground against him with hand and mouth.

Brown eyes met his gaze. His voyeurism seemed to kick her determination in gear, and she sucked harder, faster.

Her eagerness pushed him so close to the edge, but he didn't want to fall. He wanted to stay in this moment, in the feel of her tongue against his throbbing head forever. "I'm going to come, Stems. Use your hand."

She didn't stop, only used heavy suction as she worked him up and down.

"Fuck yeah, baby. Pull back."

Her nipples brushed against his stomach as she swallowed him whole.

Hips rising off the floor, he bucked as a load of pleasure shot from his body. His heart had stopped pounding as all the blood was pooled in his cock. Wild grunts erupted from his throat as

Ember continued sucking through his release. Every sensation centered on what she was doing with her mouth and tongue. He shuddered, on the verge of screaming for her to stop, but dying for her to continue, he bit her thigh to keep from promising her anything, giving her the keys to his kingdom.

He heard her purr out a, "Mmmm." And damn if that didn't make his dick jerk again.

He grunted, then licked and kissed the love bite he'd left on her thigh before collapsing back on the floor. Soft hair fell across his legs, then a silky-soft body landed with a plop on his chest. He lifted one lid.

A Cheshire grin lit Ember's face.

He reached up and tucked her well-fluffed hair behind her ear. "You're amazing, and so brave. So much buried deep inside that beautiful body, and I'm going to dig it all out."

"Want to start now?" She sprinkled kisses across his chest, his face.

Owen chuckled. "No, not tonight." With his hands, he massaged the firm globes of her bottom. "I want our first time together to be under better circumstances."

Ember closed her sleepy, sated eyes and rested her head against the crook in his shoulder.

"I'm not rejecting you. I'd prefer all conflicted feelings gone before we venture further. Come here." He lifted her lolling head and kissed her.

She tried intensifying the connection.

But, he slapped her bottom and eased back.

She sighed, rested her elbows on his chest, and met his gaze. "So, what else did the detective say?"

"I'll leave the file here. She's done initial interviews of Elliot's friends and co-workers. Next, she'll review police files and determine more details about the gun." He continued his massage of her back and squeezed the sweet cushion of her ass. He tried not picturing how hot she'd be bent over with that heart-shaped ass in the air.

"I can't thank you enough for hiring the detective. I'd like to meet her sometime. I realize that my brother...that the detective might determine he..." She shook her head. "No, I don't want to darken this moment." Quiet for a moment, she traced a finger along the outline of his lips. "I liked what we did, felt really...naughty."

Naughty Ember, now that was a vision he could get behind. "Best orgasm I've ever had."

"Aren't they all the same?"

"What?" He huffed out a laugh.

"Nothing." She swirled a circle in his chest hair with her index finger.

Backtracking, he considered her inexperience. His brain was still restocking oxygen and blood, so he was running a bit behind. He lifted her chin. "I'm sorry. Don't be afraid to ask questions. To be clear, some orgasms are more intense. Oral tends to be because I don't have control. And when you swallow, mmm..." Eyes closed, he shivered with the memory. "Plus, you didn't hold back, and that made a difference."

She squirmed and nuzzled against his neck.

"Sex shouldn't be embarrassing or shameful, Stems. Coming together is meant to feel good, and baby, that was way past good."

He'd gone hard again, absolute rock solid, radar ready since her soft body lay cushioned against his. Her scent lingered on his tongue. Every particle in the southern regions of his body begged to stake a claim. Bury all the day's strain in pleasure.

But he'd wait. Too much had happened today and he had to leave. When he was with her for the first time—her first time—the moment would be perfect and would last. He'd need to take care of her after he took her innocence, and in order to do that, they needed days and his very large bed.

"Quit squirming." He pinched her bottom. "I can't stay. I've got Chewy's day camp up north tomorrow. By coming here, I tanked on packing T-shirts and rally rags into bags. I'm sure my phone has some colorful texts."

"What camp?" She blinked and shifted against him.

Her voice sounded all husky and warm. He shifted beneath her and clenched the blanket in his fist. There had to be medals for sexual restraint. Had to be. "Chewy holds a camp for physically disabled children every fall. He's a good guy, because he actually attends his charity events."

"That's sweet. And you're sweet for helping."

"I'm not sweet, Stems."

Ember licked her lips and shot him a cheeky grin. "No, I guess you're not."

CHAPTER 25

Heart pounding, Ember escaped her freakish nightmare and blinked open her eyes. Shadows danced across her bedroom ceiling, taunting her with visions of circling demons.

What kind of dream was that?

Nightmares based on vicious fights she'd endured at the hand of her mother frequently shaded her sleep, but this was different. She shivered from the cold sweat dampening her body, and then burst into nervous laughter, still caught up in her brutal dream.

A very real something ran along the base of her foot, and squeezed her toe. "Ember."

Did someone say my name? Am I still dreaming?

"Hello? Is someone there?" Eyes wide open, she shifted a fraction on the pillow and peered around the dark room. Only a sliver of light escaped from the sides of her blinds. Familiar shapes formed gray blurs.

An odd rustle crept across the quiet. A creak.

Her breathing suspended as she listened.

Dear God, don't let there be another rustle.

Shadows widened across her wall.

A primal "No" ripped from her throat.

A strong hand slammed against her mouth, covering her nose and lips.

Opening her mouth to scream, she released only a choked gasp. She bit, kicked, and swung, fighting to escape.

The intruder landed multiple blows on her face.

Stinging, jolting pain momentarily stunned her. Ears ringing, she cried in agony.

"Quiet."

The torment continued as he shoved some type of fabric past her clenched teeth. Blocked from screaming, other instincts raced to the fore. Her body took charge and battled for freedom. Flailing for purchase against this intruder's assault, she gripped the man's arm.

Denying her struggles, he bent back her wrist and slumped over her body, smothering her with his weight.

Outmatched, she stilled, considering her options. Her escape.

Her nose throbbed, and she blinked against the pain in her battered eye.

Then he flipped her.

His merciless knee pressed against her back and pinched against her spine. Acute pain shot across every nerve-ending in her body.

Wrenching back her neck, her attacker worked the fabric out of her mouth, but left a portion across her lips, then tied the handkerchief ends at the back of her head. Strands of hair caught, as he tightened the knot against her scalp, making her eyes water.

She fought to breathe past the fabric now wrenching wide her mouth, digging and pulling against both sides. With each gasp for breath, her lungs burned. Tears drenched her face.

I can't die like this. Fight.

Bending her elbows, she fought to turn over and escape.

Her attacker's repeated full-knuckled punches against the back of her head blackened her world. Disoriented, face buried in her pillow, she blinked. White flares assailed her vision, creating a glaring spotlight on a very real nightmare.

In a muffled voice, the monster growled, "Stay still." He yanked at the knot in her hair. "I wouldn't want to accidentally nick you."

Nick me? Oh please, no.

Frozen in place, she flinched as cold, hard pressure trailed along the side of her neck, ending between her shoulder blades.

A knife? He has a knife? Dear God, please help me.

Dazed from the blows, fear pouring out through tears and

muffled screams, she once more fought to turn, to stop this madman from taking more from her than anyone else ever had. Once he trapped her body, he could do anything. Anything. Dear God, anything.

Each movement, tussle, and wrestle was blocked with a hard strike against her body. She became one with the pain, strove to push through its existence, out-rival, outdo. To descend with the unforgiving savage into the darkness, but he picked up the gauntlet and laid down the hammer over and over until a piercing pain shot down her back. For a moment, she believed she could no longer feel her legs.

His knee sharpened against her back—declaring his intolerance. Foul words from the man echoed through her ears as if traveling through a tunnel.

"Don't say I didn't warn you."

Bloody knuckles landed beside her nose, incongruent beside the laced-edged pillow. The other fist pressed against her temple. A sharp prick burned the bridge of her nose, then sliced a trail to the edge of her nostril. A metallic scent and the cool sting against her senses permitted a horrific thought to surface—he'd cut her.

"Red blood to match that red hair." Evil emanated from his hushed tone.

Would he keep slicing until she bled to death? Who would find her body? Was he going to rape her?

Steadying her breathing, she focused on a way out. Was Clayton home? Could she pound against the thin duplex walls? Blood trickled, and then dripped onto her upper lip, itching—pushing her to focus on the reality of her situation—to ignore the pounding pain heating her beaten face.

Pain erupted in her shoulders as he forced her arms behind her back.

If he bound her, she'd be finished. Strength Ember didn't know she possessed surfaced, and a scream torn from some unearthly place in her soul ripped past her throat.

Once last chance. Stop him.

Break free.

But her arms wouldn't respond—weak, so weak. She shifted her left hip and tried to use her legs to flip over. Once more, he pressed a knee against some central place in her back that numbed her legs.

Controlling her weak tussle, he shoved her face into her pillow.

Can't breathe.

She rubbed her itchy nose against her pillow, now soaked in blood, sweat, and hopeless tears. Stifled against the mattress, she struggled to breathe.

Weak, so weak.

She shook her head back and forth on the pillow, violently resisting her forced suffocation. But, maybe she should let go. Stop breathing. Release. Just die. Pressure loosened on her head, and she turned, gasping for breath.

He wrenched her hand onto the pillow beside her face. "Girls who don't listen get punished."

A blade plunged straight through her palm. For a dazed moment, Ember stared at the unreal scene of a thick knife from a Leatherman's tool embedded in her hand.

Then the blade disappeared.

Raw agony branched through every finger, jolting up her arm and slashing across her heart. A black hole opened. Screaming past the barrier in her mouth, she fell past her black world into red. Blood poured from the laceration, oozing, leaking life from her hand.

Who was this man? This nightmare personified.

Why me?

A zip sound filled the air as he bound her wrists together behind her back.

Her mangled hand throbbed unbearably.

Bound.

Helpless.

Shivers racked her sweat-soaked body and her hand violently shook in the wrist-cutting band.

What more will he do?

Sobs fueled by the unknown and the agony coursing through her beaten body tore from her throat. No more, she could take no more.

A vicious tug on her hair wrenched back her neck, making her gag and gasp for breath. Panting, wheezing for each breath. She knew…this was it.

The end.

Death.

But then the pressure on her back lessened, and what felt like a comb brushed through her hair. Fear chilled her as the atmosphere switched from blood-strewn terror to a mad house filled with warbled mirrors reflecting masked faces that could be heard but not seen.

Who was behind this mask?

Off tune with sanity, a song hummed from her perpetrator's throat and filled the room in tandem with her panting breaths and pounding heart.

Her eyes once more stung with tears as with unforgiving strokes, he worked through her tangles. That tune, that hum, filled her with more terror than a thousand jabs against her body, than any blade ripping through her skin.

That hum signed her death warrant. That creepy, horrid tune shot terror-filled ice down her spine and froze her heart. He'd likely kill her and keep her body parts in jars in his fridge. Maybe if she held her breath, she would pass out and not have to consciously suffer through the pain of dismemberment.

The cut on her nose dripped fresh blood onto her pillow. Dried blood and tears itched. A brassy smell filled her nostrils, gagging her. And the anguish—she was so far beyond any known definition. She remained still, waiting, dreading the moment the song would end, because what happened after would be the true nightmare.

A tugging. A back-and-forth motion of his hand against the back of her head. Then cool air poured over her neck.

"Now that you aren't so pretty, maybe you'll behave," the man murmured into her ear.

Something stringy drifted across her face. Her hair? Had he cut her hair? She sputtered and tried blowing past the fabric in her mouth to keep what must be her hair from sticking to her tear-drenched face. Her hand seared as hairs grazed her wound, catching in the blood still dripping down her fingers.

A seeking hand skimmed down her back.

She stilled. Not breathing. Not moving

No. No. No. Please, no.

When he reached her bottom, he squeezed her fleshy

mounds. His weight shifted and he sat back on her calves.

Using what little reserves she had, she battled to break free of his presence. Bucking, fighting, wrestling to rise from his twisted touch.

Ignoring pain.

Refusing fear.

But this monster played to win. He grabbed her hand and pressed against the damaged flesh.

Racking spasms thundered through her body, white lights flickered before her eyes, and she swallowed to keep bile from escaping her gag.

"How many licks does it take, Ember? Let's see?"

He knows my name. She shivered with revulsion and clenched her back teeth.

Over the sound of her accelerating breathing, she heard rustling, and what sounded like the whoosh of a belt through loops. Cool air struck her bottom as he lifted her nightshirt, and then kneaded.

A whip cracked.

A sting slashed against her outer thigh.

His laughter surpassed sanity. Through the pain and each crack of the belt, his heavy, excited breathing stuttered through the room. "Are you counting, dear?"

Tortuous thrashes at an unconscionable level repeatedly struck her body. Her body shook against the bed, out of her control. Her moans and pleas spilled unheard from her drooling lips. Her punishment continued.

Ember closed her eyes and thought about Owen. If she died in this moment, she wanted her last thoughts to be of him. Let this harbinger of death take her body, but he would not own her final thoughts.

The bed shifted as his weight moved away.

Her bedroom door slammed shut.

Muscles clenched, she cringed against the next assault.

Was her killer still there?

Silence. Through the haze of pain and her shivering body, she focused on one sense. Hearing. Listening. Her trembling body and pounding heart interfered.

Do this. I can do this.

A phone. Call the police.

Where is my phone?

A faint slam shot through the quiet from her apartment's front door.

Her heart jumped into her throat, pounding so loud the sound canceled out everything else. *Is he gone?*

Get up! Move.

Fighting past the pain and stifling fear, she used her face as leverage and shuffled her legs along the edge of the mattress. Stomach muscles clenched, she rose into a sitting position. When her lashed bottom grazed the bed, she shot up from the needling pain, but her legs balked and she collapsed against her nightstand. Her chin bounced against the floor. Stars lit her eyes as pain fired through her side and hand.

Adrenaline. Please, God, just give me one more burst of strength.

A muffled bang.

What was that? Is he back?

A neighbor's door? Clayton? Was that Clayton?

The room spun as fear and hope coalesced. Hysteria crept into her mind-fucked world. Black shrouded her vision, red pain poured from the walls and ceiling, sluicing over her body with stinging needles that pierced her skin. Sobs escaped and choked past the gag tearing the sides of her mouth.

No. Stop. No. Don't lose it now.

She struggled to rise and, once more, cried out against the pain as she collapsed against the side of her bed.

Focus.

He might come back.

Leveraging her body against the mattress, she stood and escaped into the living room.

Frantic, Ember glanced around the room. Dark shadows threatened her sanity, but she pushed on. Bumping her hip against the side table, she knocked the phone onto the floor.

The stupid piece of shit tumbled beneath her coffee table.

No. I don't have time.

Falling to her knees, she prepared for the jolt and dropped her upper body against the carpet. As her hand hit the floor, she swallowed hard against rising vomit and white lights once more threatened to black out her world.

Almost there.

With inhuman will, she rested her back against the couch and fought through the pain stinging her backside. She stretched her leg, and with her big toe, dragged the phone closer.

Toeing on the power, she carefully pressed 9-1-1.

A lady's voice answered.

Ember toppled next to the phone. She opened her mouth, but blocked by the cotton gag, she couldn't speak.

# # #

Stoplights blocked his path. Owen pounded a fist against the dash. No one was out at this time of night, so why even switch to red? He slowed to forty-five, checked the crossroads, and then shot through the intersection.

Throughout his life, there were only two times he'd lost his calm. Once when his father passed, and another after his high school girlfriend died in a car accident. While painful, those moments had a sense of resolution. Not this. Not now. This was insanity. This had no purpose or reason.

Panic, dread, fear—all emotions he in no way welcomed—coursed through his body, along with the wish to move quickly through time while everything else remained frozen.

Someone had violated his woman—and that someone would pay.

Guarding others was his sole purpose in life. That role defined his position on the field, his place in his family, every aspect of who he was—and he'd failed.

Since his mother shook him awake, handed him the house phone, and said Clayton "Somesuch" was on the line, adrenaline had kept him on the edge of a full-fledged Berserker rage. That heavy flow of blood remained strong as he slammed his truck into Park in the hospital ER lot. At the entrance, a nurse made him show his ID before letting him through. Didn't these people understand he didn't have time to stop?

The nurse led him to Ember's curtained area in the ER.

"She's in the second one over."

He nodded. Took a step forward, then stopped. Too much sound—beeping monitors, weeping, pained moans, all too foreign. His woman didn't belong here among all this chaos.

Fists clenched, jaw tight, he attempted to control the fathomless fury drowning his body. What would he see behind that curtain? How could he hide his rage?

Move. She needs you.

Peeking past an opening in the curtain, he saw Ember propped up in the hospital bed. Her lower body lay twisted at an odd angle. And her face—*Oh, hell, fucking no*—her face a blotched mix of purple and red. A bandage covered her entire nose.

He bent over at the waist, braced his hands on his knees, and sucked in a breath, then another. Who could do this? The bottom of the curtain ruffled, teasing him with movement, adding a spin to his already sickened stomach. He'd seen a lot of injuries on the field, but nothing like her poor face. One eye was practically swollen shut. A hard bite on his lower lip kept unwelcome tears from spilling down his cheeks.

Get a grip on it, stupid crybaby ass. Ember matters, not you. Straightening, he ran a hand through his hair and once more opened the curtain.

Clayton sat at her side, holding her hand. He turned at the movement and caught his eye.

The curtain hooks jangled across the steel rod, creating an eerie chime in the sterile room. A feeling of reverence for the beautiful, broken creature on the bed overwhelmed him. Marred with cuts and a violent array of bruising across her face and neck, yet she remained beautiful—a rare red rose cultivated in strength and strife. He saw nothing but the grace of this stricken woman. This moment of clarity, of being shown what mattered in life, would also be laid at her door. Every piece of Ember Brooks blinded him with exquisite beauty. But that didn't keep him from the knowledge that someone would pay, someone would feel as much pain as she had, and more. This he vowed.

He nodded at Clayton and stepped further into the room. But something seemed off.

Her hair.

What kind of cut is that?

Her red locks were trimmed at different angles, with one short tuft sticking straight in the air.

Ember shifted and met his gaze. Her entire body seemed to shiver uncontrollably. Tears glistened and meshed with dried blood as they trailed down her cheeks. With a trembling bandaged hand, she wiped away the evidence, leaving a smear of red and black across her face. She brushed a hand over her hair and turned away with a guttural moan.

Owen got his wish—time stopped.

He'd cut her hair.

Somehow, that violation was the last straw. His heart seethed with an emotion he'd never felt before—aching with a need to annihilate and seek vengeance, yet at the same time, wrenching over the pain Ember had suffered.

Too much. Too much.

Stomach churning, he had to leave. Without a word, he turned on his heel and blindly charged through the exit, stumbling over to a bush, and heaved the contents of his stomach.

Revolting.

Everything about this evening was vile.

The stench of the hospital—the stench of his vomit, all vile. He moved farther down the driveway and collapsed onto the curb.

The crisp autumn air did nothing to cool his wrath. He'd heard Ember's soft "Owen" as he'd departed. But he couldn't face her while crazed emotions controlled him.

That bastard had cut her hair.

That fiery representation of her inner strength—and he'd taken it. Found her Achilles heel and wrenched it from her body—her soul. Who would she be now? Would she collapse this time? Allow her tormentor to win?

"Fuck!" A string of curses that would make a pirate proud poured from his lips. He stood and paced along the sidewalk. An entire month pounding against the team's blocking sled still wouldn't be enough to remove this frustration. When he got his hands on the man responsible, he'd shear him from head to toe, string him up by his balls, and punt him into the next county.

The sliding glass doors pinged open.

Clayton charged around the corner, his hands on his hips. "You leaving?"

"No." Shooting the cop a sideways glance, he spit into the bushes.

"Go back in, then."

"Needed a minute." Once more dangerously close to tears, Owen blinked, and that enraged him even more. Fisting his hands in his hair, he breathed deep and regained control of his unstable emotions. "He cut her hair?"

"Yes." Clayton sniffed, and glanced away.

"What else?"

Clayton hesitated, knocking his knuckles together before releasing a long breath. "No sexual assault. But he...I'm not sure in your current state I should go over this. Plus, divulging case information to outside parties isn't necessarily allowed."

"Fuck allowed. What happened?"

"You have to stay cool, all right?" Clayton leaned against a cement pillar. The bright red light of the Emergency sign illuminated his face. "I need to ask one thing before I explain."

"You want to ask *me* questions? I don't have time for this. You don't have time for this. Shouldn't you be out looking for this guy? Tell me what that asshole did. How the hell is she supposed to ever overcome..." He thought about the injuries to her face. Her hair. "Fuck."

"She won't overcome anything if she doesn't have someone strong by her side. So I *will* ask my question. Are you just playing around, or are you serious?" He jerked his thumb toward the emergency room entrance. "Because that girl deserves a hell of a lot more."

Owen huffed out a laugh. Unable to believe he had to waste time justifying his intentions to this guy. "If you weren't a cop, I'd beat the ever-loving shit out of you. And I'm this close," he pinched his index finger and thumb together, "to not giving a shit what you are."

Clayton studied him for what seemed like an interminable moment. "The assailant entered her bedroom and gagged her with a scarf. With what Ember described as a short knife, the man sliced her nose, stabbed her hand, and cut her hair. The perpetrator then assaulted her with a belt. No sign of break-in. Of course those duplex locks are shit..."

On the field, Owen prepared for each hit. Each moment on the line, the raw punch of another man trying to break past his position. Shoulder pads and helmet braced against a freight train of pain, but he had no protection against Clayton's words. Each blow visited upon his woman wasn't blocked, wasn't muffled behind layers of padding.

One inconceivable statement repeated in his mind. "Assaulted her with a belt. What the hell does that mean?"

"Owen, let go of my shirt." Clayton's spoke with an even tone. "Breathe, man. Calm down. Ember doesn't need another bout of violence right now. Deal with your shit on your own time, this isn't about you."

"I'm aware of what this is about. This is about someone terrorizing my woman." Visions of Ember being stabbed and beaten were even worse now that he had a clearer picture of all she'd endured. Kicking the stone pillar, once, twice, wasn't doing anything to relieve his anguish.

Clayton jabbed his shoulder. "Stop. Get your mind straight, go back inside, and handle your business."

"You'll be getting a new neighbor soon because she's moving out."

"I'm fine with that."

Owen jabbed a finger against Clayton's chest. "Don't think you'll leave me out of the investigation either. I want to know who this guy is, and I want him to pay. Do what you have to."

"You think I don't want him as much as you? After I got the call and got to her place, I opened her door...I saw her...she was curled against the couch and I just—" Clayton rubbed a hand against his forehead. "Why am I talking to you? Get inside."

Owen nodded. Clearly, Clayton was just as overcome by Ember's condition.

Heading back inside, Owen stopped at the restroom and wiped at something wet on his cheeks. *Damn it.* After splashing cold water on his face and rinsing out his mouth, he breathed deep, in and out, past the tight ache in his chest—a clamp that wouldn't cease until he found retribution. Through clenched teeth, he tried forming a smile until he managed one that didn't make him look like a deranged serial killer. Once more, he stopped at the white curtain.

When Ember met his gaze and bit her bruised bottom lip, she pierced straight through his heart. Not saying a word, he sank beside her on the bed and eased her into his arms.

One touch on her back, and she flinched. With a gentler

hand, he settled her against his chest.

She adjusted against him, burrowing deeper and deeper.

Her movements like a frightened mole, digging a tunnel beneath his skin. She was already there, buried deep within his heart.

They lay quietly for minutes, maybe hours.

With her in his arms, he felt a slight calm return. "Ember." Her hair tuft tickled his chin. "When you're released, you'll come to my house. Sometime this week, we'll go back to your place." Her muscles seemed to tense and she whimpered slightly. "All right, all right. I understand. I'll go back with Mom sometime and pick up your things. Don't worry about going back. I've got you now."

When she didn't respond, he continued with a softer tone. "Our living together would have happened eventually, I'm just moving up the date. Don't think you're staying another night by yourself with some crazy fucker after you."

She shivered.

Regret pooled low in his gut over his harsh reminder of her nightmare.

In a soft voice that sounded as if she had a sinus infection, she responded, "I'll stay at your place tonight, but then—"

"No." Owen forced an even tone passed gritted teeth. "You'll stay, period."

She shifted against his chest and met his gaze. "But my apartment...it's mine." After pausing a moment, she winced, then lightly patted the raw corners of her mouth. "I won't let you take that away." She clenched his shirt in her fist.

"Woman, do you have any idea how I feel right now? 'Cause if you did, you wouldn't argue."

Her head rustled back and forth against his chest.

Perhaps he'd pushed her too far, but there was no way she was leaving his sight.

Wetness permeated through his shirt and dampened his chest. "Ember?"

She lifted her chin, her bottom lip quivering. "He c-cut my h-hair."

With each of her tears, he felt his own heart drip bloody beads of sorrow and anguish. "I know, Stems. You're all right now. I'm here."

Through gasping sobs, she sputtered out, "He said...he cut me... as punishment."

Unable to speak, he nodded.

"I didn't want him to."

"It's all right, baby. Shhh." He kissed the top of her head, but was afraid to offer comfort any other way. Where could he touch her without causing pain?

"But, I couldn't...it was all over and I couldn't—" She rubbed a hand under her nose.

Raw red marks marred her wrists. Dried blood matted her hair.

Steady breaths. Don't tense. Don't let her see my anger.

"Don't do this right now. We'll talk when you're feeling better. Let me find you a tissue." He straightened and grabbed a handful of Kleenex from a box on a table by the bed.

"Thanks." Her voice sounded funny with the large Band-Aid on her nose. Suddenly, her eyes shot wide and she shoved his chest. "Go away."

"What?"

"No. No. He'll come after you. He'll hurt your mom, your sister." Her bloodied, swollen eye quivered and fresh tears watered her cheeks.

"Stop. You'll hurt yourself." He gently cupped her face. "I failed you once. Don't think I'll allow such a breach again."

A nurse entered with a packet of papers for Ember's care and a couple prescriptions.

If ever Owen needed his mother, now was the time. She would know what to do. He felt swamped by helplessness, by a need to make everything better, but he'd need help to assure Ember's comfort in the coming days. "I'll handle the paperwork." He carefully unwrapped from her side.

"Owen." Ember grasped his hand.

"Don't worry. I'll be right outside."

Following the nurse out into the hall, he sat at a chair outside of Ember's room. His hand shook too much for any of the writing to be legible. "Miss, can I just pay for her care now?"

"You want to pay for all of it?" The nurse raised a single brow.

"Yeah."

"Do you know how—"

"I'm aware of the expense. It doesn't matter. Here's my address. Send all invoices there." He handed over his driver's license.

The nurse nodded and clicked back down the hall.

As he took in Ember's condition, he considered the least painful course of travel. He figured she had no clothes to wear, so he took off his shirt. "Stems, you have to get up now. Put my shirt on over your gown."

She shuffled to her side, then onto her stomach. With her legs and bottom hanging over the side of the bed, she stopped.

"What's wrong?"

Her answer was muffled in the mattress.

He watched as her chest rose and fell.

"Let me help you." He clasped her elbow.

She turned in the opposite direction. "I can't sit."

Clayton's words came back with a punch. Of course, no wonder she was lying on her side. He wanted to absorb all her pain and thrash through each ache in her body. Why had this happened? Hadn't she suffered enough? Seeing her fight through the pain was the bravest thing he'd ever witnessed. He clenched his jaw against sympathetic tears.

Damn, this woman gets to me.

Action. He needed action to break through these heartrending thoughts. "Let me carry you."

She glanced over her shoulder, met his gaze, and gave a slight nod. "Owen just be careful of my...um...my butt, 'cause he—" Shaking her head, she bit her lip.

"Excuse me," the nurse spoke from the doorway. "Mr. Killion, here's your paperwork." She smiled at Ember. "Take care of her."

"I will." Owen tucked the envelope under his armpit. "All right, Stems, let's get you home."

"Wait, sir, what are you doing? You can't carry her. We'll get her a wheelchair." The nurse glanced down the hallway.

"She can't sit. I've got her."

"We can't allow—"

"Ma'am, I realize you're doing your job, probably quite good at it actually, but I'm carrying her out of here. Right now, I don't care about hospital protocol."

The nurse nodded. "I'm leaving. I was never here."

"All right, Stems, let's get you home." Her back still to him, he maneuvered around to her side and lifted her into his arms. When his forearm brushed her bottom, he heard a slight hiss from under her breath. "Should I put you down?"

"No." Her hand clenched on his shoulder. "Please, can we just go?" Her eyes were closed and her breathing came in short pants.

The walk to his truck seemed to go on for miles, as if they were stuck in purgatory and would never reach their destination. Her body remained tense in his arms. With each step, he jolted her body and her stuttered breathing broke across his neck. Using a slow, steady tread, he paced to his truck.

Upon arriving, she said, "Put me down, please."

He lowered her to the ground, maintaining his grip on her elbow.

She stood beside his truck, staring into the unknown.

What is she thinking?

Tears rained down her face and her body shook with sobs. Kicking his tire with her bare foot over and over, she screamed, "I hate him. I hate him." She pounded her uninjured fist against his chest. "Why? Why did he do this to me? What did I do?" A battle-torn moan ripped from her throat. She collapsed at his feet and rocked back and forth. "He cut my hair. Why would he do that? Why?"

Tears of his own finally escaped and trailed a heated path down his cheeks. He wrapped his arms around her, joining her on the pavement. "I know, baby. I know." Holding tight, locking her in his arms, he let her bruised body comfort him as much as he comforted her.

CHAPTER 26

Growing up in an abusive household, she'd become immune to the fear, to the flinch before the strike. Immunity built against the fear, hate, and insanity. But pain, her dear friend, had returned with a vengeance, bringing with it a soul-stealing terror. One she couldn't seem to shake.

Half asleep the next day, her eyes drooped as Owen welcomed his co-worker and friend. Painkillers brought about extreme drowsiness, but her pal, pain, kept oblivion at bay. Peaceful rest would not come; only nightmares waited. In sleep, she would, no doubt, recall each pierce of his blade, each revolting movement on her body, each slash of his belt. She bit hard on her tongue.

Stay awake. Stay alert.

Slowly lifting her teacup to her lips, her hand shook, sloshing liquid against her bandaged hand. The sides of her mouth stung when she opened her lips even the slightest bit, but she needed the calming warmth of Earl Grey.

Her greatest wish was to be alone, but yet, she hated the loneliness. Hated monsters waiting and watching from dark shadows. And Owen wouldn't leave her. He'd remained by her side through his mother and sister's fussing.

How did he truly feel about this mashed-up world she'd opened? What did he see in a pitiful girl, beaten and bruised? Ember refused to look in a mirror, viewing the results of her living nightmare would most likely push her past some breaking point—not that she wasn't already broken. Or was she? How would she pick up the scattered pieces this time? Find sanity once more? Break past this stifling anxiety, this inability to actually breathe?

Owen stepped into the bedroom, two men in tow. He had to be exhausted, she certainly was, and yet, he had taken command. Brought her here to his castle to keep her safe. So, why didn't she feel safe? Why did she feel more exposed, more raw than ever? The anger had begun to build. Deep inside, ice crystals burgeoned across her heart. Revenge was too small a word for what she wished upon the head of the man who had joyfully served her punishment.

"Ember, let me introduce you to Doug. He's our trainer. This is his friend, Steven. He's going to fix your hair. Okay, baby?"

"I'm not a baby," she answered in a petulant tone, but someone had to be on the receiving end of her irritation. She sighed and started to apologize for her smarmy attitude, but caught sight of Steven's scissors. Her heartbeat kicked up and a flash of another knife scored across her mind.

No. No.

Black dots swam across her vision...falling...falling...

Opening her eyes, she heard Owen yelling, but his words seemed muffled.

Silver slashing, blood, pain, the whoosh of the belt, all real, all on a pinpoint.

Breathe.

Hunched in a ball, she rested her forehead against the floor.

He's not here to hurt me. Calm. Breathe.

Maybe Steven could cut her hair while she slept, so she wouldn't see the blade. "Owen." He didn't respond since he was busy hollering at someone. "Owen!"

He jerked his head in her direction. "Ember. What happened? Maybe we should take you back to the hospital." He knelt beside her and lightly patted her shoulder.

"No. Would you just hold my hand for a moment?" The pinpoint started to fade. Savage memories escaped back into the ether of her mind.

"Sure, but—"

"No. Just…could you stop? Please. I'm sorry. But…can you just stop for a minute?"

"Sure." He brushed a hand across her cheek.

After taking a deep breath, she explained her trepidation. "Will you hold my hand while he cuts my hair? It's the scissors. I can't…" She buried her face against his leg. The brush of denim stung her bruised skin, but the warmth beneath was what she sought and found.

"Of course, anything you want."

"Okay. He can come back now."

Owen helped her stand and shouted directions to all those present in the room.

She kept her gaze on the floor, embarrassed and ashamed, she was sure she looked like a sideshow freak. Sitting on her knees, she faced the back of the couch.

Scissor-wielding Steven came to stand before her. His golden highlights seemed to shimmer in the light, as if he were an angel come to save her from evil hair demons.

Too late, buddy.

"I'm Steven, honey. We'll get you fixed up, all right?" He flashed a sympathetic smile. "If you need me to stop at any time, just say the word."

"I'm sorry. Do what you'd like. Just please, do something quick."

He nodded, and then combed a hand through her hair. "So pretty and thick. We'll get you evened out in no time." He winked, which allowed a single tear to fall down his cheek.

She refused to cry again. "Doug, I'm sure you have lots of stories about Owen. Tell me what he's like at work." The mask she'd developed throughout her childhood served her well today. Don't let them see your pain or any weakness.

Her brother would understand, but her brother had succumbed to the darkness. Would she? Without having any time to process what had happened, she didn't have any idea how far gone she was. Just one moment at a time, one second, fight through. Perhaps she should call Xander and have him prescribe something that would blur her reality.

But not yet.

Doug sat beside Owen on the couch.

She smiled in all the appropriate places during his tales of Owen's antics. Rigid mask firmly in place.

Owen's mother and sister hovered nearby, laughing at Doug's stories, adding in bits and pieces.

The man himself barely said a word, only squeezed her hand and, with a smooth caress of his thumb, gave her strength. How much could he see? Was he really that aware of her inner turmoil?

Steven finished with her hair. Each pull and tug made her scream inwardly, but she refused to upset everyone with her irrational terror.

He didn't hurt me. Owen is here. I'm okay. I'm okay.

Everyone cooed and expressed their belief that her new hairstyle was fabulous and perfect for her features.

She knew better.

Even with Owen's hand in hers, she felt her will crumble.

"You tired, Stems?" Owen gazed into her eyes.

So much was written in his brown depths. Someday soon, she hoped he'd spell out every word. She shrugged. Talking hurt, her hand throbbed, and her nose itched under the Band-Aid. She'd love to rip off the stupid thing.

He nodded, then not so subtly ordered everyone to leave the room.

Alone with him once more, a thought occurred. "Your game?"

"Tomorrow." He ran a hand over his bristled chin, but avoided her gaze.

"No. Please go." Ember didn't want his life to stop, and she could use a little space.

"I can't leave you." He kissed her hand, still linked with his.

Her icy heart melted just a little. No barrier could stand against those puppy dog eyes. "No, don't miss for me." She winced against the sharp sting talking caused the sides of her mouth.

He growled in response, then rose off the couch and peered out the window.

Strong, wide shoulders narrowed into a V, well-fitted jeans emphasized his finely toned ass, white socks on his super-sized feet. He hypnotized her with his domineering presence. His stability. He would keep her safe. He was the one man in her world she could rely on.

Let go.

He's here.

"Owen."

He turned and met her gaze.

"Thank you."

# # #

Wearing a new pair of freshly laundered undies, Ember slid on loose workout pants Owen had pilfered from Maude's closet. Afraid to be alone, she'd asked him to stay in the bathroom while she showered.

After her haircut last night, she'd fallen asleep on the couch. During the night, Owen must have carried her to his bed. She woke frightened and unsure of her surroundings at first, but had felt a warm, reassuring presence at her back.

She studied Owen as he sat on the bathroom's bench with a thundercloud practically circling his head. They'd quarreled over him leaving today, until she'd cried due to her inability to properly speak her case. He'd finally agreed, more out of guilt for making her cry than anything else, she assumed. Together, they'd wiped her tears, and then fiddled with the shower panel until the flow was just short of a mist.

No sense of embarrassment occurred due to her nudity, but a quick glimpse in the bathroom mirrors did reveal her battered face and body. She'd kept that nightmare vision at bay by enjoying Owen's soap-sluiced form. During her shower, he'd been all business, getting her clean, and then instructing her to stand by the shower bench while he finished. She'd made sure he didn't get a view of her backside. He seemed angry enough.

Being clean seemed crucial to her healing somehow. She'd asked him to scrub every inch of her body, twice.

With a scowl on his face, Owen rose from his perch and helped tug on her pant leg. "I'd rather not go."

"Please." She cupped the side of his face in her hand. "You need to vent." Then she flicked his nose with a finger.

He didn't laugh, but instead gripped her hand and met her gaze. "When you're ready, you should talk to someone about what happened. I'd prefer you talked to me, but if you need Xander instead...I'll set up the appointment. Don't let this fester."

Ember nodded, and then unwrapped the plastic baggy from her bandaged hand. Concentrating on something else besides words, appointments, and talking about her feelings seemed crucial.

"Let me do that." He removed the rubber band holding the bag in place.

So kind. So helpful, seeing to her every need. She dropped her forehead against his chest and wrapped him in an embrace. Trying to say without words how grateful she was for his presence. "I'm hideous."

He simply swayed her back and forth. "What I see when I look at you isn't hideous. I can't say what I think, because I don't want to upset you. But understand this—you're always beautiful. Every part of you. You're still standing, still staying strong. Nothing could be more appealing than that."

With her bandaged hand, she pressed against his chest, easing away as her other hand slid up and rested behind his neck. "You're my only link to sanity." The truth of those words frightened, but standing bruised and torn before him, there was no place to hide her feelings. Death had come too close. "I will talk to you...when I'm ready."

Relying on another didn't come easy in her world, but with him, trusting seemed simple. She breathed in his familiar scent, and her heartbeat flickered past the cold fury and burned with desire. Could she be intimate again? Would she fear his touch? Somehow, she believed accepting him on a physical level would do nothing but create happier memories. Blissful memories.

Not today, but soon. She patted his chest. "You should go."

"Mmmm, I want to stay right here. I like holding you."

"Anytime."

"You're cute for someone on the injured list." He dropped a kiss on her forehead. "You're right. I need to cause some serious damage, might as well do it on the field." Easing back, he studied her for a moment, opened his mouth to say something, then closed it and looked away. He shook his head, and met her gaze once more. "I...I just feel...no, not today. Let's go find Mom and Maude. I've got lots of instructions while I'm away."

What had he meant to say? Her heart pounded in her chest.

He just felt what? Who left off a sentence like that? But she was too tired to over-analyze right now. The shower, combined with her meds, made keeping her eyes open a chore. He planned to play his game, and then take a return flight back. Nancy and Maude would keep her company until his return.

They'd talk when she was better. And she would get better. For him.

And those sluicing soap suds.

# # #

"Your mind right, Big-O?" Jason sank down next to Owen on the locker room bench and gave him a one-armed hug.

Owen grunted in response. After rushing to the stadium from the airport, he had no time for chitchat. Mental preparation for this game with all the outside worries beating against his mind, hadn't left him in the cheeriest of moods.

"What do you need?" Jason nudged his knee.

Owen turned down the volume on his iPod. "Make sure I don't kill anybody."

"Sore still?"

"Yeah, I'm sore still, way past sore into beyond pissed. The fucker stabbed her, beat her, and cut her hair. Better hope I never get my hands on him." He clenched his fingers around his helmet.

"Is she doing all right?"

"Would you be all right if someone broke into your home and beat the shit out of you?" His nasty attitude washed right over Jason. Good thing, because apologizing for being a massive dick wasn't in his game plan today.

"Hey, big man." Bronco punched his shoulder. "Where you at?"

"I'm here."

"Use it on the field."

"Not today." Owen shook his head, and then bent over and tied his shoes. "There's too much. I'll play the game. Don't worry."

"Hey, what's with the fucking boy-band over here?" Chewy came by and smacked Jason's head. "You bitches gonna break out in song?" He pointed his ever-present football at Owen. "They find the fucker?"

Owen shook his head. "Not yet."

"Don't kill anybody." Chewy nodded, and slapped Jason again before being sidelined by some blonde reporter in a red suit.

Bronco and Jason had hung around and caught him up on playbook changes. Now they were waiting under the stadium for the offensive line to be announced onto the field.

Bronco fiddled with the strap on his helmet, and then met his gaze. "She tell you what happened?"

"Not yet."

"He, you know, do anything?"

"No…he did enough, though." Owen banged his fist against the cement wall. "I've got a private investigator doing some digging. You should have seen her. She just—"

Bronco hauled off and slapped him across the face. "Bring the pain. Your pain. Her pain. Own it."

Owen shook off the sting. Two words. Simple.

And yet, what did he own? What actually mattered?

Real life had finally arrived on Easy Street, and he needed to grab the wheel before everything spun out of control.

He adjusted his ear buds and cranked Metallica. More than ready for this game, this challenge, to start. As he ran out on the field, he concentrated on the thumping heavy metal.

Bring the pain.

He would own this field today.

CHAPTER 27

Both legs stretched and resting on Owen's thighs, Ember breathed in the cool late-September air. An earlier rain mixed the scents of wet fall leaves and mums, planted by Owen's mother, creating that earthy aroma you could only enjoy in the fall. Shifting in her lawn chair, Ember could barely believe she'd been living with Owen for almost a week. Due to her trauma, she'd been given the entire week off work. Owen had stayed each day, never leaving her side. Each night, with every bedroom light blaring, he lay at her side, holding her close.

Tonight, she helped him wrench around on his cars. Trying to forget. Healing physically, but mentally would take much longer. Talking helped. They'd spent the past few days talking about everything, but what was really on both their minds. Who had attacked her, and why? She'd even considered the possibility her attack was related to Elliot's death. Had Owen heard anything more from the investigator?

Clayton had come by for a visit on Monday, but had no further news.

Did she really want to think about this now? "You know, I was wondering. What do you guys talk about on the sidelines?"

Owen ran his hand along her leg then squeezed her knee. "What do you talk about at work?"

"Work stuff."

"Yeah, well, so do we." After tipping the neck of his beer bottle in her direction, he took a swig.

"Like what? Specifically."

"We talk about the other team." Owen shrugged. "We adjust plays. Coach yells if we're doing good, yells if we're doing bad."

"So, you throw the quarterback the ball?"

"Snap. The center snaps the ball, protects the quarterback, and blocks for the running back. I yell out code words so that my guys can adjust to the defensive line. I'm aware of all sides. Eyes everywhere." He waggled his brows and bugged out his eyes, circling them rapidly like crazed bingo balls in a hopper. "The defense tries to shoot the gaps, so we have to block. My calls determine who each player blocks."

"Owen, why haven't you kissed me?"

Oh boy, brain-to-mouth filter malfunction.

He halted with his beer bottle halfway to his lips. "I thought we were talking about my job."

"We were, but now I want to talk about something else."

"Do you?"

"What's that supposed to mean?" She dropped one foot off his leg and kicked at loose gravel.

Owen scrubbed a hand over his face and released a heavy sigh. "Look, I don't want to upset you, so I've been hands off. You're all bruised."

"I'll always be a little scared."

"Stems—"

"No, I want to talk about this a little. Being scared might be a good thing." She ran a finger over the stitches in her hand. "This awareness will teach me to be more prepared, and I'll be able to protect myself. I want to take some self-defense classes, because I don't like feeling vulnerable, out of control. I may even buy one of those big Desert Hawks."

"Desert Eagles, babe. And if you can't get the name right, perhaps you should rethink that purchase. Besides, do you know how heavy those are?" He ran a finger along the inside edge of her sock.

"I could do it," she mumbled and counted the stitches in the center of her hand. Twenty-four total. Twenty-four she wouldn't need if she'd had a Desert Eagle.

"What's going through that red head now?"

She stood and took a swig from his beer bottle before

meandering over to the tailgate of his Ranchero. "I want another ride."

With a laugh, he hit the key fob on the air ride suspension kit, which gave the car adjustable ride height. The compressor hummed as the air bags filled and slowly lifted the back end. He stood in front of her and stopped the lift once they were eye level. Quiet for a moment, he brushed a finger across the seam of her lips. "You want to be kissed?"

"By you, yes." Smiling, she grabbed his belt loops and pulled him between her legs.

Tilting her head at the perfect angle, he bent and kissed her softly, without heat, without passion, directing, going through the motions with each skilled sweep of his tongue.

Not enough. She needed the storm to fully pass. "Don't hold back. Not tonight."

"Ember, I—"

"No. I want your hands coursing all over my body. Performing magic like you do with your cars. Down and dirty, smeared in grease, I don't care. Please." With a firm grip on the back of his neck, she drew him closer and kissed him with a violence that erupted from every raw emotion she'd buried this past week. The need to be swept away by pleasure, to dive off that cliff to bliss thrummed through her. Escape through mutual release would help seal away lingering fears of losing their connection. She may not be able to speak of her trauma, but she could allow her body to speak, couldn't she? She tamped down the very real possibility this physical outlet just glossed over her real need—the need to tell all, to trust him—but desire was simple and had one goal. Desire didn't judge or pity. Desire brought only that burst of pleasure.

Owen responded to her raw need and deepened the kiss. One hand guided her hips closer to the tailgate's edge, rocking his hips in time with each plunge of his tongue.

Panting for breath, Ember kissed the side of his neck and nipped his ear. "I like it fast."

He hissed out a breath and once more took the wheel, kissing her until she arched against him. His hand worked over her body, brushing under her shirt and up to sweep across the top of her breasts, and then teasing her peaked nipples with light tugs.

An electric sizzle shot from her breasts to her center, gathering, needing. Overwhelmed by the pure hot lust that blanked out all reason, she whimpered.

One hand worked down his zipper, almost impossible due to his heavily swollen cock. She slid her hand beneath the waistband of his boxer briefs and glanced down at the bounty she'd exposed. His thick head strained out from the top. She brushed her thumb over the tip, and reveled in his deep moan.

Retaliation came in the form of a love-bite where her neck met her shoulder. A husky whisper reached her through the haze of lust.

"I've missed you. Missed this soft, fair skin. The dazed look of hunger in your brown eyes." His fingers tickled across her stomach, before moving to caress the swells rising above her bra cups.

"Touch me." Frantic, she joined her mouth to his. Needy. Demanding. Ready to give him everything, which she tried to make very clear by wrapping his turgid flesh in her hand.

Goal achieved as his breathing accelerated and his hips rocked in time with her hand's motion. She wanted that motion rising above her. Wanted him moving in just that way between her legs. Now. Right now.

He wrapped his large hand around her wrist. His lips brushing against hers as he spoke. "You want this?"

Ember nodded and swirled a wet bead from the tip of his erection in a circle around his heavy head.

Owen grunted out, "Hold me tighter."

Power surged through her. She was in control. She made him feel. "More. I want more."

He whipped off his shirt, bent to take her mouth, but stopped and growled against her lips. "So do I. Do you understand what that means? After this, there's no turning back. I'll take more and then more again." He took his more by feasting on her neck, her lips, until his breath meshed with hers.

Overcome, she eased from their kiss, gripped his shoulders, and met his gaze. "You work on these cars, and only certain people can see the artistry behind what you've done. But I see. I see beneath your surface to the man you are inside. I want to purr like one of your engines. I want to be the gas pedal under your foot. Push me. Don't ever hit the brakes."

He said nothing, only studied her face, his deep-brown eyes searching hers.

But for what?

"I can make you purr, I promise. But inside, not here." He grinned and gently kissed her still-healing nose.

Away from the heat of his skin, a chill breeze brought about the realization they'd attacked each other in an open garage where anyone could have interrupted. "Take me inside."

With her hand joined in his, she headed to the bedroom where they'd chastely slept side-by-side for days. Not so tonight.

Ember Brooks and Owen Killion, who'd have thought? Certainly she'd never envisioned herself in such a position. *Or positions.* She burst out laughing.

"What? What's funny?" He squeezed her hand.

"Nothing. I'm just really, really ready for this."

"Really, really, huh? Well, we'll see what we can do."

She nodded and followed him into the bathroom. Trusting him with her body was the first lap on this very long race toward love.

Love. She sighed and wondered how that word had come to mind.

Love, if only.

# # #

"You're so huge."

Well, if that wasn't what every man was hoping to hear, he didn't know what was. Owen turned from checking the water temp pouring out of the tub faucet, raised his brow, and smirked. "Why, thank you."

Ember laughed and splashed him with a handful of water. "No, I meant your whole body, as far as your, um...you know...I guess ...I really wouldn't know."

"Really again?"

"Yes, really." She kicked his arm with her wet foot. Her toenails were painted a vibrant shade of red. Maude's doing, after making Ember sit the other night for a "pampering."

He ran a thumb along her big toe's nail bed. "Water warm enough?"

"Why yes, it really is." She laughed again. Her nose had a long scab down the side, and her face and body were covered in yellow, purple, and brown bruises. "You've got to come in now. You're all wet."

"That's the plan." He studied her pale body floating in his oversized tub. Full breasts lay in luscious mounds against her chest, topped by light pink nipples that begged to turn red. The tips of her short auburn hair, now wet, were darker and clumped together. Her slender stomach led down to a tuft of curly red-brown hair. Her long legs were the perfect pillow for his thighs. "Your bruises are quite colorful."

She swished her hand along the top of the water. "Aren't you joining me?"

So, they still weren't discussing her attack. He'd waited, but she hadn't said a word. Not demanding her trust and forcing her to talk was against his nature. Why wouldn't she confide in him? Had she already spoken to Xander? Keeping her suffering inside couldn't be mentally healthy, no matter what she'd survived in her past. His mother had lectured him about 'all in good time,' but that didn't ease his worry that they weren't as close as they could be. Weren't they missing out on an important step because she wouldn't share her troubles? Patience was not a virtue in his book.

"Owen? What's wrong?"

"Nothing. Scoot up."

"Up? Why? What are you doing?" She straightened from her slouch against the back of the tub.

"I'm coming in." He placed one foot on the first step along the side of the tub and nudged her forward with his hand.

Eyes wide, she shot out of the water and stood dripping in the middle of the tub. "Wait, where are...no...no...I don't want you...get out." Arms wrapped around her middle, she visibly shivered and shrank away.

She acted as if he was contaminated. "Hey, it's all right." He raised both hands, palms up, and stepped back onto the floor. "What's wrong? What did I do?"

She opened her mouth to speak, but only panted out quick, short breaths.

"Do you want me to leave?"

Her gaze flicked to his. "No. I-I-I..." After shaking her head, she continued, "I…uh… just don't want you behind me. I'm sorry."

Oh hell. In order not to frighten her even more, he kept his breathing steady and avoided pounding his fist onto every available surface. Not having someone behind her made sense. What the hell had happened that night?

"Why? I'd like to talk about this before we…why can you be intimate with your body, but not with your heart? Tell me what happened."

A single tear slipped down her cheek, before she turned and sank back into the tub. "I'll tell you if you get in, too. Just not behind me."

"Scoot to the other side then." The hot water only added fuel to the raging steam burning through his thoughts. Fury, anger, disgust, and who knew what else were swimming around in the water with him. All he knew was this wall between them had to come down.

"You're so comfortable in your own skin, Owen. You're always walking around naked. Probably 'cause of the locker rooms and stuff, huh?" She climbed up his body before resting her head on his shoulder, and running her fingertips over his chest and arm. "How come you don't have any tattoos?"

He grabbed her wandering hand and kissed the inside of her palm. Ms. Brooks always tried to change the subject, and he'd let her for a bit.

"Don't some players shave their chests?" She plucked at the hairs on his chest.

"Ow. Stop." With a finger, he lifted her chin so he could gaze into her brown depths. Without a word, he made clear distraction time was over.

"Fine," she huffed and tried to turn away.

But, he wouldn't let her. Couldn't. He had to look in her eyes as she gave her truth.

"I'd much rather be deflowered right here, right now, than go through this…discussion." So saying, she ran a hand down his stomach and wrapped her fingers around his rock-solid erection. "Sure you don't want to use this first?" With a very thorough grip on his cock, she shifted, kissed his mouth, and pressed her full breasts against his chest. Her body kept in rocking rhythm with each stroke of her hand.

A violent need sprinted through every vein in his body. Capture. Plunder. Mark.

The heat from their kiss joined the steam rising off the water, fogging his mind to all else. She seemed so desperate for more, out of control. Her whimpers and gasps heated him just as much as the teasing stroke of her tongue.

With both hands locked in his hair, she slammed his head against the back of the tub.

He glided his fingers through the water droplets on her back and cupped her ass in his hands.

She flinched and hissed out a breath.

"Damn it, Stems."

"I'm sorry."

He brushed her hair away from her face. "Stop being sorry."

Her eyes went wide, and she bit her glistening bottom lip.

Fuck, her mouth was hot, all plump and that rare shade of pink. And wet. So wet.

Wait. No.

"Tell me."

She ground out a sigh and leaned against the other side of the tub. She studied her hand for a moment, and then shook her head. "Fine." Exasperation exuded from that single word.

"Why won't you talk to me? I just need to know."

"I don't want you to." Her voice shook, and she pounded a fist against the side of the tub.

"It's killing me that I don't—"

"Killing you." She scoffed and flicked her hand through the water. "It's killing *you*."

"We're supposed to be a team, remember? Standing on the line. Eye to eye."

"Everything will change if I tell you."

This was not what he expected. "Why? What will change?"

"I'm ashamed. Don't you see that? Some man came into my bedroom and violated me, beat me, and I couldn't stop him. He touched me." Shuddering, she closed her eyes.

He watched the steady rise and fall of her chest.

She pressed her fingers against her eyelids, her palms covering her mouth so that her next words were muffled. "I feel ashamed sometimes. And if you know, then I'll repulse you."

Wait? Touched her?

Clayton had never mentioned anything about this. What the hell did "touched her" mean? "Explain, please."

She pulled the plug on the tub. The only sound in the room was water gurgling down the drain. "I'd like a towel, please."

He sighed, annoyed by her stall tactics. They weren't leaving this tub until she finished. Since he'd gathered a couple towels and left them on the floor, he just leaned over and grabbed one off the pile.

Tub now empty, he handed over the towel.

She bent her knees and wrapped the towel around her body before resting her head on the side of the tub and closing her eyes. "He came into my room. The apartment was dark, so dark, so I couldn't make him out. He overpowered me. It's as simple as that. No." Her hard word matched the slam of her fist against her knee. "No. I swore to myself I would never cry for him again. Are you happy now?"

Every muscle in his body tensed. He longed to comfort her, but knew sympathy was the last thing she'd want. "No, I'm not happy. Look at me when you're talking to me."

Ember mumbled something under her breath, and then resumed her resting place against the tub, but kept her gaze on his. "You just have to see it all, don't you? And why shouldn't you? Everyone else has picked through my brain for years."

"That isn't the case here, but however you choose to see it, I'll have it all. Now." Comparisons to Xander weren't cooling his temper any.

She picked at a stray string on her towel, and shot him a feral smile. "Well, here we go then, Counselor Killion. He sliced my nose then when I struggled, he punched me repeatedly and stabbed my hand. I remember how surreal that moment was, a knife sticking out of my hand, but...I thought about you instead, trying to quell the pain. He bound me then sang this song, or hummed it anyway." She met his gaze head on. "That's when I knew I was dead. Life over." She paused for a moment, staring off into another place. Lost in her nightmare. "He flipped me over. And I actually hoped that he did kill me after, because...but he just beat me with a belt or something. He laughed the whole time.

It wasn't funny though." Her fingers ran along the edge of the tub, rhythmically moving back and forth. "He knew my name, said he was punishing me."

"But he didn't rape you?" His breath locked in his throat as he waited for her answer.

"No, you know that."

"Okay." He hadn't really known. Was dreading the answer all along even though neither Clayton nor she had mentioned rape. Would it have mattered? Yes, at first, but, in the end, no. Now he knew, but there was so much more, more terror, more agony, so much she couldn't say or explain. So much he would never understand about that night. But none of that mattered, because he loved her. He wouldn't say the words now because the time wasn't right. Maybe would even be seen as expressed in pity. But soon, he would tell her soon.

She rose and wrapped the towel more securely around her body. "I just want to go to bed."

After he watched her leave, he remained in the tub for a moment. Chilled not only on the outside, but also down deep by the horror she'd endured. Naked in an empty tub, he took the time necessary to digest her words. The attacker had known her name. He'd been punishing her. For what? Who was he? Why such a personal vendetta against Ember? And the most important question—was he finished? Or would he try again?

While this night had not ended as he'd wished, he had only himself to blame. He'd pushed. So now he knew, and that fact essentially changed nothing. Absolutely nothing. He still loved her more than his next breath. Craved her with every red-hot blood cell in his body. He hadn't considered he could love her more, but apparently, that was not the case.

Every week, he put his mind and body on the line and got beat back, shoved, slammed, bent. But that redhead was the only one who could truly tackle him. Some hits were worth the fall.

"Sorry, buddy, not tonight." Owen patted dry his aching balls and threw the damp towel in the hamper.

Entering the bedroom, he noticed something seemed off.

All the lights were out.

This was new. Since her attack, Ember slept with every light on in the room.

"Ember?"

"I'm here."

He heard a faint rustle of sheets. "Don't you want the lights on?"

"Not tonight."

Not wanting to further disturb her by asking why, he shrugged and slid beneath the sheets. Lying on his side, he made out her form in the darkness.

She was resting on her side, facing him. "I changed my mind." Her light touch brushed over his shoulder and down his chest.

He closed his eyes and groaned as lust stirred his body once more. "About what?"

In answer, she leaned closer and kissed him. All in. Starting where they'd left off.

Easing back, he placed a single finger against her damp lips. "No, you said no." He had no idea what she was doing, what she wanted. He only knew she was driving him crazy.

"I don't want the night to end like this. I related my sordid tale as you requested. But now, I want to forget. Put your hands on my body. Make me feel clean again. Make me yours. Only yours."

"I won't say no to you. I can't." He took her lips in a deep kiss. Deeper, harder, he rose above her, lining their bodies together. They fit. Perfectly.

Owen bent down and kissed her neck, and then plumped her breasts in his hands. Working the hard nubs with his thumb and finger before taking each in his mouth, sucking each tip and then teasing with his tongue.

She moaned and rocked against him, her hands roaming his body. Arching, she clenched his ass in a tight grip and spread her knees.

With her sensuous movements, he almost spilled his seed. Once more, he captured her mouth, drowning out the sounds of her moans. Reaching down, he touched her dewy folds, and then circled her wet core. Words of love longed to escape his mouth, but he was beyond coherent thought. As he sunk a single finger deep and felt her body heat and move beneath him with each silken thrust, he prayed for patience. He brushed his thumb over her hidden nub.

Ember shot up onto her elbows. "What?" The word gasped out as her lower body swayed against his hand. "What are you doing? Stop teasing."

"I promised to make you purr, and I keep my promises." Maintaining the caress on her lower body, he brushed his mouth over the underside of her breasts, before licking and rasping her nipple against the roof of his mouth.

"Owen, it's too much. I can't... can't. I'm hot, my whole body's hot under...under my...oh yes, right there...my skin."

He removed his finger and rubbed his wet finger over her nipple, before very thoroughly licking it off.

"Oh, that's hot. Touch me again."

"Want me to check your engine, baby? Get under the hood. Bury my tool so deep." He matched action to words as he sank two fingers inside and worked them over her slick folds.

She moaned, and her breathing turned erratic.

He spoke against her lips. "I need to find just the right angle sometimes. But I'll work and work until I find the right socket. Then I grind back and forth." He brushed his palm against her nub with each thrust of his fingers. "Until everything breaks loose."

A deep hum rose from her throat before she shuddered and released a satisfied cry. She grabbed his shoulder and bit down hard.

"Did I make you rumble, Stems?" He ran his nose along her cheek and met her hooded gaze.

In response, she grabbed his neck and pulled him down for a kiss that brought back the purpose of this moment. Her body still quivered, yet she clarified her continued need with each heady kiss.

"Give me a second. I need to protect you." He fought for control as he fumbled through the side table for a condom and slipped it on. Safe now, he released the reins on his primal nature, knowing he had to claim her. He longed to feel her break again, only this time while he was buried deep inside. Shifting higher on her body, he rocked his cock against her wet seam.

She moaned his name and rose to meet his thrust.

"Open your eyes."

His own eyes, now adjusted to the dark, could see hers, which glimmered in the light—languid and dazed from her release.

Her hands explored his chest, his sides, until she caressed his long shaft and settled him at her opening.

He braced his elbows on the pillow and blocked her head between his hands. "This means you're mine."

"Yes," she whispered the word and lifted enough to receive just the tip of his erection into her body.

He shivered against the need to thrust. To claim. "Say it."

"I'm yours, Owen. Only yours, as you are mine."

"It's going to pinch a little." He thrust deep and felt her barrier give. A groan escaped from some primal place in his body. Rising from that primitive experience of claiming a mate, being the first, the only.

He peered at her face and noted she was biting her lower lip. "I'm sorry, Stems." He pulled her lip free with his teeth and kissed her long and thoroughly while his cock twitched with impatience. Testing the waters, he eased back and thrust once more.

She gasped and her eyes opened wide.

Grinding back the need to claim, he stilled, then brushed her hair from her face. "Relax. I don't know how much longer I can maintain control. Your body. You're so...fuck it...I can't." He rested his forehead against hers. Done, so done. There were no words.

But this was her first time, and she'd been traumatized only days earlier. That should have cooled his ardor, but instead lit the flame. *His* marks would be on her body—inside and out. No more memories of another. His love for her deepened as he reveled in the knowledge he alone had claimed a treasure. Not only the treasure of her body, but of Ember, everything she was, so much more than one man could ever deserve. But he'd take her, take everything she gave and return so much more.

She drew his lips back to hers and kissed him. Her nails dug deep into his backside. "Move, Owen. Please."

Love. This was love, something he'd never quite experienced in the moment. Grateful, he kissed her harder, and then gazed at the vision beneath him. Her short red hair was a dark shadow against his pillow. Her lips open and bruised red from his mouth.

Her chest flushed and heaving. Gaining her trust, her openness in mind and body, made this moment worth the wait.

He adjusted his angle, then dove deep.

She arched with him and her entire body shivered.

Together, they rocked, moved, and sealed tight their bond with sweat, with blood. Tonight, they coalesced into something more, something they would only find together, time and again.

His breathing became labored and his balls tightened. Not much longer. He needed to claim, to release his heated seed and leave his mark in her body, under her skin. Teeth clenched, eyes closed, he could no longer watch her face.

Her hands coursed over his skin, then clenched against his shoulders. She panted and shook beneath him. "Owen, oh, please...right there... I think... something...something..."

He rose to his knees and lowered his hand to massage her swollen bud in time with his thrusts.

She broke—screaming, moaning, no shame in her joy, holding nothing back.

He could feel her release, the tight squeezes against his cock. Beyond all boundaries, on another plane of pleasure, he thrust again and again. Sweat poured from his brow, control gone.

Tiny spasms from her orgasm clenched against him, and he joined her in bliss. Coming, shouting her name, pumping with abandon, lost in the pure pleasure of his spilling seed, he'd never felt so free. Unrestrained. A feral growl released from deep in his throat, and he fought to catch his breath, fought to still his grinding hips.

Damn, they'd been loud, but fuck it. If each time were like this, they'd never leave the bed.

Relaxation and satiation combined, seeping through every pore. Boneless, he rested his head against her damp chest. He licked the sweat from her skin, causing his limp, yet ever-ready cock to twitch inside her body. Damn, if he didn't want her again. But he couldn't, not tonight. She'd gifted him with enough. He didn't wish to cause her any more pain.

He circled his nose through the damp sheen on her chest, before kissing his way up the side of her neck to her mouth. Hours passed, days, as he showed her without words how wonderful the moment had been. Expressed his gratitude with each caress of his tongue, each soft brush of his lips. This kiss forged that final seal, and revealed his gentle side. He fought back words of love, wishing he could add them to this moment, but instead kept them contained.

She returned his kiss and squirmed against him.

Clearly, the mood had turned, when he'd only meant to calm and soothe.

He pulled back, kissing her with light, quick pecks once, twice, then another, deeper joining, before finally drawing back.

Running her fingers through his hair, she followed his retreat.

He chuckled. "Since there are no words to describe how I feel right now, to explain what we just shared, I'll simply say, thank you."

She glanced away, and then fiddled her fingers against his chest. After sighing heavily, she met his gaze once more. "Owen."

"Ember." He laughed once more when she smacked his arm.

"Will you listen, please?"

"I'll do what I can, but you wore me out, woman." He slapped her hip then sat up and turned on the fan, but instead hit the light button on the remote.

She blinked against the glare before burying her face against his side.

He pinched her arm. "What were you going to say?"

In retaliation, she bit his arm.

Tough little thing.

She wrapped her arm and leg around him, her body brushing against his.

Her soft parts pressing, squishing, and causing his parts to go hard. Damn, she was beautiful. He ran a hand down her arm and wrapped her fingers with his, and then kissed her forehead. "Speak."

This time, she bit his chest. "You're such a boss. I had something very serious to say, but you've ruined my mood."

He rose above her, twisted her onto her back, and lifted her arms above her head. "Spill it, Brooks"

She laughed for a moment, and shook her head. "Let go of my hands and I will. I don't like being restricted."

"Sorry." He bent and kissed both her wrists before sitting

back on his heels.

Seemingly lost in her own thoughts for a moment, she brushed her fingers against his stomach. "I was so very broken, once. But...I worked very hard to heal. Tonight, you broke me again. I'm open and vulnerable in so many ways. Frightened. So much destruction in my life, and yet, I feel...you...you could actually be the one who finally destroys me."

He swallowed hard before speaking. "Give me your hand."

She raised a brow, but held up her hand.

He gripped her fingers in his and kissed her wrist, then held their linked fingers against his heart. "Will our relationship be perfect? No. Will I hurt you? Yes. Will you hurt me? Yes. But, Ember, we will always come together, here." He held their hands against his pounding heart. "We will last. Eye-to-eye on the line. I could never destroy you. Your life will be different now, better. I'll give you everything I have, all I own—my heart, my body, my world. Everything is yours."

"Everything?" She ran a finger down his swollen cock, and then pressed the tip against her wet heat.

He rumbled out a laugh. "Everything. I'll make sure your newly awakened sexual needs are satisfied." A gentle nudge, a slight rock against her followed his words.

"They're pretty intense." She ran her fingers through the hair on his chest and clutched his shoulders, nudging him closer.

"How intense?" he whispered against her ear, before kissing her neck.

"I want everything again. Right now." She arched against him, rubbing her breasts against his chest, wiggling her hips so they fit.

And oh, how they fit. He shivered and focused on other things. *Lima Beans, I hate lima beans. They're green and slimy. Bitter.*

Ignore her welcoming body, her lush curves.

He was losing the fight. "Ember, you'll be sore." He dropped his forehead against her breastbone. "You're already a bruised mess."

"I want to try."

He growled, and released a deep breath.

"I guess you don't want to give me everything after all." Beneath him, her hand strayed to cover her left breast, and she brushed a finger against her nipple while licking her lips.

Well now, lima beans be damned. She thought to throw down the gauntlet, did she? His fiery redhead played to win. "Think you'll stroke my competitive nature, do you?"

"I'd like to stroke something. Or everything."

Was that siren's twinkle in her eye? "What have I awakened?"

"Find out."

And so he did—everything.

CHAPTER 28

6:44pm

Time ticked on. Alone. All alone, Xander sat at his desk, waiting, seething. Weeks had passed, was it weeks? When had he seen Ember last? Why did she still refuse to come? Hadn't he given her the best years? He needed to finish. His book wasn't complete. Ember had no remorse or care for what he went through every day. She was his family. His circle. No beginning, no end.

6:50pm

He sliced his letter opener across his desk calendar, ripping through the dark ink of seven p.m. Her appointment time. Their time. Was that a car door? He rolled to the window in his chair and glanced through the blinds. Nothing. Darkness. Only rain and leaves silently drifting and falling without pity or care where or how they landed, just exulting in the constant drip, drip, drip to the ground. She'd found another family. Left him behind for another. That man who was nothing but a beast, using his body, his money, to overpower her.

6:55pm

During the game, newscasters had spoken of her life and her injuries as if she were some salacious story. No one knew her, not like him. How dare they speak of her in such a familiar manner? They knew not what she'd been through. And why hadn't she called? Didn't she need his comfort? His counsel? If such an act couldn't bring her back, then what would?

His.

His.

7:00pm

Time now. Her time. Tick. Tick. The second hand moved without volition. Unrelenting, the passage of time. Waiting. Waiting for no one. Caring not who remained behind.

7:05pm

Xander poured a cup of tea and set the steaming brew by the side of the couch. Ember liked this special blend. He'd prepared the cup exactly as specified, brewing the water to two hundred degrees, and then letting the leaves steep for five minutes. But the flavor would be ruined. Become bitter and cold the longer it sat. He sank down on the end of the couch and ran his fingers over his temple. He needed to finish the chapter on her father, and begin the new one on handling grief. These headaches came and blocked out everything else. White lights would flash before his vision, but Ember could heal him. Her gentle touch across his brow would take away all the pain.

7:17pm

He sipped her tea. Cold. Ruined. She hadn't come since she started living with that man, locked away like a princess in a tower. What was he doing to her body? Had he claimed her? Touched her? The pounding in his head became unbearable. He tried to shake off the pain. Were the beast's hands marring her skin? No. No. No. He collapsed into a ball on the floor, clenching his hands in his hair. Pulling, fighting back the darkness...a kaleidoscope of colors flashed before his eyes—red, pink, black, white...then...

7:45pm

Wake up! In the middle of his office he stood, sweating profusely, his chest heaving. How had so much time passed? What had he done? Papers were strewn across his desk. His couch and chairs were overturned. Had someone broken in? Was he here alone? What had happened? He sank to the floor and steadied his breathing. His fists were bloody. Damn her. He'd have to take a pill now, and it was all her fault. Her fault.

She'd pushed him too far.

On shaky legs, he went to the cabinet where he kept his medications. After opening the cabinet and finding the right bottle, he downed two pills.

Just wait. Calm would come.

And so would Ember.

When her heart was ripped to shreds, she'd come once more.

He'd wait right here. And in that moment when she begged for his comfort, she'd pay.

7:58pm

Ember had clearly lost all sense of direction, along with all sense of time and consideration of others. He smoothed his hair and sat once more at his desk. Calm. Control. Someday soon, she would see clearly. This was only a passing infatuation—a lonely child playing with a shiny new toy.

Once the shine tarnished, she'd return.

He'd make sure of it.

CHAPTER 29

Sprawled across the sheets on his king-size bed, Owen shook his head, amused by the vision dancing on his bed.

Ember shook her hips to the beat, wearing his football jersey and nothing else. Over the past two weeks, she'd become so carefree. Her short bob bounced around her head, which had him noticing other shapes bouncing quite freely under his shirt. He'd already taken her once tonight, but damn, if he didn't want her again.

His little stem had blossomed into a lovely flower. Blooming and teasing with the silken petals of her body, spending every night in his bed eagerly learning how to please him, and he had to admit, the naughty vixen had become quite adept. Those tight curves and the way their bodies fit together preoccupied his thoughts every day. Although his focus on the field had narrowed, he strove to play stronger and smarter for her and their future. Life outside of a football field had suddenly become filled with all kinds of what-ifs.

After a flirtatious full-body flash, she dropped to her knees and ran her hands up over his chest, before reaching down to stroke and entice.

No need, he was already solid and aching again.

She'd become his everything.

With a devious laugh, she once more wiggled to the beat, then turned and flashed her sweet ass.

His redhead liked to play, so he'd let her enjoy her little

game. He'd let her do just about anything, because he loved her. Loved her with everything in his heart—deep and hard—just like when he was buried inside her. Sometimes, they'd take their lovemaking slow, and he'd ease back to look in her eyes then think, how was loving this much possible? Did she love him?

Owen grabbed her ankle and yanked.

She tumbled and laughed, then fought to break free. "Stop, I'm trying to conduct a sexy striptease." Her breath came out in short puffs, winded from her X-rated dance. She shoved at his chest, but he wouldn't budge, so she pinched him. "Let me up." When that didn't work, she tried wrestling him into submission.

He generally let her win, but not today. "No. I've got you right where you belong." He grabbed both her hands and held them above her head, linking their fingers. She tried bucking him off, but he locked her legs between his knees. Her captivity had an interesting effect on his practically cast-iron erection, so he kissed her. Deeply.

Kissing her had become his favorite pastime. He craved the connection their melding lips and crossing tongues brought, so he kissed her at every opportune, and every inopportune, moment. Most times, they ended on the floor, the couch, on top of the washing machine. Each time, he'd never planned for things to go so far, but no complaints on his end. Or hers. In fact, she liked to push him, to dare him. They'd even christened two restaurant bathrooms. As if all the love she'd never been able to give now opened and spilled onto him. Her feelings flowed with breaking breaths and rolling moans as he tilted his head and slanted his mouth over hers.

Ember returned the kiss, then broke away and arched to the side. "Did you like my dance?"

"Mmmm, I like when you're in nothing but my jersey." He ran his nose along the side of her neck, breathing in her special scent. Absorbing every nuance of her body.

"Such a pirate, marking your territory by draping me in your colors."

"How about I mark you in another way?"

An auburn-tipped brow rose, and she shifted beneath him. "Mark me how?"

"In the purest way possible. I'll brand you with words that

come straight from my heart." He brushed a swift kiss against her lips and gazed into her eyes. "I love you, Ember."

This reveal was met with a sharp intake of breath. Her head shifted to the side.

She was quiet so long he envisioned his heart deflating like a tire, gnashed open by a jagged rock.

"You sure?"

Not the response he hoped for, but what he should have expected. "Very sure."

"Can you release my arms, please?"

Knowing this moment wouldn't be easy, he let her go. Softer emotions were foreign to a girl who'd grown up without any sort of affection. Hell, he'd had to dig pretty deep, too, but love didn't hide. Love revealed every facet of his being. Everything he'd wished to keep separate and concealed refused his will and leaped at the chance to be loved in return.

She sat up, nudged him onto his back, and rested her head on his chest.

He fingered a red curl. "Did I scare you?"

"No, it's just…what does love mean to you? Explain how you feel."

"I'm much better at showing." He brushed a hand along the side of her breast.

"No, please, don't do that. Don't retreat behind sex. I'm being serious. I need to know." She rose, sat Indian-style, and peered down with confusion evident in her deep brown eyes. "I have these feeling for you, too, but are they love? How does love feel?" She shook her head and, after a long moment, brushed away a single tear escaping down her cheek. "Are you drowning? Do you feel a constant state of heat under your skin, surrounding your body? A captivation you can't escape, because your body aches in all the right places? A stabilization that grounds you as nothing has before?" She linked their fingers and lifted their joined hands against her left breast. "Are you scared this is all just a dream? I am so lost in you. Will I ever be free? Is this what love is? Lust, fear, happiness, trust, panic—all mixed with the feeling that I've finally found where I belong?"

He reveled in her continued honesty, her continual ability to reveal her deepest feelings cut straight to his heart. "If that is what love is for you, then yes, that is what love is for me, too. But add in a protective instinct a mile wide. I have never been this open to anyone. You have the power in this small hand." He drew her hand to his lips. "The touch of your fingertips bring such passion, such pleasure, but at the same time, your claws could rip my heart right out of my chest."

She bent and kissed his chest right above his heart. "No, no I won't. I'll keep you safe. Give me your hand."

Her tone suggested seriousness, so he acquiesced.

"I am bound to you." Lifting his hand, she lined her palm against his, and then tightly wound their fingers together. "If that is love, then let it be love. But understand this link represents more; my hand in yours means we are connected. This means you will be the one person who won't leave me. I leave all my past behind and give you my future." Ember brushed a kiss against their linked hands. "I bind my heart to yours. Whether you choose to care for this gift is, and always will be, your choice."

The blood in his body pulsed and raced at her words. He felt transformed, as if she'd spelled him in some way. Overwhelmed, he was encompassed by love.

And now he would show her. He couldn't stop. He needed to join with her in the most primal way. Mindless to all else, he rose on his knees, splayed his fingers through her hair and captured her mouth with a kiss that sealed every word spoken. Settling her on his lap, he tugged on her neck and met her gaze with his own. "You called me a pirate. I am that and more. I've marked you as my own now, and I'll never let you go."

CHAPTER 30

Bundled in Maude's jacket and armed with pepper spray, Ember headed through the parking garage focused on the unwelcome task before her—visiting her apartment. A brisk chill from the late northeast Ohio October evening blew through the cement corridors, which reinforced the necessity to pack up her winter things.

Her phone pinged with a text from Xander, making her heart practically leap from her chest. A very real fear still lurked in every corner of her mind. Hand shaking, she read his text.

Come by for dinner?

For weeks, she'd dished out various stall tactics in order to avoid a counseling session with Xander. He'd dig too deep and bring forth memories she'd rather forget. Then he'd babble some kind of psychological justification for the attacker's actions that she didn't want to hear. Perhaps keeping all her memories of that night inside wasn't mentally healthy, but she'd told Owen. And one night, when he was out of town, she'd gone through an entire box of tissues revealing all to his mother.

That was enough.

So no, she wouldn't be joining Xander for dinner. She texted back:

Sorry. I'm heading to my apartment to pick up winter clothes.

By yourself? Is that wise?

Point proven. He made her second-guess every decision, made her look into her past to explain her reasoning behind every action she now performed. Why did there have to be a reason?

Couldn't life just be? She settled for a middle ground. No need to strain their already tenuous relationship.

She texted: *Lunch next week?*

Sure, dear, whenever you're ready. Call me if you're having trouble at the apartment. I'll come.

Thanks.

Since their last session, she'd contacted Xander through email and text. His failure to let her break free like she'd requested left a small crack in her life. She missed his calm counsel and support. But after using him as a crutch for so many years, she had to stand on her own.

A month had passed since she'd seen him, even though some events in her life left her wishing she could knock down his door. Her mother had called, asking her to run by the grocery, which was pure Diana Brooks, lost in her own little me-me-me world. The selfish woman still had a battery charge leveraged against her, yet expected a favor?

Ember shook her head at her mother's ridiculous behavior as she made her way to her car. She'd had lunch with Bethany a few times, and they'd cried and laughed. Her life was moving forward. And she hoped that at some point, her relationship with Xander would morph into a new phase. In time, he would see she'd grown into the woman he'd sculpted, and instead of holding her back, he'd happily continue to guide her forward.

After scanning the parking lot, she dropped her phone and spray in her purse and unlocked her car door. As she sank against the plush seats of the new Audi, she tossed her purse onto the passenger seat. Owen had talked her into accepting this car. He'd gone on and on about the safety features in car speak she didn't understand, but in a way, kind of turned her on. She was mental over the man, but still hadn't said the three words he most wanted to hear. Uttering, *I love you* seemed foreign, like speaking a different language.

A pleasant shiver tickled through her body as she thought about this morning. Her hand hovered above her left breast where Owen had left his mark after taking her with a fury. He'd pounced before heading to the airport for his Monday night away-game.

Owen had no trouble repeating, *I love you.* His openness and depth of feeling made her realize a few things—if her brother had felt even a tenth of this for Bethany, he never would have left. Never would have taken his life. Would she ever truly know what happened? And why? The why of it all still managed to pierce her heart in a way that would never fully heal, but she welcomed the sting, would endure the pain until she discovered the truth.

Her phone buzzed with a text from Kelly: *@ Bandits come watch game w/ us*

Ember's thumbs hovered over the keyboard. Procrastination did seem like a good idea. She'd stay at the bar for a bit and enjoy time with her friend while Owen was out of town. He'd absorbed her every moment, and that wasn't fair to her friends. Besides, she wanted to watch him play. She hit send on her text.

On my way.

#

After a rousing evening shouting at the bar's TV screens with her friends, Ember vowed to schedule more girls-nights.

Her good mood quickly faded as she arrived at her duplex. Taking a quick dash through the light drizzle, she halted at the threshold of her door. Not ready to face the demons sure to be unleashed en mass once she opened the door, she retreated and walked through the soaked grass to Clayton's door. His car wasn't parked out front so it was unlikely he'd answer. She pounded away anyway, but after interminable minutes and a sore hand, there remained no answer. Part of the reason she had been able to come here alone was the idea that Clayton could help if she needed. But nope, she would have to face her fears without his gun-toting presence. Maybe she should call Xander back.

No. No crutch.

Hair wet, water dripping down her nose, she recalled a similar cold glide of steel.

Don't go back there.

The sooner she packed, the sooner she'd be safe with Nancy and Maude. They'd surround her and help erase any distress. They had asked to tag along, but knowing this would become an emotional trip, she had declined. No sense turning into a blubbering mess in front of the woman you hoped would be your mother-in-law.

Stomach growling since she'd skipped lunch, and two cheese

sticks at Bandits didn't count, she considered what goodies Nancy would have waiting. Brownies maybe? The thought of chocolate solace pushed her enough to unlock the door. Drawing a deep breath, she flicked on the lights, which illuminated her living room— her clean living room.

Interesting. Maybe Nancy had tidied her apartment, or perhaps Owen had hired a maid service. Still, there was that odd smell, the acrid odor of disuse. A cold and empty sensation cloyed through her bones and created goose bumps on her skin.

While flipping on every light switch and lamp as she quickly stepped to her bedroom, she concentrated on Owen. His power. His strength. She'd watched the game with Kelly, screaming like a loon after each offensive play—sure they'd won by her support alone. So, the hour was late and she wanted to get this errand over with as soon as possible, but that meant going into the bedroom.

She stepped into her room and counted to ten.

Sound. She needed sound to block out the beat of her heart pounding in her ears. "All right, what do I need? Okay. I'll open my closet. Good, good. Oh, here is my suitcase." Talking to herself pushed her further into nutty-nut coo-coo land, but the sound soothed and kept her focused. "What shall I pack? I need jeans, long sleeve shirts."

After dropping the suitcase on her bed, she quickly jammed everything together before zipping it shut. "Now, where's my other suitcase?"

She found another bag in her closet and headed for her dresser. A noise outside had her jumping so far out of her skin, she was surprised she didn't stroke out right there in her bedroom.

Is that a car door? Is Clayton home?

A knock sounded at her door.

She rubbed a hand over her chest to calm her heart. Good God, if she didn't end the night in the emergency room it would be a miracle.

With hope Clayton had seen her car and was checking on her, Ember peered through her blinds to see who stood on the front stoop.

Her father.

Wasn't this night bad enough?

Tom Brooks pounded on the door again. "Ember! I know

you're in there." The thumping continued. "Open this damn door. I'm getting wet."

In order to keep the neighbors from calling the cops, she opened the door. "What are you doing here?"

"Can't a man stop by to see his daughter?" He pushed past her, shaking off his jacket and flicking his fingers through his white-streaked red hair. "Thought maybe you were staying with that football player of yours."

Ember tightened her grip on the doorknob. "Not a good time, Brooks."

Great. He'd discovered her relationship with a rich guy. Dollar symbols practically beamed from her father's eyes. Not good.

"You're looking fit." He made himself at home in her kitchen. "Ran in to a bit of trouble, Ember. Think you could help your old man?"

"No." She slammed shut the door and followed. Grabbing a glass from the cabinet, she filled it to the top at the sink. Her mouth had gone dry. Her parents had a way of wiping all natural processes from her body.

"What do you mean, no? You got that fancy job. Sure you don't have any extra funds for your old man?"

"I have student loans, apartment bills, car payments, so, no I don't have any extra funds. Why don't you get a job?" A conundrum existed. If she got her phone and her pepper spray, she'd also alert him to the whereabouts of her purse, which contained her wallet.

"You getting sassy?" He grabbed her arm and pulled her into the living room. "Where's your purse?"

"Stop." She wrenched her arm from his grip. "I'd like you to leave."

"You pay me, I'll walk." His jeans were worn at the knees and he wore a flannel over some local bar's T-shirt.

Paunchy gut, lined eyes, and a ruddy, red-veined nose gave proof to his alcoholism. "I don't carry cash. I gave that up a long time ago because of moments like this." She flashed a tight-lipped grin.

"Get some from that rich football player of yours."

Time for a subject change, because he'd gotten only one

portion of that statement correct. Owen was hers. "Nice to see you at Elliot's funeral."

"Fool boy." He ran a hand through his damp tufts of hair. "Why would I come when he did something stupid?"

"Not willing to take any blame? At all?" *Unbelievable.*

"All that is your mother's doing." He shoved a finger against her chest. "Now let's go. I saw an ATM down at the gas station on the corner."

"Mother's doing, huh?" She scoffed. Ember more than agreed with that. But, now that the shock of his sudden appearance wore off, she wondered about the timing of his visit. Was he the one causing her troubles? Cold chills shivered down her spine. Just how desperate had he become? "How long have you been in town?"

He smirked. "Who says I ever left?"

Why was she even trying? Normal conversation with this shyster was a lose-lose scenario. "Just leave. I'm not doing this."

"Fine." He smacked the side of her head. "I'm staying at your mom's until you bring by some money."

"Is that supposed to be some kind of threat? You will never get another penny from me." She headed for the door, and then turned, waiting for him to follow. "Don't ever touch me again."

"What will you do, girl? Send your pretty-boy ball player after me? Well, he's going to pay too, or else."

She laughed and glanced away. "As if you could do any—"

Never drop your guard. Never once take your eye off the snake, because that's when they'll strike. And strike he did. He punched her hard enough to drop her to her knees then kicked her stomach, knocking the air from her body. As she struggled to breathe, she choked at her father's foul breath pouring past her nostrils.

He wrenched her up by an ear and growled, "That's what I'll do, you ungrateful bitch. I want money. You tell that football fucker he'll pay, or I'll do worse, got me?"

Pain shot down her jaw. Blood filled her mouth and took her back. So far back, to another time, another place. Terror gripped her, and she crunched into a tiny ball on the floor.

Waiting.

Afraid to move.

Don't make a sound.

Her phone rang with Owen's ringtone—"Warrior" by Disturbed. Sanity returned. She tested her jaw and, with the back of her hand, wiped blood from her mouth. "Breathe, breathe, it was only your father. You know who he is. You know that monster. He's hit you before. You have to get up. Get up and lock the door."

Gritting her teeth, she rose and kicked shut the door. The loud bang angered her even more. Why hadn't she used that force against her father? Why did the cycle repeat? "Oooo! You stupid, horrible ass." She pounded her fist against the door. Suddenly furious, she shoved the coffee table across the room, threw magazines and paperback books, venting all her anger. Why had she let him in? Would she never learn?

Finished with her fit, she grabbed her purse, which was buried under her jacket, and found her phone. She tossed the phone in her hand, considering. Should she call Owen? She had always leaned on Xander. Was she doing the same with Owen?

Owen had texted earlier. He'd been on his way to Chewy's hotel room for a post-win celebration, so maybe she shouldn't disturb him. But they were a team now, and he'd see the new bruise on her cheek tomorrow and be livid she hadn't called.

She thumbed a quick text.

Hey.

Wasn't that the most brilliant thing she'd ever written? And her college major had been Communications.

She drummed her nails across the back of her phone. Still furious, she kicked at a magazine now lying on the floor. Noting a dried blood smear on her hand, she headed for the bathroom. The smell, added to dear old dad's kick, agitated her empty stomach. Tums would soothe the building acid. Shuffling through her medicine cabinet, she found the huge plastic bottle of antacids and the ibuprofen. Double-fisting drugs was the general side effect of all Brooks family visits.

The silence was broken by Owen's ringtone.

Startled, she dropped one of her antacids onto the floor. "Crap."

"Crap? No, Stems, it's Owen. What's going on? I just tried calling you, but you didn't answer."

On her knees searching for the stray tablet, Ember put Owen on speakerphone. She had barely heard him above the loud music and people muttering in the background. "Sorry to bother you. Are you having fun? Oh, there it is." Without any deliberation, she trashed the pill. It had landed at the back of the toilet. The five-second rule didn't count in such areas.

"Stop it…Ember…will you get out of my face? Sorry, Stems, Jason's being nosy. Where you at?"

"I'm picking up winter clothes at my apartment." Female voices chanted his name in the background. "Sounds like you're busy. I'll let you go."

"What?"

"Nothing. I'm getting ready to head back to your place." Why was she shouting? She wasn't the one surrounded by female party favors.

"Heading home, good. I didn't like you going there alone anyway. You okay?"

"Owen, you in this round? I thought you were on my team, baby."

Baby? What was happening at this party? What was that girl talking about? "Um…I'll let you go."

"Hey. What's wrong?"

For a moment, she considered responding. She'd called for reassurance, but this conversation was offering nothing but…apprehension…and jealousy. As well as drawing up the deep-seated fear that her overwhelming insecurity smothered him at times.

"Ember, please tell me."

If his tone had been demanding, she would have disconnected, but his husky voice soothed and provided a coating for the pain. "I was packing up some stuff and my—"

"Hello! Who's thish? Ish this Owen's girlfriend? He misses you soooo much. Girl, you are so lucky."

Ember hung up. What was all that about?

Again, Owen's ringtone pealed through the room. She shoved the offending item into her pocket.

Why would he let a girl take his phone and talk to her like that? Was he out searching for her replacement already? Was she expendable? There were obviously plenty of other girls willing to fill her spot. Deep down, she'd known that truth. But his declarations of love had blocked her ability to see outside their bubble—a danger, because bubbles always popped.

This wasn't fair. Her mind was deranged from being in this apartment again and her Dad's jab to her face. Maybe he'd finally rattled loose the crazy cells in her brain.

Owen had never given her any reason not to trust him, but what about the long run? With all that temptation around, who wouldn't cheat just once, and then twice, before letting go completely?

She'd always been the wallflower. Never invited to the cool kids' parties. But not Owen, he charged through life, sure and strong. She strove to be more like him, but on days like today, finding courage seemed impossible. While fully aware this was a total knee-jerk reaction, she scrolled to Xander's number. On the second ring, she started to hang up.

He answered. "Ember, good to hear from you."

"Hi, Xander."

"Are you all right? It's late, dear."

Why hadn't Owen expressed the same concern?

Because he was surrounded by drunken bimbos.

Wow, she'd turned an ugly shade of green. Well wasn't that lovely, because she had no doubt the color matched the shade in her stomach, inching toward her heart, not to mention, her throat. Insecurities were ever present, and that infuriated her. One visit from her father, and she fell completely apart. Who was she kidding? How had she ever thought her life could change with people like Tom and Diana Brooks still alive?

A text appeared on screen from Owen: *Answer phone Stems.*

"Xander, sorry to bother you, but…I just…well…my dad stopped by and…" She paused and bit her lip. "He hit me. Usual stuff really, but… I thought… I don't even know what I thought."

"I'll come right now. Where are you?"

"At my apartment."

Wht R U doing?

"I'll be over shortly."

Ember, pick up

"Xander, you don't have to. I know things are complicated between us right now. I shouldn't expect you to come after how distant I've been lately."

"I want to. We'll work this out together."

Loev U

Did she have any right to be mad at Owen for talking to other girls when she'd reached out to Xander? They were a team, and he deserved to know why she was acting strange.

While calling Owen back, she heard her phone beep with another caller. Sure it was Owen, she answered. "Hi. I was just—"

"This is Nurse Bastin at Manchester General. May I speak to Ember Brooks?"

"Yes, this is Ember Brooks."

"You're the emergency contact for Diana Brooks. I'm sorry, dear, but your mother has had a heart attack."

CHAPTER 31

"We should go see your mom."

Ember massaged her temples, avoiding the bruise pounding on her left cheek. The pain brought to mind the futility of involving herself in Brooks family affairs. "Xander, I just don't think—"

"Not caring about the welfare of others is who she is, not who you are." As Xander set the teapot on the kitchen table, he placed a hand on her shoulder.

The soothing scent of mint herbal tea filled the air. She sighed and watched steam wisp from the spout. He was wrong. She was resentful and petty. Deep down, she knew she should care that her mother could die, but no bond to the woman existed.

But, she needed to get out of this apartment, and she wasn't ready to go back to Owen's house. She'd just check in on her mother, or maybe she'd ask Xander to speak to the doctors. "Fine, we'll go."

Xander sat across from her, sipping his tea. "This is the right decision, dear. Do you need to get your things? Your suitcase?"

Yes she did, but she'd send someone back for them later. She'd walked into a pristine apartment and now it was a mess, but wasn't that how everything in her life ended?

"I'll get my clothes some other time. I really don't want to visit my mom at the hospital, Xander. I know that's cruel, but I can't stop how I feel. " Ember tapped her teacup against the table, sloshing the steaming liquid over the side. She watched a single bead drip down the glass and land in a pool, and then sighed before running her finger through the wet puddle. "I don't even think of her as my mother. She's just a lady who, if I let her, will hurt me again and again. Why should I allow her to do that?"

"Because you, my dear, have a conscience. I know you. I believe you'll regret being callous to those who, in their own way, care for you. Put forth an effort. I honestly don't know how you could ever leave her behind." Xander dropped his teacup on the table, and then cleared his throat. "I'll be beside you the whole time, as always."

Feeling grateful for Xander's presence, Ember wrapped her arms around him for a big hug. "Thanks for coming."

He tightened his grip. "Of course, I'm here for you. Everything is fine now that we're together."

Her phone rang again with Owen's tone, but she didn't answer. There was too much to discuss, and texting or talking on the phone just wouldn't be enough right now. So, she'd work things out with Owen tomorrow. "All right, Xander, let's go. I just need to text Owen real quick. He's in a tizzy."

Go to bed. I'll talk to you tomorrow.

# # #

The Emergency Room door slid open, and the first thing Ember heard was her father yelling. And she hadn't even heard the bell signaling the second round. Round two with her father wasn't on her agenda tonight. Every direction she turned led back to the nightmare of her past. With a swift glance, she assessed the scene.

A nurse dressed in blue cradled a computer and tried reasoning with Brooks.

Ember noted two security guards moving toward her father from the opposite end of the hallway. Tom Brooks had been back in her life for one evening, and already the cops were involved. Unfortunately, her father saw her before she could escape.

"Ember, 'bout time you got here." After shoving papers in her hand, he grabbed her elbow and pulled her off to the side. "Thish surgery is going to cost a lot of money. Insurance ish st-still in my name. You give me the cash, and then I'll...I'll pay the bills."

His words were slightly slurred, but years of practice had

honed his speech so no one else would recognize his inebriated state.

"First off, let go of my arm, Brooks. Second, you're insane if you think I'll give you any cash."

He squeezed her arm and exhaled bourbon-laced breath next to her ear. "You think I like coming into this stinking hospital for that fat bitch? You think I care if she dies?" He waited for a nurse to pass before continuing. "You were always so high and mighty, flouncing around. You tell that boyfriend of yours to pay, or his little girlfriend might not be so pretty no more."

Stale sweat and cheap alcohol emanated from her father's body. After jerking her arm from his grasp, she slammed the papers against his chest. This time, he wouldn't get the best of her. This time, she'd fight back. "I'm not giving you anything."

He started to pull something out of his pocket.

One of the guards halted behind her father. "Is everything all right here?"

Before she could answer, she spotted Xander.

He stepped between her and the second guard. "Mr. Brooks, pleasure to see you here. What seems to be the problem?" Xander placed an arm around her shoulders and gave her a reassuring squeeze.

Her father sneered. "What are you doing here, pretty-boy? You think you got it all figured out? Well, I want my money. I held up—"

"Mr. Brooks," Xander interrupted. "Calm yourself. You've done enough damage tonight."

"*I've* done enough damage? Who you talking to, boy?"

Xander grabbed her father's arm. "I'll see you out."

After an intense staredown, they headed back out to the parking lot.

"You all right, miss?" The guard patted her arm.

"I'm sorry for the disturbance." As she spoke, she heard the old excuses roll off her tongue. "My father tends to create chaos wherever he goes."

"Will your friend be all right with him?"

"Thank you. Yes, please, go back to your other duties. Again, I'm really sorry." Her face heated with embarrassment. She glanced around the waiting room and saw people averting their gazes. No doubt, they hadn't realized their evening in the ER would feature a Brooks family drama. She should start charging. Maybe then she could pay off her student loans. With a disgusted half-laugh, she shook her head and considered leaving.

"Miss, are you related to that man?" The nurse dressed in blue stood at her side.

"Yeah, I'm sorry about my father. He's a bit...a bit something."

The woman nodded, and a sympathetic smiled lined her face. "Would you mind answering some questions?"

"Sure." Answering questions, now wouldn't that be a gift from God. So many why's of her life. Why was she here? Why was her father an alcoholic? Why did he feel it necessary to beat her down? Why was Xander taking so long?

After releasing a deep breath, she followed the nurse back to her cubicle and responded to questions for which she actually had answers.

#

Once all the admittance and consent forms were complete, Ember took the elevator to the OR waiting room. Xander still hadn't returned, and after the night she'd had, she really didn't want to know why.

He had met her father before. Even interviewed him for the book he was writing. Whatever that weird vibe was between them, she hoped Xander pressured her father to leave. When the elevator door opened, she remained in place, unsure what had possessed her to come here in the first place. Taking a step forward was actually taking a step backward. Her stomach churned as she glanced at the pale blue walls, the beeping monitors and hushed voices.

The burden of inevitability pressed her forward, and she headed for the nurse's station.

A nurse tapped her shoulder. "Miss, may I help you with something?"

"I'm not sure." Bright glare from the florescent lights scored across her eyes. She blinked, cupped her hand above her eyebrows, and wished she was asleep in Owen's king size bed and this was, in fact, only a nightmare. Maybe the nurse could dispense some ibuprofen for the dull throbbing in her cheek. Pain from her father's love tap had marched to her head and set up a full contingent of bass drums.

What am I doing here?

Biting her lip to hold back tears, Ember gazed down the long, empty corridor.

"I'm sorry, but unless you're family, you can't stay here. Visiting hours will begin at 7am."

Family. Ember almost scoffed at the word. Family was nothing but boggy ground full of slush and drudgery. And with each step back into the muck, her bond to Owen and her new path smeared with filthy footsteps.

"I do have family here. Diana Brooks, she bears the title of my mother, and believe me, she wears that crown like a queen."

CHAPTER 32

After innumerable rounds on her Solitaire app, Ember watched the black-and-white clock tick past one in the morning before her mother's doctor entered the surgery waiting room. Xander, who had returned after almost an hour with her father, stood and shook the doctor's hand.

"Your mother is stable, Ember. We've done an intervention procedure. A stent was used to open a blocked artery. Your mother's lifestyle will require a drastic change. I suggest she complete our cardiac rehabilitation program, which provides a medically supervised setting to help persons recover from their heart attack and teaches ways to further prevent progression."

Drastic change. If only the doctor knew how long she'd hoped for that very thing.

Xander took her hand. "How long will Mrs. Brooks remain in the hospital?"

"Three to five days."

The doctor gave them more general information, and they thanked him before he walked away.

Regardless of how things stood, Ember was glad her mother wasn't going to die. She ignored the inner voice that said, *you only care she's still alive, because she can give you answers about Elliot's death.*

Even knowing what she would find, she checked her phone after the doctor left. Three texts from Owen, each increasingly heated, which practically burned a hole through her hand. Avoiding her feelings of frustration, jealousy, fear, and helplessness wasn't how she'd agreed to handle her relationship with Owen. He promised to meet her eye-to-eye. Causing him worry wasn't fair.

She texted back: *My mom had a heart attack so I'm at the hospital*

Owen's ringtone immediately filled the lounge.

Xander took the phone from her hand and stuffed it in his pocket. "Let's go see your mother before you answer any calls." He took her hand and led her down the hall. "You seem exhausted, dear. We'll get some coffee after this."

Sounded like a plan. She wanted to get this visit with her mother over with and go home. Owen's muffled ringtone seemed to scream through her mind as it played from deep in Xander's pocket.

"Xander, I really should answer Owen's call. He's really upset."

Xander shook his head. "Answer after this chat with your mother, dear."

"All right, but...I think...I think hearing his voice will help me get through this."

"Ember, look at me." Xander stopped and gripped her shoulders. "You and I have been through so much over the years. You know I'll be here for you. I always have been. Say what you need to say to your mother."

Perhaps in her weakened, drugged state, her mother would express the truth about her brother. A vicious and heartless thought, yes, but desperate times and desperate measures made her a bit cold-blooded.

"Xander, please wait out here. I need to speak to her alone." Intent on finding the truth, she didn't want anyone witnessing her horrid deed.

"I'm not sure." Xander hesitated by her side, his hand still linked with hers.

"Please." She squeezed his hand then loosened her fingers.

"Fine. I'll wait out here, but remember, Ember, she's heavily sedated."

She hugged him. "Thank you, Xander. For everything." Flashing a thin-lipped grin, she stepped away and pushed open the door. Various machines beeped and filled the room with soft green-blue light, which illuminated her mother's bulk. Ember's plan to block any softer emotions wasn't quite as easy when facing the poor woman spread out on the bed. "How are you?"

Her mother slowly opened her eyes and croaked out, "Water, please."

"I don't know if you can have that."

Her mother wheezed in a breath and moaned, wrapping her hand around the bedside metal bar in a white-knuckled grip.

"I am here only because of Xander. I will speak to the pastor at your church and see if anyone from your congregation is willing to help once you get home."

"Not you," her mother whispered.

Ember wasn't clear if those two words were a question or a statement. "I've asked you many times about Elliot's death, perhaps now that you've almost died, you'd like to clear your conscience."

Her mother laughed, which led to a long coughing fit, causing her monitors to light up.

Temporary guilt assaulted Ember.

"Ask him," her mother rasped.

"What?" She glanced over her shoulder. "Who?"

Her mother's gaze looked past her.

Ember spun around. Xander stood in the doorway, watching. *What?* Had her brother talked to Xander about his problems? What did her mother mean?

"I think your mother should rest." Xander stepped in and pulled Ember from the room.

With an overload of questions firing through her mind, Ember skidded to a stop halfway down the hall. "Wait. What did she mean? Did Elliot ever talk to you?"

Xander ran a hand through his hair and rubbed the back of his neck. "She was babbling, dear. Perhaps your mother believes I can determine what was going through your brother's mind, but at this point, that's impossible. It's also quite feasible the drugs were making her hallucinate, and she thought I was Elliot." Locking both arms across his chest, he narrowed his eyes. "And I find your questioning your mother right after a life-threatening surgery quite callous. Whatever were you thinking?"

For the first time in her life, she caught a glimpse of a ruffled Xander. Shame shot through her, grinding her already sour stomach. But still, she'd gotten something new, even if her mother's statement didn't make sense. Perhaps the time had come to discuss her brother's emotional state with Xander. Maybe he could offer some closure. Yet, something niggled. Both her father and mother seemed to have had private conversations with Xander. What had her father said earlier? Something about money? And now her mother? She studied Xander. Was she missing something?

Xander tugged her down the hallway to the lounge and practically shoved her in the seat. "Sit here and rest your head. I'll grab some coffee."

Ember grabbed a magazine off the table. Perhaps, delving into the lives of the rich and famous would distract her from all the questions bouncing around in her head.

Xander returned and handed her a paper cup.

"I'm sorry, Xander. I'm just desperate for some kind of explanation for Elliot's death. I'm tired and overwhelmed by everything." Lightly blowing across the surface of the steaming liquid, she watched the waves bump against the plastic cup. If only she could be a wave, floating along for days, weeks, months without bumping into a solitary thing. Heaving a sigh, she combed her fingers through her hair. "I need to get some rest, and so do you, but perhaps I could come by on Thursday and talk, just like old times."

Xander ran a hand over her hair. "I'd like that."

"I'll drop you off at your car, and then I can pick up some things at my place before I head to Owen's house." Since she needed to be alert on her drive home, she quickly finished her coffee. "Mmm…that was nice and warm. Thanks, Xander."

A moment of companionable silence passed as he sipped his tea alongside her.

She took his hand and squeezed lightly. "I will get my mom established with her church group, and even though I know this is harsh, I won't do anything else."

He turned and raised a single blond brow.

"All right. All right. Who am I kidding? I probably will check on her. Why do I even try, Xander?"

"Because of my guidance and my counsel, you are a perfect lady." His grip on her hand tightened. "We'll take care of your mother, and anything else that gets in our way. Now, rest your head for a moment."

Yawning so hard she heard her jaw crack, she shook her head and fought to stay awake. No wonder, since she hadn't slept due to worrying about Owen, her father's arrival, and her mother's heart attack.

What had they been talking about? Was that Owen's ringtone again?

A hand pushed against her side, and she tumbled—falling, drifting until her head landed upon a hard cushion.

"Relax." A soft brush of fingers combed through her hair.

She shivered, suddenly frightened of the darkness she couldn't escape. She tried to speak, but her tongue was thick in her mouth and wouldn't follow her direction. Her limbs felt heavy, as if weighed down by anchors.

And that quiet hum…where had she heard that tune before? Heart pounding, she fought to surface through the sludge weighing down her mind. There was something…something…

Then nothing.

# # #

Shifting in the hard metal seat, Xander let a small grin cross his lips. Finally, his prize was exactly where she belonged.

Such flawless skin. Such pale beauty.

Xander traced a finger along Ember's jawline, along her plump lower lip. To the victor come the spoils. He smiled and drank from his tea in quiet celebration.

The day had come. She'd returned.

He brushed his fingers through her short hair, wallowing in triumph. His strategy of time and patience had paid off. The natural order of their relationship would soon resume. How fortuitous, everything aligned just as he'd planned, and the best, the true fall, was yet to come. When fighting for his future, he couldn't be overly secure, so he'd quite masterfully set the stage for a final act. As he trailed a hand along her hip and over her bottom, heat coursed through his body and hardened his already swollen erection. He arched against her head resting in his lap.

Ember shivered, seemingly disturbed even in sleep. Poor girl. At every turn in her life, she required his guidance. No one else could lead her through her current muddle, or the coming storm. Her infatuation with that heathen had gone on long enough. That man had probably soiled her body from the inside out, but no matter. There were ways to become clean again. He would scour that man's filth from her body, and then cover her with his mark.

He gripped her shirt in his hand, ready to rip it from her body, ready to claim what was his—only his. After a quick glance around the room to make sure they were still alone, he lifted her mouth to his and kissed her. Eyes closed, he imagined her lips moving under his, and he pressed harder, punishing her for making him put her in this state. He'd done what was necessary, followed his plan, but he'd take this reward now. Desire overwhelmed his self-control and he moaned against her mouth. As he kissed his way down her neck, he stopped just short of biting into her creamy flesh. They'd discuss roles and expectations soon.

She belonged with him. She was his prize. His creation.

When he heard her phone ping, he jolted out of his fantasy and settled her back on his lap. Her skin pinked from where his stubble rasped across her skin, and her lips glistened.

After shifting his heavy, aching erection in his jeans, he removed her cell from his pocket and checked the text. That man thought to interfere. Too late.

Enough already, Stems. Are you still at the hospital?

He held back a giggle as he texted back. *Xander is here. No need to come*

I'm on my way from the airport now. Give me 60 min.

An hour. A day. A month. Time didn't matter. Ember was his again. Xander texted back. *I feel we need a break*

Will discuss when I get there

No. I don't need you

Not going to happen

I need Xander.

What?

Xander laughed and shoved the phone back in his pocket. The man was so confused, but let him come and see there was only one winner in this game.

No other man would take Ember.

He smiled, anticipating the moment when that man would

see the truth—see with whom she'd sought solace, who she'd turned to in her greatest moment of despair.

Him.

Ever and always.

The final act had begun.

CHAPTER 33

"Thanks, buddy." Owen fist-bumped Jake.

Jake just grunted and wiped the sleep from his eyes.

"I owe you one."

"Good, 'cause I want next Friday off, with pay."

"We'll work it out." Owen grabbed his gym bag out of the truck's backseat, and then double-tapped the side, saluting as Jake drove away from the hospital.

Pissed beyond anything, Owen shouldered the bag's strap and headed for the revolving door. He cursed a blue streak, trying to squeeze into the pie-shaped space. Finally, he held the bag between his legs and stepped sideways. Weren't people tortured enough visiting the hospital? Panic attacks while walking through the front door must be a side business they'd tapped into with the funniest video people.

After Ember's text regarding her mother's heart attack, he'd taken an earlier flight. When she'd called him at the party, he'd thought her voice seemed wobbly, as if fighting back tears—and now these bullshit texts. What the hell?

He'd see her and calm her down. She'd let her past undermine her belief in their relationship. They'd discussed her issues many nights while lying together in the semi-dark, since she still slept with both side table lamps lit. While resting her head upon his chest, she expressed her fears. She asked him not to give up when she got lost in doubt.

He'd made clear over and over he would lead her back from

the dark places in her mind.

She'd made her bond, so why was she pushing him away? Was it due to jealousy? If so, he'd soothe her worries quick enough. Those girls cooed over him all night, checking out his pictures of Ember, and teasing him about his sexy redhead until he'd headed back to his room. Alone.

The elderly lady behind the Information counter smiled, and wrinkles crinkled at the corner of her eyes. Owen spent a few minutes chatting her up and viewing a round of grandchildren photos on her phone before he asked for Diana Brooks's room number.

Stepping off the elevator onto the fifth floor, he stopped and rotated his neck in a circle. Airplane seats were not conducive to a comfortable night's rest, especially after a game. After following the directional signage to Ember's mother's room, he peeked in, but her mother was alone, sipping what looked like water from a straw.

Owen turned on his heel and headed for the nurses' station. Two brunettes stood behind the counter discussing a popular TV show. "Excuse me. Is there a lounge on this floor?"

They turned in unison and smiled. The younger one said, "Aren't you Owen Killion?"

"If I am, would you tell me where the lounge is?" He flashed a lopsided grin.

"Sure, if I can take a picture with you first."

After taking pictures with the nurses, he was directed down the hall. Upon making his way to the lounge, he stopped at the entrance and surveyed the open space. Padded metal chairs, magazines, TVs with early morning news shows, and Ember resting her head on Xander's lap—not quite the breakfast of champions.

Xander peered down at her face while running his fingers through her short hair.

Owen refrained from charging over and snapping every one of those fingers in two. Before this moment, he'd felt a tick of gratitude for the guy since he had helped Ember through her rough times, but that appreciation didn't allow his acceptance of another man touching his woman. He dropped his bag on the floor with a thud.

Xander lifted his head and met his gaze. "Good morning, Owen." He removed Ember from his lap and gently placed her back on the seat cushion.

Huh, why isn't she waking up? Owen moved toward Ember, but stopped when Xander tightly gripped his forearm. Owen glanced at the hand on his arm, then once more met Xander's gaze.

Xander released his arm. "Whatever it is you're thinking right now, or even considering doing, I wouldn't. I've sedated Ember because she's—" Brow furrowed, he shook his head and paused for a moment. "She wasn't ready for you. I warned her. Relationships are complicated for her, because she tries to please everyone. Did you know her father is back in town?"

Owen shook his head. "I'm going on very little sleep here, Kane. Don't push me."

"Oh, of course not...but you see...well, I'm afraid she's made quite a mess of things. I've been worried, because she's been weaning herself off her meds."

"What meds?" Owen had brushed past Xander but turned back at his odd statement.

"Ahhh." Xander nodded. "You see, Owen, Ember is a very unstable girl, and this relationship you've begun was never going to end well. I believe I warned you in the beginning. And now she's, well, I'm afraid she's done something unforgivable. In her mind, she won't see her actions that way of course, she's not rational...I'm sorry you've been brought into her world. I hadn't realized..." Xander sighed and massaged his temples. "She's... she's been lying again. A practice I thought we'd worked past."

"What are you talking about? There's nothing wrong with her." Owen crouched down beside her, and then lifted her in his arms. "Ember, baby, wake-up." Settling into the chair, he brushed at a pink blotch on her cheek. "What happened to her face?"

Her head lolled in his hands.

"What kind of drugs did you give her?" Owen supported her neck. "What in the hell kind of person are you?" Anger and frustration added to aching knees and a lack of sleep did not equal an understanding of why Kane thought he had any right to drug Ember. Owen wanted nothing more than to drag the walking drug store outside and pound a fist through his supercilious face.

Xander sank onto the coffee table and pinched the bridge of

his nose, eyes closed. He sighed deeply again, then met Owen's gaze. After a moment, he said, "Ember has made a horrible mistake. One I'm afraid you'll find hard to forgive."

This man's smooth manipulations grated on his last nerve. *Too bad, psycho, she's already taken.* Owen's phone rang with his sister's ring tone. "What mistake? Ember hasn't done anything wrong." His phone continued to chime.

Xander waved a hand. "You should probably get that. I imagine it's related to what I've been trying to tell you."

Owen removed his cell from his pocket and answered. "Maude."

"Owen, where are you?" Maude's voice sounded congested.

"At the hospital. Why?"

"Which one?"

"Why? What's wrong?"

"I came over this morning and Mom…she…well…a couple guys broke into the house last night, and Mom—"

"What?" Ice ran through his veins. He narrowed his gaze at Xander.

Xander moved around the chairs and peered out the window.

"Mom was knocked around…and they…they…." A series of sniffles and raspy breathing followed.

"Maude, calm down, it's all right. They what?"

"They are transporting her to the hospital."

"Who?"

"The ambulance. We're—"

"No. Who broke in?" Owen eased Ember off his lap then stood and paced in front of her sedated form.

"I don't know, but the police already caught one guy at the pawn shop, trying to sell your ring."

"What?"

"Oh, Owen, I'm so scared."

"I'm here. It's going to be fine. I'll wait in the ER."

He hung up and combed his fingers through his hair. "How much longer will Ember be incoherent, Kane? I've got to head downstairs. Can you wait here until I get back?"

Xander tapped a finger against the window's ledge. "She didn't mean to cause any harm. She was only trying to please her father."

"You know what?" Owen stalked over and stabbed a finger against Xander's chest. "Enough with the vague statements. Spit out whatever the hell you're alluding to. I'm this close to kicking your ass anyway for drugging her."

Xander flicked away his finger with one of his own. "In your current state, I thought to break the news gently. But since you'd prefer otherwise, I'll be blunt...I believe Ember spoke to her father about you and, under pressure, agreed to help him obtain much-needed funds."

"Told him about me?" Owen scratched his chin. "Told him what?"

"I'm sorry, Owen. She reverts to childhood behavior when around her father. This personality change stems from an obsessive need to please him so he won't leave." Xander glanced out the window. "I do not know how long she's been off her meds. She may not recall what she's done."

"Are you implying Ember had her father rob my house? That's ludicrous. Her father probably got the idea after seeing us on the news together." This man had drugged his woman, his mother was on her way to the ER, and his knees were killing him, so this accusation was a rotten cherry on top of a seriously fucked evening. "How could you possibly think that? Do you know her at all?"

"Do you?" Xander raised a single brow. "I am not certain of the depth of her involvement. Her actions may have been inadvertent, but before she drifted off, she admitted what she'd revealed to her father. Her words were jumbled, but I worked them out."

"Ember wouldn't betray me. There isn't anything wrong with her, other than the drugs you gave her tonight. We'll talk about that when I get back."

Xander folded his hands together, then tapped both index fingers against his chin. "Apparently, I need to simplify my point." Xander's icy-blue gaze shot chills down Owen's spine. "Ember has perfected a very special skill. A skill honed from years with that family. She'll make you believe there's no pain while she's driving a stake in your back."

CHAPTER 34

Overcome by nausea, Ember swallowed hard, then shot up and clasped a hand over her mouth as she scanned the lounge's surroundings for a bathroom. With shaky legs, exacerbated by dizziness, she wobbled to the door marked WOMEN. Blasting past the stall door, she dropped to her knees and retched. Her body filmed with sweat as she clutched the toilet's cool rim. Shaking and shivering uncontrollably, she emptied her stomach. With a deep moan, she sank back on her knees and tugged on the toilet paper. As always, the stupid roll was caught up, and only one square came off at a time. After smashing four or five squares together, she wiped her dripping nose. Stomach rolling and her breathing coming in short pants, she shook her head, trying to deny the backwards flow, but once more grasped the rim.

Empty, trembling, her head throbbing, she fought against the tissue roll, and then collapsed upon the cold tile floor. Wrong— everything seemed backwards and wrong. Tea, she needed tea, a long hot shower, and sleep.

A knock sounded on bathroom door, before it creaked open and black boots appeared. Clayton's voice landed like a stampede of raging elephants across her brain. "Ember? You all right?" He crouched beside her.

"She must be having a physical reaction to her emotional trauma." Xander leaned against the door frame. "She's in my care, Clayton. I'll see that she gets the help she needs."

The only help she needed included a toothbrush, the "Earl,"

239

and a soft bed. She refused to open her eyes or move. Had Owen called? Was he here? Her stomach churned once more, but, this time, with regret. Jealousy and insecurity made people do crazy things.

A warm hand brushed against her sweaty forehead, and she heard the toilet flush.

"Ember, do you remember what happened last night?" Xander's calm voice was accompanied by another light stroke across her hair.

"Please leave," she croaked without moving or opening her eyes.

"I can't, Ember," Clayton responded. "It's your father. He's been accused of breaking into Owen's house."

Surprise! This morning could actually get worse.

Ember sat up, then attempted to stand. Dizziness threatened once more, so she braced both hands against the wall. Taking a series of deep breaths, she fought back the fresh wash of nausea and the elephants still gallivanting in her head. Trembling and covered in sweat, she tried to grasp what was wrong. Had she caught some hospital bug?

Without acknowledging Clayton or Xander, she shuffled to the sink. In the mirror, red-rimmed eyes and an equally red nose greeted her. She flipped on the faucet, gathered cold water in her palms, and then splashed her face. After letting the cool water pour over her wrists for a moment, she glanced at Clayton.

He yanked a paper towel from the machine and handed it over.

As she dried her face, she breathed in and the earthy stench of cheap paper towel swamped her senses. "I should have known my father would do something like this. I'm so sorry." She stared down at the sink for a moment before glancing at Clayton. "Did he destroy Owen's house? He came by the other day asking for money, gave me a slap and a kick in the gut, and then left. I didn't think he'd—"

"Ember..." Xander placed a hand over her mouth. "Don't say anything else."

She swatted at his hand. She didn't like people blocking her breathing. "Why shouldn't I say anything? My father coming by asking for money isn't news. I can't believe he went after Owen."

She flipped the faucet back on, cupped water in her hand, and rinsed out her mouth.

Clayton met her gaze in the mirror. "I need you to come to the station."

Ember shook her head. "I'm not posting his bail." She tossed the wadded paper towels in the garbage and mumbled, "of course, he'd come along and ruin everything."

"Dear, we'll get you the help you need." Xander patted her shoulder.

Xander's patronizing attitude was not mixing well with her current mood. Why did he keep touching her? Hadn't he seen her lying next to the filthy toilet? Why couldn't they just leave her alone so she could sink back down on the floor and sleep? She didn't care what germs thrived on the tile squares.

Clayton took her hand. "He said you were involved, Ember. We need to ask you some questions."

"I'm sorry, but involved in what?" Her stomach churned again, which must be attached to some pulley system in her heart because it churned as well.

Xander placed both hands on her shoulders. "You've been neglecting your psychological care and not taking your medication. I hadn't realized you were this unstable."

"I'm not unstable. What do you mean?" Irritation surfaced and she shrugged off his hands. Xander always treated her like an errant child. He always did this, made it seem like she couldn't survive without hours of therapy. Her brain was not mush. She remembered her conversation with her father almost word for word, because it was the same every time.

"Don't worry." Xander patted her cheek. "I'll help you through this. I thought we were making progress."

Ember eased away from Xander's irritating counselor persona and turned to Clayton. "I'm sorry. I'm not feeling well, and I don't understand what you're implying. Why am I going to the police station again? Is Owen outside?"

"No, but I spoke to him earlier. Your father claims you were involved in planning the robbery at Owen's house." Clayton ran his fingers through his hair. "Ember, there's something else...his mother was assaulted and brought to the hospital last night."

"What?" She staggered then set her back against the wall, slid down, and focused on Clayton's words. "When did his house even get robbed? I mean, I'm living there now, so when did this happen?" Panic raced through her mind. "Is his mom okay? What about Maude? Is she all right?"

"Ember, honey." Xander knelt beside her and took her hand. "Your father knew where all the valuables were."

Ember braced a hand against Xander's chest. The blows kept coming, and too many questions whirled through her aching head. Where was Owen? Did he believe these lies?

Will I go to prison?

Xander wrapped her in his arms. "It's going to be all right. I'll take care of you."

"I'm so confused." Where had this stomach bug come from? Why was she standing in the women's restroom speaking to two men? Perhaps, she was still dreaming. "I'm not feeling so well."

"I know." Xander dropped a kiss against her temple. "We'll work things out."

She sighed. Of course things would work out. Owen wouldn't believe her capable of such a thing, would he? And what had Xander said about meds? What meds? She'd stopped taking drugs over two years ago. Trust her father to come back and create this whirl of chaos. And yet, deep down, hadn't she always known something like this would happen? Fairy tales weren't real. In real life, the heroine's glass slipper splintered under pressure, and all she had left was a bloody foot.

CHAPTER 35

After enduring an endless round of questions at the police station, Ember was dropped off at her duplex by Clayton. She'd asked Xander to give her some space.

She lodged a chair under the bathroom doorknob and showered. If only the cleansing bubbles could wash away the shattered pieces of her heart, but no, they remained, piercing and ripping through her chest, blocking her breathing.

Owen hadn't returned her calls.

At least, she wouldn't have to sit in the dark, covered in spent tissues, and wonder why, because all the evidence pointed to her. It was her word against her father's, and only by Clayton's interference was she able to come home as they gathered more evidence.

Stepping out of the shower, she whipped the towel off the counter and quickly patted her body dry. The only thing keeping her standing was Owen. What was he thinking? A love like theirs couldn't be broken by her father's greed.

But how had her father known where to find Owen's valuables? Even she doubted her innocence when presented with all the facts. One thing niggled like an acid-laced worm in her mind. How had her father planned this robbery? He wasn't smart enough to come up with this sort of scheme alone. Maybe she'd call that private detective Owen had hired, perhaps that woman could provide some answers.

But first things first, she needed to visit Nancy. They were friends of a sort, even if her son was angry, or whatever emotion was ruling him at the moment. Plus, she considered Owen would be more likely to listen with his mother present.

This is where love got you—stuck in an endless haze of eternal optimism, even when the light at the end of the tunnel remained unseen. And she very much feared she'd be lost in the dark for a very long time.

# # #

Once at the hospital, Ember's lack of food, sleep, and sense of impending doom created a nervous shaking she couldn't stop. The cold October evening hadn't helped with the chill. A late-night drizzle had dampened her hair and clothes, but she refused to care.

After getting Nancy's room number from the Information desk, she headed to the fourth floor, which was eerily quiet since she'd come near the end of visiting hours.

Would there be security? She peeked around the corner, but didn't see a guard.

For a moment, she considered turning tail and running back home, but the need to know overwhelmed everything else. She knocked with a single knuckle. No one answered, so she pushed open the door a few inches and peered into the room.

The shades were drawn and the only light came from the machines and open door. Nancy's pale face was visible and her eyes were closed.

Ember spotted a blemish on her cheek and a bandage on her forehead.

Owen was not in the room and neither was Maude.

Perhaps this was for the best. Ember would just leave the flowers and search for Owen in the visitor's lounge, or wait outside the door until he arrived.

Guilt, shame, and embarrassment filled each tear that poured down her cheeks. She placed Nancy's flowers on the table with all the others, and promptly knocked over a box of tissues.

"Ember?"

"Oh my gosh." Startled, Ember whipped around and knocked a vase off the table. Flowers and water crashed, and then spilled across the floor.

"Oh, no. I'm so sorry, Nancy." Ember bent and gathered the

broken pieces in her hand.

"It's all right. Just toss the pieces in the trash."

Ember's hand shook almost uncontrollably now as she dropped the glass in the garbage before gathering the flowers and stuffing them between two vases. This was a huge mistake. "I shouldn't have come. I just want...you see...I don't want to distress you by being here, but please let me explain. This may be selfish because my words are more for me than you, but could I please have a moment of your time?"

Nancy waved her closer. "Of course, dear. I was hoping you'd come."

Ember plucked a few tissues from the box and wiped her face and nose. She heard a deep male voice in the corridor. Her vision blanked, and every whoosh of her heart drummed through her ears.

He was coming.

"I-I-I...um...I needed...you see...please understand, I had no part of my father's despicable plans." She cleared her throat and tried to ignore the heavy footsteps coming down the hall. "Mrs. Killion. I wish I'd never brought your son into my world. People get hurt there. And it kills me you are another victim. I'm so sorry."

"I'll agree this hasn't been the most pleasant experience. I've never been so frightened in my life." Nancy smiled and offered her hand—the one not in a cast. "But you aren't to blame for your father's actions."

"You were targeted because of me, Mrs. Killion." Ember stepped closer and clasped Nancy's hand. "I'm sorry."

A charge filled the air. Owen loomed in the doorway. His dark shadow filled the rectangle of light cast onto the floor from the bright hall. "I'll let you say I'm sorry now, because the words are meaningless, just like every word from your mouth."

The bed engine whirred as Nancy adjusted her position. "Owen, I don't think—"

"No, she doesn't think. She conspires."

Owen's unforgiving gaze reached her from across the room. His severe stance exuded fury and disgust, mixed with the stench of sickness lining the hospital corridors. Her cracked heart, dripped with anguish.

He believed the lies.

"Owen, you misunderstand—"

"No," he lashed out. "I understand completely. You betrayed my family."

Ember's mouth went dry. How could he believe her capable of such malice? She had to fight, to try—just once make him see she wasn't guilty of anything. "Owen, when I said I was sorry, I meant—"

"I'm this close...this close..." He whipped a chair around and banged it against the wall, and then he stopped and visibly took a deep breath. "Get out."

Those two words shattered the remnants of her fractured heart.

"Owen Robert Killion, you listen to me. I'll—"

"No, Mom. No." He kicked the chair across the room. "She is the reason you're lying in that bed."

Ember was immobilized by her fear that one step forward would result in her falling at his feet and begging for forgiveness, understanding, and that ever-elusive word he'd so freely spoken for weeks—love.

Hands balled into fists, Owen stepped to the other side of his mother's bed. "I've taken many, many hits in my life, but never one so low. I didn't see the blow coming, but that's on me." He paused for a moment and finally met her gaze. "There won't be a next time."

She wanted to scream. Hold him down until he listened. Make him see...just see.

A thousand blows, the cut of a knife, all nothing, nothing compared to this...pain ripping like buckshot through her chest, eviscerating everything. Deep down, she'd known this highpoint in her life would end in the lowest of lows. But did this heartbreak have to hurt so much? Did it have to feel like the walls had crumbled? Suffocating. Removing every breath from her body. What was left of her now? Why always nothing? Nothing.

Ember wiped at the tears pouring down her cheeks and took a deep breath. He wanted her to admit her duplicity? Well then, she'd give him that. "Owen, please...just...I agree, it is my fault. I accept the blame." Her voice faltered as she held back a sob and whispered, "I never should have loved you."

"Love, fuck that. You don't even know what that word means." Owen pounded his fist against the bedside table. "Leave. Now. You've put my family through enough."

Flinching against each sharp word, Ember struggled to hold his gaze. "Owen, please...could we just—"

"Enough. There is no we. Not anymore. You've...you need to leave. Now."

"Please stop yelling. Just stop." Ember covered her ears with her hands and fell to her knees. Her whole life, she'd lived on the edge of madness, and with each of Owen's words, punching like blows, she finally fell and tumbled into the abyss.

Don't do this. Not here.

Leave.

Now.

Ember stood, flashed Nancy a tight-lipped smile, and whispered, "I'm sorry...for everything," and left, all while disregarding Nancy's pleas to stay.

At the door, she dared one final glance at the man who had opened her heart—now a solid, impenetrable wall.

He met her gaze briefly, and then turned away, staring at this clenched fist.

She didn't blame him.

And in the end, when she could breathe again, she would even wish him well.

But, not now.

Not today.

# # #

"Owen Robert Killion, that was absolutely uncalled for."

"Uncalled for? The girl beat you, and you almost died." Owen paced the room by his mother's bedside.

"*She* did not touch me, her father did. Now, if you're going to act like a two-year-old you might as well leave. I'm not having it." His mother waved him off.

"Not having it?" He scoffed, and then picked up the chair and sat. Elbows resting on his knees, he pounded his folded fingers against his forehead. "How could she just waltz in here like that?"

"Owen, I love you, but you're an idiot. That girl didn't dupe anyone."

"Her father put you in that bed." He jabbed a finger toward the doorway as if Ember were still there.

"That's right. Her *father.*"

"Her father might have been the one at the actual break-in, but that duplicitous bi—"

"Stop, stop right now." His mother lifted her hand, palm out. "I won't hear you speak such foul language."

"But she—"

A tissue box hit the side of his head.

"What the he—"

"I have heard enough, Owen Killion. Ember had nothing to do with her father's plans, and that's the end of it. She loves you, and she's devastated by this whole business. And what do you do? You just ripped her to shreds."

Owen scrubbed both hands over his face. "How else did her father know those things?"

"Ffffffttt." His mother snapped her fingers in his face. "All nonsense."

"As much as I wish her father's break-in was nonsense, it isn't. I failed in my job to protect you, and I let a psycho into our lives."

"Why are you so set on believing her capable of such a thing? Think it through, Owen. None of this makes any sense." She plopped her head back on the pillow and was quiet for a moment, picking at the blanket with her fingers. "I know what it's like to lose someone you love." She met his gaze and a single tear slid down her cheek. "Don't let her go. I know you love her. You're suffering. She's suffering. That girl has been through enough."

"Don't cry, Mom." Owen leaned over and kissed his mother's cheek, and then took her hand. "The only thing I understand right now is you are in this bed because I made a bad choice."

"No." His mother squeezed his hand. "I'm here because Ember's father chose to take advantage of a situation. Just imagine growing up with such a man as a father. And now he's destroyed her life again. The cycle keeps repeating. It's a wonder she makes it through each day. I admire her for coming here. I also admire her for saying she loved you in the face of so much animosity.

Where does she get such inner strength? She's like a canyon that's been torn apart by water and air over thousands of years and now stands alone, beautiful and brittle, crumbling under each storm, but remains standing, always."

"Mom, you're high on something, and you don't know all the facts."

She patted his hand. "Oh now, that's where you're wrong, son. Mothers know everything."

# # #

Owen punched the elevator button. After receiving that verbal spanking from his mother, he wondered that his ass didn't hurt as much as his head—or his heart. He didn't know which play to make, and he feared he'd made a huge misstep with Ember.

After speaking with Clayton and hearing Ember had been freed due to lack of evidence, he'd walked back to his mother's room and there she was—Ms. Deceiver—in the middle of a confession. He'd never felt such a violent range of emotions. He only knew she had to leave before he said or did something he could never take back.

Clayton had made a comment that only now could he take a moment to reflect upon.

There something else at play here. I'm missing something. Ember's had a series of unfortunate events. One or two I could ignore, but when you look at the whole…something's not adding up."

Owen sighed and massaged his knee.

What is taking the elevator so long?

When the elevator doors slid open, Rachel Harris stepped out. "Owen, good. Clayton told me you were here. I've been calling all day."

"Been a little sidetracked."

"Then you'll go off the rails with this." She grabbed his arm and hollered at the nurse inside, "Hey, hold that please." She tugged him into the elevator. "Let's get some coffee. You look like you could use some."

Coffee wasn't even close to what he needed. He rubbed at the ache in his breastbone and that pissed him off, because he didn't want to feel any heartbreak for the girl who had deceived him.

And yet, Clayton had a point. So many misfortunes in such a short time meant something. Ember's tires, her coil wire, her attack, her brother's death, her father's reappearance—if you laid them out like puzzle pieces, what picture would they form?

Maybe it was a good thing Rachel was here. Perhaps she could help piece everything together. After stepping off the elevator into the lobby, he followed her to the coffee shop.

As the ever-vigilant detective, she picked a table farthest in the back, and she sat with her back against the wall.

He hated these tiny round tables with their flimsy plastic-and-metal chairs. He tapped the saltshaker on the table. "Unless you can explain how two assholes broke into my house, I could give a shit, Harris."

Rachel plopped her bag on the table and pulled out a folder. "Oh, we're feeling a little pissed this evening, are we? Looking for a target for those frustrations? Ain't gonna be me, sugar." She laid a hand over his on the saltshaker. "I'm getting a coffee before we start this little bed time story. You want one?"

Owen shook his head. He grabbed another chair, spun it around, propped up his feet, and considered whether or not Dougy would deliver ice for his knees.

Rachel returned with a steaming cup of coffee and sank into her seat. "You asked me to look into the death of Elliot Brooks, and I did." She flipped open the file with her pinky finger while pouring three sugars into her coffee. "After reviewing the evidence, I understand why Elliot's death was ruled suicide, because essentially it was. But then you asked me to look into Xander Kane. Well, that's been a whole lot more fun." She rubbed her hands together. "Following that guy around and digging into his past has been a dream assignment."

"Following him? Why?" Owen fiddled with his thumbnail. The last person he wanted to talk about was "Ken-doll" Kane.

"You asked me to investigate him, remember?"

"He's some kind of all-knowing psychologist. Drugging people. Always creeping around."

"Creep is a very accurate depiction of Xander Kane. He's visited some interesting places the past couple of weeks."

"Like where?" Owen pushed the chair out from under his legs and straightened in his seat.

Rachel flashed a cocky grin. "Glad to see I've got your attention." She sipped her coffee and grimaced. "Gah...so gross. Anyway, let's start at the beginning. Essentially, Xander Kane has lied about his past. After interviewing people who know him now and people who knew him as a child, I discovered a huge discrepancy. If you were to ask him, he'd say he had a happy childhood, but the truth is much, much different." Rachel sank back in her chair and took another drink of her coffee. Her tiny nose scrunched up, and she stuck out her tongue. "Shall I continue?"

"I'm still here." Finding out Xander wasn't perfect was one point back on his previously unblemished ability to easily judge people. But he still had one blemish, and it stung. Would for a very long time.

"Kane was raised by his mother's sister. Those who knew her don't recall her with high regard. Apparently, his aunt was a psycho neat freak and made it clear having to raise her sister's child interrupted her strictly ordered life."

"Why would he lie about being raised by an aunt?"

Rachel shrugged. "Maybe his childhood was so traumatic he replaced it with another. But here is where the tale gets interesting. He went to a pawn shop and purchased a 1911 in .45 caliber around five months ago. You tracking with me?"

Owen's heart pounded in his chest as the puzzle pieces rearranged in his mind. "A .45. Wasn't that the caliber Ember's brother used?"

"Right. Ember's statement to the police claimed her mother had no guns, so where did it come from, and where is it now? Also, Xander recently visited the corner at 38th and Vine, a well-known street pharmacy. He's been there twice since I've watched him. The first purchase was Super K or Ketamine, and the second was GHB. I had to grease their palms a little, so expect a little bump on the next invoice, Killion."

"Fine." At this point, money was a moot point. "What do they do?"

"They're kids from homes that—"

"No, not that. The drugs. What do they do?"

"GHB kind of acts as a relaxant, slows the heart rate and respiration. It can sometimes create a coma-like sleep, depending on how much you take."

Coma like sleep? Owen shot out of his chair and paced. "The other day, Ember was completely incoherent. Xander mentioned something about her meds. Thing is, I don't know if she really takes meds or not."

"Then this makes sense. He's got drugs, a .45, and you're really not going to like this—three days ago he bought a KA-BAR knife. I realize this isn't the same knife used in Ember's attack, but Xander's penchant for sharp objects doesn't give me the warm fuzzies."

Owen stopped in his tracks.

Xander bought a knife.

His stomach dropped, and that one perfectly formed piece that never seemed to fit, fell off the table and landed in another box completely—Xander.

The other pieces shifted and aligned. Everything now made sense.

Harris continued. "Third thing to consider, and this may clear up one issue, Kane has been on four dates with Tracy Knox. That name ring any bells?"

Tracy Knox.

His ex.

Puzzle complete.

CHAPTER 36

Xander settled against Ember's headboard and opened the paperback book where she'd left her bookmark.

The pirate threw her down in the hold.

"You'll not keep me here." But all the while, her heart was pounding with desire. Who was this man? Not a Duke, but a pirate?

"You chose to stow aboard my ship, my lady. So, I will, in fact, keep you."

"I'll escape."

"You'll try."

Satisfaction flowed through him. This was what she wanted. This was proof Ember wanted to be seized and carried off into the sunset.

"I'm leaving, Xander. As soon as I get another job, I'm out." Ember tossed clothes across two open suitcases placed on her bed.

"Running away from your problems doesn't solve anything, dear." He tapped the book against his thigh.

"Should I stay here? In this apartment, where I was beaten and violated? Should I stay in this town where he lives, with memories of our time together stirring every time I turn around? Should I stay in the place my brother died, and my parents continually destroy everything? I'm sorry, but running away from this constant nightmare is a great option." She wadded a T-shirt into a ball and threw it across the room.

"Ember, calm down. Use the breathing techniques I taught

you."

"Oh, that's good," she scoffed. "Breathing techniques for a person who can no longer breathe. My lungs froze up hours ago. Your platitudes won't work. Nothing helps. My life is cursed by someone who finds joy in my torment."

"Whatever do you mean? What's happened?"

"I've discussed a lot of things with you, Xander, but my love life remains off-limits." She huffed out a laugh, and mumbled, "Love life, whatever."

"Ember, we've worked through so much before, let me help you again."

"Why, Xander? Why?" She swept the suitcases onto the floor. "You want to dissect me? Put me in your little book and close the cover? I'm real, not wrinkled pages. I bleed, I cry. I am not your test subject." She slashed a hand through the air, and then kicked her suitcase across the room. "So no. Just no."

"I don't appreciate taking the brunt of your anger. This childlike fit is quite disgraceful." How dare she speak to him so callously? He'd ripped her from the dregs. Formed her out of unmolded clay. Her denial of his influence over her life was more than a slap in the face. "Ember, let me explain—"

Her home phone rang.

Ember visibly tensed when her mother's brittle voice sounded from the answering machine. *"Ember...I'm ready to talk about Elliot...are you there? Come by the hospital and I'll explain...Ember?"*

So, the woman hoped for redemption after looking death in the face. Just what did she think to reveal? Who would believe her anyway? Disgusting pig, he never should have relied on her to keep her mouth shut.

Xander rose off the bed and came to Ember's side. "Your mother never did have good timing. This is obviously a plea to keep you hanging on. She knows she needs your help once she returns home. Don't let her manipulate you with this distasteful scattering of crumbs. While sad, the plain truth remains—your brother committed suicide. It will never make sense, and you need to let go of your irrational belief there was a reason." He ran a hand down her back. "You were right when you said we need to move on, and we will."

"Exactly. I don't know why I even let you talk me into visiting her. I'm glad you are finally seeing her as I do. That's why I'm moving as far away as I can." Ember slammed shut her dresser drawer, turned, and stared at the underthings in her hands. "Except."

"Except?"

"Why?" Ember sank onto the bed. "I've always suspected my mother knew more than she'd admit. Why tell me now?"

"She almost died. She's using the one thing she knows will lure you in." Sweat trickled down his brow. Ember was getting too close. He'd never let her speak to her mother. He clenched his jaw. *She's almost yours. Don't blow it.*

"But what if she does know something?" She stood and grasped his shoulders. "I have to know what happened. I have to hear her out. These questions have been burning since Elliot died. I need closure."

"Don't take this on as well. She'll only disappoint you again. These actions prove you're not thinking clearly. Why would you believe anything your mother says?"

Ember tilted her head and studied him.

"Is this about Owen? Has he hurt you?"

She glanced at her feet.

"Now I understand. He gave up on you. Believed the lies." Xander braced his thumb under her chin and kissed her, locking her lips with his, showing her how much passion they could create. "I would never doubt you. We are one and the same. Stay with me." He ran kisses along the side of her neck. "We'll erase him together."

"Xander, please…I can't…" Shaking her head, she eased out of his arms and continued speaking of her ridiculous plan. "I need to hear what my mother has to say. I have to know."

But she wouldn't. *Ever.*

"Would you mind…I hate to ask, but I'm terrified of being here alone, so could you wait for me while I shower?"

"I'll always be here for you." Xander ran a hand through her hair and kissed her forehead. He smiled and waved her off as she headed for the bathroom. He plopped back onto the bed and lifted her pale, pink bra. Closing his eyes, he imagined releasing each snap, brushing his hand over her soft skin.

Her phone rang.

Killion, Owen.

"Sorry, you're too late." Xander powered down her cell and stuffed it in his pocket, then took out his own phone and made a call.

"Alice, hello…yes, it's Xander…we've yet to discuss your fee structure for staying in my apartment…I'd like to meet, are you free?…Good, I believe I've come up with an arrangement that will suit us both."

# # #

Even as the lukewarm shower spray poured over her skin, Ember still experienced a dry emptiness in her heart. She stared as the soapy washcloth fell from her hand and dropped onto the floor. Her legs gave out, and she followed the cloth down.

Sobs wracked her body as she succumbed to the pain. Sitting on the base of her shower stall, she couldn't get warm. Four ibuprofen pills hadn't come close to cloaking the sting of Owen's words.

The spray turned cold, so she rinsed out the cloth and wiped her face. If she stayed in here, would the water just continue to pour? If she remained locked away, would the world continue around her?

Maybe she could find an iota of relief if she spoke to her mother. And though Xander could be right about her mother's intentions, he could also be wrong. If nothing came of this discussion, then she wouldn't ask again. She'd go with her other plan to visit the detective Owen had hired. Moving ever forward. What other choice did she have?

Ember cranked off the faucet and grabbed her towel off the hook. After carefully patting dry her face and the rest of her body, she avoided looking in the mirror and glimpsing the pitiful image of red-rimmed eyes. Pain lived in the eyes, and way too many truths—neither were welcome. Her shower breakdown was enough. *Enough.* Gritting her teeth, she fought back emotions that refused to stay locked away. Biting her tongue, she sank deep with her teeth until the taste of blood filled her mouth.

She reached for her toothbrush—but something caught her eye.

A long, red hunk of hair curled around the bottom of her sink.

Her hand shook as she lifted it by the creepy pink polka-dot ribbon tied around one end.

Was this her hair?

Where had it come from?

Oh, my God. He's come back.

She dropped it.

The bathroom door swung open. Xander stood in the doorway.

Her heart thumped. "What are you doing?" She secured her towel around her body.

He met her gaze but said nothing.

"I'm not dressed."

"I see you've found my gift." He waved a hand toward the sink.

A mental block lifted. Calculations raced across pages in her mind like an old dot matrix printer.

Adding.

Adding.

Two plus two equaled four.

Xander plus her ponytail in the sink equaled…"You."

CHAPTER 37

"She won't pick up." Owen dropped his phone on the bedside table.

"When's Bronco supposed to get here?" Waving the discharge papers in front of her face, his mother perched on the side of the bed. She got up to look out the window every five seconds.

"He'll be here soon. Take it easy."

"You don't need to wait here with me. You and Rachel should go to Ember's place, now. Go."

Harris had called Clayton and filled him in on all she'd learned about Xander. They were waiting to hear back while he did his own digging.

Bronco blustered into the room, wearing jeans and a faded T-shirt that belied his wealthy upbringing. An ever-present hardback book was cradled in his hand. "Hey, sorry it took me a bit." He ran a hand through his tousled hair. "Semi accident on I-440."

"What are you reading?" Rachel flicked the binding of Bronco's book.

"Mystery novel. It's a library book."

Rachel raised a brow. "Aren't you a professional football player?"

"Yes."

"Then why don't you buy them?" She stood with her hands on her hips, staring up at him like he'd committed some crime.

Bronco's brow creased between his hazel eyes. "What's wrong with going to the library?"

"What in the hell are you two talking about?" Owen shot out of his chair and paced by the door. "There is a potential madman armed with guns, knives, and who knows what else, and you're discussing the library? Would you like some tea and strumpets to go with that?"

"Crumpets," Bronco mumbled.

"What?"

"You said strumpets, the word is crumpets."

"Why the hell do I care, and why the hell do you even know something like that?"

Bronco shrugged. "If you're going to yell, at least be accurate."

"You're friends with this guy?" Rachel crossed both arms across her chest and jerked her thumb in Bronco's direction.

"Who are you again?" Bronco stared down at the petite brunette from his six-six frame.

"She's the detective I hired to look into Ember's brother's death."

Rachel's phone rang with the *Hawaii 5-0* theme song. "That's Clayton." She stuck her finger in her free ear and shifted closer to the door.

"What do you need?" Bronco slapped him on the back.

His mom piped up from the bed. "He needs to get his ass in gear."

"Mom." Owen flicked a glance at his mother and shook his head.

"Go get your girl, before something awful happens." His mom sniffled a bit and wiped at the corner of her eye.

Rachel returned, not smiling. "Xander isn't at his apartment. Clayton is heading to Ember's duplex now."

"Why isn't he sending in the troops?"

"He can't," Bronco interjected, tapping his book against his palm. "Not officially. Xander hasn't done anything wrong. I'm getting a twitch. You should leave."

Not even before a big game had Owen's heart raced like this. What if he was too late to save Ember? He glanced at Bronco.

"I've got this." Bronco saluted with his book. "Go."

Rachel was already halfway down the hall.

Owen caught up with her by the elevators. She was doing some kind of braid with her hair.

"In Xander's mind, it isn't over. He needs absolute control. Past patterning suggests he'll try to contain her somehow." She pulled a hair band from her pocket and secured the end of her ponytail while pacing before the elevator doors. "He'll need to mark his territory, so to speak, until he's got her under his control. He won't stop. Ember is his, and only his. If he has to destroy her to keep her, he will. He feels he's created the perfect companion. Someone who worships him, and only him."

Owen ran a hand through his hair as he realized a horrific truth. "He's going to kill her, isn't he?"

The elevator doors opened.

Rachel entered and punched the button for the lobby. She studied the elevator panel for a moment then met his gaze. "Most likely. Yes."

CHAPTER 38

"You," Ember whispered once more.

"That's right, Ember. Me." He absorbed her shock and smiled.

Time for her to understand who was in control, and what would happen if she crossed him. "I tried to make you understand. I feel I was quite gracious in allowing your little dalliance, but then you left, and that is something I won't tolerate. Ever. We'll talk about our future once I get you home. For now, I believe we should consummate this new beginning." He laughed and stepped farther into the bathroom. "Oh, I feel so free now that you know, now that you understand." A weight that had pressed upon him for weeks lifted. Only one detail remained. "Wash out your mouth."

"I-I-I don't understand. What have you done? Was it you that night? Did you fucking attack me?" Her voice faltered, and her hand shook as she raised it between them.

"Such a filthy mouth. We need to get it clean." Dirty, so dirty. She was his, but soiled by that other man. Cleaning her mouth would be a good start, and then she'd have to scrub her entire body with soap and hot water.

Don't touch until you're clean.

He pushed her shocked form onto the toilet seat and rustled through her cabinets until he found mouthwash. "Use this. Swish for two minutes."

"Xander, you beat me, you stabbed my hand. You-you-

you…my hair. I don't understand why you're doing this." Her eyes were wide, and her hand was clenched on the towel between her full, heaving breasts.

"I am doing nothing. You are to blame. You've fouled yourself with that man and now must be cleaned." The voices were back. Contain. Keep her or she'll discover the truth.

The truth.

White.

White.

White.

The truth was white.

He grabbed her arm and shoved the mouthwash bottle against her lips. "You can only stay if you're clean."

Ember grabbed his wrist and twisted her head.

Intent on her sanitation, he tugged on her short locks and shoved the bottle past her clenched teeth. "You're nothing but filth. You make me do this. Make me punish you over and over."

She shoved free, stood, and backpedaled toward the door.

"Where do you think you're going?" He grabbed her arm and yanked her closer.

She spat out the mouthwash and bucked against him, arms flailing as she struggled to reach the doorknob. "Xander. Enough! I won't let you do this again. Let me go."

"Why fight me?" Wrapping both arms around her from behind, he shivered as he breathed in her sweet scent and his nose tickled from the damp hair on the back of her neck. "We've been here before, and I believe we both know who won that round." The more she struggled, the more she inflamed his already heated body. He thrust his heavy erection against her towel-covered bottom.

He tightened his hand around her throat, ran his other hand up under the towel, then pinched her bottom. "Stop struggling. The more you resist, the worse your punishment. You will be mine. Tonight."

Twisting, she shoved back with an elbow and groped for the door.

Her attempts were futile, yet arousing. Rough foreplay had always been his cup of tea. He grabbed her elbow and knocked her against the wall.

She lost footing on a throw rug, and stumbled.

Xander watched, as if in slow motion, as her head bounced off the side of the shower stall.

Blood trickled from the gash on her forehead, and her body rested at an odd angle on the floor. One arm was raised and slumped against the toilet seat.

"Quiet now, aren't you? You deserved this!" Xander shoved her with his foot. "*I MADE YOU.* Don't think for one second, I'll forget what you've done." He slicked back his sweat-soaked hair and tugged down his shirt collar. "We'll discuss this at home." After washing his hands, he knelt beside her and lifted one end of the towel—

A persistent knock sounded on her door.

Who the hell?

The knock continued.

Ember's cell phone rang in his pocket.

Xander stood, yanked open the bathroom door, and then paused for a moment to regain his calm before heading for the front room. Who kept pounding on the door? Wasn't one series of knocks quite enough? Such rudeness was entirely uncalled for.

Peering through the front window blinds, he spied the man's sister standing on the stoop. He'd made a point of knowing everything about his competition, every weakness—and Maude Killion was definitely an Achilles heel.

Won't it be fun to teach her some manners.

Remaining hidden behind the door, he unlocked the bolt. "Come in."

"Ember?"

He choked back a giggle until she stepped parallel with the door's edge.

Then he slammed the door against her.

A scream tore across the room as she toppled to the ground.

Xander jumped on her back and bashed her face against the wooden threshold between the entryway tile and the living room carpet.

Blood spatter colored the floor in various hues of red and black

Giddy, he stood, kicked shut the front door, and then peered around the room.

Dizziness threatened. He blinked and leaned against the wall. His legs gave out, and he slid to the floor.

What am I doing here again?

His hands. They were filthy. Crusted in red.

Oh no, she would see.

He had to get clean.

Another knock sounded on the door.

Xander jerked to his feet and peered out the window.

Another knock, harder, more impatient this time.

He scurried back to Ember's bedroom and yanked open her blinds.

At this point, he couldn't tell if the knocking was coming from the front door, or his heart banging against his chest.

After flipping open the window locks, he sliced through the screen with his knife, slid through, and jumped to the ground just as he heard the front door open and her neighbor, Clayton, yell, "What the hell?"

His car. He had to get to his car.

In preparation for a quick getaway with Ember, he'd parked his car in the back lot of a shopping center behind her duplex. No security cameras were back there, and he could have easily carried her over his shoulder the entire distance. The man's sister had ruined that plan, however. "I'll just come up with another."

He whistled a tune and strolled to his car, all the while forming Plan B in his mind.

Ember wasn't lost to him. He'd always find a way.

Sirens blared in the distance.

He smiled and pulled out his phone. "Alice, meet me at Manchester General. Room 514."

CHAPTER 39

"What happened?" Owen rushed to Clayton's side after fighting his way past the police barrier. Rachel remained behind, asking questions.

Three police cruisers sat at the curb outside Ember's duplex. Their lights hit the side wall of the duplex in alternating splashes of red and blue. On his way here, he and Rachel had passed one ambulance. Another sat on the curb, EMTs moving swiftly around the vehicle.

"Killion. Glad you're here." Clayton pulled him into the yard, closer to the ambulance.

"Where's Ember? Is that her in the ambulance?" A cold chill raced down his spine. What had she suffered this time? Guilt lay across his heart. This was his fault. He'd left her unprotected and she'd taken the hit, and the fall. "Is she...is she..." He licked his dry lips. "Wh-what did he do?"

Clayton caught his arm. "Ember's gone."

Owen heard the words and stumbled, clutching tightly onto Clayton's arm. He bent over at the waist and tried to catch his breath. *Gone. Oh, God.* A vice squeezed every ounce of blood from his heart, and left him in a dizzy world empty of everything but the pain. *No. No. No.*

"I'm sorry, Killion. I got here too late. I arrived and the door was wide open. I found...I found your sister first. Then went back and found Ember in the bathroom. She was...I found her by the tub." Stalling for a moment, he rested a hand on Owen's shoulder.

265

"She was unconscious due to a severe head injury. She hadn't regained consciousness by the time the guys loaded her up."

"Unconscious? Not dead?" Owen kept his tone even as he straightened and met Clayton's gaze. Everything hinged on Clayton's next words.

Clayton's brow furrowed. "No, not dead."

"Not dead." Owen let those words sink in for a moment, and then realigned what Clayton said in his mind now that the oxygen and blood once more flowed through his body. "What did Xander do?" He stepped toward the duplex, intent on doing something…he had to keep moving or he'd crumple to his knees. "Wait…what did you say?" He halted his forward motion as Clayton's initial words registered. "Maude was here?" He searched for her through the crowd of uniformed bodies coming in and out of the duplex. "Are you sure?"

"Yeah." Clayton pointed at the ambulance. "That's her the medics are loading now. She's suffered a broken nose and busted upper lip, along with a gash along her forehead and a broken wrist. "

As Owen listened to the litany of injuries his sister had attained, he suppressed a roar of fury. "I will kill him with my bare hands. Where is he?"

Clayton shook his arm. "Don't go jumping to conclusions. And you're not killing anybody."

"Don't pull that cop bullshit. We both know who did this. Where. Is. He?" If he didn't find an outlet for all this adrenaline pumping through his body soon, he feared his heart would explode.

"You let me worry about finding Kane." Clayton jerked a thumb toward the ambulance. "Get your ass back to the hospital."

Owen stepped into Clayton's space and shoved his shoulder. "You think I'm backing down from this, Copper? You best think again. I want that fucker found, and if you don't, I will, and I can't be certain of the consequences."

"You might want to check that tone." Clayton planted his legs in a wide stance.

"Check *my* tone?" Owen rocked back on his heels, and then waved a hand at Clayton. "You're the one letting psychos beat helpless women. Harris told you he was mental."

"And I'm doing my job. Get your shit straight, Killion. And let go of my arm before I cuff your ass and drag you down to the station."

Owen shifted closer. His need to expel his anger at an object that could withstand the beating, rose to the forefront.

Rachel shouldered in between them. "What the hell's going on over here, Killion? Your sister needs you. Quit messing around."

A tense moment passed as he glared at Clayton.

Clayton's jaw clenched, but he stepped back. "I'll figure this out. If you see Xander Kane, do not engage, Killion. Let me handle this." He glanced at Rachel. "Harris, I'll need to see all your files on Xander Kane."

Owen stomped across the grass to the ambulance, leaving Rachel with Clayton.

A paramedic waved him off. "Sir, you can't be over here."

"Maude's my sister."

The guy nodded, and then moved aside.

"Owen?" Maude's voice sounded like her face was covered in pillows.

All his women were injured. Why didn't this coward come after him? Why prey on the weak? Why did this man get away with breaking all the rules of decency?

"Hey, don't talk, okay? I'm here." He hopped into the ambulance, and then took her hand.

"Sir, I'm sorry. You'll need to sit on the bench so we can do our jobs."

Maude tried to offer a reassuring smile through her cracked, bloody lip. Dried blood matted her hair against her cheek and forehead. The middle of her face was marred in red and black clumps and smears.

He set his rage from boil to simmer. One second, one minute, one hour at a time. Order had to exist in this constant round of chaos.

After a few minutes, the ambulance took off. The paramedics remained standing, hooking his sister up to an IV. Hearing each of his sister's moans and sniffles, he wished he could absorb her pain. What was she doing at Ember's place anyway? How could he protect these women if they didn't stay put?

Focus, Killion.

Game plans formed in his mind. He needed to set his players in position so he could do his job—protection.

He texted Rachel. *Meet me at ER. Will discuss game plan then.*

Next on his list, he called Jason. "I need you to come to Manchester General's ER."

"Why?"

"Maude's been attacked."

"I'm sorry, what did you say?"

"Stop fucking around, I need you at the ER. Call Bronco." He disconnected and held onto the edge of his seat as the ambulance made a tight turn.

The dark-haired paramedic sitting beside him bumped his shoulder. "You're Owen Killion, right?"

"Yeah." His head hurt. Hell his whole body hurt. He'd been wrong, so wrong. He'd do anything to get Ember back—to hold her safe and secure in his arms again. The words he'd said. He couldn't even think of his foul accusations. He'd been cruel and unyielding when deep inside he'd known the truth, hadn't he? He heaved a deep sigh and rubbed his aching temples.

"You all right, man?" The guy dressed in all blue shook his knee.

"No. I've taken too many hits today. Real life isn't like the playing field." He scratched his bristled jaw and huffed out a breath. "I have no idea what play to call."

"Your sister, right?" He jerked his thumb toward Maude.

"Yeah, and here I sit, perfectly fine." Owen closed his eyes and rested his head against the van's side panel.

"The police will catch who did this. Clayton's one of the best."

Owen just nodded. Not in the mood for idle chit-chat about Clayton, football, or anything else.

His mind was too frozen with fear. Fear of the unknown. Fear of asking for forgiveness. Fear of what he'd find when he arrived at the hospital. Would Ember even see him? Was she in some kind of coma? What was the extent of the injuries this time?

This time.

Wasn't that just the kicker, especially since he'd been the one to wound her earlier. And which wounds were worse—internal or external? One faded with time, but the other, those scars on the heart, remained unseen. The words he'd spoken couldn't be called back, and now he had to live with the consequences.

CHAPTER 40

As Xander slid the needle into the IV, he reached down and shifted his aching erection—the plunge so much like sex. Euphoria shivered across his skin as he absorbed the power of taking a life. His hand no longer shook as he removed the lethal injection of morphine.

The woman in the bed hadn't twitched since he'd entered the room. Unfortunate, as he'd hoped the image of him as the Grim Reaper would be the last thing her eyes would see. "I never should have trusted you. Deceitful bitch. Ember is mine." He scratched at the red wig on his head and twisted on his high heel as someone entered the room.

Alice tiptoed to his side and whispered, "What are you doing?"

"What am *I* doing? You're supposed to be keeping guard." He shifted his hand behind his back. "Go back to your position in the hall." He shooed her away with a flick of his fingers and waited until she left before returning his attention to his patient. "Good help is so hard to find these days. Don't you agree, Diana?"

As morphine trickled through Ember's mother's system, death would creep with silent steps. Her respiration would slow, then her overtaxed heart would slug along until it stopped beating altogether. Though Xander wished he could stay and watch as death overcame the stagnant sow, he needed to visit Ember's room.

That man's sister had interrupted before he could finish.

Hooking onto Alice's elbow, Xander tugged her down the corridor and into an unconscious man's room that he'd noted earlier was empty of visitors. The fossil on the bed had surely already seen one century pass, and would lie on this bed through another.

Xander sank onto a seat by the bed and used a magazine like a prop, adding to his "visitor" façade. He dangled his heel by his big toe. He'd had Alice bring some of her clothes. She was a tall, chubby one, like his Ember had once been, so her clothes fit him well enough to fool any passersby.

"So, we'll just wait in here?" Alice hovered next to him, pacing.

Her constant motion rattled his already frayed nerves. "Yes, we need to wait until a nurse comes by, and then you'll bring her in like I explained. All right?"

"I don't like this." Alice fiddled with her fingers and bit her bottom lip.

"Did you like living with your father? Perhaps you would like to move back home?" Fighting to remain calm, he glared at the silly girl before flipping the page. "I'm sure he'd welcome you back into his arms."

Her gaze flashed to his, and she shivered. "That's not fair."

"You chose to move in. I chose my compensation. Either that, or I'll send you back to Daddy."

"No, please." She knelt before him and grasped his hands. "I'll do as you ask."

"That's right, you will. Now quit whimpering. I hear someone coming. Peek out and see if it's a nurse."

Alice flounced over to the door, waved the nurse inside, and then shut the door behind her.

Xander smiled as Alice lifted the syringe and plunged.

"What's going on in—" The nurse's hand flew to her neck.

Xander shifted in his seat. Too bad, he found Alice repellent, or he'd use her to relieve his aching erection. Power was quite the aphrodisiac. "Good job, Alice." His whole body shivered in anticipation. "Hurry. Let's prop her in the bathroom." He grabbed the woman under the shoulders.

Alice stood still, just staring at the woman on the floor.

"What have I done?"

"Be quiet and grab her legs."

After they settled the sedated nurse on the toilet seat, they stripped off her clothes.

"These clothes are probably too small for you. You really should do something about your weight."

"I'm a healthy size nine, Xander," Alice huffed and shook out the shirt. "So yes, these clothes will fit. Will she be all right?"

Xander smacked Alice on the back of her head. "Don't question me. She is a means to an end. That is all you need to know."

"But—"

Xander grabbed her arm and wrenched it around her back. "I tire of your whimpers and questions. I will send you back to be Daddy's little plaything if you don't shut up and do as I say. One call is all it takes." He tightened his grip on her arm until he heard her hiss. "He's already been snooping around looking for you. Shall I tell him where you are? Leave the apartment and give him a key?"

Tears poured down Alice's cheeks. "No, please." She struggled to free her arm. "You're hurting me. I'll help. I'll help."

Xander shoved her out of the bathroom. "Quit sniveling and get dressed. We still have a lot to do." He adjusted the strap of his purse. He enjoyed this playtime. He'd never got to play dress-up as a kid. Too messy. Too dirty.

Once he got Ember home, he would play with her all the time. She'd be dressed in her costumes when he got home each night, anxious to hear every part of his day. She'd fix his dinner and settle beside him. He'd teach her how to please him as an ever-eager student. Together. They'd be together. No longer would he share her with another. Her indiscretion and disobedience was over.

Sure, he'd frightened her, but she had to understand he was the one in charge. He expected obedience.

Alice spun in a circle before him. "See, Xander, I told you the clothes would fit."

Alice's smart mouth would be dealt with, as well. Once she'd served her purpose.

"This next mission won't be as easy, but I'm counting on

you, love. Don't do anything but what I tell you, and everything will be fine." He brushed a stray hair behind her ear. "I'm sorry I was so harsh with you earlier. I guess I'm just excited Ember will finally see my home. Grab my pack and we'll go." Xander peered down the corridor before ushering Alice past him, and then shut the door.

Alice tucked in the nurse's shirt, which was patterned with colorful medicine bottles and syringes. "I've met Ember before, when she was leaving one of the counseling sessions. She's nice."

"Nice?" Xander scoffed as he clicked down the corridor to the elevators. "She hasn't been so nice lately, Alice. But she will be. That, I can promise."

# # #

After Owen settled his sister with a very unnerved Jason, he finally made his way to Ember's room. He ran a hand over his face and rubbed his eyes. Worry over Ember's condition had driven him to his knees already today, and he'd gladly fall again if she'd wake and accept his apology. He refused to lose her.

After releasing a shaky breath, he stepped into her room. Love and gratitude for this amazing woman settled deep in his heart as he watched her chest rise and fall. A huge bandage covered her forehead. Bruises marked her neck and arms. Leaning over the bed, he kissed her forehead. "I love you, Stems. Please, wake up." He brushed the barest kiss across her dry lips.

Flooded with remorse, he sighed and sank into a chair by her bed before resting his elbows on his knees and studying the cracks in the tile. What terrors had she suffered before her fall? Would she survive this time? Xander, her friend and confidant, had turned on her in the most heinous way—and so had he. So had every man in her life.

"Ember, baby, I'm so sorry." He lifted his gaze and took her hand. "You've been through so much. Too much. I'm going to make it all right though, Stems. Just come back to me." He choked back a sob. This girl was ten times stronger than he would ever be, and he loved her with everything he had. "I know now that love isn't enough. I'm sorry I failed you. Sorry I didn't trust. But I'll never do that again. Never." He kissed her palm, and then brushed her hand against his bristled chin.

Owen told her about his mom and his sister. Told her about Rachel's investigation of Xander. Through it all, she remained silent—unmoving. Lost in a world with no pain.

"Did I ever tell you about the time Bronco and I streaked through campus? Well, Bronco streaked through, I strolled." He chuckled at the memory. Story after story, he filled her in on every part of his life. Time passed, but seemed to remain still. Waiting. Waiting. Nurses came and went after offering reassuring smiles and words that all jumbled together in his mind.

Stroking a finger over her brow, he ached to see Ember's brown eyes again. Yearned to see her teasing smile as she wore nothing but his jersey and danced above him on his bed. Why hadn't he appreciated those times more? A simple moment of happiness, those rare glimpses of perfect bliss, they never seemed as important as they did in this moment, but that would change. He would change.

Back aching, he sank back in his chair and studied the hypnotic rise and fall of Ember's chest. Eyes half-closed, he started when his phone rang. He hurried to remove it from his pocket so the peal wouldn't disturb Ember. Not that she would wake.

Rachel was on the other end. "Killion, where you at?"

"With Ember. Why? What'd you find?"

"There was a message on Ember's answering machine from her mom that suggested she had information on Elliot's death, so we sent a patrolman to her room."

"And what'd she say?"

"Well, that's the problem, Killion. Dead people don't talk."

CHAPTER 41

Owen stared out the hospital window and banged his knuckles against his forehead. This whole situation had tumbled into a major cluster. Clayton and Rachel were on their way to the hospital. A guard was on his way over from the precinct, too, just in case Xander tried to enter Ember's room. "Come on, pretty-boy. I'd love to have you stop by."

"Who are you talking to?"

Owen jerked, and then turned to face the speaker. "Fahhh…you scared the living shit out of me."

A nurse stood right beside him with an odd, teeth-baring smile. Her shirt was pulled taut over her full chest. She shifted and itched at the elastic band on her tight pants.

The hairs on the back of his neck rose. He wasn't in the mood for advances from an over-excited Marauders fan.

She took his hand, and then ran her fingers up his arm. "Are you doing okay?"

"Uh, a nurse just came by and said Ember's doing fine." He pulled away from her grasp and rubbed the goosebumps on his arm. Offering comfort was one thing, but this chick pushed the personal space boundaries.

She shifted closer, brushing her body against his side. "Go ahead and sit while I check her vitals."

"Right." Grateful for the escape, he moved his chair around to the other side of the bed. His discomfort level hit another notch as he felt her at his back. He flashed her a tight-lipped smile as he settled in his chair.

She unhooked the stethoscope from around her neck, but dropped it at his feet. "Oops." As she bent to retrieve it, she steadied herself by pressing her hand against his groin.

What the hell? A stinging pain shot through his thigh.

"I'm sorry about this, but he gave me no choice." A bead of sweat trickled down her temple.

Gritting his teeth, he reared up and grabbed her wrist.

She struggled and kept her hand on his thigh.

A hot burn screamed through his leg. He twisted her wrist and shoved her away.

She yelped and landed on her butt, and then scrambled to her feet.

A needle stuck out of his leg. When he yanked it out, it broke off in his leg.

"You bisssshhh." His tongue seemed anchored in his mouth. All his muscles locked, and he collapsed against Ember's bed.

Sideways on the ground, muscles twitching with spasms, he watched a pair of ladies' shoes enter the room and halt. As he watched the door close, Owen fought to scream. His worst nightmare was playing in full-color right before his eyes.

The heels stepped close, and then stopped beside the white shoes of the nurse. "Good job, love."

Xander's voice pierced through his ears, straight through his brain, down to his heart. *Oh, God no. Where is that guard?*

Owen struggled to move, but couldn't. Paralyzed by a fucking needle. He tried shouting, but no sound passed his frozen vocal cords. Surely every blood vessel had burst in his face as he struggled to speak, to move.

Damn it. A string of curses and punishments for those shoe-wearing psychos ripped through his mind.

The nurse whispered, "I didn't give him all of it. It broke off in his leg."

"My special concoction will only keep the man down so long. We'll have to hurry."

Feet shuffled around the bed. A duffel bag dropped onto the ground. White shoes left, and then came back seconds later with a wheelchair.

And still, he couldn't move. Owen had underestimated

Xander's desire to win. The sadistic bastard had balls of steel, coming here. But, based on the guy's meticulous movements and calm voice, he wasn't worried in the least. Arrogant fucker thought he was smarter than everyone else. And what pissed Owen off the most was—he was right. Cold calculation had just scored big time.

Ember would never be safe from Xander's psychotic imaginings. Never.

And he'd failed to protect her. *Again.*

"Wheel her to the parking garage. I'll meet you there, dear. Do not speak to anyone," Xander snapped out.

"I'll handle it," the nurse snapped back. "Don't worry."

Both pairs of shoes followed the wheelchair to the door.

No, no, no, please, God, no. Where the hell is that guard? Where are Clayton and Rachel?

Then, he felt it. A burning tingling, and then his fingers twitched. Every ounce of power in his body focused on his hands. The fingers in his right hand bent, but his left hand remained useless.

"What are you doing?" Xander's contemptuous tone pushed Owen to try harder.

He clawed at the floor with his hand.

"Put that cap over her head, Alice." The heels clicked across the floor. "There, that's better. Do I have to do everything? Now go."

Owen's entire arm shook as he braced his right hand on the floor.

White heels clattered across the tile and stopped in front of his face. The shoe's tip touched his nose.

"Look at you." Xander's patronizing voice filled the room. "Frozen in time. No need to fret, the drug will wear off shortly. But this, however, may last a little longer."

The heel crashed against his face.

Black-out.

# # #

The taste of blood lined the back of Owen's throat. Sharp pain ricocheted from his nose to his forehead. Rage and fear meshed with the taste of copper. He swallowed, loving every earthy tinge as it traveled down his throat.

A fierce argument assaulted his ears, adding to the agony throbbing through every muscle in his body. *What kind of drug did that walking pharmacy give me?*

"Absolutely not. You are not going to that house and facing that madman alone." Bronco's voice rumbled through the room.

"It is my job. It's what I do, big guy, so back off."

Ah, Rachel, of course. Why were they here, and not looking for Ember? He had to move. Get up. Fight past the pain.

Owen tried wetting the inside of his dry mouth with his equally dry tongue. "If you're here, who's with my mom?"

"Oh good, you're awake." Another pair of shoes appeared in his vision. Shoes were really starting to piss him off.

"Chewy and Jake are with your mom." Bronco was smart enough to crouch. "Chewy was pissed he couldn't come to the hospital. Thinks he should be in charge of the rescue mission."

Rachel scoffed. "As if."

"Lady, you aren't—"

"Enough! Where's Ember?" This arguing was getting them nowhere. "Bronco, help me up. How long was I out?" Dizzy, his thigh screaming, he fought through the pain long enough stand. He wobbled for a moment, then stumbled to the toilet and heaved what was surely everything he'd ever eaten. He thought of every kind of torture—every kind of pain—he would inflict upon Xander.

The gloves were definitely off.

After rinsing out his mouth, he stumbled back into the room. Moving, keep moving. Get the blood circulating again. No pain. No pain.

Bronco grabbed his chin. "Might have a broken nose."

"How long?" Owen slapped away Bronco's hand and wrenched the needle out of his leg.

"You were out fifteen, maybe twenty, minutes. What the hell happened?"

"Xander had this nurse helping him. She stabbed me with something. I couldn't move. I couldn't..." He whirled a chair across the room. Chest heaving, he growled out, "I can't let him win."

Rachel stood before him and clasped his shoulders. "I need you present, Killion. Shake it off. I have an idea of where Xander took her—his aunt's house. He's been there a lot lately."

"How would you know?" Bronco tugged her arm off Owen's shoulder.

Hands braced on her hips, she shot a glare at Bronco. "I'm being paid to know." After a blatantly irritated eye-roll, she headed for the door. "Let's go, Killion. I'll drive. We'll grab you a Red Bull, or something with an intense amount of caffeine on the way out. Maybe that will get your blood pumping."

Owen followed her out the door. "My blood pressure is fine, Harris. We don't have time to stop."

"If you two think you can leave me behind, you best think again." Bronco stormed down the corridor behind him.

"This isn't your fight, Bronco." Owen shook his head.

Bronco jabbed his shoulder. "Who the hell are you talking to?"

"Let him come, Killion." Rachel blasted open the door to the stairs. "We need an outside man."

"Outside man..." Bronco mumbled.

"Shouldn't we call Clayton?" Holding close the terror in his heart while refusing to accept the discomfort in his body, Owen focused on each step. He had to keep moving. Each step brought him closer to Ember.

"We'll call Clayton once we're there. Flashing lights and sirens would spook this guy." Rachel glanced over her shoulder. "That's the last thing we need."

Owen bumped shoulders with Bronco as they exited into the lobby.

He let Rachel drive, knowing in his mental state, he'd break every traffic law known to man. And a police chase through the city streets would only slow them down.

Owen refused to consider what the freak was doing to his woman. Refused to consider that the mental case had already...

No.

Ember would not die thinking no one loved her.

She would not die.

Owen closed his eyes and prayed for one more chance on the line.

One more play before the lights went out.

CHAPTER 42

"It's that one with the red brick and round staircase." Rachel drove past the house, made a left at the next street, then turned down an alley and parked her ancient Ford Taurus behind a metal garbage bin.

Owen opened his door and met Rachel in the shadows at the back of her car.

"I have to grab some tools." She popped the lock on her trunk. "Bronco, we need you stationed outside of the house. Give me your phone."

For a second, he hesitated, but handed it over.

"I'll program Clayton's number. As soon as we breach the back door, call him. Tell him where we are, but no lights, no sirens. Clear?"

"Crystal." Bronco took back his phone and shoved it in his front jean pocket.

The chill October pre-dawn air did nothing to cool Owen's nerves. Yellow eyes glowed from some nocturnal creature hiding under the wheeled-metal garbage container. In that moment, Owen understood feral. His entire body thrummed with survival instincts. The distinct click of a gun clip locking into place echoed down the alley.

"Owen, I know what you're thinking, but you've got to let me lead. You're of no use to Ember if you're thinking with your heart instead of your head. Clear?"

"Oh, I'm way past crystal clear." Owen stayed in the

building's shadow as he made his way down the alley to Xander's aunt's house in the downtown historic district.

Bronco broke off and hid within the cover provided by a copse of trees.

At the house, only one light shone downstairs, and another in a room on the backside. They couldn't see any other angle as they made their way along the side fence, and then crossed the yard to the back door.

Following behind Rachel, Owen froze as the wooden steps cracked and creaked under his weight. The sound was like cannon shot across the still morning. Four am may seem like a good time for burglary, but the bustle and noise during the day would undoubtedly provide better cover.

Rachel whipped out a pin light and a black leather case filled with slim metal tools with various hooks on the ends. "Lock picking kit," she whispered. "Never leave home without it." Within seconds she had the door unlocked.

Owen held his breath as he watched her twist open the door handle. *Don't let there be an alarm.* Couldn't just one thing go their way?

Rachel squeezed his arm and met his gaze, then mouthed, three, two, one before swinging open the door.

Nothing.

All quiet.

Her long exhale proved she had worried over the same.

The door opened to the kitchen. A faint mint aroma filled the air. The scent reminded Owen of the tea Ember drank at night. A quick glance at the stove showed a teakettle on the burner with two ripped tea bag packets on the counter.

Rachel tapped his arm and lifted an index finger to her lips. She pointed to his feet while slipping off her shoes.

He followed her lead while every instinct screamed to storm this castle and reclaim what was rightfully his.

With her gun raised, Rachel moved further into the room, stopping every few moments to listen.

An instrumental played upstairs, which sounded a lot like "Little Red Riding Hood" by Sam the Sham and the Pharaohs. Trust that mental case to play an appropriately creepy song.

Owen's cohort halted by the kitchen door. Her shoulders

rose and fell as she took a deep breath before stepping into the hall.

When he followed her, he halted when the wood floor creaked beneath his feet.

Rachel glared and murmured, "Don't step. Shuffle."

Sliding down the hall, they peeked into each room. Everything was concealed under white slipcovers.

Rachel halted at the bottom of a winding staircase.

Unprepared for her quick stop, Owen jostled what was likely a table covered with glass vases. The tinkling clatter reverberated through the room. He received an angry glower from Harris. His breathing suspended as he waited for Xander to rush down the stairs with guns blazing.

Luckily, the music blaring from one of the rooms up there likely hid his clumsiness. With that hope in mind, Owen pressed his mouth close to Rachel's ear. "He won't hear us with the music so loud. Go."

Still cautious, Rachel took her time climbing the stairs.

He didn't think she blinked the entire time as she kept her gaze focused on the landing.

At the top of the staircase, the upper level broke off in two directions. Since the music was coming from the left, they crept that way. Each door was shut. Light poured from beneath the room at the end of the hall.

Rachel reached for the handle.

The music stopped.

She remained frozen with her hand on the handle.

Owen heard her gulp. Though, how that was possible over the racing of his heart, he'd never know.

After a long moment of silence, Rachel opened the door and stepped through—her gun raised and ready.

Damn, the girl was brave.

She waved him through, but grabbed his arm and pressed him behind her. Side-stepping so her back faced a corner, she kept him in place with a tight grip on his arm.

Owen glanced around the room. Long red silk curtains were drawn. A mini fridge hummed in the corner. A stack of paperback books sat in a chair and a small flat screen TV was set up at the end of the bed—the occupied bed.

A lump was under the shiny red comforter—Ember. A wave of relief rushed through his body. Only her head appeared from under the covers. He couldn't decide if he was glad she was still unconscious, or if that worried him even more. Or was she unconscious? Maybe she was—

No, don't go there. He stepped forward.

Rachel shot a glare over her shoulder and dug her nails deeper into his arm. She shook her head and mouthed, *No.*

Steps sounded across the wooden floor. The same girl that had stabbed his leg earlier came out of what must be the bathroom.

Rachel trained her weapon on the girl. "Stop where you are. Where is Xander Kane?"

The girl yelped, and a wet washcloth slipped from her hand. "No. You can't be here." Eyes wide, she raised her hand, palm up between them. "Leave. He's insane. You have to—"

A suppressed pop shot through the room.

The nurse's eyes went wide as a red bloom appeared on her chest. She crumpled to the ground.

Xander stood behind her with a silenced gun raised in his hand. He was dressed like a woman, still wearing those high-heels.

Owen surged forward. "You motherfu—"

"Stop, or I'll kill her right now." Xander pointed his weapon at Ember.

Although it went against everything in his nature, Owen stilled.

Rachel shifted forward and lifted her weapon. "Kane, put down the gun."

Xander flashed a wicked grin. "I'll be put under psychiatric care, you know. No matter what I do, I'll be found criminally insane. I won't go to prison, no matter how many people I kill—Elliot, that fat bitch, Diana Brooks, Alice. I know how to play at insanity. But that's only if they catch me. If not, I'll creep up and take her when you least expect it. No need to wonder about that." He scratched at the red wig on his head, tilting it askew.

Owen considered his options. Could he take down Xander without getting shot? What would Harris do?

"At the care facility, I'll be surrounded by patients and, eventually, after receiving my skilled counseling, all the patients will improve. Then the administrators will have no choice but to hire me on as staff. So you see, it's a win-win. I win. You lose. Win-win." The gun waved in time with his words, and then he heaved a deep sigh as he unscrewed the silencer from his weapon. "I've decided Ember isn't special enough. I had such high hopes for her, but she let me down, time and time again. So, what do you do when you create something faulty?" He leveled the gun at Ember's head. "You destroy it."

"Xander Kane, drop your weapon." Clayton stood in the doorway, gun raised.

Xander smiled. "Well, if it isn't the neighbor. Some cop you are, letting crimes occur while you rested your head against your pillow."

"Kane, I'm giving you to the count of three to place your weapon on the ground. Harris, stand down." Clayton kept his gaze on Xander. "One."

"What are all you people doing in here? Don't you know you'll get the place dirty?" Xander's high-pitched voice screeched across the room.

"Two."

Rachel groaned, "Oh, hell."

Xander looked right at him with ice in his gaze. "I've still won."

A cold vise clamped over Owen's heart. *Won what?*

Clayton shouted, "No!"

Xander raised the gun to his forehead and pulled the trigger.

An ear-ringing blast resonated through Owen's body. The unique smell of gunpowder roasted through his nostrils, and the only sound he could make out was a thin ringing.

Xander's body crumpled to the ground.

Clayton rushed into the room and rounded the bed.

Bronco hustled through the door behind him and glanced at Rachel who, with a shaky hand, lowered her weapon to her side.

Owen watched in a daze as Clayton kicked the gun away from Xander's body.

Bronco shook his arm. "Owen. Owen! Check on Ember."

No other words could have focused him more. He stumbled across the room to Ember's bedside.

Still and pale, her eyes remained closed.

He wrapped her icy body in his arms. *Why was she so cold? Was that his blood, or hers?* "Oh, my God. I think she's bleeding."

Ember jerked against him and moaned in pain.

"Ember, baby, can you hear me?" He couldn't have come this far to lose her now. As he lightly shook her arms, he fought back a crashing wave of panic. "Stems, please wake up."

Her weak hands struggled to fight him off.

That's when he saw it—a cut leaking blood from her right wrist.

Her breath rattled in her chest, and she took in short pants of air.

"Move out of the way, Killion." Clayton knocked him aside. "It's horizontal. Rip your shirt and tie it around her wrist."

"How the hell did you get here so fast?"

Clayton narrowed his eyes, jaw tight, before turning and waving over an EMT. "Bronco texted me from the hospital. We'll be discussing that in more detail later, Killion."

EMTs and police officers filled the room. Rachel was on her phone. Bronco stood beside her at the door. The police were asking him questions as they pointed at the poor girl on the floor.

Overcome by the cacophony, words became indistinct. This insane vision couldn't be real. Impossible to believe one man had caused so much damage.

Then, a soft whisper became the only sound in his world.

Owen met Ember's gaze. Fear blazoned from her deep-brown depths, and tears trickled down her face. She blinked, each glimpse of her beautiful eyes shorter than the last, as if her lids were too heavy.

"No!" He shouted, and grabbed her face between his hands. "You will not die on me. Stay with me. Eye-to-eye, Stems. Keep those eyes on me."

She whispered words that tore through his heart—words she'd repeated over and over since the first day they'd met. Words he had denied her only hours before. "I'm sorry."

Then her gaze glassed-over, and her head lolled back in his hands.

Owen closed his eyes and whispered, "No, Stems. I'm the one who's sorry." He released her back into a paramedic's arms, lost in a daze as he watched them carry her from the room.

He'd considered the possibility that he'd lose her.
But not like this.

CHAPTER 43

A loud moan startled her awake.

Fear kept her paralyzed until Ember realized *she* had made
the sound. With wide eyes, she quickly inspected the room
without shifting her head—too afraid to move or make another
sound.

Where am I?

Where's Xander?

On that thought, she shot upright. Pain lanced through her
head. Taking short breaths, she fought back nausea. The bandage
on her head crinkled. She reached up and patted the wide binding.
What had happened? She remembered struggling for her life, but
then nothing.

Oh, God.

What had Xander done? What kind of hospital was she in?
Breathing through the pain, she gripped the blanket closer to her
chest. Another quick glance around the room reassured her a little.
Seemed like a regular hospital room.

Her pea-sized bladder said good morning, or was it good
evening? What time was it anyway? For that matter, what day of
the week?

Had Xander been caught? Did they know he was responsible
for her attack? She shivered when she remembered the crazed
look of pride and possession in his eyes as he'd stood in her
bathroom doorway. Why had she never before noticed his
insanity?

After taking a deep breath, she shifted her legs over the side of the bed and waited. She tried to guess the necessary steps to get to the bathroom—maybe six?

A realization occurred when she shifted to stand. She was attached to a catheter. *Gross.* How many days had she been out? Dizziness waved through her, and a film of sweat covered her skin. She closed her eyes, lowered her head, and caught sight of the bandage on her right wrist. *Great.* What new injury had she sustained there?

Oh, Earl Grey, I need you. Where art thou, my caffeinated master?

She should compose some kind of love song to the man so she could sing the tune at times like these. Loopy didn't even begin to describe how she felt.

Movement outside the rectangular-shaped window in her door caught her eye.

Owen was there, talking to Clayton.

Where was Xander?

Shivers racked her body.

Owen slashed his hands in the air. He pointed a finger at Clayton, and then ran a hand through his hair.

Clayton waved both hands in a downward motion.

Was he trying to placate Owen? A brunette stood at Clayton's side. Why was Owen so agitated? What were they arguing about? Was it whether or not to drag her to the police station? Did he still think her guilty of robbing his home? How had she gotten to the hospital?

Light-headed from all her unanswered questions, she slumped back onto the bed. Tears trickled down her cheeks and she whispered, "I'm so tired of being weak."

Just that small glimpse of Owen reminded her that while her body may be bruised, her heart was absolutely broken. Biting down on her blanket, she held back a sob. A few tears she could handle, but not a full-blown breakdown.

Why was he here? Hadn't he done enough? Must he witness her continued downfall? She could never mend if he was in the vicinity. She closed her eyes and dreamed of escaping all the men in her life.

Her brother had committed suicide, her father accused her of conspiracy, Owen thought her a liar, and Xander had tried to kill her.

"I just want to leave. I don't want to be here anymore." She sniffled and wiped her nose on the stupid blanket.

Another town. Another job.

Maybe she'd even change her name.

Ember no longer suited her. She was all burned out.

No longer a living flame.

#

"So, you believe the girl dressed as a nurse was one of his patients?" Owen scrubbed at the stubble on his chin. When was the last time he'd slept? It was going on four o'clock now, so almost twenty-four hours.

Clayton nodded. "Her name was Alice Flemming. Our detectives found her things in the spare bedroom of Xander's apartment. Her parents have been notified. Xander must have manipulated her. We don't know how yet, but we'll figure it out. We assume the clothes Xander was wearing were hers, and the nurse in Ember's mother's room ID'ed Alice from a photo." His jaw clenched. "I can't believe the guy was right under our noses the whole time. He orchestrated everything."

Owen heaved a weary sigh. "One good thing to come from this is, now Ember will know her brother didn't leave her. She always knew he hadn't committed suicide, and she was right. Though, I'm sure she'd rather have him back."

"She'll need time to take all this in. Take it easy on her, will ya, Killion? She's a rare woman." Clayton jabbed his shoulder.

"Talking about me again." Rachel wobbled three coffee cups and one soda bottle in her hands as she returned from her caffeine run. "I know I'm one of those fine, rare ladies." She winked. "No need to fight over me, boys."

Bronco scoffed. "Need more meat on those bones if we're going to scrap over anything."

Harris flipped him the bird. "How's Ember doing? She wake up yet?"

Owen took the soda Bronco handed over. "She's unconscious still. Probably for the best."

"Well, Rach, you ready to head back downtown?" Clayton bumped her shoulder with his. "Got a nice stack of paperwork to muddle through. Since you decided to head out on your own, the least you can do is help me work through the mess."

Bronco frowned. "She needs some rest, man. Do your own paperwork."

Owen studied Rachel. She seemed to be holding up well, after almost shooting a man. "Rachel, I want you to know how grateful I am for all you've done for Ember and my family. I fully believe Xander would have killed Ember had we not arrived when we did. His intent was clear." He wrapped the petite thing in a tight hug. "If you ever need anything, I'm here. I don't say things like this to just anyone. You're in my circle now, and that's the end of it."

"Thanks, Big-O." Rachel's voice was muffled against his chest.

Owen just nodded. He never thought he'd wish for another man's death, but he had. He wasn't proud of the feeling, but the man had injured his woman and killed her brother and mother. Not to mention what the crazy man had done to his own sister and mother. Yeah, Xander had deserved to die. The horrific vision replayed in his mind of the gun being pointed at Ember's head. And the shock in young Alice's eyes as she fell to the ground was tattooed across his mind forever.

"Killion, let her breathe." Bronco eased Rachel out of his arms.

"You going to be all right, Slim?" Owen patted her head. "You saved Ember's life."

"Lost one, though." Rachel shook her head, and then hooked her arm through Clayton's. "Take me downtown, officer."

Bronco pulled her away from Clayton. "Come on, Harris, I'll drive you to the station."

"Who the hell do you think you are? I don't appreciate being manhandled."

"Uh-huh. I'll keep that in mind."

"And another thing, don't think you can herd me around like catt—"

Owen tuned them out as Bronco and Rachel continued to argue on the way to the elevators.

"Hey, Killion," Bronco hollered down the corridor, his phone against his ear. "Your mom wants you to 'answer your damn phone' and come down to the third floor to see your sister."

"I'll head down in a minute." Owen waved him off, and then turned back to Clayton. "Clayton, can you—"

"Yes, I'll stay with Ember until you get back. Doc did say she should come around any time. I imagine she'll be pretty confused at first."

"She lost a lot of blood. Every time I think of all that blood...the blood on Alice's shirt...the blood from Ember's wrist...what was wrong with that guy, anyway?" He combed his fingers through his hair and glanced at Clayton. "How do you deal with that kind of stuff day in and day out? No wonder cops are assholes."

"We're only assholes because dumb shits like you take off on their own while trying to play the hero."

Owen chuckled and bumped against Clayton's shoulder. "I believe Rachel is the heroine in this tale, and Ember, of course."

"Bump me again, Killion, and you'll see a real asshole. Up close and personal. I'm half-ready to haul your ass down to the station." Clayton studied him for a moment, and then scrubbed both hands over his face before jamming them in his pockets. "Ember may need counseling."

"Oh hell, no. Any pampering or talking she needs, she's got me."

"Right, 'cause you're Mr. Understanding."

CHAPTER 44

The glare of sunlight scored across Ember's eyes. Was it morning? How much work had she missed? Millicent was going to kill her. Not to mention the medical bills. Her stomach churned, and she bit her bottom lip to hold back the rising nausea. What was her deductible again? What kind of life was waiting outside these hospital doors? Focusing on mundane matters kept her from considering the man in the seat beside her, or his heavy hand clasped on her arm over the hospital bed rail.

Owen slept in the chair beside her bed. He must have been really tired, because he was snoring loud enough to rattle the building, and his mouth could've sucked in a full squadron of flies—or spiders. After the way he'd last spoken to her, he deserved to choke on at least one spider. Lack of caffeine had turned her evil, or at least, she'd use that as her excuse.

Ember studied his face. What did he want? Why was he here?

Having him in the room offered a much-needed sense of safety. It'd be nice if he stayed, but maybe he was only here to make sure she didn't escape. The only thing that mattered at this point was, as long as he was here, Xander wouldn't return. She hated this constant heart-stopping panic, hated each memory of the horrors Xander had visited upon her body. When would her fear end? Could she ever again take a shower alone? Or even enter a bathroom? Maybe she'd get a dog. A Bassett hound. The least vicious dog ever, yes, but they had a pretty deep bark.

She'd pick a wiggly, long-eared pup and together, they'd go

on all kinds of adventures. Definitely a female puppy. No more male species for her. She wanted a companion who would be happy to see her every day. Deep brown eyes and a wagging tail were all she needed at the end of each day.

Owen stretched and caught her studying him. "Ember. You're awake."

His voice was still raspy from sleep. God, he was sexy stretching like that, his body so strong, muscles bulging in his arms. "Yeah." She could barely croak out the word. "Could I have something to drink?"

"Sure. How long have you been awake?" He poured a glass of water and handed it over. His hand was a little shaky, and he spilled water on her hospital gown. "Sorry." As he wiped it off, he brushed against her breast. "Oh..crap...sorry."

Her traitor body responded to his touch. *Too bad, double D's, he's no longer interested.*

She drank the entire glass of water without stopping. "Is...is...um...is Xander around?"

"No, Stems, he isn't." His hands curled into fists.

"Oh...do you know where he is?" She cleared her throat and glanced at her empty cup—her now half-crumpled cup. "This water is really good. Can I have some more?"

"Yes, I know where Xander is, and yes, you can have more water." Owen stood, and then removed the destroyed cup from her hand. "Let's get you better first. Then we'll talk, all right?"

"Talk about what?" She eased away from his touch. Why did she have to get better before he'd tell her what happened? Concentrating on where the pain emanated strongest, she fought to understand what had happened to her body.

"Ember, you just woke up from—"

"I woke up yesterday."

His eyes widened. "You did?"

"For a little bit. I don't know what's wrong with me. I'm so tired. Do you think I could have some tea?" She plucked at the bandage on her wrist. "What are all these bandages from? What happened?"

"When I get you home, I'll explain everything. You—"

"That's not fair." She pounded a fist against the bed. "I deserve to know what happened." She stilled. Did she really want to know? What if it was something truly horrific? "Do you know about Xander? He was the one, Owen. In my house that night, the attacker was Xander. Then he was in my bathroom, and there was hair in the sink, and I tried to get away…he was saying all these things and I…and I…couldn't…I couldn't—"

"Sh-sh-shhh, calm down." Owen lifted her hand and kissed her palm. "We know what happened. He's gone, and will never hurt you again."

"But how?" Her stomach rolled and growled. Panic coursed through her system, and a clammy chill covered her skin. The not knowing frightened her more than anything else. What had Xander done? "Owen, please, I need to know."

"You should probably eat something." Shifting his gaze, Owen brushed a hand across the top of her head. "Can we give it a bit? At least until a doctor comes in or something." He glanced at the door, as if hoping reinforcements would enter.

"Owen, please, what happened to me?"

He sighed and shuffled over to the window.

Real nice when her world sat on the edge of an abyss. "Wouldn't you want to know? If you were wrapped up in a hospital bed, wouldn't you want to know how you got there?"

Owen was silent for a moment before he turned. "All right, but if my telling you about Xander gets too much, say the word and I'll stop."

"Thank you." Ember pushed the button on the bed to raise her back.

"Oh good, you're awake." A nurse stepped into the room. "How are you feeling?"

The nurse spent an interminable moment looking her over, doing whatever nurses do. And the entire time, Ember kept her gaze on Owen. He made a great study of whatever fascinating scene there was outside the window. She couldn't see anything but buildings, so she didn't understand what he found so compelling. She thanked the nurse as she left, then turned her attention back to Owen. "See, she says I'm fine. Now tell me."

Owen scrubbed both hands through his hair before turning and meeting her gaze. "Remember, though, too much, and I'll stop."

Ember nodded and straightened in the bed.

For a moment, he paced beside the window. "I'm not sure...the whole story is so messed up, Stems. I have no idea where to begin."

"Start from when you kicked me out of your mother's room."

Owen halted in his march, frowned, and then scratched his head. "Ember, I'm so—"

"I don't want to go there now, please, just what happened after I left." She hoped the nurse hurried back with her tea. This story was obviously going to require a triple dose of Dr. Grey.

"After you left." He stopped and glanced at her.

She gestured for him to continue.

"Fine." He shook his head and huffed. "After you left, Rachel came by. She'd found some suspicious info on Xander. We asked Clayton to stop by Xander's place, and then yours. When Clayton got to your place, he found my sister knocked out on the floor, and you were in the bathroom with a head injury."

"Maude?" Her headache went nuclear, and she licked her suddenly dry lips. "What happened to Maude?"

"She came by your place because she wanted you to know she didn't believe any of your father's lies." He met her gaze and cleared his throat. "Xander must have attacked her on his way out."

"Oh, Owen, I'm so sorry." Ember clenched the bed railing. "Is she all right?"

"Feisty as ever. She wants to see you. Both her and Mom have been worried half to death."

"And your mom, is she better?"

"Yeah, she is. She's back home. So..."

"Good."

"Good." Owen cleared his throat again. "So anyway, after that I rushed to the hospital, got Maude settled, and then came to your room. Xander had a friend helping him. She was dressed as a nurse and came in here and she...ah...she...um...stabbed me."

"What?" Ember shot upright, ready to rumble. Her pain was one thing, but hurt someone she loved—the gloves were off. "Who stabbed you? Where is she?"

Owen flashed a tight-lipped grin. "She helped Xander take you to his aunt's house."

"I don't care about that. What did she do to you? I don't see any Band-Aids." Ember gave him a quick once-over.

"She got me with a needle, Stems. The shot rendered me immobile. Pissed me off more than anything. I didn't realize how diabolical Xander could be, or how desperate he was to secure you."

"But he did." She longed to say, *I'm sorry*, but understood those words were the last he wished to hear.

After releasing a heavy breath, he nodded. "Yeah, he did."

"Oh." Her world suddenly seemed a little woozy. She blinked, and then refocused on Owen, her rock. Her center.

"Rachel and I followed him, though, and then we brought you back to the hospital." He poured another glass of water, and handed it over. "Want me to see where the nurse is with your tea?"

What? My tea?

Something wasn't adding up here. While true, she'd been unconscious for however long and not all her circuits were firing, she still knew he was leaving out a ton.

"I'll go see if any of your nurses are down at the station." He avoided her gaze as he headed for the door.

"Hold on a second, Mr. Run-off-for-my-tea." She waved a finger. "You said, *and then we brought you back?* And then?" Glaring as she beckoned with her index finger, she stifled the urge to tackle him, then hold him down until he revealed all. "Why do I feel like there's a whole line of dot-dot-dot in between the *and* and the *then?* Would you rather I fill in those dots with my imagination, or would you like to come back here and finish the story? Obviously, you think I'm some weak willow. And just as obviously, you are wrong. I survived. I am here. Now the only question that remains is—*WHAT DID I SURVIVE!?*"

"Ember, please calm down."

"Owen, do you have any idea the amount of pain I am in right now, and how much screaming adds to that pain? But I'll do it if you don't answer my question *RIGHT NOW.*"

"Fucking hell." Owen pounded his fist against the wall, but remained standing by the door, jaw clenched tight. "Xander wanted to keep you as his own, like a trophy or a doll...or a pet...whatever. We tracked him to that house, and he did and said…things."

Anger reached a boiling point, and she was so close to leaping out of the bed and pounding against Owen's chest until he just spat the truth out. "Did and said things? Things? What did he do to me, Owen? What did he do? Did he rape me, is that why you can't say it, because I need to…" A sob erupted, but she choked it back. "I need to know."

"Oh, baby, no. Not that." In two steps, Owen had her in his arms and he rocked her back and forth. "He killed the nurse right in front of me, Stems." His voice cracked a little on the words. "And he said… he said… he admitted to killing your brother, and before he took you from the hospital…he killed your mother."

Ember released her grip on his back. Numbness tingled from her fingers to her toes. Shock kept the flow of tears at bay. "My brother? B-b-b-but why?" Movement, she needed to move. The room became nothing but a filmy blur.

"Rachel believes he fed off your angst. Each chapter of his book on your life dealt with your traumas. Apparently, he didn't have enough pages."

After taking a deep breath, she belted out. "He killed my brother for a book? Did my mother know?"

"I can't answer that, but you did say she rarely left the trailer."

"He killed everyone for a book about *me*?" She glanced at the door, ready to run, to escape this nightmare, these words pouring out of Owen's mouth. Why had she asked for the truth? And why was the truth suddenly so obvious? Who was she that she hadn't seen their duplicity? Could she have saved her brother, if she'd just opened her eyes? What other truths was she missing?

"Ember—"

"No, no, no, no, no. I need…would you please…please, leave." A living plague, a blight on all who knew her, that was who she was. Everyone she knew, everyone she touched fell into despair and death, but no more—never again.

"I'm not leaving you. Not now." Owen brushed a finger down her cheek and across her upper lip.

Ember turned away. "I want you to go." She'd brought death into his life, and she wouldn't allow him to stay in her living, horror-filled world.

"I told you it was too soon to tell you," he grumbled and lifted her chin to meet his gaze.

No, she wouldn't get lost in the comfort offered in those brown depths. He'd suffered enough because of her. And her brother...had died...because...because...

No.

No!

"Get out." Ember threw her water pitcher, her cup, and her pillow. "I left. I did as you asked and left. Do the same for me. Just go!"

Owen remained by her beside, his hand wrapped around her uninjured wrist. "Ember—"

"Enough harsh words have been spoken between us. I don't want there to be any more. Just leave." Each word was forced past her clenched teeth. Each word kept the torrent of tears from releasing. *Wait until he leaves. Don't break now.*

"What's going on in here, Owen?" A brunette who looked like a living Tinker Bell fluttered into the room. "I could hear yelling all the way down by the elevators."

Owen shifted and scratched his chin. "I told her some things."

"Things?" The pixie shot him a glare.

"Don't you start in on me, too."

The brunette shot her a glance, and then tugged on Owen's arm. "Come with me."

Ember heard snippets of their whispered argument.

"What did you tell her...you *WHAT*..."

"...she wanted...I don't...fine...Xander is...*SHE ASKED*."

"You know what, Killion?" The pixie's voice rose. "She's right, just leave."

"Fine." Owen stuck his head back in the room. "I'm grabbing some breakfast, but I'm coming back later. Harris, *do not* leave her here alone."

"Aye, aye, captain." She saluted him and slapped his butt.

Ember studied the girl as she came to stand by her bed. "You must be the detective."

"You must be one, too. Look at you, figuring all that out after being comatose for days." Rachel gestured toward the empty chair. "Mind if I sit?"

Ember shrugged. "I'd rather be alone. I don't mean to be rude, but I don't want you here."

"I brought you some tea."

"Thank you, but I'd still rather be alone." On the verge of erupting like an overdue volcano, Ember watched in amazement as Rachel settled into the nearby seat. For a detective, the women seemed a tad clueless.

"I'm Rachel Harris. Owen hired me to look into some things. I can't begin to imagine how you're feeling right now, so let's hear it. Scream if you need to. I won't mind."

"Let's hear it?" Ember huffed out a laugh.

"I did bring you tea." Rachel handed over the steaming peace offering with a bland smile.

Ember took the lid off the cup and breathed in the rising steam. She blew on the top, and then took a tentative sip. An overload of information was stacked in a jumbled pile in her mind. But only one thought penetrated all others. Her brother had died because of her. How many ways could a heart break? Did it splinter, crack, or simply die slowly in portions while turning from thriving red to a mottled black with each rip and tear? She breathed in, then out, and focused on finishing her tea.

Rachel flicked on the TV.

Ember wiped at the tears falling down her cheeks before pushing the mute button for the TV on her side panel. "I have questions."

Rachel nodded then clasped her bandaged hand in her tiny, pink-tipped fingers. "I have answers."

They talked for hours, cried, laughed, shooed away Owen and his friends, and cried some more. Rachel didn't judge or pull any punches. She was like a hummingbird, flitting from one topic to the next, but you were happy to follow her along because she hypnotized you with her vibrant wings.

"It's all my fault." Ember sniffled and pulled the last tissue from the box.

"I live by this quote from George Bernard Shaw: 'You don't learn to hold your own in the world by standing on guard, but by attacking and getting well hammered yourself.'"

Ember scoffed and shook her head. "I think I've been hammered enough."

"Oh, I'm sure. I've seen Owen." Rachel smirked and waggled her brows.

They collapsed into giggles.

"I shouldn't be laughing, or smiling. Not when Elliot can't do the same."

"Ember, you are one of the bravest women I've ever met. I believe in you. I'd like to call you friend, if I may."

"I'd like that." She sniffled into the tissue.

"Good, because I was sort of wondering…do you think I could interview you for my next book?"

Ember stared at Rachel, narrowed her eyes, and then threw a scrunched tissue at her head.

"Gross." Rachel laughed as she sank back in her chair. "I'm sorry. I was truly only joking."

"Gotcha." Ember laughed, and then groaned. Her ribs ached. Her face ached. "Absolutely no interviews. No more stories about my life. I'm going into seclusion."

CHAPTER 45

"We can stop by the drug store on the way to my place." Rachel dug through her purse and pulled out her keys.

"What's going on?" Owen sauntered in wearing workout pants and a ragged T-shirt with some shoe brand plastered across his left pec.

Ember's heart sank. She really didn't have the mental capacity to fight right now. She'd hoped to escape before he arrived. For the sake of honesty, she did agree she'd been a little unfair earlier, screaming down the hospital walls with her frustrations and fears. But, damn it, he hadn't trusted her. You don't say you love someone, and then walk away. But maybe, just maybe, they should try again without the shroud of Xander hovering above them like an ominous blanket of death.

Rachel patted her shoulder. "Ember is staying with me for a while."

"The hell she is." Owen charged across the room. "What are you talking about, Harris? She's coming home with me." Hands braced on his hips, he shifted to glare at Rachel.

Ember slanted her gaze to his high-dollar tennis shoes. For a man, he sure had tons of shoes. Did he get them free from companies? What size was he, anyway? Definitely a bigger size than her brother. She closed her eyes at the thought. Poor Elliot. He'd done nothing wrong except be her brother, and because of that, there would always be an empty hollow in her heart that nothing would ever fill. No one would ever convince her that his death wasn't partially her fault.

"You have no idea what she needs." Rachel shook her keys at Owen. "And you didn't trust her. She needed you to believe in her, and you just snubbed her."

"*She* is right here, guys," Ember announced without much vigor.

"Ember, your place is with me." Owen knelt beside her wheelchair. "Mom's dying to pamper you, and I'm sure Maude will smother you, too."

"Killion, you can't just storm in here after tearing apart this girl's heart. You owe her a huge apology, and I'm not leaving until I hear it." Glaring, Rachel tapped her toe and planted her hands on her hips.

"Butt out, Harris."

Ember waved her hand between them. "Rachel, it's all right. Give us a minute."

Rachel sighed, then raised her hand for a quick fist-bump. "Stay strong, sister. Killion, I'm watching you." She forked her fingers at her eyes then waved them back and forth.

"Yeah, yeah, you've watched too many De Niro films." Owen chuckled as he watched Rachel leave.

Silence reigned after the door closed behind the petite detective.

Ember's buffer against discussing everything and all now waited in a huff outside the door. *Which way to turn now?*

"Ember."

"No, I need a minute." Rising from the wheelchair, she headed to the bathroom and closed the curtain. After staring at her bruised face in the mirror, she took two deep breaths. Why was there always such a struggle between your heart and your head? Why couldn't they simply agree? Either choice she made could lead to more pain. Shouldn't she start fresh someplace new? Away from all this madness.

"Ember? Babe, you ready?"

The concern and touch of fear she heard in his voice loosened the tight fist around her heart. She sighed. "It's rude to bother people when they are in the restroom, Killion."

She didn't need Owen. Not really. But what in life did you really need besides water, food, and sleep? Once you looked death in the eye, the basics became very real. So, where did that leave her? What basics should she allow back into her life?

Nothing about the man hovering outside her bathroom was basic or easy. Basic was a saltine cracker. Owen was a chocolate-covered graham cracker, dipped in caramel. If you need to eat, might as well enjoy the good stuff. Hadn't she learned that life was too precious? That everything could be stripped away at a moment's notice.

Hiding behind Rachel wasn't fair, nor was embroiling her in their quarrel. As her new friend, Ember should at least wait a few days before Rachel became even more involved in her completely insane life. But maybe her world wouldn't be insane anymore. Maybe Owen could be her one safe place. Maybe all she had to say was, I forgive you. Ember straightened her hair band and stepped out of the bathroom.

Owen waited behind her wheelchair. His head tilted to the side as he read messages on his phone. Handsome, as always, though his hair was a bit of a mess, and he had the makings of a full beard, but somehow that just made him sexier. His facial hair had red highlights, which seemed odd since his hair was brown.

Her head still throbbed, but the pain was manageable. She stared at the bandage on her wrist, still stunned Xander had sliced her open. What was his purpose? Every time she thought about what he had done to her after all their years together, her stomach churned and she barely held back the urge to scream until the paint peeled off the walls.

Rachel explained Xander was likely responsible for all her other troubles, as well. He wanted her distressed so she would turn to him and only him. Ember's mistake had come when she'd replaced him with Owen. Someday, she hoped to understand Xander's unconscionable behavior and come to peace with his death, but not today. Right now, she wanted to sleep for days. Block out everything, but that wasn't possible. The time had come to settle her relationship with Owen.

He stuffed his phone in his pocket and smiled as he met her gaze.

She tried to smile back, but bit her lip when she felt the rise of tears. Intent on having this discussion, she decided not looking at him might be the wisest course of action. So she plopped into the wheelchair and set on her lap the plastic bag of travel toiletries Rachel had thrown together. "I think I might quit my job."

Great way to start, Ember. Brilliant.

"Go ahead."

Owen's husky murmur quivered down her spine. "No, I mean after I find another one." She glanced over her shoulder. "Or, I don't know, maybe I'll see if I can switch to a different department."

He shrugged. "If that's what you want, Stems. Do it."

Sliding the zipper up and down on her oversized Marauders jacket, she stalled and tried to think of other things to say. "Think I could pop a wheelie in this thing?" She lifted the front wheels and almost knocked the chair all the way over. Would have if Owen hadn't caught her. Smiling at his face above her, she said, "Thanks for the save."

He settled her chair on solid ground and kept his hands on her shoulders. "No problem." Those words were whispered right by her ear, along with a kiss on her temple.

"I...uh...think it might be best if I stayed with Rachel. I'll go back home as soon as I get things settled. I may even—"

Owen spun her around. "If you think you're going back to that duplex, you're wrong. I had Bronco and Jason pack up all your things and take them to my place."

"So, well then...we'll just... Rachel and I will just come pick them up." She poked at the toothpaste tube in her plastic bag. "How do they get toothpaste into these little containers anyway? Is it like an automated system, you think?"

Owen released a hefty growl and ran a hand through his hair.

Ember heaved a heavy sigh of her own. "Can we address the elephant in the room? I need to know why you are here. What does it mean? The last words between us were pretty...uh...harsh, to say the least. Harsh enough to do what no one else has ever done—break me."

Owen closed his eyes and tapped his index finger against bottom lip. "Please don't say that." When his brown eyes appeared again, they seemed deep pools of despair and regret. "I'm so sorry, Ember. I was broken, too, and I lashed out. There is no excuse for my words. What I said wasn't fair."

"No, it was fair." Ember shook her head. "Everything I

touch goes sour or dies. I think it's better if I'm not in your life. I've caused enough damage. I appreciate all you've done for me, and I wish circumstances were different. My world is a black hole, and anyone too close to my sphere gets sucked in and eviscerated. I don't—"

"You *are* my life." He dropped to his knees by the wheelchair's side, clasped her chin in his hand, and slanted his mouth over hers. Light kisses against her cheek followed before he worked his way down her neck. "My world is a black hole *without* you. If I'd only listened to you that night, then Xander couldn't have hurt you again. Talk about living in the darkness, I'll have regrets about that night for the rest of my life."

Ember eased back and braced a finger against his lips. "You can't know what Xander would have done. He was unwell. I do forgive you, Owen. We were caught in an evil person's web. We couldn't have foreseen Xander's grand plan." She fiddled with her fingers and whispered, "It was all because of me."

"Stop." Owen cupped both sides of her head in his hands. "Xander's behavior wasn't because of you. Never you." As he tugged her toward the edge of the chair, his mouth descended slowly, as if he were giving her time to ease away.

But the pull between them was too strong.

Ember watched as Owen's mouth landed on hers, then she closed her eyes and let go.

Owen dove deep with his tongue, savoring every corner of her mouth. "I've missed you, Stems. I can't wait to get you home." He scattered kisses across her face. "I will take such good care of you." He ran a hand up her thigh and squeezed. "In so many ways." His eyes were full of wicked desire this time as he rested his forehead against hers.

"Owen." Ember brushed her hands through his thick hair. "You deserve so much more than this. Than me."

Owen shook his head and brushed a swift kiss across her damp lips. "There is no deserve. We just are. We live. We move on each and every day. Life is a struggle, and I want a beautiful, strong woman by my side. I want *you*. I love *you*."

"Fairy tale love isn't real, is it?" Ember eased back to meet his gaze. "I sometimes think we should work harder on saying 'I like you' more than 'I love you.' Because liking someone is harder.

Liking someone is down in the trenches. It's the day-to-day fight. There are some days I just won't like you, but I'll always love you." She wrapped a hand around his neck and tugged him closer. "I may need you more in the coming weeks. There is a lot I still don't understand. I need to know I can rest my head on that strong shoulder and let everything go. That you'll hold me until I stop crying, and listen when I need to talk out this mess. I need you to make love to me until I explode with pleasure. I'm asking for everything and, in return, I'll give you all that I am." Ember kissed the tip of his nose. "But in the end, it's just me, Ember Brooks from the trailer park, who had a rough childhood and still has a heart full of insecurities. I'm not perfect, but with you, I've found a place where I can just be me."

Owen gripped her hand in his and kissed the underside of her bandaged wrist. "I'll meet you on the line every time, Ember Brooks. Every time."

Ember's heart felt free. Once more, she'd handed over her world to Owen, and while their path ahead may be bumpy at times, she had no doubt she'd always see his footsteps by her side. "Let's renew our pact to always love each other, and when we don't like each other, we'll step back and consider why."

Owen brushed a finger along her lower lip. "I forgot love is about trust. I knew I was wrong the whole time. I won't make the same mistake again."

"I hope so, because I love you." She placed a hand upon her chest, above her pounding heart. "My feelings are a crazy, colorful combination inside me. But, it's love, so help you now, Killion. You're stuck. You're one of the basic facets in my life."

"Come home with me." Owen kissed their joined hands.

"Only if you promise me one thing."

"What's that?"

"You'll always be my center."

EPILOGUE

With a swipe of her glove, Ember brushed the snow from Elliot's tombstone.

She could finally say goodbye. After three weeks of Owen, his friends, and his family hovering, she was finally outside on her own. Well, not really, she'd asked Dean Jordan from Xander's college to meet her for coffee, and asked if he'd accompany her to Elliot's grave.

"I appreciate you coming, Dean Jordan, especially after trudging through all this snow. I don't know how to feel about everything Xander ever said to me, but at the same time, I'm still here. He did help, but at the expense of so much. I wish I had never met him. No matter what anyone says, I'll always feel responsible for his actions. I can't help that." She shook her head, and then placed a dozen yellow roses across Elliot's engraved name.

"I understand why you feel that way. I'm sorry I didn't see the danger signs earlier." Dean Jordan patted her shoulder.

"He was my counselor for years, and I didn't see them either. Please don't blame yourself." Ember placed her hand on top of the Dean's.

"I feel just as responsible as you, and like you, will always feel as if I should have done something different."

Ember nodded. "I'm healing. I'll always miss my brother. I...I loved him." She pulled a tissue from her pocket and wiped at the tears pouring down her cheeks. "I'm sorry...it's just...just...it was so unfair, you know? Elliot was happy. And after our childhood, that was an amazing thing. Then Xander took away everything. From him. From me. I get to live on though, right? That's supposed to be my consolation. Well, sometimes it sucks."

She choked out a sob and fell to her knees by Elliot's stone. "I'm so sorry, Elli. So sorry. I'll do better though, baby brother— for you. I'm looking after Bethany. I'm trying. But it's hard sometimes, 'cause I miss you like crazy." She ran her hand over Elliot's name, and then glanced at Dean Jordan. "I'm sorry, I promised myself I wouldn't do this, but I'm still a bit of a mess about everything."

Jordan sank down on his haunches beside her. "You're a lovely, bright young woman. I imagine your brother would want you to be happy. Happiness is not a guarantee in life. We have to work for it every day. I want you to try every day to find one thing that makes you happy."

"Oh, sir, I can't do counseling assignments anymore. I'm afraid I've soured on the subject." Ember blew her nose and dug in her pocket for another tissue.

"Maybe so, but I'd hope you're not soured on happiness."

"Sometimes, but I'll try to see the bright spots, I promise."

He nodded and remained quiet while she reined in her emotions.

"I think I'm ready now." Ember shuffled her purse over her shoulder.

They walked back to their cars, their breath forming white puffs in the frigid early-December air.

Her phone pinged with a text from Owen. *I'm home, Stems.*

"Well, Dean Jordan, this text just made me happy. Owen is back home after his away game. Oh, and Monday, I start my new job. It's with the same company, but I'll have a new boss." She twirled in a circle. "That *really* makes me happy."

"Good. If you're not willing to talk to a professional, maybe keep a journal. Write those happy moments at the top of every page. Then, on bad days skim back through your notes."

Ember wrapped him in a hug. "Thanks again. You really helped."

"I'm glad. You've got my number."

She watched him walk back to his car, and then called out, "Wait...Dean Jordan...I wanted to ask...um...do you know if

Xander was properly buried?"

"Yes, I took care of it."

"Oh. Thank you for telling me." There hadn't been an opportunity to ask anyone else. And being aware of how Owen felt about Xander, she hadn't asked. Though she despised Xander for what he had done to her, her family, and Owen, she felt a sense of finality knowing he rested in a grave somewhere.

Jordan nodded, got in his car, and drove off.

On the drive home, Ember contemplated the dean's information on sociopaths. He said they have no sense of social or moral obligation. Their sense of entitlement was due to an underlying rage and resentment. Their lack of genuine compassion allowed their belief they could act in whichever way they chose. Nothing was off limits. Underneath Xander's polished social self lived a rigid, calculating agenda. Xander's world existed in win-win, with no care for how he obtained his goal.

But that was the problem—no one had won.

Her father was out on parole for attempted robbery. She still slept with a light on, still had nightmares of each vicious attack at Xander's hand, still missed her brother, and even her mother on days when she was feeling generous. She pitied that poor girl Alice that Xander had killed. Apologized over and over to Maude and Nancy for his machinations. Xander's manipulations even made her question her judgment, and she found herself leery of forming new friendships.

There was one bright light at the end of the tunnel. She'd won Owen Killion's heart. And that was the championship game and a gold medal all tied up in one. Owen wouldn't let her retreat into a shell of guilt. He brightened her days and fired her nights.

Ember flipped down the visor and wiped the smeared mascara from under her eyes. If Owen saw her ruined makeup, he'd know she'd been crying, not that her red-rimmed eyes wouldn't give her away. "Well, Ember Brooks, that's as good as it's going to get." She grabbed her keys and headed inside.

She'd had her goodbye cry today, but would probably have another. Her tears for her brother were a private thing, between her and Elliot only—and the Dean, but he didn't really count.

She entered the mudroom and slipped off her shoes while digging through her purse for gum. After unwrapping a stick of cinnamon, she popped the gum in her mouth and dropped her bag on the kitchen counter. "Owen?"

"In here."

Following the sound of his voice to the living room, she glanced around, but didn't see him. "Owen?"

"Down here."

Well, if he wanted to start their evening on the living room floor, who was she to argue? She threw her jacket on the couch and spotted him lying on the floor with two tiny gray balls of fluff on his chest. Their little mews gave away the creatures beneath the puffy fur—kittens. "Oh, my gosh, they are so cute."

Owen smiled and tugged on her leg.

She dropped beside him before she fell over.

"What do you want to name them?"

"I'm not sure. I've never had a pet before."

"I know." He flashed a grin.

Lord, she'd missed him. And now he'd brought her kittens. "Today, I like you."

"I like you, too." He settled her beneath him and kissed her with seductive skill. The kittens weren't the only ones purring when he finished.

She arched against him and found him just as revved as her. She ran a hand across his jaw, grabbed his chin between her knuckle and thumb, nudged him closer, and—got batted in the ear by two tiny paws.

They laughed and straightened their backs against the couch.

Ember picked up one kitten and stared in its little mewling face. "I need some attention, too, little kitty. My man's been gone too long."

Owen chuckled and took the ball of fluff from her hand. There was an odd expression on his face. What kind of trickery did he have planned? She hoped kinky trickery.

"Did your visit with the Dean go all right, Stems?"

"I'd rather talk about it later. Right now, I want to do other things. Naughty, dirty things."

"Is that so, Ms. Brooks? Naughty *and* dirty. Hmmm... let me consider the options." The kittens pounced on a toy Owen dragged across the carpet on a string.

At the end of the string was—a ring.

Ember gasped, and her heart beat erratically in her chest. Oh, she really liked him today.

"Cat toys are really expensive these days." Owen caught her gaze and grinned.

That lop-sided smile always drove her crazy. "Yes."

"Yes?" Hope unveiled on his single word.

Did he really think it'd be that easy? "Yes, I think cat toys are expensive." To hide her smile, she buried her face in warm, gray fur. "So, how was your game?" She kept her gaze on her fingers as they stroked through the soft fur.

He joined his fingers with hers. "Gonna play coy, are you?"

"You're the one playing."

Owen tackled her to the ground and kissed her until she couldn't breathe. Knowing they'd get too caught up in each other, she pressed a hand against his chest. She wanted this moment to happen right here, not later in bed, or later when their clothes were strewn across the floor, and she was mid-orgasm. "Ask me now, please."

"Ask what?" He arched a single brow.

She flipped him over and braced her elbows against the solid wall of his chest.

Thinking they were playing, the kittens pounced as well.

He laughed, but sputtered when he got kitty fur in his mouth. "Ember Brooks, will you take care of these kittens with me?"

She rolled her eyes, laughed, and pinched his arm. "Do it better."

"I love to hear you laugh. Ember Brooks, will you—"

A kitten batted his nose, then jumped on his head.

"Damn it, cat, I'm trying to propose here."

Ember laughed, and felt the rumble in his chest as he did the same. "Yes, I will marry you." She covered his face in smacking kisses. "Now, quit being mean to my kitty."

"Your kitty? Is that what you're calling it now?" Flashing another grin, he pinched her bottom.

She squealed, sending the kittens scurrying to all corners of the room.

Owen rolled her beneath him once more, as always, a dark Marauder, claiming his treasure.

And she was more than ready to be plundered.

Thank you for reading *Ember's Center*. I hope you enjoyed Ember and Owen's story. If you did, please leave a review at your purchase site. Reviews are very appreciated by the author.

Please turn the page for an excerpt *Fire's Field*, Book #2 in Jillian's paranormal Elementals series. *Water's Threshold*, Book #1 is now available at all major book retailers.

Please enjoy the following excerpt from *Fire's Field*, Book #2 in **The Elemental Series**. Jillian's Paranormal with Suspenseful Elements coming, First Quarter 2015.

"Good evening, Violet." A deep male voice tinted with a faint Russian accent drifted into the kitchen and fired goose bumps across her skin.

Heart pounding, Violet fumbled the grocery bag in her arms before placing the paper hindrance on the counter. "How...How did you find me?" She peeked around the corner into the living room, and there he sat.

Flint.

Dressed in a fine-fitting, black suit. A large bouquet of yellow roses wrapped in purple tissue paper rested on his lap.

"Pillar told me you were staying here." His raven-wing hair and amber eyes were only discernable by the flickering light dancing across his sculpted features.

"Giving her up, just like that." Violet snapped her fingers.

"I don't owe that salty square my allegiance." Flint shifted his finely-honed, blacksmith body in the chair, crinkling the florist tissue.

"You've known her for many years."

"Unfortunately, yes." Flint sniffed, and picked at a yellow petal. "She may have led me here, for reasons of her own, but I would have found you. Pillar's sudden need to redeem herself now that her leader's been shot back to where he came from, doesn't concern me, or allow for any pity. She's been against us for a long time."

"And you don't forgive." Violet folded both arms across her chest, remaining in the doorway between the kitchen and the living room. Caught between her wish to flee, and her curiosity to learn more about this Elemental being.

Please enjoy the following excerpt from **Blue Falcon**, **Tia Catalina's** Suspense with romantic elements, available now.

"He wiggled the knife in front of my face. "There's no need to be afraid. I just want you to hold the knife." He reached out, grabbed my hand and forced the knife under my clenched fingers. "Excellent. Now, let's do a little blood splash and you'll be good to go." He shoved me backward and I tripped over the mother and child. A bright red smear stained my hands where I'd tried to stop my fall. Gore marked my pants—wet and sticky.

"Let me help you." He bent down and dipped his gloved hand into the blood pool. Leaning over me, he flicked blood off his gloves onto my shirt and face.

I backpedaled. *Not quick enough.* The bloody spray sobered me like a splash of cold water.

He laughed and captured my chin with his hand, tilted it at different angles, and announced, "The artistry of the blood arc is superb. I believe my work here is done." He brushed his hands together as if dusting off the grime of a hard day's work, and moved back toward the kitchen. Stopping in the doorway, he said, "One last thing, Grace. I left your instructions on the wall. Be sure to read them before you run off. Wouldn't want you to meet the same fate as Angel." He disappeared into the kitchen and the back door slammed.

The smell of death surrounded me. My breath caught in my chest and I closed my eyes against the sight of the massacred bodies of my perfect family.

They were beyond my help.

ABOUT THE AUTHOR

In the spring of 2013, Jillian Jacobs changed her career path and became a romance writer. After reading for years, she figured writing a romance would be quick and easy. Nope! With the guidance of the Indiana Romance Writers of America chapter, she's learned there are many "rules" to writing a proper romance. Being re-schooled has been an interesting journey, and she hopes the best trails are yet to be traveled.

Water's Threshold, the first in Jillian's Elementals series, was a finalist in Chicago-North's 2014 Fire and Ice contest in the Women's Fiction category.

Jillian is a: Tea Guzzler, Polish Pottery Hoarder, and lover of all things Moose.

The genres she writes under are: Paranormal and Contemporary romance with suspenseful elements.

CONNECT WITH JILLIAN JACOBS ONLINE

Website: www.jillianjacobs.com

Twitter: @GreenMooseProd

https://twitter.com/GreenMooseProd

Facebook: www.facebook.com/AuthorJillianJacobs

Made in the USA
Charleston, SC
10 May 2016